Books by Charlie Higson

SILVERFIN
BLOOD FEVER
DOUBLE OR DIE
HURRICANE GOLD
BY ROYAL COMMAND

DANGER SOCIETY: YOUNG BOND DOSSIER

MONSTROSO (POCKET MONEY PUFFINS)

SILVERFIN: THE GRAPHIC NOVEL

THE ENEMY
THE DEAD
THE FEAR

THE
FEAR

CHARLIE
HIGSON

PUFFIN

PUFFIN BOOKS

Published by the Penguin Group
Penguin Books Ltd, 80 Strand, London WC2R ORL, England
Penguin Group (USA) Inc., 375 Hudson Street, New York, New York 10014, USA
Penguin Group (Canada), 90 Eglinton Avenue East, Suite 700, Toronto, Ontario, Canada M4P 2Y3
(a division of Pearson Penguin Canada Inc.)
Penguin Ireland, 25 St Stephen's Green, Dublin 2, Ireland (a division of Penguin Books Ltd)
Penguin Group (Australia), 250 Camberwell Road, Camberwell, Victoria 3124, Australia
(a division of Pearson Australia Group Pty Ltd)
Penguin Books India Pvt Ltd, 11 Community Centre, Panchsheel Park, New Delhi – 110 017, India
Penguin Group (NZ), 67 Apollo Drive, Rosedale, Auckland 0632, New Zealand
(a division of Pearson New Zealand Ltd)
Penguin Books (South Africa) (Pty) Ltd, Block D, Rosebank Office Park, 181 Jan Smuts Avenue,
Parktown North, Gauteng 2193, South Africa
Penguin Books Ltd, Registered Offices: 80 Strand, London WC2R ORL, England

puffinbooks.com

First published 2011
This edition published 2012
001 – 10 9 8 7 6 5 4 3 2 1

Copyright © Charlie Higson, 2011

The moral right of the author has been asserted

Set in 12.7/15.8 pt Bembo Book MT
Typeset by Palimpsest Book Production Limited, Falkirk, Stirlingshire
Printed in Great Britain by Clays Ltd, St Ives plc

British Library Cataloguing in Publication Data
A CIP catalogue record for this book is available from the British Library

ISBN: 978-0-141-32506-4

www.greenpenguin.co.uk

MIX
Paper from
responsible sources
FSC
www.fsc.org   FSC™ C018179

Penguin Books is committed to a sustainable
future for our business, our readers and our planet.
This book is made from Forest Stewardship
Council™ certified paper.

ALWAYS LEARNING   **PEARSON**

For Amanda — for everything

I would like to thank Alex Lawson for a great day out behind the scenes at the Natural History Museum.

And Doug Kempster at the Port of London Authority for talking me through the workings of the River Thames.

The Collector

Stuff . . . more stuff . . . Get more stuff . . . good stuff . . .

It was dark outside, safe to leave now. He squeezed his great bulk down the hallway and out through the front door, sniffing the air. A curtain of greasy hair flopped in front of his eyes, and he pushed it back with an enormous fat hand, smearing a shiny yellow streak across his face from a burst pustule on his cheek.

He smiled. He was going out to find stuff.

More stuff.

All he had ever really been interested in was stuff. Things. Kit. Gadgets. Toys. Gizmos. His tiny basement flat had always been full of it. Days and nights he had spent down there on his computer – TV on, music blaring, playing games: playing and playing and playing until he lost all track of time. He had been so happy, surrounded by his stuff, his shelves of DVDs, CDs, old vinyl, comics, *Star Wars* figures, manga figures, *Star Trek* collectibles, books and magazines, takeaway food cartons, toy robots, keyboards and amps and screens . . . Nothing ever chucked away. Old computers piled in corners, mobile phones, cameras, tangled piles of leads and plugs . . .

Stuff. A life of stuff.

Eventually he had made holes in the walls, burrowed out

of his flat, taken over the basements on either side, and when they were full he had moved upwards, floor by floor, filling the building ever fuller with stuff.

And now he was off out to find more stuff. It was so easy now. Everything was just lying around waiting for him to come and pick it up. He held a sturdy carrier bag in each meaty hand, though he didn't think he'd need them tonight. Tonight he was looking for toys. His last toys had got broken beyond repair. They'd stopped moving, stopped entertaining him with their jerky actions. Stopped making their funny noises. What use were toys if you couldn't play games with them any more?

When they no longer worked, he simply ate them.

Collecting stuff and eating, that was all he did now. When his toys broke, he slumped on his sofa and stared at the blank screens of his TVs, waiting for night to fall. Sometimes he'd sit at the computer, tapping away at the keyboard, some deep memory stirring inside him. For hours on end. Tap, tap, tapping. Making a strange kind of music.

But now he had a purpose.

He waddled slowly down the road, taking great care with each step. There was just enough light from the thin moon and distant stars to pick his way along. He didn't mind the dark. In truth he had always been nocturnal, sitting with the curtains drawn, no interest in sunlight or fresh air or other people.

He was careful, though. If he fell down, it would be hard for him to get up again. His bare feet landed solidly and squarely on the filthy surface of the road he knew so well. Night after night he would come out here and move from shop to shop, house to house, looting them for more stuff.

Like some huge clumsy bear ransacking people's dustbins, his strong arms ripping and tearing to get at what he needed.

He was tempted by the massive building down the road. The department store. So many nights he'd spent in there removing stuff. But it was getting too dangerous now. Others had got in and made nests and they sometimes tried to attack him as he trundled about searching for anything he'd missed. They couldn't do him any real harm – he was too big, too heavy, too solid – but he liked to hunt for his stuff in peace. So he had taken to breaking into houses instead. There was always stuff in them. This had been a rich neighbourhood. He would tear out hi-fi systems, pull flat-screen TVs from walls, dig through drawers for cameras and sat-navs and iPods and mobile phones, cramming them into his bags to carry home and add to his collection.

Not tonight, though. He had to concentrate, not forget what he was looking for.

Toys.

He'd heard them the night before. Smelled them. On his way back home with bulging carrier bags. He'd tried to get at them where they were hidden in a building, but the sky had started to brighten over the tops of the roofs and he had slunk back to his cellar to hide until the darkness returned.

He hated the sun. It burned his skin, blinded him, sent his thoughts spinning so that he couldn't think straight. The darkness was warm and comforting, like an old blanket. He would sit slumped on his sofa through all the long day: waiting, dozing, dreaming. And now . . . Now he had the whole night to break in and get at the toys.

3

He smiled as he pictured all the fun he was going to have when he got the toys back to his collection. Prodding them, and making them skitter about on the floor. Letting them get away, then pulling them back. He chuckled, the sound a wet gurgle in his throat.

Stuff . . .

He only wished they would last longer and not break so quickly, because it was hard work catching them. They ran about and made too much noise. Most broke before he could even get them home.

He followed the scent down the street, wiping away the snot that bubbled permanently from his nose. He was dribbling too. Sticky saliva falling on to his stained T-shirt.

Stuff . . .

It took him ages to make his way down the street, round the corner and on to the next road. Each footfall landing softly on the tarmac. He hoped no one had got there before him. The smell of the toys was very strong.

Here was the place. A shop he used to come to a lot. A gadget shop. Long since cleaned out, but the toys had got inside. He'd come past it last night and the good sweet smell had hit him like a hammer blow. He'd tried to get in, but there were wooden boards nailed across the front.

He had plenty of time tonight, though.

He smiled again.

Stuff . . .

Good stuff. Cool stuff. More stuff. Nice stuff. More stuff. Stuff stuff stuff.

There was nobody else around. The streets were quiet tonight. He walked over the road, his legs making a swishing sound as they rubbed together. He put his face to the gap between two of the wooden boards and breathed in.

He had to be sure. Sometimes their smell could linger for days, even if they'd moved away. *No.* They were still in there. His toys. He leant his weight against the boards, heard them creak and groan, felt them bend. He moaned with delight. That was the way to do it. Last night he'd made the mistake of trying to pull the boards down with his hands. Better to push. He walked backwards. Put down his bags. Then moved forward, not exactly running, but gaining speed. Until . . .

THUD.

He hit the boards, heard a crack and then sounds on the other side. Scurrying. Whispered voices. The toys were awake.

He backed off, further this time, then went forward again, the breath hissing through his nose.

THUD.

And again. Again and again and again – slow, unthinking, patient – until at last the wood splintered and fell away from him and he was inside. In the dark.

Stuff . . . Come on . . . Where's the cool stuff?

The smell of the toys was more intense now. Filling his head and making him feel drunk. He closed his eyes and smacked his lips together, then stuck out his tongue, tasting the air. They were nearby. If he could just catch two, maybe three, of the toys, he would have the whole night ahead of him to play with them before he went to sleep. After that? How long? A few days maybe before they broke.

But where were they? He stopped moving and stood very still so that he could listen. There was a scraping sound, a rattling and banging. More whispers. Ssss-sss-sss-sss-ssssssss . . . He moved towards the sound, groping his way through the darkened shop, past the empty shelves and on into the back.

There they were. Four of them. Trying to open a back door. They'd barricaded themselves in with no way out. He spread his arms wide and belched. The toys all turned round together, their faces white blurs. One of them ran at him, but he barely felt it. Like a moth, bumping at a window. They were shouting. Why did they always shout? Why not just come quietly?

Come on . . . stuff . . . make it easy for me . . .

They were on the small side, easy to carry but easy to break too. He picked one out, trying not to be distracted by the others. The smallest one. He backed it into a corner, while the rest of them battered at his back. Just moths.

There. He'd got it. He picked it up and tucked it into his armpit, the weight of his arm holding it still. The rest of them carried on hitting him, shouting, their thin voices irritating him. Maybe if they'd run they might have got away from him because they were faster. He would have tracked them all night, slowly and steadily, following their scent, and he knew that the smaller ones couldn't keep going for long – they always got tired before he did. But these ones had stayed to fight, so this way it would be easier.

Two of them had sticks. The biggest two. Their blows fell harmlessly on his flesh, no more than a tickle. He sighed and swept his free arm wide, flinging one against the wall. He knew that would break it, but he couldn't take all of them home anyway. The smashed toy fell to the floor and he managed to scoop up the other small one. Two was enough. He tucked it away neatly in the great folds of his flesh.

Maybe he should try for a third, hold it by the neck. Sometimes they broke, though, if he did that.

No. He'd leave the other one. Maybe it would stay close and he could come back for it tomorrow.

He sighed again and headed back towards the front.

The fourth toy followed him through the shop. It had found a bigger stick. It was sharp. The toy was screaming very loudly as it jabbed at him with the stick. It might follow him out on to the street, all the way home, and its noise would attract the others. Then they would fight him for his treasures.

He stopped, turned and pushed his huge belly against the toy, forcing it against the wall. He pressed harder and harder, watching the soft blubber fold itself round the toy until it was invisible. He could feel it wriggling feebly.

It wriggled and wriggled and then, at last, was still.

The collector moved away and the small body stayed pressed into his gut. He took it by the hair and trudged out into the street. It would be no good for playing with, but he could dump it on his food pile.

And so, with a toy under each arm, he dragged the third broken toy down the street towards home.

He would leave the carrier bags where they were. He had plenty more. He had stacks and stacks of them among his stuff. He felt a little pang, though. He hated to leave anything behind.

The toys under his arms kicked and struggled, but by the time he had got to his front door they had stopped, exhausted. He was pleased with himself. This had been a good night's work. He had more cool stuff. New toys. They would keep him happy for a few days. He dreamt of all the things he would do with them, all the games he would play. First, though, as soon as he got them inside, he would have to snap their little legs. He had learnt the hard way that they could escape if you didn't do it. Why did they always try to run away? Why wouldn't they just stay and play nicely? Why did they always have to make things so difficult?

And why, in the end, did they always have to break?

THE ACTION IN THIS BOOK
BEGINS FIVE DAYS BEFORE THE
INCIDENTS DESCRIBED AT
THE END OF *THE DEAD*.

1

All the kids had nightmares. It would have been crazy if they didn't. They'd seen so many strange and terrible things, after all. Disease and death, fire and darkness and chaos. Their world turned upside-down. They'd seen people they loved destroyed by the sickness – mothers and fathers, older brothers, sisters, best friends. None had escaped its touch. They'd all lost someone and some of them had lost everyone. How could you not have night-mares if you'd watched your parents slowly lose their minds? If you'd watched their bodies being taken over by the disease, watched it blistering the skin, eating away at the flesh, watched it kill them?

Or worse.

Because when they didn't die, when they lived on as mindless, shambling creatures with decaying bodies and a taste for fresh meat, it was much, much worse.

The kids who'd taken shelter in the Tower of London tried to forget. They tried to delete the memories of all they'd lived through, but when they slept some deep part of their brains kept on reminding them, and suddenly they were back there, reliving it as a loved one got taken by the disease, or as friends were attacked by the hungry things that had once been human. Suddenly they were hiding again from their own families, trying to get away as a mother or a father reached out for them with rotting fingers . . .

They would talk and struggle in their sleep. They would cry out. There would be screams in the night. Some would sleepwalk and be found in strange places spouting gibberish. More than once someone had woken to find a friend with their hands round their throat.

DogNut was no different. On the night before he was due to leave the Tower he had his old familiar nightmare once again. Why this one? This same dream, night after night? Why would his brain not leave this memory alone? He'd survived more dangerous attacks. Lost closer friends. So why, in the darkness, did the dream come creeping like some low shadow creature into his brain? So that even he, tough and wiry and street-smart and seemingly scared of nothing, would jerk awake, tangled in his bedclothes, crying like a little baby and calling out for his mum.

Every night the dream ran its course. He could never wake himself before that final terrible moment . . .

Maybe it was the weirdness of what had happened, the fact that he'd seen nothing quite like it before or since. The slow, disgusting, unreal nature of it. It had even felt like a dream at the time.

It had happened soon after he'd arrived at the Tower, when they were all still learning about their surroundings, before they'd turned the business district to the north and west into a forbidden zone. All the big office blocks and skyscrapers were here, even though it was the most ancient part of the city, founded by the Romans some two thousand years ago. It was an area where far-out, modern, hi-tech buildings of glass and steel rubbed up against medieval churches and solid, stone-clad eighteenth- and nineteenth-century buildings decorated with pillars and columns and statues.

This part of London seemed to contain a special sickness all of its own.

But all those months ago they hadn't realized . . .

In his dream DogNut is back there, out on patrol with his friends Ed and Kyle and a boy called Leo. Leo is a chatty kid who's pretty tough, but also more than a little clumsy. So, although he loves fighting and is always the first to volunteer to go out hunting for food and supplies, he is as much of a danger to his own side in a fight as he is to any attacking sickos. DogNut is always nervous going on patrol with him – he doesn't pay attention and is noisy and too sure of himself – but today a lot of the other kids are laid up with the flu and he's the best available.

They walk along a wide street. In his dream it's black and white, like an old film. Bank notes are blowing in the breeze like confetti. The four of them laugh and try to catch as many of them as they can, even though they are completely worthless now. They follow the trail of money and it leads them to a fancy-looking Victorian building with an imposing front that reminds DogNut of a Greek temple. It's the money that brings them here. There's smoke rising from the building, but the boys are curious to look inside. To find the source of the money.

The revolving doors at the entrance are locked. The window next to them, however, has been smashed, and, carefully avoiding the broken glass, they climb inside.

They are in what appears to be a posh bank of some sort. There's a wide marble floor, with a circular pattern of tiles set into it that looks something like a compass. There are pillars and carved wood, and paintings on the walls, a couple of big dead trees in pots. At the back is a staircase leading up from the lobby, to the left an empty reception desk. There are no signs of any human activity.

Leo is keen to explore further.

He says something about looking for gold.

Notes aren't much use, but gold will always be valuable . . .

They walk towards the stairs. And as they get to the middle of the tiled pattern on the floor, there is a crack and the floor begins to crumble beneath their feet. DogNut instinctively grabs on to Leo and they hold each other as the floor collapses. In the dream it happens slowly, they almost float down, but at the time they must have fallen hard and fast.

Right down to the basement.

Miraculously they are unhurt. They've landed on something soft. The air is filled with dust so for a few moments DogNut can't see anything, despite the sunlight filtering down from the floor above.

Ed and Kyle had been walking a little way behind them and haven't fallen through. DogNut hears Ed calling down to him, asking if he's all right.

DogNut shouts back that he's fine.

We landed on something . . . He tries to work out what exactly the two of them are standing on . . . or rather *in*. He's sunk up to his waist in something warm and slimy. And it's moving, like some giant animal.

'What is it?' says Leo.

'It's bad is what it is,' says DogNut. 'We got to get out of here.'

'But what is it?'

'I don't want to know. I just want to get out.'

As the air clears, DogNut notices that there's a sort of

luminous glow down here. It helps him to gradually make out his surroundings.

Faces. Too many to count. Looking up at him. He's sinking in a sea of faces. He realizes that the sticky mess he's fallen into is *people*. They're all squashed together, and it's as if they've melted into one single, shapeless blob. They are stacked on top of each other. He can see more faces underneath. Bodies crushed and trampled and squashed beneath the feet of those people at the top.

They're smartly dressed in business suits, although the suits are filthy and ragged, and some of the men and women wearing them are obviously dead. Not all, though. Hands wriggle up from the gloopy mass, fingers worm towards him, heads crane over to try to get closer, but the bodies are so tightly packed that none of them can really move.

DogNut looks around; the whole basement is crammed full of these people. How they live down here, what they eat, he has no idea. Maybe they eat whatever drops in on them. But then he sees to his horror that they are eating each other. Where they are able to they've clamped their mouths on to their neighbours. Over there a head has three or four other heads clustered round it, sucking and chewing. And there – two heads eating each other. He watches in appalled fascination as a mouth peels the cheek off a woman, exposing her gums. She has long since lost her teeth. The only sound is a squelching, slurping noise. There's something cold and dead-eyed about these people, as if they didn't care. They look like lizards.

And now DogNut realizes that they are trying to eat him too. There are three mouths sucking at his legs. He pulls one leg away and it comes free with a plopping noise.

He frantically kicks and wriggles, but as one person is knocked away another fills the gap.

'This is disgusting,' he shouts.

'Go up,' says Leo. 'We have to go up!'

The ceiling is nearer than DogNut had expected. God knows how deep this human pool is. He forces his way up, standing on shoulders, heads, jerking away from gaping mouths. Ed is leaning over the edge, his hand extended downwards. DogNut reaches up and his fingertips touch Ed's. But then the panicking Leo pulls him back.

'Let me go first!' he screams, and climbs up DogNut's body, using him as a ladder. DogNut swears but tries to help him, pushing him from below. In his panic, though, Leo slips and tumbles sideways, falling into a field of upturned baby birds' mouths. He thrashes about and only succeeds in sinking deeper into the human bog.

DogNut tries to get hold of him and manages to get a grip on his shirt. With his other hand he reaches out for Ed who is dangling down over the hole supported by Kyle. DogNut tries not to lose his grip on Leo. It's impossible, though. Leo now has at least seven grown-ups hanging off him like leeches.

DogNut knows that if he lets go of Leo he will die. It's up to DogNut to save him, but he's in danger of being pulled back down himself so in the end he lets go of Leo and watches helplessly as he sinks for the last time beneath the sea of faces, which curl in on him, enveloping him.

Every night the scene is repeated, and every night the same thing happens. Leo falls and sinks out of sight into that horror.

And that night, like every other, DogNut woke gasping for air, still watching poor Leo disappear. He sat there, soaked in sweat, shaking, his head bobbing on his long neck, telling himself that it was all right. All right. Just a dream. Just a stupid dream. He wasn't back there. It wasn't real.

It *was* real, though. It was his fault Leo had died . . .

DogNut had yelled so loud his throat had bled. Ed had hauled him up and he'd flopped down on to the tiles. They'd checked his body. He was covered with saliva, but none of the sucking mouths had broken his skin. Ed had tried to reassure him, told him it wasn't his fault.

It was, though. He had let go of Leo.

And his guilty brain wouldn't let go of the memory.

No.

He had to put it out of his mind. Push it away like all the other bad memories. Tonight, of all nights, he needed his sleep, because in the morning he was leaving.

He'd been at the Tower of London a year. Building a new life with Jordan Hordern and Ed and Kyle and all the others who had made it here after the battle at Lambeth Bridge. Why did he never dream of that night? When half of London had gone up in flames.

Because it wasn't his fault.

No.

Come on, DogNut. Don't be a wuss. Don't think about it. Suck it up. Be a man. Move on. Think of Brooke. Beautiful, stroppy Brooke. *Yeah.* He smiled. Always look on the bright side of life, as the old song went. The nightmare wasn't the only regular dream he had, was it?

Some nights he dreamt of Brooke, the mouthy blonde girl he'd got split up with at Lambeth Bridge. It had been mad. Sickos, driven on by the fire, had attacked them. Half of his group had got away over the bridge, the rest of them,

17

DogNut included, had ended up on a tourist boat floating down the Thames . . .

A year since he'd last seen Brooke. And in all that time he'd never been able to forget her. In his dreams she was impossibly good-looking, her hair clean and golden, her clothes immaculate, but she was just as rude and unwelcoming. Somehow that only made him want her more. So now he was doing something about it. He and a gang of kids from the Tower were going to go upriver and search for lost friends.

As he lay in the darkness now, though, in the bleak early hours of the morning, he wondered for the thousandth time if he wasn't crazy. Why leave the safety of the Tower? Why leave his friends? He had it made here.

Ha. Good one.

He'd never be a general like Jordan Hordern. He'd never be respected like clever Ed who everyone loved. He was just daft deputy DogNut. Cooped up inside this gloomy castle. This couldn't be it. For the rest of his life. There had to be something more. He was going to go out there. He was going to make something of himself. He was going to find Brooke, the prettiest girl in London, and return a hero.

Hold on to that, DogNut – that's your future.

You're gonna show everyone.

You're gonna show Jordan Hordern, and Ed . . . and Leo.

You're gonna be a hero.

2

It was morning and DogNut's crew was down by the Thames packing a big rowing boat with food and water, weapons, sleeping bags and clothing. DogNut was wearing his leather American flying jacket from the Second World War. Like a couple of the others he was bringing along a steel breastplate, but that was stashed in the bottom of the boat along with everything else. It was too heavy and awkward to row in.

The day was bright and clear. Sunlight sparkled on the dirty water of the Thames, turning it from muddy grey into a shifting carpet of silver and gold. DogNut knew it was probably just tiredness and a trick of the dancing light, but he kept seeing shapes out of the corners of his eyes and try as he might he couldn't quite chase away the last shadows of his dream and concentrate on what he was supposed to be doing. He needed to be careful. Sure, it was a lovely day and all that, and the river might look like something out of a Disney film right now, but he knew it could be very dangerous. It was wide and deep and powerful and criss-crossed with unpredictable currents. He'd seen its dangers first hand. On the night they'd arrived here last year the boat they'd been on had hit a bridge and sank. Several kids had drowned, including Brooke's friend Aleisha.

And only last month a boy had been playing near Traitor's Gate, right next to the river, showing off to his mates, and had slipped off the wall. The Thames had looked as if it was hardly moving, but the poor guy had been snatched away in an instant and never seen again.

You had to respect the river. The kids had spent their time at the Tower organizing themselves, learning about their surroundings. Lately they'd been studying the river. Learning its ways and learning not to fear it.

DogNut had carefully chosen this time for their departure. Although the sea was miles away the Thames was still affected by the tides. When the tide rose in the North Sea, it forced a huge volume of water up the estuary where it funnelled into the Thames and reversed its flow. The level of the river at the Tower could rise as much as seven metres. Then as the tide went out the waters would begin to drop and be sucked out to sea.

Their route was upriver, to the west, so they'd had to wait for the tide to turn so they could go with the flow and not against it. There was a twenty-minute lull at low tide when the river didn't flow in either direction, but now it was starting to flow strongly backwards as the incoming tide pushed it inland. This would make rowing upstream much easier.

DogNut would have preferred to set off earlier, but it wasn't until late morning that the tide was right. They'd found the boat at a rowing club in Rotherhithe to the east, and it was part of the small fleet of vessels the kids had collected and now kept at the Tower. It was an old-fashioned skiff, wide and deep, with space for six at the oars and one more at either end. The kids who were going on the expedition had been training hard on the water for the last two weeks, but they were hardly experts, so they were all a little nervous as they packed the boat and prepared to set off.

They were a mixed bunch. The youngest was a ten-year-old girl called Olivia who'd got separated from her older brother during the battle at Lambeth Bridge. She was desperate to find him, though, and had been miserable at the Tower this last year. She was a skinny, nervous little thing and DogNut hoped she could hold it together. Still, she was brave enough to risk the journey, despite how frightened she obviously was – DogNut gave her some credit for that. Just so long as she didn't slow them down . . .

Olivia wasn't the only girl coming along. There was Jessica as well. Jessica was DogNut's age. Like Olivia she'd lost contact with the group she was travelling with in the confusion of the battle and ended up at the Tower. She said she wanted to find her friends, but DogNut reckoned the main reason she was coming along was that she'd recently split up with her boyfriend and wanted to get away from him. She was moody and hard work at the best of times, but now she was miserable as hell and not great company. They were limited to eight people so DogNut was glad of three strong fighters: Marco, Felix and Al. Marco and Felix were two of DogNut's old mates from the Imperial War Museum who were mainly coming along for the adventure and to help him. They were very close but couldn't seem to stop arguing and putting each other down. Marco was nice to everyone, and pretty popular; Felix, on the other hand, was always getting into fights for speaking his mind. Al was a lumpy-faced kid with a fat nose and big teeth who wanted to find his sister, Maria. DogNut referred to the three of them as the Good, the Bad and the Ugly, though never to Al's lumpy face. He had a mean temper and was a vicious fighter.

The best fighter of them all, though, was a giant of a boy called Finn. It was just a mighty shame that he'd cut his forearm a few days ago, and the wound had become infected. His arm was bandaged and in a sling. He couldn't fight and he couldn't row, but he was determined to come along anyway. He'd been travelling across south London with a group of friends from his school in Forest Hill when they'd been caught up in the fire. They'd separated, some had gone west and one or two, including Finn, had travelled north where they'd eventually come to the Tower. He was hoping to find out what had happened to the others. Finn didn't say very much and was even quieter since his injury. DogNut was hacked off that he was out of action. He was very strong for his age and looked about eighteen. He'd always been a good guy to have at your side in a fight. DogNut could hardly stop him from coming, though, and even with a dodgy arm he'd be way more use than Olivia.

The final member of the expedition was Courtney, who would be sitting next to DogNut on the boat. Courtney and Aleisha, the girl who'd drowned when the sightseeing boat sank, had been best friends with Brooke, and DogNut knew that Courtney was desperate to be reunited with her. They'd been inseparable and Courtney missed her terribly. She was a big, heavy girl who had grown into a tough and fearless fighter, and DogNut was glad to have her along.

Five fighters and three passengers. Not bad numbers. But eight fighters would have been better . . .

DogNut supervised them as they stowed food and water, blankets and armour and weapons in the bottom of the boat. He was their boss and was pleased to see that they all did what he told them without grumbling. Here at the Tower he was captain of the Pathfinders, the name Jordan Hordern had given to the kids who went out scavenging, so he was used to giving orders. They were all taking orders from General Jordan Hordern, however. He was the big man. DogNut would only ever be second or third in line. Not this time, though. No, on this expedition he would be number one. He had to make sure the kids remembered that and did as they were told.

He smiled to himself. Numero Uno. Admiral of the Fleet. Top Dog.

There was a shout from the riverside and he looked over to see a small group of kids walking on to the metal pier where they were loading the boat. It was Jordan Hordern and Ed and three of the Tower guards carrying halberds. DogNut went over to meet them.

'You all set?' Ed asked.

'Guess so.'

'You sure about this?' Jordan squinted at him through his thick glasses. DogNut shrugged.

'You're a useful man to have around,' Jordan went on.

'I'll be back,' said DogNut theatrically. 'Bringing treasure from around the world!'

Jordan didn't smile. He didn't have much of a sense of humour.

'Take care of yourself, won't you?' Ed gave DogNut a big hug.

'Gay,' said DogNut, and Ed hugged him again, harder this time, and lifted him off his feet. They laughed. Ed's face looked crazy when he laughed. The scar down one side went white and tugged his mouth and eye out of shape.

'It ain't too late for you to change your mind,' said DogNut. 'Come with us.'

'I'm staying, Doggo. They need me here. Besides, you got a full crew.'

'I could kick someone's arse off. Finn ain't much use with his arm in a sling.'

'Nah.' Ed shook his head. 'This is your gig.'

Olivia ran over and threw her skinny arms round Ed's waist.

'Please come with us!' she squealed.

Ed picked her up and sat her on his hip.

'I can't come, Livvie. You'll be all right with the Dog.'

'I'm scared.'

Ed handed Olivia over to DogNut. 'DogNut will look after you, won't you?'

'Course I will.' DogNut beamed at Olivia and carried her to the boat, then passed her down to Marco and Felix who settled her at the front.

DogNut turned back to Ed.

'Feels good to be doing something, man,' he said, breathing in deeply and turning his face up to the sun. 'It's safe here, but I been feeling more and more boxed up lately. All we do is get from one day to the next. I'm taking control of things. Hitting back. Not letting the sickos rule my life.'

Ed raised an eyebrow. 'And of course there's Brooke.' He leered at DogNut. It wasn't a good expression for him.

'Yeah, Brooke,' said DogNut. 'You missing out, man. I'm gonna get in there before you.'

Ed raised his hands in surrender. 'She's all yours, dude.'

'All mine,' said DogNut.

'All you got to do is find her.'

24

'You had to bring me down, didn't you,' said DogNut. 'Bust my bubble.'

'You'll find her.' Ed sounded very sure of it. DogNut slapped his palm and clambered down into the boat.

'But a year's a long time,' Ed called after him. 'Maybe she's changed?'

'Pop, pop, pop,' said DogNut, sitting down next to Courtney. 'All my bubbles is busting.'

Jordan came and leant over the side of the pier, his face unreadable behind his glasses. They were held together with a dirty Elastoplast and were so scratched DogNut wondered how he could see anything through them.

'I'll keep your position open for you,' he said. 'You can pick up where you left off when you get back.'

'Cheers,' DogNut shouted, as he pushed the boat away from the edge. He grinned at Courtney, picked up his oar, slipped it over the side and looked down into the water. And that was when he saw them, looking up at him from the murky depths, with their gaping mouths stretched wide, hands coming towards him. The creatures from his dream.

DogNut closed his eyes to shut out the image and moaned quietly, as if he'd hurt himself.

Then he grunted. Shook himself. Opened his eyes. He had to stay focused on what he was doing. It was time to let the daylight burn off the memories and let the fresh air blow the black tatters of the fading dream away.

Bad thoughts. They couldn't help. They'd only poison his brain. He was going to leave them behind. Leave Leo behind. Leave his guilt back there in the basement of the bank. He was going to come back stronger.

He looked around the boat at the other kids. They didn't

seem to have noticed him losing it. They were all too wrapped up in themselves, dipping their oars in the water, settling on the benches. Good.

'OK, let's do this,' DogNut shouted, and they were off, pulling fast through the shimmering water.

3

Apart from Finn they'd all arrived at the Tower floating down this stretch of river. After their sightseeing boat had hit a bridge and sank, they'd made it to the Tower on a flotilla of life rafts. The memories of that day were confused and the story of the fire and the battle had been told so many times that it had taken on the status of a myth. Things had been added, kids had enlarged their parts, so that now DogNut wasn't sure what bits of the story were real and what were made up.

It was going to be interesting travelling back upriver to Lambeth Bridge – where they planned to put ashore – interesting to see what memories it stirred. Brooke's crew had escaped north over the bridge in a supermarket lorry, and DogNut intended to follow the route they'd taken and try to find out what had happened to them.

They'd packed enough supplies to last them a week if they were careful. DogNut reckoned that any longer than that wouldn't be safe. If they hadn't found anyone in that time, they'd return to the Tower and try again at a later date.

He twisted round and looked at the others. Olivia sat up at the front like some kind of mini-figurehead. She was trembling slightly, whether from cold or fear he couldn't tell. Her face was set in a determined expression. Marco and Felix sat side by side on the first bench, already bickering and criticizing each other's rowing style. The next bench was taken up by Ugly Al and moody Jessica, rowing steadily and not talking to each other. DogNut and Courtney were on the last bench and Finn was at the back. As the only one of them facing the front, he was in charge of steering. He sat there, a huge silent presence. DogNut knew he was gutted about not being able to use his swollen arm, so it was good that he was some help to them as a navigator.

A fresh breeze was blowing in their faces as they manoeuvred into the middle of the river and they were soon passing the great blue-grey hulk of HMS *Belfast* to their left and pulling steadily towards London Bridge. Out here they could forget about the problems that were going on all around them in the city. The disaster might never have happened. It could have been just another day. From a distance the buildings looked just as they did on all the old postcards. The best thing was that no sickos could get to them here. They could row and row and keep on rowing until they'd left town, right out into the countryside if they wanted, and no diseased mothers or fathers could stop them. The kids had been using the river more and more lately, and were beginning to understand what a useful thing it was to have right next to the Tower.

It was still hard going, though, digging into the choppy water, trying to keep the strokes even and not tangle the oars. Slowly they began to work together as a team and drop into a steady rhythm.

DogNut was soon caught up in it, in sync with Courtney: leaning forward, dropping the oars, pulling back, lifting the oars, forward, back, forward, back. DogNut had always been happier when he was doing something. He could switch his brain off and not worry about things. He didn't like thinking.

He smiled.

'You thinking about Brooke?' Courtney asked.

'Wasn't.' DogNut grinned at her. 'But now I am.'

'Do you think we'll find her?' she asked.

'I dunno,' said DogNut. 'I hope so. That's all I got, though, just hope.'

'You like a dog, ain't you?' said Courtney. 'You'll sniff her out.'

DogNut lifted his chin and howled.

'Not so loud.' Courtney laughed. 'She'll hear you coming and run a mile.'

DogNut grew serious. 'D'you think she likes me at all?'

'We better hope for your sake she does.'

'You don't reckon she likes Ed better?'

'I ain't seen her for a year,' Courtney protested. 'I don't know what she likes, do I?'

'Before then, though,' said DogNut. 'What about before?'

'Who knows the workings of that girl's mind?' Courtney raised her eyebrows. 'She always went for good-looking boys, though.'

'Like Ed,' said DogNut. 'Before he got that scar.'

'Yeah,' said Courtney. 'Always the cool boys that everyone wanted to go out with. She'd track them down, show them no mercy. Then mostly she'd get bored of them after a week. Move on.'

'Ed thinks she went off him when his face got cut up.'

'Maybe.'

'D'you think we've left it too late?' DogNut asked. 'D'you think we should have come looking for her before?'

'Dunno,' said Courtney. 'But we was too busy just trying to survive. Wouldn't have risked it before. Wouldn't have risked it with anyone else, either.'

'You mean it?' said DogNut.

'I mean it. You're a good guy, DogNut. Used to think you was just some idiot, you know? But you've grown up. Not too much, mind. You're still a good laugh. I mean, I like Ed, but sometimes he's, you know, he looks like there's a cloud hanging over him. You act like nothing's a hassle.'

'So, what sort of boys do you go for?' DogNut asked, and Courtney just made a grunt that could have meant anything.

'Well?' DogNut pressed her.

'I don't have a type.'

What she wanted to say was *skinny, funny boys who don't take things too seriously*. Boys like DogNut.

Courtney *did* miss Brooke. She *did* want to see her again, but the main reason for coming along on the expedition had been because she saw it as an opportunity to be alone with DogNut for a few days. Well, yeah, all right, not completely alone, but more alone than you ever could be in the Tower with all the other kids around. And now here she was, squeezed up against him, shoulder to shoulder on the bench. OK, so she was sweating too much and couldn't help puffing and panting as she worked her oar. Already her shoulders were aching, her hands were getting sore and the wooden seat seemed to be getting harder and harder. Despite all her padding.

Her big fat arse.

She was still closer to him than she'd ever been before.

Yeah. That was the truth of it. If it wasn't for how she felt about DogNut, she would never have come along in the first place. It was just too dangerous. She had a reputation as a fighter, as a big tough girl that you didn't argue with, but she still got scared, and the idea of leaving the safety of the Tower and setting off across London quite frankly terrified her. She was amazed that her feelings for DogNut were stronger than her fear.

Of course it was stupid. What hope did she have? She knew DogNut's reason for the trip was to find Brooke and try to persuade her that the two of them were meant for each other. Still, Courtney had this time with him . . . Maybe she could change his mind? She had pictured all sorts of things happening on the trip.

Like saving his life . . .

Pathetic.

What were the chances that a skinny pin like DogNut would go for a fat girl like her? Cos that's what she *was*: fat. Wasn't nothing she could do about it. She was born that way. She didn't eat any more than anyone else, she got exercise, she wasn't lazy or nothing. She was just fat. Her friends tried to reassure her, tell her she wasn't fat, that it was all muscle and bone . . . And she *was* muscly, stronger than any other girl she knew. It was just that when she looked in the mirror in her little room at the Tower – which was something she tried not to do that often – what she saw there was a big fat lump.

With a big fat arse.

She glanced round at DogNut, working away at the oars. He was a scraggy, stretched-out thing. His arms like twisted ropes. What did he see when he looked at her?

A mate? A soldier? A lump?

31

She was pathetic.

She didn't have a hope.

Pathetic and screwy.

Well, they were *all* screwy, weren't they, and this whole trip was screwy. Courtney fancied DogNut, DogNut fancied Brooke and Brooke probably still fancied Ed. Despite what DogNut thought.

Who did Ed fancy then? She had no idea. Ed kept himself to himself.

Yes, this was one screwy expedition. And who even knew whether Brooke was still alive? Funny how Courtney could have that thought without feeling anything. It wasn't a nice thought, let's face it, but for the last year she had been reminded of the reality of death nearly every day. She wasn't totally hardened to it. It still got to her when someone died. She still cried a bit, but she was much tougher than she had been before. A part of her could sit back and look at it coldly – Brooke might easily be dead. The part of her that might have been sad was pushed out of the way. She didn't want it to get any more battered than it was. Another part of her – a nasty, dark, sneaky part – secretly hoped that they wouldn't find Brooke, that she might be dead – that way DogNut was hers.

I don't really mean it, God. It was just a thought.

It was all right to have nasty thoughts, wasn't it? As long as you didn't hold on to them. And, really, come on, what were the chances of finding Brooke? One girl, out there in the whole of London. If she was even *in* London still. Brooke and the others had all got away on that big lorry full of food. What would have stopped them from just keeping on going, driving right out of London? All the stories were that it was worse in the countryside, but even so . . .

'I hope we find her,' she said. Trying to convince herself.

'We'll find something,' said DogNut. 'It's gonna be an adventure whatever.'

Yeah, thought Courtney worriedly . . . *whatever*.

4

'Didn't realize it was so close.'

'Me either.'

They were passing between the Tate Modern, the huge old power station that had been turned into an art gallery to the south, and St Paul's Cathedral, set back from the river to the north. St Paul's was gleaming white in the sun and was a solid reassuring sight. It had stood there for hundreds of years and looked like it would stand for hundreds more.

It was a shock to find it so close, though. The kids had learnt to avoid the area between the Tower and the cathedral. It was part of the no-go zone, the old financial district. Weird things happened there. Like what had happened to Leo. The streets this way were far too dangerous. Some time ago a couple of groups had set off to explore in that direction, and had never come back. Jordan Hordern forbade anyone else from heading there. Nowadays, if the kids at the Tower wanted to go further than the surrounding area, they headed east, or south, across Tower Bridge. The fire hadn't made it this far along the river and there were rich pickings in the houses and shops over the water.

'What was his name?' said DogNut who had been following his own train of thought.

'Who?' said Courtney.

'The nutjob who wanted to go to St Paul's? Crazy freak who made that stupid flag and was always spouting, like, religious stuff.'

'Matt.'

'That's it, Mad Matt. Wonder if he ever made it there?'

'I hope he drowned,' said Courtney flatly.

When they'd escaped from the fire on the tourist boat, Matt had gone crazy and tried to change their course down-river to the cathedral. It was his fault that the boat had crashed and sunk and Aleisha had been sucked into the river. Matt had last been seen floating away on a piece of wreckage with his followers.

Courtney wondered if he'd made it, if he'd been living in St Paul's all this time. So near, and yet a million miles away. It was weird to think of all the other kids who must be out there, in their own small groups dotted around London, trying to survive, only knowing their own patch.

A thought struck Courtney.

'We're doing a good thing,' she said. 'Isn't it?'

'Is it?' said DogNut. 'I don't think I ever done nothing good before.'

'Exploring,' said Courtney. 'Seeing what's out there. Meeting other kids. Pulling everything together.'

'You jumping ahead of yourself,' said DogNut. 'We ain't met no one yet.'

'But we will.'

'Look at that,' said Jessica, from her bench directly behind them.

DogNut and Courtney looked round. They had reached the edge of the fire damage. The buildings all along the south side of the river were blackened and broken – it was

35

a desolate wasteland. With no emergency services to put the blaze out it had raged for days, eating away at the city until rain and a change in the wind had finally halted it. A haze of smoke had hung over London for months after it had happened but now the skies were clear.

As the kids stared in fascination at the ruins they lost concentration and the boat was quickly out of control and turning in the water. It took some shouting and cursing until they finally got it straightened up and moving smoothly again, but they still couldn't help looking as they slid past the seemingly endless devastation. It brought it home to them all just how dangerous their mission was. Just how much London had changed.

As if to ram the point home, two dead bodies floated past. A little girl who must have been no older than five or six, her body puffy and bloated, her eyes eaten by fish, and a middle-aged man, his greenish skin covered in lumps and boils and swellings so that he looked like nothing so much as a giant dead toad.

The boat fell silent, all their efforts now focused on rowing, which was much more tiring than they'd expected, despite all their practice. It had felt easy at first, but they were becoming all too aware of just how big the river was, how heavy the boat was and how far it was to Lambeth Bridge. The bench seemed to dig into DogNut's backside so that he could feel every knot and ridge of grain in the hard wood. His back and arms ached; his hands felt raw.

They'd come to Waterloo, where there was a big bend in the river. They realized they would have to fight the fierce current that wanted to pull them to the north bank. Marco and Felix, who had been muttering at each other for the whole journey, raised their voices.

'You got to row harder,' Felix snapped.

'It's you who ain't rowing hard,' said Marco. 'The boat's, like, twisting round. You got to dig into the water.'

'What with? A spade?'

'No, with your oar, stupid.'

'I am digging in with my oar, you spaz. What do you think I'm doing?'

'Don't call me a spaz, you spaz, you're gonna get us drowned.'

'Will you two shut up!' DogNut shouted. 'And concentrate on not hitting the bridge. If we don't hold our line, we'll smash up against it.'

'You know you shouldn't use that word,' said Olivia to Marco and Felix.

'What word?' said Marco, fighting for breath.

'Spaz. It's a bad word. Paul hit someone once who said it.'

'Who's Paul?'

'He's my brother. He's the one we're going to find.'

'Right.'

'We had a cousin who was disabled. He was always getting bullied and Paul was always sticking up for him.'

'He sounds like a nice guy, your brother,' said Marco kindly.

'He sounds like a dick,' Felix murmured under his breath. Marco tried not to laugh. Luckily Olivia hadn't heard him.

'He's brilliant,' said Olivia. 'When my mum and dad died he looked after me.'

'We'll find him,' said Marco.

'The dick,' Felix added, slightly too loudly, and Marco snorted.

Olivia was about to say something else when Finn spoke for the first time.

Two words.

'Big Ben.'

'Nearly there,' DogNut gasped. 'Lambeth Bridge is right after the Houses of Parliament.'

But the rising tide was starting to lose its energy and no matter how hard they pulled on the oars it was almost as if they weren't moving at all. It got harder still as they passed under Westminster Bridge. The water here foamed and churned as it bunched up by the stonework. If they weren't careful they'd be swept on to one of the supports. Nobody said a word as they strained to keep the boat straight.

At last, nearly an hour after setting off from the Tower, they dragged the boat clear of the swirling, roaring water and emerged into the light at the other side of the bridge.

DogNut felt a surge of relief, but noise and movement made him look up and he saw a row of people craning over to peer at them from the terrace that ran along the back of the Houses of Parliament, overlooking the river.

He had a moment of panic, but was relieved to see that they were all kids. They must have spotted the rowing boat and come out to see what was happening. There wasn't a sick adult in sight. It gave him hope and renewed strength. He urged the others on. They had planned to row across to the south bank and land at Lambeth pier, but the kids along the embankment were shouting at them and gesturing towards their side of the river.

DogNut looked at Finn. There were still strong currents in the water and they were struggling to control the boat.

'Maybe we should go closer and see what they want.'

Finn said nothing, just gave a brief nod.

'Over to you,' said DogNut. 'Guide us in.'

Finn nodded again. 'There's a set of stairs leading up from the water,' he said. 'At the other end of the buildings. Might be a safe landing place.'

'We could give it a shot.'

Whatever happened, they couldn't stop rowing. If they did, the current would take over and pull the boat sideways along the river past where they wanted to land. So they kept close to the edge and Finn directed them towards the steps. They could hear the kids shouting down at them from the terrace.

'Where are you from?'

'Where did you get the boat?'

'Who are you?'

He couldn't make out the rest – they were talking over each other. And DogNut had a question of his own.

'Are those stairs over there safe?' he yelled.

'As far as we know.'

'They should be.'

'Haven't you never used them?'

'We don't have any boats.'

'What do you reckon?' DogNut asked Finn. 'Shall we risk it?'

Finn shrugged, squinting ahead and scratching his arm in its grubby sling.

'No reason why it's gonna be any more dangerous than the pier on the other side,' said Courtney. 'This is as far as we was gonna go. I say if there's steps here we use them.'

'We're gonna try and land at the stairs then,' DogNut shouted up at the kids on the terrace. 'Can you give us a hand?'

The kids above started running back into the building and through to the other side, so that by the time the rowing boat had reached the stairs there was a small crowd waiting for them, all shouting directions at the same time in a very unhelpful manner.

The stone steps sloped gently down to the water and although they looked slimy and wet they also looked pretty solid. They must have been used for hundreds of years by boatmen arriving at the parliament buildings.

Finn came alive, shouting instructions to the rowers, but this was the trickiest part. They knew that if they went too close to the edge too early their oars would simply crunch against the embankment wall that rose several metres above them. At some point, though, they were going to have to raise the oars and drift in to meet the stairs. If they overshot it, it would mean trying to row back against the current, which they all felt too tired to even think about.

They heaved at the oars in grim silence, concentrating hard. No one wanted to make a mistake.

DogNut's arms ached all the way up to his shoulders. They were rigid with tension. He risked looking round. They were only a couple of metres from the stairs. Finn was guiding them in expertly. He allowed himself to relax.

'Get ready to raise your oars on my side,' he said, and just then the boat jolted and there was a horrible scraping sound along the bottom. He felt it through his bones. As if something was gouging into his own body.

'We've hit something,' Olivia screamed.

5

The boat nearly tipped over, and the kids scrambled madly to right it, tangling their oars in their panic. Then it gave another lurch and there was the sound of splintering wood.

'Crap. Must be a wreck, or something,' said DogNut. 'Pray it ain't done too much damage.'

But even as he said it he knew they were in trouble. Water started to bubble into the bottom of the boat. Then there was another rending crack and a ripping sound and this time they could see a metal spar tearing through the planks at their feet.

The kids in the boat were thrown into chaos, floundering about and yelling at each other. They completely lost control and a couple of them dropped their oars over the sides. Now they were paddling and poling and splashing inelegantly as they struggled to get the sinking boat to the edge.

The skiff rocked madly from side to side and the stern was lower than the front. There was a real danger now that they might not make it to the bank. And if they fell in . . .

Courtney remembered what had happened to Aleisha when the tourist boat had sunk not far from here. How the water had seemed to reach into the cabin and grab hold of her. How quickly she had been dragged away.

DogNut tried to hold his nerve and not give in to the fear that was causing the others to be totally useless. He needed to try to think straight. He was their captain, after all. He lifted his oar from the water and held it out towards the knot of kids on the steps who were all shouting at the same time.

'Someone get a hold of this!' he shouted back at them. 'Pull us over!'

A big lad wearing a T-shirt with a Coke logo on it managed to get a hand to the oar, then his other hand, and he grunted as he tugged with all his might. A couple of his friends joined in and the boat, weighted down and sluggish with all the water in it, slowly drifted closer to the edge. Marco saw what was happening and was clear-headed enough to offer his own oar to the kids on the stairs. For once Felix didn't have a go at him; instead he gripped Marco's oar and the two of them held it hard.

Now the boat moved more quickly and at last bumped against the stonework. Helping hands took hold of the side as DogNut and his crew desperately chucked their soaking-wet belongings ashore. Bags of food and water, backpacks, spare clothing, sleeping bags, blankets, armour and weapons were passed in a chain from the stricken boat and up the stairs to dry land.

Finally, to a chorus of cheers from above, the kids scrambled ashore. DogNut was the last one off, and he jumped clear just as the edge of the boat dipped beneath the swirling grey water. It was too heavy now for the kids to hold on to. They let go and it disappeared into the murky depths. They all thought that would be the last they saw of it, but a few seconds later the prow bobbed up and skimmed along the surface like a shark's fin for a few metres, before it slowly sank and was swept away with all the other debris that was floating on the river.

DogNut swore. Unless they found another boat they would have to walk all the way back to the Tower. It had been going so well. If only he'd stuck to their original plan and gone over to the pier on the other side. He was suddenly filled with a vicious rage.

'Why didn't none of you tell me that wreck was there?' he blurted into some poor kid's face, spraying him with spit.

'We didn't know.'

'Yeah . . . well . . .'

DogNut stopped, deflated. There was no point in taking it out on this lot.

'Who's in charge?' he asked, looking around.

'I am,' came a voice from above and he looked up to see a girl with pale skin and a bright flash of flaming red hair leaning over the wall. The sun caught in it and it looked like a golden mane around her head. DogNut smiled. The sight of a pretty girl always lifted his spirits. He bounced up the steps and offered her a high five.

She returned it self-consciously – this was obviously not her style. She stood there slightly unsure of herself, a group of guys standing around her holding clubs. DogNut sucked his teeth, giving the girl the once-over.

'Pleased to meet you, gyal,' he said. 'The name's DogNut.'

The girl raised her eyebrows, but didn't smile. She looked very serious.

'Was my gamer's tag,' DogNut explained. 'And it, like, stuck.'

The girl looked none the wiser.

'You know what a gamer's tag is?' he went on.

'No. Do I need to?'

'Not really.' DogNut laughed. 'I ain't played no computer games in ages. So, what's your name?'

'Nicola.'

'Cool.'

Nicola had a posh voice, which only made DogNut fancy her more. He'd always been attracted to posh girls. Although they weren't always attracted to him. Not wanting to be caught staring at her, he checked out his surroundings. As well as the guys with clubs there were about twenty other kids arranged in a loose circle round DogNut and his crew. They were in a long triangular park surrounded by trees that extended from the end of the Houses of Parliament. The kids had added to the original fence with poles and spikes and barbed wire to keep out intruders, and the lawn had been dug up and planted with vegetables. The planting looked much more professionally done than their efforts back at the Tower.

DogNut spotted the equipment that had been rescued from the boat piled up a few metres away.

'We better get our gear,' he said, and made a move towards the pile. Nicola put up her hand, halting him.

'In a minute.'

Now it was DogNut's turn to raise his eyebrows.

'You got a problem?' he said, keeping it polite for now.

'You tell me.'

'I ain't got a problem.'

Nicola turned to the watching kids.

'Get back to work,' she said, and the kids drifted away in ones and twos. Only the ones who were armed stayed with Nicola. They didn't look very welcoming.

Nicola turned back to DogNut. 'We need to talk.'

6

'Do I look like a sicko?' DogNut threw up his arms in protest. 'Do I look like a grown-up? A zombie? Whatever you might call them. Do I?'

'No.' Nicola held DogNut's gaze.

'Well then.'

They were in the middle of the park, DogNut and the other kids from the boat crew surrounded by the boys with clubs. Other boys and girls were busy working at the rows of vegetables: digging, weeding, checking for pests. A few more patrolled the perimeter along the road. They weren't as well-armed as the guards back at the Tower, and carried an odd assortment of spears, knives and clubs. DogNut was trying to stay cool, and the rest of his crew were angry rather than scared, except for Olivia who was holding on to Finn's good arm.

DogNut reckoned they might be able to rush the guards, overpower them and get to their weapons. He and Courtney and the Good, the Bad and the Ugly were all tough fighters. But for now he was holding back, waiting to see what was going to unfold here.

'We have to be very careful,' Nicola explained. 'We don't know who you are –'

'But –' DogNut tried to interrupt, but Nicola cut him off.

'We're always under attack from other children.'

'You're joking me.'

'I'm deadly serious.' And she looked it. 'We don't know anything about you.'

'Do we look like an invading army?' DogNut laughed. 'There's only eight of us.'

'True. But most of the attacks on us are sneak attacks, by small groups. There's a bunch of kids have set up camp in St James's Park. They're not very nice. They're always sending raiding parties down here, trying to steal from us.'

'Well, we ain't from St James's Park.'

'Where *are* you from?'

'Look,' said DogNut, 'you being bare rude here, sister. You need to jam your hype and tell your boydem to stand down. They making me uncomfortable. Then we all just shake hands, sit down somewhere cosy like and have a nice civilized chat. What do you say to that?'

Nicola thought about it for a moment then relaxed.

'OK,' she said, nodding to some benches at the edge of the park. 'Over there.'

Once they were seated DogNut explained who they were and where they were from. Nicola seemed satisfied, but still a little wary.

'So you're looking for friends,' she said when DogNut had finished.

'You got it.'

'They came over the bridge well near to here, in the fire,' said Courtney. 'That's why we come up this way. We mainly looking for a girl called Brooke. Blonde hair and a big mouth on her.'

Nicola looked around at the five boys who were still with

her. 'Don't think we have anyone called Brooke here, do we?' Her friends shook their heads.

'When she come over the bridge she was in a big Tesco lorry,' said DogNut. 'With a load of other kids.'

'I remember the lorry,' said a tall boy with a wispy growth on his top lip that wasn't quite a moustache. He was missing his front teeth and wore his hair in a ponytail. 'I came over Lambeth Bridge at the same time.'

'What happened to it?' DogNut asked.

The boy shrugged. 'It didn't stop. Far as I remember, it just kept on going.'

'And none of you know where it went? What happened to the kids on board?'

'What about Paul?' Olivia chipped in. 'My brother? Paul Channing? He wasn't on the lorry. He might have come here? We're not only looking for Brooke.'

Suddenly the boat crew were all talking at once. Asking after friends, relatives.

Nicola held out her hands and had to almost shout to be heard.

'OK, listen,' she said. 'We'll call a session of parliament.'

'You'll do what?' said DogNut, taken aback.

'Parliament,' said Nicola matter-of-factly, as if it was the most normal thing in the world.

DogNut didn't know whether to laugh, but chose not to. Nicola had such a serious expression on her face.

'That's how we run things here,' she said. 'We vote on everything. If we call a session, everyone has to attend and we can ask if anyone knows anything about your friends.'

'You vote on everything?' said DogNut.

'Yes.'

'So they voted you in charge then?'

'Yes,' said Nicola. 'I won the vote. They made me prime minister.'

Now DogNut couldn't stop himself from laughing. It sounded too much like a game, or a school project. But Nicola looked more serious than ever and DogNut's laughter died away.

'I know it sounds a bit silly,' she said, and at last she did smile. 'But we have to start setting up some sort of order in the world. There are lots of children here and they need things to be normal; they need to have some kind of structure in their lives.'

How quickly they'd had to grow up, DogNut thought. It was a simple choice, behave like adults, or die like babies.

'True dat,' he said. 'Just like Jordan Hordern is big man at the Tower. He's a general, though – he ain't no prime minister.'

'Doesn't matter what we're called,' said Nicola. 'But it made sense, as we were all living here, to set up an old-style government.'

'So why *are* you living here then?'

'It's safe,' said the boy with the ponytail. 'The Houses of Parliament is one of the most secure places in the country.'

'Guess so,' said DogNut.

'It's too big for us, really,' Nicola added. 'But more children arrive all the time.'

'A lot of us were already here when the fire broke out last year,' said Ponytail. 'And then hundreds more kids poured across the bridges. Some of them stopped here.'

'But not Brooke?' Courtney asked.

'Sorry,' said Ponytail. 'Don't think so.'

'As I say,' said Nicola, standing up, 'we'll call a session. You make up a list of names of the people you're looking for. There are nearly a hundred of us here – someone might know something.'

An hour later and all the kids were assembled on the rows of red leather benches in the House of Lords. It was gloomy and cold, despite the light streaming in through the high stained-glass windows that ran down either side of the hall.

'Fancy,' said Courtney as she sat down next to DogNut and looked around at the carved wood panelling that covered the walls, the gold leaf, the chandeliers, the oil paintings.

'It looks like a film or something,' said DogNut. 'At least they ain't wearing any fancy robes and wigs.'

The boat crew had been given their gear back, but Nicola had insisted she keep hold of their weapons and armour until they were ready to leave.

Nicola was sitting on a golden throne at one end, her ministers on the benches nearby. She called for quiet, explained the purpose of the meeting and then read out the names that DogNut had given her, adding a brief description of the lorry crossing the bridge.

A murmur went around the assembled kids and Nicola let them talk for a couple of minutes. It was soon clear, though, that nobody was going to jump up and say, 'That's me!' or, 'I know where they are.' Slowly the noise died down and Nicola spoke again.

'So nobody knows anything about any of these children?' she asked.

There were shaking heads and mumbled 'no's all around. Courtney felt a mixture of disappointment and relief. She still couldn't get her mixed-up feelings about Brooke and DogNut straight in her head. And then, to her surprise, she found herself standing up and calling out into the echoing space of the hall.

'Did nobody even see what way the lorry went then?'

'I saw it,' someone shouted. 'It just carried on going.'

'There was some other boys walking with it,' said Courtney. 'Posh kids all in red with rifles. What about them?'

'Everyone knows them,' said a girl at the back.

'What do you mean?' Courtney looked confused.

A stocky kid with a shaved head stood up and called over to her.

'You see their leader? Was he a weirdo called David?'

'Yeah, that's him,' said Courtney. 'You got it. He was in charge of them.'

'He a friend of yours then?' said the stocky kid.

'Not exactly,' said DogNut. 'He was guarding the lorry. Wherever he is, the lorry ought to be too.'

'They're at Buckingham Palace then.'

A noisy hubbub of chatter broke out among the assembled kids. Nicola stared across at the new arrivals.

DogNut leant over and muttered to Courtney. 'So David's at Buckingham Palace. That makes sense. This lot have set themselves up as the government – David's set himself up as the bloody king.'

Courtney laughed and DogNut straightened. 'How far is it to the palace from here?' he asked.

51

'It's only about ten minutes away,' said someone sitting nearby.

'Sorted!' DogNut punched the air. 'So do any of you mugs want to come with us? Show us the way? Keep us safe? We don't know this area . . . Anyone?'

Nobody made a move to volunteer, and DogNut sighed.

Waste of time. This bunch might have been well organized, but they weren't exactly the most adventurous kids in the world.

'I have to ask you again,' said Nicola. 'What is your relationship with David?'

'I don't have no relationship with David,' said DogNut with a smirk. 'You calling me gay?'

A ripple of laughter spread among the seated children.

'I just want to know what he is to you,' said Nicola patiently.

'He ain't nothing to me,' said DogNut. 'He tipped up at the War Museum just before it all kicked off, looking for guns, yeah. When everyone had to get out on account of the fire, he kind of, like, volunteered himself to guard the lorry. Wanted a piece of what was on it, the food and that. Why you ask? You got a problem with him?'

'You could say that. David's always trying to take over here.'

'He one of these raiders you told us about?'

'No. He's got a lot of kids at the palace. He wants more, though. Keeps trying to make a deal with us. But you can't trust him. One of my promises when I was standing for government was that I wouldn't ever have anything to do with him.'

'Well, you telling us how to get there ain't exactly gonna break no promise, is it?'

'No. But I can't let anyone go with you.'

Courtney shook her head and looked at DogNut.

'What other promises did you make?' DogNut asked. 'Just so's we know.'

'My only other promise was that I'd never attack any other kids.'

DogNut laughed. 'That why you took our weapons and set your soldiers on us then?'

'That was self-defence.'

'If you say so.'

'So you ain't none of you gonna help us?' Courtney shouted angrily.

'We're not fighters here,' said Nicola.

'No, you're talkers. And talking ain't no use to us.'

Courtney left her place and headed for the doors, telling the others to come with her. They hesitated for a moment, then drifted after her. DogNut followed her and put a hand on her arm, slowing her down.

'Ain't so bad, gyal,' he said. 'We got us a lead. At least we know where David went. Can't blame these kids for not helping more. They got problems of their own.'

'Maybe.'

'Wait a minute!' It was Nicola, hurrying to catch up with them. She looked flushed and slightly embarrassed. Courtney gave her the cold shoulder, but DogNut waited for her.

'I'm sorry,' she said. 'But you must understand. I've got to look after my people. It's not far to the palace. You should be OK.'

'Yeah?'

'You're welcome to stay with us here for a bit if you want. As long as you stick to our rules.'

'Thanks but no thanks,' said DogNut. 'Is a cool offer, like, but we come up this way to find old friends. We ain't gonna crash just yet. We gotta keep moving. So what's it like round here? Many sickos?'

'Sickos?'

'Grown-ups. Mothers and fathers . . .'

'Oh, them. We call them oppoes – short for the opposition.'

'The enemy?'

'Yes.'

'They bother you any?'

'There's always some around. Less than there used to be. David's actually done quite a lot to clean the streets up. And lots of them have just starved to death, I guess, or been killed by the disease. It's not too bad in the day, but it's certainly not safe out on the streets after dark.'

'Sounds familiar,' said DogNut.

The gap-toothed kid with the ponytail – he seemed to be Nicola's deputy – had joined them.

'We've tried to clear out the area as well as we can,' he explained. 'But they're starting to come over the bridges again, from the south. Real mean ones. As Nicola said, we're not really fighters here; we've fallen back on our defences instead. There are some gangs out there, though. Hunters. They wander the streets looking for oppoes. We sort of rely on them to keep us safe.'

'If you bumped into a hunter gang out there, they might be able to give you some more information,' said Nicola, trying to be helpful. 'They cover a lot of ground.'

'So you wouldn't consider breaking your rules and borrowing us an escort?'

Nicola looked embarrassed.

'I can't order anyone to go with you. I can let everyone know that if they want to help I'm not going to stop them, but . . .'

'But you ain't fighters. You gonna stick behind your strong walls.'

'I'll give you your weapons back, and it's our lunchtime in half an hour. I can offer you a meal and some water. How's that?'

'Deal. Then we on our way, sister.'

8

They were ready to leave. They'd had something to eat, picked up their weapons, strapped their extra belongings to their backpacks, put on their bits and pieces of armour and now they stood by the Sovereign's Entrance in Victoria Tower.

Being in the Houses of Parliament, among the lush trappings of the old world, had felt like a dream. She had never realized just how big the place was. Almost like a small city within a city. They had only seen a tiny part of it. She had heard some of the kids call it the palace of Westminster. And it was a palace – full of paintings, and gold, and marble floors. More than ever Courtney felt like London had been turned into a giant playhouse and they were just silly toddlers dressing in their mum and dads' clothes and parading about pretending to be adults. What hope did any of them ever have of building anything like this in the future? How would they even know where to start? Massive carved stone pillars rose above their heads, supporting arches and beams and statues and huge windows. Even the Lego buildings she'd tried to make as a kid had always collapsed. She remembered learning about the Romans at primary school (they always seemed to be learning about the Romans). About how when they left England everything had started to go wrong; all their fine buildings, with mosaics and central heating and toilets and murals and whatever, had fallen apart. The Brits went back to their old ways – living in mud huts, huddled round fires, eating crap – and everything the Romans had brought here had been forgotten. They called it the Dark Ages. Must have been a rubbish time. Well, they were in a new Dark Age now, weren't they? That was for sure.

And the Romans had left them to it again.

Actually, no, the Romans hadn't all done a bunk. Some of them had stayed behind. Some of them had become monsters.

Courtney looked around her little group. Apart from Marco and Felix who were having an argument about who had the heaviest backpack, they were silent and tense. Olivia was sticking close to Finn, comforted by his size. Al and Jessica were slumped against the wall, waiting for the off. DogNut was standing at the entrance, looking out into the thin spring sunshine. They'd all been eager to press on, but now they were holding back. Nervous. Unsure of what lay in wait for them out there.

'We gonna go then, or what?' she said, approaching DogNut.

'Guess so,' said DogNut. 'Let's get rocking.'

They trooped down a wide row of steps towards the iron gates, DogNut and Courtney leading the way. Behind them came Al and Jessica with Olivia and Finn; bringing up the rear were Marco and Felix, seemingly the only two glad to be getting out of here. They hadn't come along on the expedition to listen to a lot of chat and watch a bunch of snotty kids pretend they were the government. They wanted to explore and chase sickos and fight and have some good stories to take back with them.

At the Tower Jordan Hordern made them all do two hours' military training every day, but they hardly ever got the chance to use any of their combat skills. Most of the sickos had been cleared out of the area around the Tower, apart from the no-go zone, of course.

But the thing about a no-go zone was that you never went there. That was the whole point.

A scruffy boy wearing a tall blue policeman's helmet was waiting to let them out. The helmet was way too big for him and it hung down over his eyes, his hair sticking out untidily at the back and sides. He was nervously tapping his leg with a truncheon and as he saw the boat crew approaching he unlocked the gate and swung it open.

'I like your helmet, boydem,' said Marco, 'but it don't fit you too good.'

'It's not as cool as yours,' the kid replied.

Marco was wearing a First World War German helmet with a spike in the top. As much for show as for protection. He'd found it at the Imperial War Museum and was never without it.

'Ta,' he said. 'It's a real babe magnet.'

'Is it?'

'What do you think? Has a girl ever said to you she really likes a man in a stupid helmet?'

'Guess not. But there's a joke in there somewhere.'

'Save it.'

The boy was about to say something else when there was a sudden movement and he fell back.

DogNut stiffened like a hound spotting a rival.

'What is it?' asked Courtney.

A group of kids had appeared from a nearby hiding-place. They rushed the gates and barged past the kid in the

58

helmet, throwing him to the ground. They were a dirty, mean-looking bunch, armed with metal bars.

They stopped when they saw DogNut's crew. Getting the measure of them. Their leader stepped forward.

'All right?' he said. 'We come to collect our tax.'

He had a dirty bandanna tied round his head, and wore a shirt with the sleeves cut off, long shorts and heavy boots with no socks. He was casually dangling a machete from a leather-gloved hand. His arms were lean and suntanned. He had the look of someone who had been living rough on the streets.

DogNut sniffed and stepped towards him.

'You got something to say?' said the kid with the bandanna.

'This ain't my beef,' said DogNut.

The boy in the policeman's helmet struggled to his feet.

'Why don't you all sod off?' he said, and one of the marauders knocked his helmet off, then, as he bent over to pick it up, booted him in the backside, sending him sprawling into the iron railings.

'Leave him alone,' said DogNut.

'Thought you said this wasn't your argument,' said Bandanna.

'It will be if you keep dumping on that kid.'

Bandanna gave a little nod to one of his friends who gave the poor kid in the helmet a vicious whack in the side with his club. The kid groaned and curled up on the ground.

'Don't get involved,' Courtney hissed at DogNut.

'I am involved,' he replied, and now it was his turn to nod at his team. Marco, Felix and Ugly Al came forward. Marco carried a short spear, Felix had a sword and Al was armed with a heavy mace. There were five guys with

Bandanna, so he had a numerical advantage. It was clear, though, that if there was a fight it would be bloody. Someone could easily wind up dead. It wasn't a risk any of them wanted to take. They stood there, taunting each other, hurling insults, and in the end DogNut went toe-to-toe with Bandanna. Their faces millimetres apart.

'We'll take you down, you skonky ratburger!' DogNut yelled.

'Yeah, well, I'll cut you first.'

'Pretty tough with that chopper in your fist, ain't you?'

'All right!' Bandanna dropped the machete and threw his arms wide. 'You want some of me? Come on then! Take it!'

DogNut couldn't believe the guy was being so stupid and quickly punched him hard in the throat before he had a chance to defend himself. Bandanna gasped and collapsed. The Good, the Bad and the Ugly saw their opening and rushed forward, crowding the rest of the gang out. Then, with threats and shoves and raised weapons, they hustled them through the gate, two of the intruders holding up Bandanna, who was struggling to breathe.

As they retreated down the road, DogNut picked up the machete and hurled it after them.

'Take your pencil sharpener with you!' he shouted, and laughed as they danced out of the way of the whirling blade. Bandanna wrenched himself from the hands of his friends and croaked hoarsely at DogNut.

'You shouldn't of done that. We'll be back. And there'll be more of us next time. The taxes have just gone up!'

'Yeah? Tax my arse!' DogNut shouted, and waggled his rear at them.

They helped the local kid to his feet and he straightened his helmet, thanking them over and over.

'Who were they?' Courtney asked.

'Kids from the park,' said the boy. 'They're raiding us more and more lately. They wait for an opening then steam in. I thought it was all clear, but they must have been hiding behind one of the old security barriers. Basically they get inside and try to get hold of food and stuff. The kid you punched out's called Carl, one of their gang leaders. I guess I owe you one.'

'Save it,' said DogNut. 'You want to help us you can tell us the best way to Buckingham Palace.'

The boy scratched an armpit and pointed with his truncheon.

'Across the square and straight up Birdcage Walk. That's the way I'd go.'

'Cheers.'

'You'd have to be stupid to go my way, though,' the boy added.

'Why's that?'

'Cos Birdcage Walk runs along next to St James's Park, which is where your new best mate, Carl, and his crew came from.'

'So why'd you say you'd go that way, then?' DogNut asked.

The boy made a dismissive farting sound with his lips. 'Dunno. I always get things wrong on behalf of I'm a bit thick.'

'What's your name?' Courtney asked him.

'My mates call me Bozo.'

'Why that?'

'Told you. Cos I'm a idiot.' Bozo hit his helmet with the truncheon, hard enough for it to make a loud thwack. He went cross-eyed.

DogNut pressed him. 'Do you want to tell us the best way or not?'

'If you were cleverer than me you'd go up Victoria Road and swing round to hit the palace from the side. Is a bit further, but you'd avoid the mugs in the park.'

'We'll go the clever way then,' said DogNut.

'Thought you might,' said Bozo. 'But be careful. I was at the palace before I came here. David's bad news. He's a creep. He don't like anyone to disagree with him. Keeps everything locked down. It was well hard to get away, I can tell you. And he keeps trying to get children from here to go and join him. You know, like Facebook? Everyone used to try and have the most friends. It's like that. He wants the most followers.'

'Kids like David don't bother us,' said DogNut, leading his gang out of the gate. 'We'll be fine.'

Bozo saluted them and wished them luck.

'Dick,' said Felix as they marched off across the road. DogNut laughed and led them round the great bulk of Westminster Abbey and on to Victoria Street, the wide road on the other side. They kept to the middle and formed into a loose bunch, with nobody really taking the lead. None of them seemed to want to be the one out in front.

Marco and Felix were the most relaxed, they chatted to Finn, who carried Olivia on his shoulders.

'What did you reckon to the talent back there?' Felix asked.

'Didn't really notice,' said Finn. 'Other things on my mind.'

'Tell you the truth, man,' Felix went on, 'the main reason me and Marco come along on this trip in the first place was to see if we could find us some new wifeys. Know what I mean? The maths ain't so good back at the Tower. There's way more boys than girls.'

'I'm a girl,' said Olivia.

'You don't count, darling.'

'We sick of the same old faces day in, day out,' said Marco. 'And nothing much has changed since the sickness, has it? The peng girls still go with the popular guys, the fighters, the leaders, the good-looking ones. The *lucky* ones. The rest of us . . . We do what we can.'

'There's always Jessica,' said Finn, nodding towards her. 'She just split up with her boyfriend.'

'Yeah, Jessica,' said Marco, making a face. 'To be honest, I always thought she looked kinda . . . sour.'

Al was stuck with Jessica again. He'd had no choice on the boat, but he'd been hoping that once they hit dry land he could dump her and hang with Marco and Felix who always made him laugh. Jessica had latched on to him, though, and wouldn't stop going on about her ex-boyfriend, Brendan. She went over, again and again, all the details of their break-up. Al hoped to God she wasn't interested in him. He much preferred having a laugh with the guys than chatting to girls about all the things they were interested in, like emotions. He was pretty sure she wasn't interested in him as a potential boyfriend. Girls never went for him that way. He was just a handy ear to babble into. He almost felt jealous of Finn, carrying Olivia. He bet she didn't go on about emotions and ex-boyfriends and who said what to who and why. Probably too busy banging on about her perfect brother, Paul.

Courtney, meanwhile, was taking the opportunity to talk to DogNut.

'You scared at all?'

'Yeah. I guess. Our likkle pleasure cruise was the easy bit. Bummer that we lost the boat, but in the future that's gonna be the way to do it.'

'The future?' Courtney protested. 'I ain't doing this again.'

'No. Don't you feel it, gyal?' said DogNut excitedly. 'This is about more than finding lost friends.'

'Is it? News to me.'

'Come on. You said it on the boat. We're explorers. What were we gonna do? Sit on our arses at the Tower growing old and fat? Dying there? No way! There's a big world out here, and I aim to see some of it. We got places to go. Mysteries to solve. We need to know what's going down.'

'Do we?'

'Yeah. We gonna go back to the Tower as heroes, explorers. I'm gonna be important, Courtney. I'm gonna change things. We gonna blow this town wide open. The Thames is gonna be, like, our main road. We can easily link up with other kids like the ones at the Houses of Parliament.'

'I quite liked the sound of sitting safe behind the walls at the Tower growing old and fat,' said Courtney. 'Well ... *fatter*. I mean, do you think we're really ready for this?' As she said it, she glanced nervously around at the big buildings looming up on either side of them, half expecting a bunch of sickos to jump out from every shadowed doorway.

'We ready,' said DogNut, and his confidence spilt over into her. 'Last time we come up this way was a year ago. We know better now how not to get whacked. We've had a whole year more of learning about the sickos, of learning the best way of fighting them.'

'Or running away,' said Courtney.

'That's how you know, sister!' said DogNut. 'When to fight, when to run. I ain't dumb! I know it's not gonna be no picnic. So, *yeah*, I'm scared, but I'm not scared, if you know what I mean. What about you?'

Courtney just shrugged, letting him think she was tougher than she was. Someone he could rely on.

'I remember one time, back at the museum,' she said after a while. 'Me and Brooke and Aleisha was talking. We'd been out and found the lorry, we was all feeling good, reckoned we could handle the sickos, no problem. Anyway, we was talking – and I always remember it for some reason – maybe it was the last time we was all together and happy. I said the only problem with sickos was if you got overwhelmed. Only I couldn't remember the word at the time. Overwhelm. It's a weird word. We all had a laugh about me trying to remember it. *Overwhelm*. It ain't a word you get to use that much. And whenever I think of Brooke and Aleisha we're back there, the three of us, laughing.'

'It *is* a weird word, *overwhelm*,' said DogNut. 'I can't get it out of my brain now thanks to you.'

'You know what I mean, though,' said Courtney. 'Don't you? They're only really dangerous, the sickos, when there's loads of them. One or two you can handle, but when there's, like, hundreds . . .'

DogNut nodded, didn't say anything for a moment, because he was suddenly right back there at the bank, and Leo, poor clumsy Leo, was being overwhelmed by sickos.

No other word for it.

He shook his head, dragged himself back into the present.

'We gonna make sure,' he said, 'that whatever happens we ain't overwhelmed. All right? Deal?'

'Deal.'

And as they slapped palms, almost as if it had been arranged by a God with a sick sense of humour, they saw movement ahead and watched open-mouthed as a large group of adults crossed the road in front of them.

'Oh crap,' said DogNut, and he drew his sword.

9

Marco licked his dry lips. His chest felt tight. This was all beginning to get a bit too real. It had been easy, fun even, rowing up the Thames, and they'd never been too scared of the kids at the Houses of Parliament. They were a bunch of wimps really. He and Felix had started to think that perhaps the world was a safer place than they'd imagined, stuck inside their castle. As they were getting ready to leave, they'd laughed about it together, complained that they were getting bored. Now, seeing the sickos crossing the road, it didn't seem quite so funny.

And, Jesus, there were a lot of them.

The kids froze, hoping they hadn't been spotted. But then something alerted one of the sickos and he turned. A moment later all the other adults stopped. They were too far away for Marco to see them clearly, but he'd glimpsed enough of them to be able to tell that they were fast-moving for sickos. That meant they were younger and not as badly diseased.

The most dangerous type.

'What do we do?' he said.

'We run, I guess,' said Felix. 'There's way too many to fight.'

Marco turned round to see if the road was still clear behind them. 'Back to the Houses of Parliament?'

'Or we could go up a side-street,' said Courtney. 'Try and get round them.'

'Good idea,' said DogNut and they dodged up a smaller road called Broadway, pushing on in a fast jog, their packs rattling on their backs.

As they crossed over the next junction, however, they saw another group of sickos running towards them from the side. The kids swore and picked up their speed, only to find the way ahead blocked by yet another gang so that they were forced to duck into an alleyway that branched off to their left. Things were happening too fast for them to get scared, and as long as they kept moving, they were in with a chance of getting away without a fight.

DogNut was hot and angry. It would be a mighty pain in the arse if his expedition fouled up on day one. He wanted to be remembered for something heroic, not for leading his friends into a hopeless dangerous mess.

But that's exactly what he *had* done . . .

The alley turned a sharp corner and came to a dead end. A literal dead end – there was a pile of ancient corpses here, lying on top of each other, dried out in the sun at the base of a brick wall.

Courtney cursed loudly. 'Now what do we do?'

'We hope they didn't see us,' said DogNut. 'Hope they run past.'

'No such luck,' said Marco, who'd been keeping a look-out at the corner. 'Here they come!'

The kids dropped into a defensive huddle, DogNut, Marco, Felix and Al at the front with Courtney, Olivia, Finn and Jessica behind them. Olivia was whimpering. Jessica put an arm round her and tried to comfort her, but it only seemed to make the little girl wail louder, her thin piercing voice bouncing off the high walls of the alley.

DogNut turned round and told her rather too harshly to shut up.

They waited in silence now, breathing hard, tensed, weapons held out in front of them, watching as the group of sickos came down the alleyway towards them.

Courtney tried to stop her short spear shaking in her hands. She didn't want DogNut to know just how terrified she was. There was a hotness spreading down her thighs beneath her jeans where she'd wet herself. All she wanted to do was curl up in a ball on the floor. But she told herself that she had to stand there. Stand and fight.

As the sickos drew nearer, she was able to get a good look at them. They were young, mostly in their twenties, she reckoned, and for sickos they were fit. Lean and toned and tough-looking. They mostly wore sports gear – tracksuit bottoms or shorts, tight vests and T-shirts – some were half naked, displaying taut, well-defined muscles. They looked for all the world as if they'd just come from the gym. One appeared to have iPod headphones stuck in his ears; another wore a sweat band round his head. Most had the usual covering of boils and sores, but one or two of them looked completely untouched by disease.

They weren't human any more, though.

It was their eyes that gave them away. They were dead, like sharks' eyes.

No, they weren't human. They were animals, intent on one thing and one thing only: catching and eating their prey.

They were also better organized than most sickos. There was a young mother at the front who was acting as their leader. She was bolder than the others, who seemed to be following her lead. She wore jogging pants and had her hair pulled into a crude ponytail. She also appeared to be wearing make-up. It was smeared over her face in a complete mess of eyeshadow and lipstick and pink blusher. Like a little girl who'd been at her mum's cosmetics.

DogNut didn't take his eyes off her. He gripped his sword tight with both hands. It was a civil war Roundhead sword, heavy and strong enough to split a skull. He had a breastplate protecting his torso and wore heavy leather gauntlets. He wished he'd brought a shield along with him, but he hadn't wanted to be too weighed down. Sickos didn't carry weapons. It was their teeth you had to watch out for. Any small cut could get infected.

The biggest danger was getting bottled up like this. If there were enough sickos, they could get in past the kids' weapons and DogNut and his crew would be swamped. No, what was the word Courtney had used?

Overwhelmed.

'Come on,' he growled quietly, trying to think of a plan.

If he could take down the mother, maybe the others would back off. If he made an attack now, while they didn't expect it, if he took the fight to them, he might just be able to finish it before it got going.

He yelled and ran at the mother, sword sweeping down from over his head. But he'd waited too long; she was ready for him. She shrank back to the safety of the other sickos. DogNut's stroke swished harmlessly down through thin air and he couldn't risk advancing into their ranks. There must have been at least twenty sickos crammed in here.

He lifted his sword again and bellowed a war cry. The lead mother tilted her head to one side, watching him like a bird. The father with headphones nodded and opened his mouth to let out a strangled yowl.

And then they attacked. Hurling themselves at the kids.

DogNut and the boat crew were used to fighting, and the sickos were unarmed so their first wave was easily thrown back. There was the sound of metal striking bone, hacking flesh, and then a skeletal mother lay dead at DogNut's feet; a father was crawling away, bleeding heavily from a spear cut to his shoulder; a young mother in a bright yellow tracksuit had lost the fingers from one hand and she was shaking it in confusion, watching the blood as it sprayed up the sides of the alleyway.

So far none of the kids were hurt.

DogNut allowed himself to believe for a moment that perhaps their chances of survival weren't as low as he'd feared.

He didn't have long to enjoy the feeling as the bravest of the sickos came forward again: four fathers with bare torsos and grubby shorts. DogNut could see the sweat lying thick on their skin, saliva drooling from their mouths, the whites of their watery eyes mottled red and yellow and brown. They came in a pack, fast and hard. It wasn't so easy to knock them back this time. In the cramped alleyway DogNut couldn't get a good swing and was scared of hurting one of his friends with his sword. He spotted Al lashing out with his mace, repeatedly battering one of the sickos who wouldn't give up. Courtney and Felix were hemmed in, stabbing and shoving. Then Marco's spear was knocked flying and he quickly drew a long knife from his belt, but the lead mother had been waiting behind the four fathers and she darted out and clawed at his wrist with long fingernails. Marco yelped in agony and tried to stab the mother. Somehow, though, she wrenched the knife from his grasp and was just about to bite his forearm when Al hit her from behind with his mace. She spun round with a snarl of fury but, before she could go for Al, Finn punched her hard in the side of the neck with his good hand. At last she retreated with the second wave of sickos.

All except for one short father who lay still on the ground next to the dead mother.

Two down, eighteen to go.

And now the lead mother was armed. She raised Marco's knife above her head. DogNut felt his heart sink and his energy drain away. Sickos didn't usually know how to use weapons, but this mother must have been smarter than the others. And if she was smarter then she was more danger-ous. It was now more important than ever to take her out. Easier said than done. She was protected by the knot of fathers around her.

She tipped her head back, shook the knife and let out a long high-pitched wailing scream. The other sickos joined in, hissing and gurgling, the less diseased managing a sort of sick animal whine.

The sight of the mother waving the knife seemed to give them courage and they massed for another attack. Normal human beings would have been too scared of the kids' weapons. Sickos were stupid, though. No matter how many of them died the rest would keep on coming if they were hungry enough.

Marco straightened his German helmet. He'd managed to pick up his spear, but his face was twisted in pain. The mother had wrenched his arm and holding the weapon was obviously difficult for him. Felix had taken a knock to the head. His left ear was bleeding badly. The spear in Courtney's hands was shaking, its bloodied tip drawing a crazy zigzag in the air. Olivia was whimpering again. The sound was dispiriting, but DogNut didn't have the strength to tell her to be quiet.

He tried to focus all his concentration on the sickos. Tried to anticipate their attack. Pick his targets.

He knew, though, that if the sickos attacked with enough force, and threw as many bodies into the assault as they could, the small group of kids wouldn't stand a chance.

He swore. The sickos moaned, shuffled forward, twitching and dribbling . . .

'Come on,' DogNut muttered. 'Come on, you butters freaks, come and get some . . .'

And then there was no more time to think. A great press of bodies surged down the alleyway. DogNut slashed once, cut a father's head half off his shoulders then found himself squashed up against the wall by three bodies – foul, stinking, diseased sickos. Up close he could see that their skin was worse than it had looked, eaten away by disease, lumpy with growths and boils, their gums bleeding, their eyes weeping yellowy white gunge. He headbutted one of them, felt a splash of snot and saliva and pus across his face. Spat. Tried to drag his sword up, cutting through soft flesh. He had no idea how the others were doing, stuck as he was in this desperate, hot, sweaty huddle.

'Get off me! Get off!' he grunted, feeling teeth on his arm . . . and then there were shouts from the other end of the alleyway, the snarling, yelping sound of dogs. The sickos dropped back, turned, milling around in confusion. The lead mother broke away. Something had rattled them – the kids had their chance.

'Charge them!' DogNut yelled. 'Force them back down the alley and let's get out of here.'

'You heard the man,' Marco shouted. 'Let's go!'

The kids raced down the alleyway with a roar, smashing sickos out of their way. As they chased them into the road they saw that another group of kids was attacking the grown-ups from behind. That was what had startled them.

This new bunch of kids was heavily armed and wore various bits of homemade leather armour. They also had five big dogs on chains: three staffs, a bull terrier and a massive Rottweiler. The dogs were jumping up at the fleeing sickos, snapping and barking wildly.

The sickos scattered, limping off in different directions, howling in fear and frustration.

The two groups of kids joined together and chased the largest pack of sickos, cutting down the slowest ones. But when they came to Birdcage Walk, the wide road that ran along the side of St James's Park, the sickos broke up and their leader, the mother with the knife, got away.

A tall boy wearing a leather mask hissed a quick order to two girls who were smaller and more agile than their friends.

'Stay on them! Don't lose their scent.'

The girls sprinted off, light on their feet, keeping their distance, but staying on the tail of the command group.

The dogs now turned their attention to DogNut's crew, and strained at their leads, snarling and barking and spitting foam from their bared teeth. Their owners shouted at them and lashed them with short whips until they calmed down.

Courtney checked out the gang of kids who had saved

them. There were about fifteen of them and they were a heavy-looking bunch. They wore a mixture of leather and fur and camouflaged material, and carried spears, bows and clubs. Several had helmets or masks.

Their leader came over. He was carrying a wooden club banded with metal strips. His mask resembled a human face.

Courtney gasped. It didn't *resemble* a human face – it *was* a human face. Gnarled and leathery and stiffened by the sun. It had to be. She felt a wave of nausea and swallowed the bile that was rising in her throat.

He pulled the mask down. His own face wasn't much better – it was scarred and pockmarked from old acne. He looked quite old, maybe sixteen, and stared at DogNut's crew without any expression.

'You a'right?' he asked.

'Yeah,' said Marco. 'Thanks to you.'

'We been chasing that lot all day,' said the boy.

'Are you hunters?' Courtney asked, remembering what Nicola had told them.

'Yeah. The gym bunnies moved into the area 'bout two weeks ago. Is our job to move them out.'

'Gym bunnies?' Felix looked like he didn't know whether to laugh or cry. The last few minutes had been pretty intense, and these new kids didn't make him feel too comfortable.

'Yeah, gym bunnies.' The boy nodded up the road after the retreating sickos. 'They look like they work out. Toned. They're much fitter and less diseased than most of the mothers and fathers we hunt down. They're hard work. We been chasing them all over trying to get them out of the area. Finally found their nest this morning. Must have been about fifty of them in there. An old fitness centre.'

75

Courtney spotted a string of what looked like dried mushrooms hanging from the boy's belt. The boy caught her looking.

'They're ears,' he said, still with no expression. 'Trophies.'

'That's sick,' said Courtney, and the boy shrugged. His friends were squatting in the road, staring at DogNut's crew in silence.

'You don't worry you might catch something? Their disease?'

'Nah. We ain't none of us got sick yet.'

'But those are human ears . . .'

'So what? The mothers and fathers are just scum to be hunted down.'

'And made into decorations for your outfits.'

'We need proof of what we do,' the boy explained.

'I don't get it,' said Marco, rubbing his arm where the mother had scratched him.

'You not from round here?' said the hunter.

'No,' said Courtney. 'We've come up the river from the east to look for friends, yeah?'

The boy whistled. 'Cool. But if you was from round here you'd know that us hunters work the streets; we get hired by the local settlements. They give us food and water and supplies – clothes, weapons, whatever we need – so long as we chase off any mothers and fathers that come sniffing around. But these gym bunnies is giving us a right headache. My name's Ryan Aherne, by the ways. Don't you forget it. You in trouble you ask for me. Other hunter gangs is nothing compared to us.'

'I'll remember that.' DogNut bumped fists with him and introduced his crew.

'Which way you headed then, Dog?' asked Ryan.

'We're going to the palace,' said DogNut. 'We hoping the kids there might know something about what's happened to our friends.'

Ryan spat on to the pavement. 'We can get you close,' he said. 'But we won't take you to the doors. We don't like the man.'

'David?'

'That's him. We did some dirty work for him one time and he never paid us. You can't trust him. He your friend?'

'Not really,' said DogNut. 'But our friends was travelling with him.'

'OK, listen up, tourists. We mercenaries. We work for whoever pays us best. But this one time we'll get you up near the palace for nothing. Special Introductory Offer.'

'Thanks, blood,' said DogNut, and they high-fived.

'You be on your watch up there in the palace, man,' said Ryan. 'Guy's got eyes and spies everywhere, geeks with guns. Check the exits. Your man has a habit of not letting people out once they in.'

'No worries,' said DogNut. 'I reckon I can handle him. He's just a kid. We'll be there and gone before he clicks.'

'Yeah,' said Finn, walking past DogNut and heading off up the road, Olivia back on his shoulders. 'This David guy can't be any worse than the sickos.'

10

Despite the hunters' skill, despite the fact that they'd learnt to read the signs and always be alert to any danger, despite the fact that they never relaxed and always knew what was going on around them, they none of them had noticed that they were being watched. All the while that they'd been talking to DogNut's gang someone had been spying on them.

He was sitting alone among some bushes in the shadow of a big plane tree at the edge of St James's Park, utterly still and utterly quiet. He had a homemade cloak wrapped around his body, the hood pulled over his head so that only his eyes showed. And they were narrowed to slits. He wasn't taking any chances that he might give himself away. The cloak was camouflaged for the city, with splotches of grey on a dull green and brown background. His face and hands were smeared with soot so that they too were grey. Hidden beneath the folds of his cloak was a long, narrow knife. He gripped the handle in his right hand, ready, not that he thought he would need to use it, but it was always better to be safe than sorry.

He could stay like this for hours if necessary. He was used to it. He had learnt to live in the shadows. When he moved, he moved unseen, patrolling the streets around the palace.

There was nothing that went on around here that he didn't know about. He knew where all the settlements of kids were, where the grown-ups crawled away to sleep, where there were secret stashes of food, where all the good hiding-places were: the dark places.

He'd always been like this – a watcher. Hanging back. It had earned him the nickname Shadowman a long time ago and the name had stuck. He didn't always use the name now when he mixed with other kids. He used a variety of aliases. A different one for each group so that nobody could properly know him. Even when he was among people he was hidden.

His real name was Dylan Peake. He sometimes wondered how many living people knew that. Maybe four at the most. In this new world, without documents and forms, without parents, teachers, doctors or policemen, without addresses, you were free to be whoever you wanted.

So, in a way, Dylan Peake was someone else altogether. Separate to Shadowman. He thought of him as someone he used to know. That other boy had been born in Wales but brought up in West London. He had lived in a big house in Notting Hill. His father had been a film producer, his mother a make-up artist. Both dead. He had two brothers and two sisters.

Also dead.

Thinking of Dylan Peake as someone else, a character in a story who had lived in the mythical old world – that lost paradise of easy food and clean water and non-stop fun and games – helped him to deal with the pain and loss.

It hadn't happened to him.

Even back then, though, Dylan Peake had been an unusual boy. As the middle child of a large family, he had learnt to be invisible and hide among his brothers and sisters. His bedroom had been at the top of the house and he'd taught himself to recognize all the sounds that the building made. The creaking of boards as people moved about, the clanking of pipes as taps were turned on and off, the individual sound each door made as it opened and closed. Sometimes he would creep around the house and listen at the doors. Trying to find out what everyone was saying. Spying on his own family.

And not just his own family.

He had taken to roaming the streets at random, following people, going into shops and cafés, eavesdropping, working out the secret patterns and rhythms of the city. He longed to know what people were up to without actually joining in. He developed a knack for gatecrashing. Entering places he had no right to enter. Other schools. Parties. Offices. Concerts. Events. Nothing was closed to him. He could pass unnoticed wherever he went.

He was also a great mimic; within minutes of meeting someone he could impersonate them. It had been very useful on the phone, but also meant that he could mingle in any group, and fit in, pretending to be older or younger than he was, or posher, or more street, on a couple of occasions even foreign.

He moved freely and left no mark.

So in a way Dylan Peake had *never* really existed. He was made up of all the other personalities he had mimicked. And now Shadowman was just the name for an organization, a collection of personalities.

As the kids moved on, he waited until it was safe then stood up and followed. Keeping behind the railings. If they came into the park, he'd keep on their tail; if they went away, he'd let them go. He recognized Ryan. He'd been keeping tabs on him for months. He'd even run with him for a few days some time back, but he doubted Ryan would remember him. He'd learnt a lot in that time. Noted all the kids' names. Worked out their strengths and weaknesses. Ryan's hunters were probably the best in the area. One day they might be useful to Shadowman.

The other kids were strangers. He'd never seen them before. They intrigued him. He wanted to know where they'd come from, but he could only take on one job at a time. He needed to stay focused. Right now he was getting close to the group of wild kids who'd set up camp at the eastern end of St James's Park on the drill square at Horse Guards Parade. They'd made themselves a messy little shanty town of tents and shacks built from bits and pieces – old timber, corrugated iron, plastic sheeting – anything they could find.

As far as Shadowman could make out, they'd been on the move around London, stripping an area of anything usable then moving on. He needed to find out all he could about them. So these new kids could wait. One thing at a time. He'd learnt that. Don't rush. Do things properly. Cover your tracks.

Stay alive.

A lot of kids hadn't managed to do that.

11

One of his toys was moving about, scuttling across the floor, all jerky. Annoying.

It had woken him up when it had knocked against his legs. He'd been sitting on his sofa. Sleeping. Dreaming. He always slept well after a meal. He'd nearly finished eating the broken toy he'd brought back with him the other night. They didn't taste so good if you left them too long. Sometimes they started to smell and then they'd make him sick if he ate them. He'd probably had the best of it now. He'd put what was left of it into one of his bags, and the next time he went out collecting he'd take it with him. It was useful if any of the others were around. He could throw them scraps and they'd leave him alone. Some of them had even got used to it. They waited for him, then followed him around like pets, expecting to be fed. He'd had a pet before. He remembered it now. A cat. When he'd got ill, and there was no food left in the shops, and everything became confusing, he'd had to eat the cat. He wondered now if he would have to eat all his new toys before they were broken. This one was pesky, always moving about, trying to get away, dragging its broken bits behind and making that noise, that horrible irritating noise.

Annoying.

He nudged the toy with his foot and grunted at it. Why wouldn't they just stay still when he wasn't playing with them? Stupid toys.

He sighed. Belched. A thin trickle of sticky brown liquid squirted from his throat and dripped down his front.

It was a stupid world. Such hard work. He loved his stuff. His collection. He loved to go out searching for more. But it was hard. Avoiding the sun. Always hungry. Always thirsty.

His toys gave him pleasure, except this one. This one was making his life harder. Hard work. Hard, hard work. He'd always hated hard work.

He needed his sleep, needed his rest. Couldn't his toys see that? Why did they have to be so mean to him? It wasn't fair. If he was always having to wake up and put his toys back in their box, it was annoying.

He shouted at the toy.

''Noying!'

The toy made some stupid snivelling little noise and carried on crawling across the floor. The Collector groaned, shifted his weight and hauled himself up from the sofa. He would have to stop this toy from moving about like this. He had broken its legs, but it was still able to get about by wriggling and shuffling them.

''Noying!'

Well, he thought, as he leant over to pick his toy up, if it didn't have any legs then it would have to stay still.

12

'The fact of the matter is your friends abandoned us.' David spoke in a very formal grown-up manner, his pale, freckled face comically serious. 'We kept our side of the deal, but they simply chose to drive away and leave us to our fate. So, you see, your friend Brooke is not exactly on my Christmas-card list right now.'

The boat crew was sitting with David on a terrace over-looking the gardens of Buckingham Palace. The sunlight glinted off the lake on the far side of what had once been neat lawns, but was now a muddy field of various different vegetables. A small army of kids was busy tending the vegetables, working away with forks and spades and trowels.

If it had felt odd being in the Houses of Parliament with a bunch of children pretending to be the government, it felt odder still to be here in Buckingham Palace. DogNut and his friends had come in through the parade ground, where four of the boys from David's school, wearing their distinctive red blazers, had been on guard in the sentry boxes at the front of the palace. They'd been suspicious of the new arrivals at first, but luckily one of them had remembered DogNut from when they'd met at the War Museum before the fire. Finally they'd unlocked the gates and DogNut had led his little band across the parade ground into the shadow of the massive building. David had met them inside, in one of the staterooms, and he'd made a big show of welcoming them as if they'd been his oldest and dearest friends. Then he'd given them a tour of the palace, showing off everything, and going on and on about what a good thing they had going there. Finally he'd taken them out into the garden at the back. He called it a garden, but it was more of a small park really, what with the lake in the middle and all the trees and shrubs everywhere. Once again his main aim seemed to have been to show off. He went on and on about how organized they were, how many of them there were, how much food they were growing, how safe it was here.

He'd even got someone to go and make a pot of tea for them all.

Now DogNut, Courtney, Olivia, Finn, Al and Jessica were sitting on white cast-iron garden furniture, sipping tea as the afternoon sunshine slowly faded. Marco and Felix had settled themselves on the lawn, enjoying the last of the sun.

It had all been going so well. David relaxed, bigging himself up, upright in his chair with his cup of tea. Talking of nothing, chitchat, gossip, catching up, and then DogNut had told David about how he was searching for Brooke and David had suddenly turned.

Now he was glaring at DogNut, who had to stifle the urge to laugh.

'Brooke can rot in hell for all I care.'

DogNut had never met another kid who talked like David.

'How d'you mean they abandoned you?' he asked, trying to get to the bottom of David's anger.

'I mean exactly what I say. The deal was that my boys and I would escort the lorry over the river in return for a share of the food it carried.'

'For real?' DogNut shrugged. 'I don't know about none of that. Wasn't my food. Wasn't my lorry. I did help capture it, though. Don't remember seeing you there.'

'I wasn't there,' said David patiently. 'You know I wasn't there. As I say, the deal was –'

'Yeah, yeah, yeah, you excort the lorry over the river, they give you some of the food. That must have been something you fixed up with Ed and Brooke. Nothin' to do with me. That wasn't my crew.'

Two of David's red-blazered guards stood nearby with rifles at their sides. DogNut remembered those rifles. They were from the museum. He remembered what a fuss David had made about trying to get hold of them, and how proud he'd been when he finally managed it. He also remembered that they'd been given hardly any bullets for them. Were these ones even loaded? Or were they just for show?

'We kept our side of the bargain,' said David. 'We got the lorry over the bridge, which wasn't easy – it was jammed with children trying to escape from the fire – and then as soon as we got to the other side the lorry accelerated and pulled away from us. We chased after it, but it was no good . . .'

'They abandoned you.'

'Yes,' said David matter-of-factly.

'This is something that means a lot to David. He's talked about it a great deal.' They'd been joined by an intense kid with a crazy tangle of sticking-up hair who was wearing a coat that looked like he'd made it himself out of many different mismatched patches of material. He was standing behind David, leaning on the back of his chair.

'Your friend Brooke hurt David quite deeply,' the boy went on.

'Yeah, well, as I say, I don't know nothing about that,' said DogNut. 'I'm sure they had they reasons for driving on.'

'I'm sure they did,' said David. 'And you know what I think their reason was?'

'Tell me.'

'They never intended to share any of their food. They used me when it was convenient and then dropped me, as they had always intended to do.'

'I'm sure it wasn't like that,' said Courtney.

'Were you there?'

'No, I wasn't there. That's the whole point. We got split up. That's why me and DogNut is looking for Brooke now. But, you see, I *know* Brooke. I know she's mouthy and that, but she's got a good heart.'

'A good heart?' David scoffed. 'You sound like some awful American TV programme. From what little I saw of Brooke I'd say she was a mean and selfish bitch.'

Courtney jumped to her feet and leant over David with her fists clenched. His two guards twitched, but he waved them back with a dismissive little hand gesture. He smiled at Courtney, which only made her madder.

'You didn't ought to speak about my friend like that!' she bawled. 'I don't care who you are, and how many mates you got with guns, I'll break your stupid butters face.'

'Sit down,' said David calmly.

'Not till you apologize.'

'It's all right, babes,' said DogNut, who could tell that David would never apologize. 'He ain't worth it.'

87

'Yeah, well . . .' Courtney jerked her chin at David and sat back down.

'Maybe I was a bit rude,' said David, who remained completely unruffled. 'But you can understand my anger I hope? A deal's a deal.'

'Yeah . . .' Courtney gave him her best cold stare.

'And she obviously means a lot to you all,' David went on, 'if you've come all the way over here from the Tower of London to look for her. That's quite an impressive feat.'

'Wasn't so hard,' said DogNut.

'Tell me about it,' said David. 'Tell me all about life in the Tower. I'm interested to know what other children are up to.'

OK, thought DogNut, *you asked for it, pal*. Now it was his turn to show off. He launched into a long explanation of how they lived. Some of it was exaggerated, but he didn't tell any outright lies. He painted a picture of a well-fed, well-armed, happy bunch of warriors living in luxury beside the Thames in the ancient castle.

His friends chipped in, fleshing out the picture with their own memories and experiences. David listened intently, asking a lot of questions. In the end DogNut put up his hand.

'All right,' he said, 'we've answered your questions, bruv. Now you answer ours, yeah? Leaving aside your bad vibes for one moment, do you got any idea what happened to Brooke and the others off of the lorry, after they *abandoned* you?'

'Even if I knew, why would I tell you after what they did to us?'

'Why not? We all in this together. Kids ain't the enemy – mothers and fathers is.'

'Exactly,' said David. 'But they didn't seem to remember that when they drove off, did they?'

'Maybe if I can find Brooke I'll ask her why she done it, and then let you know.'

David offered DogNut a smile. 'To tell you the truth,' he said, 'I have absolutely no idea where she went. As I say, she can have gone to hell for all I care.'

DogNut let out his breath noisily through his mouth, like a balloon deflating. 'For real?'

'*For real*,' said David, copying DogNut with more than a hint of scorn in his voice. The boy in the patchwork coat sniggered.

'All right,' said DogNut. 'I can see you all don't want to help us none. But what about my other bredrin here?' He gestured towards the rest of his crew. 'What about Olivia, and Al and Jessica and Finn? They wasn't with us at the museum. Their friends wasn't on the lorry. What about them? Can you help them any?'

Olivia and the others all now clamoured at once, throwing out names and information. David and the patchwork boy went into a huddle and whispered to each other. Finally the patchwork boy spoke.

'Hi there. My name's Jester,' he said. 'I'm David's right-hand man.'

The boat crew muttered some half-hearted hellos.

'I know everything that goes on here. The names of everyone, where they came from, what their stories are. All the info. Anything you want to know in future you come to me. OK? We don't want any hard feelings. And you're right – we can't blame any of you for what happened with the lorry.'

He shook hands all round, making an effort to learn the

names of everyone. He got to Al last and held on to his hand a little longer than the others.

'Al, my friend,' he said, with the broad smile of a game-show host. 'You are in luck. Your sister is here with us.'

Al shot out of his seat as if someone had put a rocket up his arse. His ugly, lumpy face was made almost good-looking by a huge soppy grin, and he was shaking with excitement.

'Really? She's here? Maria's here?'

'Yep.'

'And she's all right?'

'Everyone's all right here. We look after our own.' Jester clapped Al on the back and called one of the guards over. He gave him a quick order and the boy nodded and hurried off. This got the other kids even more worked up, and once again they bombarded David and Jester with questions.

Olivia was tugging at Jester's patchwork coat.

'Are you sure my brother's not here?' she piped. 'He's called Paul Channing, he's got black hair, he's older than me, he's very tall . . .'

'Sorry, precious.'

'Can you double-check? You might have made a mistake . . .'

David silenced her. 'Believe me,' he said, 'Jester should know. He knows everything. If he says your brother's not here, he's not here. Same goes for the rest of you.'

'But we can ask around, yeah?' said Jessica. 'Talk to the kids here? They might know something.'

'I'd rather you didn't go pestering everyone. Let Jester talk to them.'

'Don't be a dick,' said DogNut, standing up. 'You can't stop us talking to people.'

David made an empty-hands gesture. DogNut gave him a dirty look in return and stormed off down the steps and over to a group of kids who were weeding one of the vegetable patches. As he approached them, they stopped what they were doing and stood up, wiping their hands on their trousers.

'We're looking for some friends,' he said, slightly more aggressively than he'd wanted. 'Any of you know where they might be? David says we got to go through him, but . . .'

A thin girl with a muddy face and hands glanced over at David before speaking. DogNut saw him shake his head. 'If David says he doesn't know anything, then neither do we,' she said.

'That's right,' said the girl next to her. 'We can't really help you.'

DogNut swore and went over to the next group, but got the same response. Nobody was willing to talk to him. After a few minutes he gave up and looked back towards the terrace where David was watching him with a self-satisfied expression.

The two of them locked stares. DogNut was fuming, his chest rising and falling. David had made him look like an idiot.

And then the tense mood was broken by a girl running out of the building, laughing and shouting. She ran straight into Al's arms and they hugged each other, both in floods of tears. DogNut tried to picture himself and Brooke hugging like that, her crying into his shoulder, him stroking her hair . . .

Somehow the picture never quite came into focus. They

were neither of them the blubbing, hugging type. For the hundredth time he wondered where she was and what she might be doing.

Each step closer seemed to take him two steps further away.

13

'Listen, why don't you all have something to eat and then stay here for the night?'

It was a moment before Courtney realized that David was talking to her. DogNut was still down among the vegetable growers looking sulky and cross. David was standing with his arms folded, watching him.

'We need to move on,' Courtney said flatly.

'But where will you go?'

'That's not your problem.'

David turned to her, unfolded his arms and smiled.

'I'm sorry we got off to a bad start. I've no argument with you. It was Brooke and the others who let me down. Maybe I've come across a bit angry. I'm sorry about that. I'll calm down. It was just . . . hearing Brooke's name brought up some bad memories for me.'

'She was my best mate.'

'I know. Please don't think that I don't care.'

'Whatever. I'm going to find her.'

'Yes, I appreciate that, but you can't just go wandering around out there. I would have thought that what happened to you on the way here would have shown you how dangerous it is on the streets still. Can I make a suggestion?'

'OK . . .'

'Why not stay here with us for a while? Not just tonight. We've plenty of food and water and it's very safe here.'

'Yeah, but I just said I want to –'

'Let me finish.'

'Sorry.'

'I'll send Jester out. He has contacts everywhere. He knows these streets really well. If anyone can track Brooke down, it's him.'

'Maybe . . .' The thought of staying at the palace for a while, resting, eating well, not being scared, being alone with DogNut with no Brooke around to spoil things . . .

'I thought you said you didn't want nothing to do with her?'

'I can be a grown-up about it,' said David, and he smiled. 'Actually, sorry, no, bad choice of metaphor. Not a grown-up, but you know what I mean. Maybe it's time I forgave her, moved on. Or maybe seeing these two reunited has made me go all gooey inside.'

David nodded towards where Al and his sister Maria were sitting on the grass, excitedly chatting away to each other as they caught up on all that had happened in the last year.

'At least stay the night, anyway,' said David. 'We can offer you better food than you'll have tasted since before the disaster. You can have a wash, get some clean clothes.' He looked pointedly at Courtney's jeans, stained dark where she had wet herself.

Courtney blushed and stared at a patch of grass, feeling about three years old.

'In any case,' said David, 'get rested, think about things. We'll talk again at dinner.' He moved in closer and spoke quietly to Courtney, fixing her with his pale clear eyes.

'Maybe you don't really want to look for Brooke. Yeah? Maybe that's the past? You don't necessarily want to hold on to it. This is the future. Here in the palace. And we need children like you – tough and experienced, with a good understanding of how things are out there. You'd fit in really well here, Courtney – you could make a good life.'

'I'll think about it.'

'Do that.'

David walked away a few paces, stopped and turned round.

'Whatever happens,' he said. 'You *will* stay here tonight.'

'Oh, but –'

'It's the safest thing for you.'

David left them to it and went inside. Courtney was confused. She needed to talk to DogNut, but when she looked for him he was gone.

14

The gardens at the palace were ringed by tall trees, so that standing by the lake in the centre you could imagine you were deep in the countryside, especially now that there were no sounds of cars or aeroplanes to spoil the illusion.

While David had been distracted talking to Courtney, DogNut had ducked into the shadow of the trees and was now skirting the outer wall. If for some reason David tried to keep them there, it was worth knowing whether there was any easy way out.

It wasn't looking good.

The wall itself was about five metres high and topped by rotating steel spikes. Above the spikes there stretched another couple of metres of barbed wire that sloped outwards towards the road on the other side.

The walls had been designed to keep people out. After all this had been a royal palace, the Queen's home in London. DogNut had heard tales of nutters breaking in, but it was still a pretty impregnable fortress. And these walls could also, of course, keep people in.

Worse still, some of David's guards seemed to be patrolling the perimeter. DogNut had seen one a couple of minutes ago. His bright red blazer had given him away.

DogNut had easily hidden behind a tree until the boy had wandered past. Despite the rifle slung over his shoulders, he didn't look like he was taking his job very seriously, and why should he? No sickos could scale that wall from the outside. This was all just for show, to give the other kids a feeling of security.

Or was there something more to it? DogNut wondered how many of the kids might be being held here against their will, like the hunters had said.

It was almost like being in some kind of concentration camp.

'Oi!'

Dammit. DogNut had missed a second guard, who had sneaked up on him from behind and was aiming his rifle at his belly. DogNut smiled at him.

'A'right?'

'You shouldn't be back here.'

'Why?'

'David says so.'

'Why?'

'It's dangerous.'

'Why?'

The boy lowered his gun and shrugged, evidently feeling a bit silly. He had a big nose and didn't look the fighting type.

'Don't you get bored doing that?' DogNut asked him.

'A bit, yeah. But it's better than digging up sodding vegetables.'

DogNut laughed. 'What's your name, soldier?'

'Andy. You're called Dog's Bollocks, or something, aren't you?'

'Close enough.'

'I remember you from the museum. Your lot gave us these guns.'

'Yeah. You ever fired it?'

'Nah.' Andy laughed and they slapped palms.

'I always wanted to stay with you lot,' Andy went on. 'David wouldn't let us, though. Said we had to stick together. Between you and me, David's a prick.'

'*For real?*' said DogNut in mock amazement. 'You learn something new every day. But tell me, Andy, my manz. Has anyone ever got over these walls?'

'Nah, it's impossible.' Andy didn't sound that convincing.

'For sure? No one's climbed in – no one's climbed out?'

Andy made a face, deciding whether to keep a secret. He looked around, checking nobody could see them.

'If I tell you something, will you promise never to let anyone know it was me that told you?'

'Sure, bruv.'

'There is a way over. Some of the kids worked it out. They jammed the spikes so they won't turn and cut a section of wire. They fixed it back up again so if you didn't know what to look for you'd never know. David never looks, anyway.'

'Why'd they do that?'

'To get in and out. David doesn't let us otherwise.'

'To get away from here?'

'No. But some of the kids take stuff, food and whatever, and they trade it with other kids out there from the other settlements.'

'Not you, though, soldier?'

'Never had the guts. Besides I've got a blazer, so I have privileges. Wouldn't want to lose them.'

'So are you going to tell me where this safe way out is?'

Andy shook his head and looked at his shoes. 'I've told you too much already. If David found out . . .'

Andy fell silent as they heard someone approaching through the trees. He looked miserable. Like a kid waiting to see the headmaster. It was only Courtney, though. Andy relaxed and smiled at her.

Courtney nodded dismissively at him and turned her attention to DogNut.

'There you are,' she said, sounding tired and grumpy. 'I been looking all over.'

'Just taking a likkle stroll,' said DogNut. 'You know. Stretching the old pins.'

'Yeah, right.'

DogNut said goodbye to Andy and walked back towards the palace with Courtney.

'David wants us to stay for dinner,' she explained. 'But Al's got some news that might change things.'

'Cool,' said DogNut. 'Hit me with it.'

'I'll let Al tell you himself.'

15

Shadowman was in his tent, zip down, sitting cross-legged on his sleep mat, checking his belongings before going out for the night. He could hear loud voices all around. It was always noisy here in the shanty town at the end of the park. There was always a cacophony of barking dogs, laughter, shouting, arguments, joking, singing. Even babies crying. He couldn't imagine bringing any babies into this mad world, but a couple of the girls had got themselves pregnant and somehow survived childbirth.

The tent was tiny. It had been advertised in the camping shop where he'd found it as a two-man, but it could barely fit one. That was fine with him. He didn't want company. He worked alone. Was happier that way. Didn't want to be weighted down with people, belongings, responsibilities. He travelled light. Everything he owned except for his sleeping bag could fit into his slim backpack. It had been designed to carry a laptop and suited him perfectly, as, slung across his back underneath his cloak, it lay flat against his body. Nobody could tell he was carrying it.

He had emptied his pockets and tipped out the contents of his pack on to his sleeping bag and was sorting through them, something he did regularly. It was a habit, really, or an obsession. A little ritual to bring him luck and keep him safe. He would touch each of the objects, remind himself why he carried it and carefully, lovingly, put it back in its place. Like a labourer with his tools, a soldier with his kit.

There wasn't much to it.

Some emergency food – beef jerky, dried fruit, stale chocolate, a mini A-to-Z book of every street in London, a Swiss Army knife, a compass, a cigarette lighter and a box of matches in a waterproof bag with a couple of small candles, a sewing kit, a knife sharpener for the sheath knife he carried on his belt, a small set of tools that packed away into a neat flat box, a tin plate and cutlery set designed for campers, a torch, spare batteries, a tiny compact pair of binoculars, a couple of biros and some paper, a first-aid kit with bandages and antiseptic cream and painkillers, a paperback novel that he'd throw away when he'd finished it and replace with a new one, gaffer tape for repairs, a spare pair of socks and thermal vest. He didn't bother to lug about any other clothes. He hardly ever washed and it was easy, in this new London, to pick up new clothes in any one of the hundreds of abandoned stores. He wanted to be able to ship out and move on at a moment's notice. He slept in his clothes, with his boots and his backpack safely stowed away in the bottom of his sleeping bag. He could be up, into his boots, with his pack across his back, his water canisters clipped to his belt and his cloak wrapped around him in less than a minute. He'd timed it and practised his technique every week or so.

He wouldn't take the tent with him when he left the camp. He'd leave it for someone else to use. It was easier to find a new one if he ever needed it. Quite frankly, he preferred sleeping indoors under a proper roof. He'd take

101

the sleeping bag, though, rolled up and slung across his shoulders.

He wondered why these kids had chosen to live in tents and makeshift huts rather than in buildings. It was certainly more dangerous. Though the kids seemed to welcome danger. Perhaps they wanted adults to attack? They did seem to love fighting. A mother and a father had got into the camp last week and they'd been chased around by a jeering mob armed with sticks and stones. By the time the kids had finished with them their battered and pulped bodies looked barely human.

That was what they thought of adults, and maybe they lived here in their camp because they didn't want anything more to do with the world of grown-ups, though Shadow-man doubted they could ever explain that. They weren't given to deep thought. They lived day to day, hand to mouth, didn't look forward or back, didn't question what they were doing. They were like him in that way.

He filled his pockets and slotted the last couple of items in his pack, which had lots of little compartments. Everything had its place and the vest kept it all from rattling about. Satisfied, he stood up, slipped the single wide diagonal strap over his head and put on his cloak. The kids in the shanty town wore a bizarre mix of stuff that they'd looted, bits of military clothing, odd fashion items, punky stuff, leather jackets, fancy dress, as if they were all trying to outdo each other with their wackiness, so Shadowman didn't stand out in his cloak. In other circumstances, with different kids, he might have taken it off, rolled it up and worn it over his shoulders as if it was a blanket, but here in the camp he felt he could wear anything he liked and not be noticed.

102

The camp was its usual chaotic, squalid mess. The biggest problem kids had since the disaster was boredom. This must have been what it was like going to war, the stories he'd read about soldiers whose days were filled with unrelenting boredom, punctuated every now and then by brief moments of extreme terror and violence. That was what life was like now for everyone. There was no TV, no computers, no mobile phones or Xboxes; there was nothing to do except try to stay alive.

The shanty town had been largely built on the solid footing of the parade ground, but it spilt over on to the grass in the park where a group of kids was playing football. The ball was a bit flat; that was a permanent problem. Balls were too easily punctured and very hard to repair. A fully pumped football was something of a precious treasure.

Other kids were playing different games: the younger ones chasing each other around; some of the girls had invented their own elaborate games that involved hopping and skipping, jumping, clapping, singing and counting. Most kids, though, just lounged around on whatever they could find to sit on – broken chairs, logs, bits of rubbish – and chatted to each other, just like the bored contestants on *I'm a Celebrity . . . Get Me Out of Here*. Of course they couldn't talk about what they'd watched on TV last night, or a piece of music they'd heard, or something they'd seen on YouTube, the latest video game, the premier league . . . It was all gossip. Who'd said what to who and what they'd said back at them, who they liked, who they didn't like.

That was another reason why Shadowman preferred to keep himself to himself. So he didn't have to talk to anyone. He kept on the move, strolling around the camp, settling now and then by one of the fires that they kept burning day and night, letting the smoke wash over him. He'd learnt early on that the grown-ups could smell kids, so he did all he could to mask his own scent. It also hid his smell from other kids. Smoke was the best deodorant around. It got into your clothes, your hair, your skin, and drowned out all the unmentionable smells that unwashed bodies accumulate. He'd rubbed most of the soot from his skin and now just looked like one more grubby boy among a camp full of grubby boys.

A group of kids was making music – banging boxes, clapping, rapping – one had a battered guitar with three strings. Occasionally one of them would break away and do a little dance of some sort, showing off, trying to outdo the others.

Nearby two boys were fighting, a small crowd gathered round them. They were really battering each other and the onlookers were laughing. Shadowman smiled. All of this served one purpose. To take their minds off the thing they all thought about all the time. *Food.* Where was it going to come from, what was it going to be, how much was there going to be?

There never was enough, of course. And it was never very nice. A lot of it would be stale or rancid.

Half the kids from the camp were out on the streets still, breaking into houses and shops to see what they could find. There was always excitement in the camp when these groups returned, like fishermen back from the sea or hunters back from the wild. Would they bring back a mammoth today, or just a couple of rats?

Another reason why Shadowman liked to work alone. He could find his own food and look after himself, not have to worry about any other mouths to feed, not sharing or waiting his turn, hanging back to see what crumbs he could pick up after the bigger, tougher kids had had their fill.

He saw one of the kids he'd made friends with, a little Irish bruiser called Paddy. He was sitting alone playing with some broken action figures. Shadowman sat down next to him and Paddy said hello.

'What are those guys?' Shadowman asked, nodding at the little men.

'They're Halo figures. I found them in a comic shop months ago. I could really do with some new ones.'

'I used to love playing Halo,' said Shadowman. 'My mum used to shout at me all the time. Stop playing that bloody game . . .'

'Yeah,' said Paddy. 'Me too.'

'My favourite was Fable, though.'

'Never played that.'

'It was good. Good story. Good acting.'

'I just like games where you blow things up and shoot people.'

'Yeah.'

There was a commotion on the edge of the camp. Someone was coming in. Shadowman looked over to see John and Carl striding on to the parade ground carrying boxes wrapped in plastic. Big grins on their faces. Behind them came several other lads also carrying boxes.

John and Carl were the two guys in charge here. John was the overall boss. As far as Shadowman was concerned, he was a skinny, wiry, ugly, gap-toothed, mean, shaven-headed little bastard. His character was a lethal mix of bone-stupid and streetwise smarts, and he was prone to terrible acts of random violence. The other kids were scared of him and he used that fear to keep some sort of control in the camp. There was a kind of screwy order and the kids seemed happy to have him boss them around. He made them feel safe.

Carl was his deputy. Cleverer and altogether nicer, he dressed a bit like a pirate, with a bandanna permanently tied round his head, and had no ambition to be number one. He seemed to be the only person who could stop John from getting out of order. Shadowman reckoned that John was seriously unhinged and probably dangerous. If the disaster hadn't happened, he would have been locked up somewhere. But now, in this upside-down new world, psychos like John were leaders and generals.

As the foraging party got nearer, Shadowman saw that the boxes they were carrying contained not food but cans of beer and cider. John started shouting triumphantly about it.

'Look what your Uncle Johnny has got for you useless tossers. Don't say I don't look after you. There's going to be a big party in the old town tonight and there ain't no adults gonna stop us! No mums, no coppers, no sleep till morning.'

Paddy jumped up and ran over to him.

'Give us one!' he shouted happily, and John casually kicked him in the balls, sending him sprawling across the gravel, spilling his action figures everywhere. John walked on, laughing, and crushed one of the little men under his heavy boot.

'Later,' he said. 'And you can wait your turn, you Irish loser. We're gonna have a riot and we're gonna do it properly. I ain't had nothing to drink in days.'

He went to his own shack and dumped his box on the ground. The other kids piled theirs around it.

'Listen up, goons and goonettes,' John shouted, jumping up on the boxes. 'I want a really big fire, I want some music and I want some grub. Get on it. Sort me out. And when I'm happy you can all have a drink. Well, not all of you, only the ones that make me happy.'

He jumped down, laughing, and tore his box open to get at a can, which he popped open and clamped to his mouth. As he glugged away, he caught Shadowman's eye.

'What you looking at?'

'Nothing.'

Shadowman dropped his gaze, embarrassed that John had spotted him. His cloak of invisibility had failed.

'Come here.'

Shadowman had no option but to go over to John who glared at him over his beer can, looking right into Shadowman and making him feel naked and foolish.

'I seen you around. I ain't sure I like you.'

Shadowman shrugged. Decided to try to change the subject.

'Where'd you get the beer?'

'What's it to you?'

'Just interested.'

'Yeah – interested. You're always interested, ain't you? Listening in, poking your nose everywhere. *Interested*.'

John took a sudden swing at Shadowman, lashing out with his left hand. Shadowman instinctively ducked and backed away. John grinned.

'You're fast, ain't you?'

'Fast enough.'

John bent down and for a moment Shadowman wasn't sure what he was going to do. But he simply grabbed another beer can and chucked it at Shadowman, who caught it neatly.

'Cheers,' said John.

'Thanks,' said Shadowman. 'What's the catch?'

'No catch. We found this lot in a pub cellar, seeing as you asked. It was rammed full of booze. Which was lucky, as Carl's little pillaging expedition earlier got banjaxed. I'm sending another gang back to get some more. Drink up.'

Shadowman opened his can and put it to his lips. As he did so, John whipped out a knife and held the point to Shadowman's throat.

'Dropped your guard, there, Snoopy,' he said, and then pressed his face very close to Shadowman's, keeping the knife hard to his skin and causing a small trickle of blood to run down his neck.

'I'm keeping my eye on you,' he said.

'OK,' Shadowman gulped, trying to keep his tone neutral.

John took the knife away, gave Shadowman a dismissive smile, then walked off, chuckling. One of his girls ran up to him, and John shoved her over.

'Leave me alone,' he said. 'You'll get your booze.'

He sat down on the boxes and lit a cigarette. Around him the other kids were madly busy, trying to get everything done to John's satisfaction.

Shadowman wondered if this was a vision of the future. Was this what was going to happen to mankind? Was everything going to fall apart and degenerate into this desperate day-to-day existence? Or was it going to be more like how David ran things at Buckingham Palace?

It was funny, really. Mankind had such a powerful urge to survive at any cost. He'd read about kids in some Third

World countries who lived on rubbish tips. Kids as young as five and six earning a few pennies to support their families by sorting crap all day for recycling. What for? So that they could grow up and have children of their own who would have to live on the rubbish tip as well.

Given the choice of living on in squalor and starvation, sickness and danger, or simply putting an end to it all, most people would choose life.

There had been a man who lived on Shadowman's road when he was growing up. He'd lived there all his life, was one of the last of the original residents of Notting Hill. Everyone else was waiting for him to die so that they could buy his house cheap. If the old geezer had sold it, he'd have probably got a couple of million quid for it. But he didn't want to sell it. He didn't want to move. He wanted what he was used to.

Shadowman would see him sometimes setting off for the shops in the morning. He was impossibly old and walked bowed over, his hands twisted with arthritis. He could barely move and shuffled forward at an agonizing snail's pace all the way down to the end of the road. It would take him all morning. And then, with the few pence he had, he'd buy a half a loaf of bread, some cheap biscuits, a pint of milk and some eggs, and then he'd shuffle home again.

Shadowman couldn't imagine what kind of a life the old man had lived, and what he must have been thinking as he dragged himself to the shop and back, but he knew that if anyone had asked him if he wanted to end it all he would have said no. He was still alive, still moving, and he wanted to live as long as he could.

There seemed to be a deep-down urge in all living things

to carry on whatever the cost. These kids were living, and they would go on living. Perhaps they would rebuild the world. Who knew? Diseases had struck before. The Black Death had wiped out half the population of Europe, but mankind had come back from that. This new disease had probably killed more. Three quarters maybe? Provided the kids were immune they would survive and somehow they would build a new world. And so far it looked like they were immune. Shadowman was fifteen now and had displayed no signs of illness. No sores or boils or crazy thoughts. That wasn't to say that it might not all change, of course . . .

Nobody could see into the future.

Well, if he wanted to guarantee his future he needed to keep out of John's way for a bit.

He drained the can and tossed it on to a pile of rubbish.

Dark soon. Better get moving.

Things to do.

People to see.

16

David was standing out on the balcony at the front of the palace with Jester. This was his favourite place in the whole building. On big occasions in the past, like weddings and birthdays, or jubilee celebrations, the royal family used to come out here to wave down at their public. Now David liked to come here and look out across St James's Park. There was a good view of London and he saw it as his kingdom. His world. The only thing that spoilt it was knowing that the squatters were down there at the far end of the park in their filthy camp. A group of kids he couldn't control. He needed to find a way to bring them on to his side.

In the meantime he had concerns closer to home. The eight travellers who had turned up on his doorstep.

'So, they've agreed to stay the night?' he said, without looking round at his second in command.

'Yup.'

'That's a relief. We don't need to keep an eye on them for the time being then. I'll keep working on that Courtney girl. I can tell she wants to stay here. At least for a while. Do you think she bought my story about sending you out to gather information?'

'I think so.' Jester nodded and leant on the balustrade

next to David. 'She doesn't seem to be the brightest spark in the box.'

'We'll make a big show of you going to find out where Brooke might be,' said David. 'They don't have to know it's all a sham. It won't be too hard to hold them here till you come back, and hopefully by then they'll have got used to the good life and won't want to leave. I'll offer DogNut a position of power. Make him a general or something.'

'Stupid name,' said Jester. 'How does he ever expect to get anywhere with a stupid name like DogNut?'

'He's the key to this,' said David. 'They follow his orders. If necessary, we'll let him leave and keep the others here. Without him around they're much more likely to do what we tell them.'

'And what about me?' Jester asked. 'What do *I* tell them when I get back? Do I tell them the truth? That Brooke and the others are living just down the road in the Natural History Museum?'

'Don't know. It'll come out one way or another eventually, I suppose. I'll think about it.'

'So how long do you want me to go away for?'

David switched his attention from the view of St James's to Jester. 'I want you to do a bit more than just keep out of the way for a few days, Jester.'

'Yeah? What exactly?'

'DogNut said he's just here looking for Brooke.'

'Don't you believe him?'

'I'm not sure,' said David. 'I mean . . . I think he's definitely looking for her, but what if there's more to it than that?'

'Like what? I don't get it.'

'You heard what he said about how things are at the

Tower of London? How that weirdo Jordan Hordern has made them into a sort of army?'

'What of it?'

'I'll bet DogNut and his gang are spies. Checking us out.'

Jester gave a snort of laughter. 'You're just being paranoid, David.'

'It's good to be paranoid,' said David.

'Don't tell me you want me to go and spy on the Tower? It's miles away.'

'No. Not that.' David shook his head. 'But there are obviously more kids out there than we thought, surviving in different places round London.'

'I guess so.'

'And if we want to be in charge we have to get them on our side,' David went on. 'We have to show that we're the toughest, the best-organized, I don't know, the best-fed group in London. We have to build an army, Jester, just like Jordan Hordern's done. So there's no argument. We're already stronger than all of the groups round here that we know of. Like Nicola and her ninnies at the Houses of Parliament. They have to rely on hunters like Ryan for their security. Not us. But we *do* need more fighters.'

'I still don't get what you want *me* to do,' said Jester.

'It was DogNut gave me the idea,' said David. 'Basically I want you to go out there and explore like he's doing.'

'Explore?'

'Yeah. I'll give you some troops, don't worry, but I want you to go out there and find me some more fighters. Look for big settlements. Offer them whatever you like. Tell them whatever you want. Just get them to come here. Until we're in control of all of London we're never going to be really safe. And to do that I need a proper army.'

113

David stopped and pointed towards the park.

'That lot there,' he said. 'John and his bloody squatters. We have to deal with them first. We have to show them that no one messes with us. We'll smash them. And then we'll smash Brooke and Justin and the rest of the losers at the museum.'

'What about Justin's offer to join us?' Jester asked. 'I thought the kids at the museum wanted to form an alliance of some sort?'

'They'd like to,' said David. 'Sure. But I'm not interested. I want to teach them a lesson. I want to break them, Jester, make them suffer for what they did to me. Then, and only then, when they know who's boss, once they come crawling to me on their scabby knees, will I let them join us. But to do that I need more fighters.'

He banged his fists on the stone balustrade of the balcony.

'Sun's going down,' said Jester. 'It'll be dinner soon. We need to go and get ready.'

'You and I,' said David, straightening up, 'will have to work really hard tonight. We have to be as charming as we can. Butter these stupid new arrivals up. We should dig out some of that wine as well, get them drunk. We have to persuade them to stay at least until you come back. I'll give you a week.'

Jester laughed. 'You've got a devious mind, David,' he said as the two of them went back inside.

'I've got the mind of a leader, Jester. And that's what the children of London need, a powerful, decisive, ruthless and clever leader.'

Yeah, thought Jester, *powerful, decisive, ruthless, clever and more than a little bit nuts*.

17

If only David and Jester had been standing at the back of the building at that moment and not the front, they would have seen DogNut and the boat crew slipping out of the palace and hurrying across the terrace towards the gardens.

They darted across the small patch of surviving lawn, between the vegetable beds and into the trees, heading for the spot in the north-east corner of the garden where the secret way in and out was.

In the end DogNut had had to force Andy to show him exactly where the spot on the wall was and how to get over. Poor Andy hadn't wanted to say at first, but DogNut had threatened him, said he'd tell David everything, and Andy had cracked.

The boat crew ran as fast as they could through the trees until they hit the wall, then followed it round, looking for the old compost bin that marked the way out. The only one of them who was missing was Al. He'd chosen to stay here with his sister, Maria.

It was Maria who had told them that David had been lying to them. She'd talked to DogNut and Courtney in one of the staterooms as she got a long table ready for supper, their conversation masked by the clatter and bang of plates and cutlery.

'He knows exactly where Brooke is. Has done for ages. And he's been trying to cause problems for her ever since. He's even talked of attacking her base, apparently, he hates her so much.'

Maria knew all this because her boyfriend, Pod, was one of David's generals, and he told her stuff he shouldn't to try to impress her.

'So where is she based then?' DogNut had asked.

'She's in the Natural History Museum with a load of other kids. They've got a good set-up there as far as I can tell, though they've got a problem finding enough food.'

'Is that far from here then, the Natural History Museum?'

'Not sure. A couple of miles, I think. I'll get someone to draw you a map . . .'

They reached the compost bin and DogNut pulled a scrap of paper from his pocket. The map was pretty basic, little more than a straight line linking the palace with the museum, with a few crude markers along the way.

Two miles. Half an hour maybe, if they were quick. It had been a long and tiring day, but they were all anxious to get going again. There was a feeling that if they didn't get away now they might never leave, and the thought that they might find Brooke on their first day out, and be with her by nightfall, gave DogNut a powerful urge to keep moving.

But night was coming fast.

Marco stood on the old compost bin and Felix scrambled up on to his shoulders so that he could reach the barbed wire, being careful not to impale himself on Marco's spiked helmet.

Just as Andy had said, the wire had been cut at one of the supports and then loosely fixed back in place. It only took Felix a few minutes to untangle it and push it to one side, then he pulled himself up using the steel spikes on the bar that ran along the top of the wall as hand holds. This section of spikes had been blunted and jammed in place so that they didn't turn, but it was still tricky getting over them and dropping down on to the roof of the van that had been parked on the pavement on the other side.

One by one they made it, though, until only DogNut, Finn and Jessica were left. As DogNut made ready to help Jessica up, she put a hand on his arm.

'I don't want to go.'

'What? You're joking. Why?'

'I don't know that my friends are with Brooke and that. They could be anywhere.'

'But they're not here, Jessica.'

'No, I know . . . Only, I'm scared, Doggo. Being chased by them sickos today, fighting them off, it freaked me out. I ain't used to this. I ain't never properly left the Tower before, not since we first arrived. I can't deal with what might be out there. I can't handle it. I only really left the Tower cos I was pissed off with Brendan.'

'We should stick together, Jess.'

'No, DogNut, I made up my mind. I ain't going.' She gripped his arm tighter. 'If you hear anything, though, if you find them, you'll tell them I'm here?'

'Yeah. Course. It's all right, babes, I get it.'

'And maybe someone here might know something if I ask around, and then that Jester guy might go out and –'

'That is a *stupid* name,' said DogNut. 'How can anyone go around being called Jester?'

Jessica laughed. 'But you're called DogNut!'

'DogNut is a cool name.' DogNut kissed Jessica and

117

hopped up on to the bin. He didn't want to waste any more time. If David realized they were gone, he might come after them and try to stop them.

'Spin them some crap, Jess, won't you?' he called down to Jessica as he helped Finn up on to the compost bin. 'Throw them off of our scent.'

'I will. And Doggo . . .?'

'What?'

'Be careful, won't you?'

'Nah. I ain't never been careful. See ya!'

DogNut made a stirrup with his hands and hoisted Finn up so that he could use his good hand to grab a spike. With DogNut pushing from below and Finn pulling he was soon up and Marco and Felix helped him over and down the other side. Then DogNut quickly scrambled up the wall, made sure Finn was clear and dropped down on to the top of the van. He helped Felix fix the wire back in place and then he stood up there a moment longer, looking at the outside world.

The sun was dipping below the tops of the buildings to the west, making it some time between seven and eight o'clock. It was a chilly evening. It had been a cloudless day so the heat was draining away fast. Summer was coming, and as far as DogNut was concerned it couldn't come fast enough.

A dog chased a rat across the road.

There was still just enough light left to see that it was a different world out here compared to the palace gardens. The streets were strewn with rubbish. Weeds grew in the cracks between paving slabs. Cars sat where they'd been abandoned. DogNut remembered how shocked everyone had been at how quickly the petrol had run out once people started getting ill. And now London was a ghost town.

It was a harsh jolt back to reality. Being in the palace had been like staying in an enchanted secret sanctuary. Like the boring bits in *The Lord of the Rings* when the fellowship stayed with the elves. DogNut smiled, picturing David with pointy ears and silly long hair.

Elrond.

He slithered down off the van. They were at the roundabout by Hyde Park Corner. In the middle of it was a white triumphal arch with a statue on the top of some kind of giant angel standing in a chariot waving some flowers about.

A chariot would be useful right now.

'This way,' he said, hurrying over the road towards the arch. They cut across the roundabout, heading for the north-west corner. They were all breathing heavily, their hearts pounding against their ribs. It had been hard enough on their nerves just trying to get away from David, but at least with him the worst they had to fear was an argument and maybe a scrap.

Out here it was different. The darkening sky, splashed red in the west, made them all fearful. It took them back to caveman days when humans must have been terrified of what lurked in the dark. Now, when the sun went down, every kid in London had learnt not to go out on the streets, learnt to be scared again.

For a start there were no streetlights. The dark really was the dark, in a way it hadn't been in London since the blackouts of the Second World War. The main thing, though, was that the sickos came out at night. On the whole they shunned the sunlight. Bolder ones, healthier ones like the gym bunnies, braved it, but most of them, the least human, the most diseased, stayed hidden until it was safe for them to crawl out of their hiding-places and roam the streets looking for food.

Any kids who hadn't found somewhere safe for the night were prey. Over the last year most kids had joined together into larger groups and found their way into easily fortified camps like the palace, or the Tower, but there were still smaller groups living scattered in the houses, preferring to look after themselves. And they were more vulnerable.

No one knew how many sickos were still alive. But you could hear them at night, gangs of them on the prowl. Even in the daylight you had to be careful that you didn't disturb a nest of them. They were everywhere – in cellars, in the underground tube tunnels, in the sewers, anywhere dark. They didn't need light. They hunted by smell. DogNut knew that he and his friends would have to keep moving or risk attracting the bolder sickos who would be emerging from their lairs now that the sun was disappearing.

'Keep to the middle of the road!' he called out as they jogged along. 'And stick together.'

They headed west, towards Knightsbridge and the blood-red sky that hung above it. This had been one of the most expensive areas of London, with tall old buildings and expensive shops. Now all derelict.

They passed a super-modern Jaguar car showroom. The building that rose above it looked like a Lego building, all pointy roofs and tall chimneys and fancy walls made of rows of red and cream bricks. Other buildings had turrets and towers, or pillars across the front. Now and then they passed a new one, all glass and steel.

God, thought Courtney, London just went on forever,

so many houses, offices, shops, banks, restaurants, so many people. What had happened to them all?

As if in answer to her question, she heard a howl and the kids staggered to a halt, looking around uncertainly, trying to see where the sound had come from. Courtney edged closer to DogNut, gripping her spear tighter.

'We need to keep moving,' said DogNut. 'It's getting darker every second.'

'Maybe we should go back,' said little Olivia.

'No way,' said DogNut. 'We carry on. We always knew it wouldn't be easy. We can't go running back to Mummy every time we hear a noise.'

'I'm scared,' said Olivia. 'Let's please go back. I liked it at the palace.'

'You want to find your brother, Paul, though, don't you, love?' said DogNut, and Olivia nodded tightly. 'Then we need to push on.'

'Besides, that sound could have come from anywhere,' said Courtney, trying to be helpful. 'It could have come from behind us.'

She instantly knew it had been a mistake to say anything because Olivia grew even more fearful. She started to shake and sob. Courtney didn't want her to freeze and put them all in danger. She grabbed her hand.

'It's all right. We'll be all right. It's not far.'

Olivia nodded again, biting back tears.

They carried on. Moving slower than before, not wanting to rush into danger, listening, looking, smelling the air for the telltale sour, rotten odour of sickos. There was so much filth on the streets, though, it was hard to pick out any one particular smell.

They heard another howl. It sounded more distant than before.

'See,' said Courtney, squeezing Olivia's hand. 'It's going away, whatever it was.'

'Was it a sicko?'

'Could have been a cat or fox or anything.'

'I wish we'd waited until the morning.'

'We'll be all right. We'll find your brother, OK?'

Olivia's eyes went wide. 'What if he's dead?'

Courtney sighed. 'Can't you think of something nice? Don't think of bad things all the time.'

'I can't help it.'

Courtney was beginning to regret holding on to Olivia's hand. She was stuck with her now and the little girl was being a real downer. All she was doing was making her more scared and depressed. Everyone probably felt the same way as Olivia, and it really didn't help spelling it out. She was about to say something to the little girl when there was a crash from the side-street they were passing.

'What was that?'

'Probably nothing.'

It wasn't nothing, though – it was three sickos, who, a moment later, stumbled into the road, carrying an unidentifiable dead thing. They were all three mothers; two of them very tall and skinny, the third much older, bent over, bald, her belly hanging down to her knees. The sickos were as surprised to see the kids as the kids were to see them. They stopped, eyes goggling.

'Run!' wailed Olivia.

'No,' said DogNut firmly. 'We ain't running. If they want an argument, we'll give them one.'

As he said it, he tugged his sword from its scabbard, and

Felix and Marco formed up on either side of him, weapons at the ready. Courtney let go of Olivia and joined them, trying to appear braver than she felt. Finn took charge of the little girl and kept behind the others, cursing his useless, swollen arm in its sling. The slightest touch sent daggers of hot pain all the way up to his shoulder. In the last couple of days it had become a lot worse. He couldn't hold anything – in fact, could hardly move the arm at all, and his fingers had become fat and puffy. He also felt slightly feverish, which frightened him.

Stupid thing was, it hadn't even happened in a battle – he'd slipped on some wet steps at the Tower and gashed himself on a piece of jagged stone.

'Come on then,' said DogNut, waving his sword at the mothers. 'You want some? Come and get it then. What are you waiting for?'

The older mother drew her blistered lips back, exposing toothless gums, and hissed at the kids, then waddled forward, her companions joining her in a clumsy charge.

'Don't look, Olivia,' Finn said kindly, covering the girl's eyes. 'Turn away.'

The fight lasted less than a minute. The kids laid into the adults with a ferociousness born out of stress and tension. The three sickos went down fast and stayed down, bleeding into the gutter.

The kids cleaned their weapons and carried on, almost hysterical from their victory and the sudden flood of relief. They were laughing as they walked, talking over each other in a mad, excited jumble as they recalled the events of the fight.

'Did you see the look on the old bat's face when I twatted her on the side of the head . . .?'

'I thought my spear was gonna get stuck! I forgot to twist it . . .'

'You got to be well careful with a sword and all, better to slash with it than to stick the point in . . .'

'How did they ever think they could win?'

'They ain't had to deal with kids like us before. Only the wimps from round here. We're Jordan Hordern's soldiers; we're trained, we're the elite . . .'

'We're kings of the streets!'

'Hey, look at that,' said Courtney, and they all stopped walking.

They had come to a fancy pinkish-brown building with a big dome on the top. Tatty flags hung along the front above a row of ragged green awnings.

'Ain't that Harrods?'

'Yeah.' Felix whistled. 'You wanna go shopping?'

'I went in there once,' said Courtney. 'It was mad. The poshest place I ever been, even posher than Buckingham Palace. You could buy anything you wanted in the whole world, even a helicopter, probably, and you should have seen the food they had in there. Mental. All the staff, like, looked at me like I didn't belong, though.'

'You could go in there now,' said Marco. 'Own it.'

'I could, couldn't I?'

'Except it's probably full of sickos,' said Felix.

'Yeah, thanks for pointing that out, or I might have forgotten,' said Courtney grumpily. 'I might have, like, gone in there with my credit card on a shopping frenzy. I was having a nice memory, yeah? A nice dream. And you spoilt it, man.'

'Yeah, Felix, you're so dumb sometimes,' said Marco.

'Oh, right, and you ain't?' Felix gave Marco a pitying look.

'Yeah,' said Marco. 'Compared to you I'm like triple A star.'

'Compared to me you are just like a piece of snot dangling off some manky mother's nose,' said Felix.

'Yeah?' Marco made a dismissive gesture. 'Compared to me you are the pants some father's been wearing for, like, a year, and he ain't never wiped his arse in all that time.'

'Why don't you two hush your gums,' said Courtney. 'You are, like, year *four* kids sometimes. Year *three*.'

Four floors above them a mother was sniffing the air, watching from one of the Harrods windows. She was moaning quietly, her tongue slobbering against the grimy glass. She was so hungry. She was imagining the taste of the children. Imagining sinking her teeth into their soft flesh. The blood in her mouth. The feel of the meat as she chewed it . . .

But they were too far away. She couldn't get there in time. This was one meal she would never eat. Because others were already there. She could see them, moving towards the children from every direction.

Lots of them.

A tear ran down her cheek, between the blisters and the holes where the disease had eaten into her face.

So hungry.

'You keep out of this, Courtney.' Felix was almost shouting. 'This is between me and Marco.'

'No, it ain't!' Courtney looked like she couldn't believe what she was hearing. 'This is between me and you.'

'Shut it you lot,' said DogNut. 'We've got to keep moving.'

'Pick your own argument, Courtney,' said Marco, ignoring him.

'I thought you was on my side!'

'I ain't on nobody's side.'

'You are just as bad as Felix.'

'Jesus, Courtney, get off my case –'

Suddenly there was a yelp from Finn. Something had snatched hold of his sling, and he lashed out instinctively with his right elbow. The pain jarred his whole body and he thought he was going to be sick.

The sound alerted the other kids who spun round to see a good twenty or so sickos spread out across the road. The adults had been shadowing them, attracted by the sounds of the battle and the smell of fresh blood.

Olivia was too frightened to shout 'Run' – the word froze in her throat – but DogNut shouted it for her.

'Run! Get the hell out of here!'

18

One thing the older kids had learnt was that if they pushed themselves they could always outrun a sicko. The problem was Olivia. She was smaller than the rest of them, slower, and had less stamina. As a group, they could only move as fast as the slowest member. At first none of them was thinking about anything other than getting away. They all headed in the same direction, with DogNut in the lead, working on animal instinct, simply trying to survive.

As he ran, though, and recovered from the initial shock, DogNut realized it wasn't as simple as that. He had brought these kids here. He was responsible for all of them. If he was going to return to the Tower as a hero and kick Leo's ghost into touch, he was going to have to act like a hero.

But heroes in books weren't tied down by ten-year-old girls, were they?

He looked back. Olivia was three or four metres behind them, her face ugly with fear. A thought flashed through DogNut's mind. If they left Olivia behind, they would be much more likely to get away. Should he sacrifice her for the good of the rest of them?

Felix saw him looking.

'Leave her,' he grunted.

'No!' DogNut yelled it much louder than he had

intended. So the decision had been made for him then. He ran back to Olivia and grabbed her hand, jerked her off her feet as he pulled her along. The nearest sickos were almost close enough to touch.

Olivia was screaming.

'Shut up!' DogNut shouted at her, and miraculously she fell silent. 'Save your breath. I ain't leaving you.'

Her little skinny legs were bouncing and skittering as her feet tried to get a grip on the road. Marco saw what was happening and pushed past Felix to help, taking hold of Olivia's other hand.

He had heard what Felix had said and he gave him a dirty look as they drew level.

'Wanker . . .'

The main road was full of sickos, so they veered off and ran down the side of Harrods where in the fading light they could just make out that the way ahead was mercifully clear. DogNut saw Courtney up at the front, in the lead now, pounding along. She was one powerful girl and moved fast despite her size. Finn was between Felix and Courtney. DogNut, Marco and Olivia were at the back, dropping steadily behind the others.

'Try and catch up!' DogNut gasped, and the three of them accelerated.

They were quickly in a more residential area, where they bombed round a corner into a terraced street of grand, white-painted houses.

'I gotta stop,' said Finn, and he doubled over, clutching his chest. 'I can't run properly with my arm like this. Stitch.'

The rest of them slowed, then also stopped. They stood in a loose group, their eyes constantly searching for any movement in both directions. At this time of the evening, as the last of the light drained from the sky, it was easy to see things in the shadows. They all felt jittery, panicked. DogNut sent Felix back to the corner to keep watch.

'We need to get off the street,' Courtney panted. 'Keep under cover for a bit. Wait for them to go away. If we stay out here, we'll just attract more of them.'

'Over here!' Olivia was shouting and pointing at one of the houses. 'There's people in there. Kids. I seen them.'

'Are you sure?' Marco looked where she was pointing.

'I seen them. Sitting at a table. One of them waved at me.'

DogNut trotted over to the pavement. The building was set back from the road behind railings. He peered in through the windows and could just make out in the gloom three kids sitting at a kitchen table that looked like it was covered with plates of food. One of the kids did indeed have his arm raised.

'They're coming!' Felix hissed from the corner, then ran back to join his mates.

'Inside. Quick,' said DogNut. 'Come on. All of you.' The front door was open a crack, the lock dangling uselessly. Maybe the kids had just broken in. DogNut tutted. He'd need to teach them a thing or two about security.

There was a bad smell in the house, but they were all used to bad smells. Hardly anyone washed regularly or changed their clothes. Toilets and showers didn't tend to work any more. Without refrigeration food quickly went off.

The hallway was filled with heaps of magazines and newspapers, stacked up on either side so that there was only a narrow corridor running down the middle.

Finn remembered how the newspapers used to pile up

at home before someone cracked and left a big stack out for the recycling.

Well, Jesus, someone needed to take this lot out something bad.

Felix was the last one in. He quietly pushed the door shut then noticed that there was a heavy stone bust of Shakespeare standing on the floor, with scrape marks leading across the floorboards. It must have been put there to keep the door closed. It wouldn't stand up to much force, but it would at least stop the door from blowing open. He slid it over and jammed it up against the door.

He wondered why the kids in the kitchen hadn't put it back in place.

There were other questions nagging at him, but he was too panicked and desperate for this to be a place of safety to think about them too closely. He followed the others down the hallway into the kitchen.

The first thing he noticed was that the room was totally rammed with junk. There were teetering piles of saucepans and frying pans and dirty plates, bin bags bursting, overflowing with rotten food, as well as toasters, microwaves, scales, deep-fat fryers, mixers, juicers . . . Every appliance you could imagine was stuffed in here, like a junkyard. And not just kitchen equipment – there were things that shouldn't have been in a kitchen: Hoovers, TVs, bicycles, footballs, golf clubs, clothes, musical instruments, books and magazines, garden tools. It was as if someone had taken the contents of every house on the street and emptied them all into this room. You could barely move.

The next thing Felix noticed was that the three kids at the kitchen table were dead. And worse. Mutilated. One of them, the boy who had appeared to be waving at them, had been torn in half, so that his body was missing from the waist down, and he had been plonked in the chair on the bloody stump of his torso. The waving arm didn't belong to him at all, but had been ripped from one of the other kids, a girl, and stuck upright in a heavy milk jug on the table. Felix's brain started turning fast. There were no signs of decay, which meant they hadn't been dead long, which meant that whoever had done this to them might still be around.

Felix clamped his hand to his mouth to prevent himself from gagging and spoke through his fingers.

'Oh, man, this is whack,' he moaned. 'We got to get out of here.'

'We can't.' Courtney was at the window, crouched down and staring out. As the others saw her, they instinctively ducked down also.

'They've come. There's loads of them in the street.'

DogNut crept over to join her, walking bent double.

'Shit. D'you think they know we're in here?'

'I don't think so. Not yet.'

DogNut could just see what was going on outside. There were indeed about thirty sickos there, spread out and shambling aimlessly around. One or two had their heads tilted back as they sniffed the air.

'D'you reckon they can smell us?' he whispered.

'With this stink in here? Who knows?'

'There must be a back way out,' said Felix. 'A posh place like this will have a garden of some sort. Must do.'

'Yeah.' DogNut and Courtney moved away from the window and joined the others. They were all trying not to look at the dark shapes of the dead kids at the table.

They moved back into the hallway and headed towards

the back of the house. Olivia was sobbing and snivelling, making little whispering noises. Marco pulled Felix aside and punched him in the arm.

'You was gonna leave her,' he hissed, letting the others go ahead.

'Shut up,' Felix replied.

'No, you shut up. We stick together. We're a team. We look out for one another. We all got to know that. Or none of us is gonna feel safe.'

'Yeah, dickface, cos, like, I feel really safe right now,' said Felix sarcastically. 'We're in some kind of house of horrors here with an army of sickos outside and it's night time, and I can't see a sodding thing, so, yeah, *safe*!'

'Shut up.'

'No, you shut up.'

They soon discovered that the garden at the rear of the house was lower than the street level. One floor down.

'There'll be a back door downstairs, probably,' said Finn.

'Yeah, and what else is down there?' said Felix.

'Shut up, Felix.'

'You shut up, Marco.'

The stairs leading down to the basement were dark. DogNut fished a torch out of his pocket. He reckoned he could risk switching it on as it wouldn't be visible from the street back here. Even so, he shielded the beam as he pressed the button and then moved quickly to the top of the stairs. They could see straight away that there was an even worse jumble of stuff in the basement than there was up here; even the stairs were piled with junk.

The torch beam was dancing about all over the place and DogNut realized he was shaking badly.

'Come on,' he said, trying to hold his voice steady.

'I'm not sure,' said Courtney. 'Someone messed up those kids in the kitchen. What if they're down there?'

DogNut hauled out his sword. It would be hard to use it in these cramped conditions, but it gave him confidence.

'Any sicko down there is gonna get owned,' he said, and set off, the rest of them crowding behind him.

The chaos at the bottom was unbelievable. Like the hallway, there were books and magazines and old newspapers piled right up to the ceiling, leaving only a narrow tunnel between them, giving the effect of being in a maze. DogNut crept cautiously ahead and as he turned the first corner he fully expected to see some kind of monster waiting for them. All he found, though, was another short length of tunnel, and another corner to turn.

There were black smears along the walls where someone had repeatedly passed by. Someone large and dirty.

DogNut took a deep breath through his mouth and pressed on.

As they explored further, they discovered that there were little pockets of space carved out of the stacks, like rooms within rooms. One was obviously used as a toilet, the floor was thick with excrement and filthy shredded paper. Another had piles of bones and half-eaten body parts in it, another was, weirdly, full of toy cars. Hundreds of them. One room contained hundreds of CDs and DVDs.

Felix was getting hysterical. This house was crazy.

'I didn't think anyone collected CDs any more,' he giggled. 'I thought everyone downloaded everything these days.'

'Shut up, Felix,' said Marco, though he was laughing too.

They realized that the maze extended under several

houses, where holes had been knocked through the walls, and they soon lost all idea of where they were. The likelihood of finding a back door was getting ever more remote. Finally they reached the end of the maze where they discovered a sort of den, with a greasy sofa that had long since collapsed, a huge flat-screen TV and a desk with several computers on it. There were no windows, though, or doors, no way out other than back the way they had come. The kids were so disorientated now they had no idea which way the garden might even be, so there was no point in attempting the dangerous work of burrowing through one of the precarious walls of paper.

'I guess we'll have to go back upstairs and climb down into the garden,' said Marco. 'I don't fancy being stuck in this maze when whoever lives here comes home.'

'I hate this,' said Olivia.

DogNut had to stop himself from snapping at her, telling her it was her fault they had come in here in the first place. It wasn't her fault, really, was it? He was in charge. He was a kid, though – kids always tried to blame someone else. His torch beam was zigzagging more wildly than ever, skittering over the details in the den. Landing now on the black stain on the sofa, now on a small human hand underneath the television, now on the broken remains of a Scalextric set, now on an empty bottle of whisky.

The image of the sicko, sitting down here, watching the blank TV and drinking whisky was ridiculous. Ridiculous and creepy.

He clamped his elbow against his side to try to stop his hand from shaking. He hated showing fear in front of the others, but he knew they were all feeling the same. The smell and the lack of air down here was awful.

'I want to go,' said Olivia, and she spoke for all of them. 'We're going.'

They set off, retracing their steps. At least they knew what to expect on the way out. They hurried through the maze, trying to avoid the filth on the floor.

A few minutes later they came to the top of the stairs and DogNut had to switch the torch off or risk being seen from the street. It must be totally dark outside now. No light came through the frosted glass in the front door.

He went to the back window. It was locked and barred. Of course it was. In his hurry DogNut hadn't registered it before when he'd looked out. This was a very rich part of town and the houses were plastered with security to keep burglars out.

'This is no good,' said Felix, joining him. 'All the other windows is gonna be the same.'

'We could try and break the locks,' said Marco.

'Too much noise, dumb-ass,' said Felix. 'They'll hear us out there and break in before we could get this lot even half off.'

'You got a better idea, wasteman?'

'Why ain't it so dark out the back?' DogNut interrupted before they could get into another one of their pointless arguments.

'What d'you mean?' asked Felix.

'There's more light here than at the front.'

'Shut up,' said Courtney.

'I'm only saying –'

'Shut up and listen!'

'What?'

'Just shut up, will you!'

They all fell silent. It was then that they became aware

135

of a strange rasping, gurgling sound, like some old piece of machinery ticking over.

'What is it?' said Olivia. She had to get out of here. She was going to faint. She knew she was. She was so frightened she was going to throw up any second now.

'Central heating maybe?' said Marco. 'A boiler or something.'

'How could anyone be running a boiler, you moron?' said Felix.

'I don't know . . .'

'It seems to be coming from over by the front door,' said Courtney.

They listened again. The sound was closer than they had first thought.

Or else it had *moved* closer.

'There's something there,' said Felix.

'I don't want to see it,' Olivia wailed.

'Put your torch back on, man,' said Marco.

'I can't risk it,' said DogNut.

'We have to see what that is,' said Courtney, in such a way that DogNut knew he had no choice.

He took out his torch again. His hand was shaking so uncontrollably that he was worried he might drop it. He held his breath and snapped the light back on.

For a moment the kids couldn't make sense of what they were seeing.

And then DogNut understood that it hadn't grown completely dark out the front. There was someone in the hallway, blocking the light.

Someone huge.

A man.

He completely filled the gap between the piles of

newspaper and was staring at them with yellow-rimmed eyes.

He was monstrously fat, with two great naked legs like tree trunks. He was wearing a pair of shorts with no shoes or socks and the remains of a vast sweatshirt that was ripped and full of holes. Barely able to contain his obscene bulk, the sweatshirt cut into his body like the string round a trussed-up chicken ready for roasting. Fat bulged out of the holes and his vast belly hung down over the top of his shorts.

He had great pendulous breasts and his hair was long and matted, with bits of food stuck in it. If it wasn't for the straggly beard that framed his bulbous, sweating face they might have mistaken him for a woman. His skin was so dirty it looked black; his eyes stared out brightly, like the eyes of a coal-miner. There was snot streaming from his nose and into his half-open mouth. The noise they had heard was his breath rattling in his throat.

'Stuff . . .' he said. 'Stuff . . .'

19

Courtney psyched herself up and ran at the giant with a roar, her spear aimed at his juddering belly, but he swatted it aside and the point stuck fast in the wall of newspaper. Courtney swore and abandoned it. As the man advanced on her she thumped him with her forearm. The blow bounced harmlessly off him, sending a ripple through his upper body.

'Stuff . . .' he said again, his voice squeezed into a wheezy high-pitched croak. He looked to be in his late twenties and he stank powerfully. He didn't look badly diseased. There were a few spots on his face, but no major boils or sores. There was green mould growing on him, though, in all the folds and creases of his exposed flesh.

'Stuff . . .'

As he moved along the hallway his sides rubbed against the walls of newspaper, making a rustling sound. Felix darted past Courtney and clumsily jabbed at him with his sword, but the blow was lost in the layers of fat.

DogNut ran through their choices. Stay here and try to fight the monster, try to push past him towards the front door, retreat into the basement with its maze of newsprint, or go upstairs. This last option seemed the safest choice, even though they had no idea what might be up there.

The giant plodded on, slow and steady, repeating the same word over and over.

'Stuff . . . stuff . . . stuff . . .'

DogNut stared at him and his mind was filled with one stupid thought, the one that Courtney had planted in his brain. This man could overwhelm them.

'Upstairs!' he yelled. 'Now.'

He charged at the waddling hulk, hoping to hold him back long enough for his friends to reach the stairs. He hacked uselessly with his sword; there wasn't enough space for a full swing. And having seen what happened when Felix and Courtney attacked him, DogNut was scared to jab him with the point in case he lost his weapon. As it was, his blade did little against the sicko except split his skin. The fat that swelled out of the superficial wound was bright pink against his dark skin.

DogNut turned and joined his friends, who were scrambling up the stairs. The last to make it was Olivia, and even then DogNut had to grab her by the arm and jerk her away from the approaching sicko.

They clattered upwards, hoping to find a room they could get in and barricade. Behind them they could hear the sicko place his fat foot on the first step with an almighty thud.

'More stuff . . .'

The rooms on the next floor were too crammed with junk to even get in. Electrical appliances, mostly, and computer hardware, monitors, keyboards, hard drives and miles and miles of cable. DogNut swore and ordered the gang up to the next floor. It was a similar story here, except that most of the junk consisted of toys of some sort, many still in their packaging. They were mixed up with other bits and pieces, sporting equipment, expensive luggage, clothing and more books.

'Maybe we could get on to the roof, or something,' said Courtney. 'Let's try the top floor. We can always come back down again.'

'I don't want to go up!' Olivia screamed. 'I want to get out of here. We'll be trapped.'

'We'll be all right,' said DogNut. 'We'll get out. Don't worry.' He grabbed her arm again and roughly pulled her up the stairs. They could hear the steady *clump*, *clump* of the man coming after them.

They thundered up to the next level. It immediately looked more hopeful. It was still full of rubbish – carrier bags, cardboard boxes, more toys, empty bottles and cans – but there was a lot more room to move around. Obviously, being so heavy, and not too keen on climbing stairs, the huge sicko was filling the house from the bottom up.

The room at the back had a small balcony overlooking the garden. Felix and Marco stayed to secure the door to the stairs while the rest of them went over to the sliding glass balcony windows and figured out how to open them.

Felix found a key in the bedroom door just as Courtney opened the latch that released the sliding windows, and they both yelled in triumph at the same time. There was a rush of clean fresh air and the kids were reminded just how badly the house stank. Finn, Olivia, Courtney and DogNut hustled out on to the balcony and looked down. They were five floors up.

'Can we climb it?' Courtney asked.

'I can't,' said Finn bluntly, and he shook his head. 'I'll stay here and try to hold him off, if you lot want to try and climb down.'

DogNut was looking at the long drop.

'We don't need no heroic sacrifices, Finn. What we need's a bloody ladder.'

'I can't do it either,' said Olivia. 'I can't climb. I can't do it. I'm scared of heights. I can't. I won't.'

'It's way too dangerous for any of us to try it,' said DogNut. 'So don't worry about it.'

'What about up?' said Felix, who had come out on to the balcony to see what was happening. 'Is there a way up on to the roof maybe?'

But that looked hopeless as well.

'So what do we do now?' said Felix, looking accusingly at DogNut. 'You got us up here.'

'Shut up and let me think,' said DogNut, and Felix muttered something under his breath.

'What did you say?' DogNut glared at Felix, who rubbed his face nervously.

'I said thinking's not your strong point,' said Felix. 'I should have stayed at the palace. At least David knew what he was doing.'

'Ignore him,' said Courtney, putting a hand on DogNut's back. 'He's just scared like the rest of us.'

Olivia was ignoring the argument. She had sat down with her back to the balcony wall. She was ignoring everything. Hoping it would all go away. She closed her eyes and covered her ears with her hands. She wasn't here. She was back at home in her room, before any of this had happened, with Paul and her dad and his new girlfriend. And her new stepsister. Kira. She always forgot about Kira. She hadn't been around that long. She was all right, but not like a proper sister.

That was better. Take yourself back. She could picture her old room. She imagined she was sitting on her bed and slowly her things came into place around her. Her pink CD machine that also played tapes and woke her up in the mornings with the radio. Her posters. Her old dressing-up box. Her clothes all neat in the cupboard that Dad had built for her. And Dad was there too, reading her a bedtime story. That was nice. He didn't do it much, but she loved it when he did. She could see him there now. His hair all messy as usual. The smell of him. A warm smell. She tried to listen to the words. Her favourite Cathy Cassidy book. *Dizzy*. She smiled. She was sure she could hear his voice in her head. So familiar. She was hardly aware of footsteps around her, hardly felt it as someone jostled her, and she went deeper into her memories, humming quietly to block out the sounds.

So she didn't hear Felix yelling that the sicko had arrived at the top of the stairs. Didn't see the others run back into the bedroom. Didn't see the door bulging as the man leant his enormous weight against it.

Didn't hear the panic in their voices.

'He's gonna get in.'

'We're trapped here now.'

'What do we do?'

'All right.' DogNut got their attention by clapping his hands. He had put his sword back in its scabbard. It would only get in the way. He was grinning.

'It's like this, OK? Listen to me. It's easy. We fox him like we did downstairs. We let him come in, yeah? Right into the room. Make sure he gets away from the door.'

'I get you!' said Marco. 'We can do it. We just have to get past him and we'll be down the stairs before he can even squeeze his great fat arse back out through the door.'

'OK,' said Courtney, who was grinning too. 'OK.'

She had found a golf club among the rubbish in the room, and felt more confident with a weapon back in her hands.

The door stopped bulging for a moment, there was a moment's silence followed by an almighty thump as the sicko threw himself against the woodwork with more speed. The frame cracked. The panels split.

'Wait for it,' said DogNut. 'Wait for it.'

'I'm gonna whack his lardy butt,' said Felix.

'Like that'll make any difference, you nunce,' Marco scoffed. 'He don't feel nothing.'

'I'm gonna whack him anyway, show him who's the big man.'

'Oh, he's the big man, all right, Felix,' said Marco, and the two of them giggled nervously.

'Don't bother trying to fight him,' said DogNut angrily. 'Just don't waste your time. All we got to do is get round him, that's it.'

Before he could say anything else the door gave way and burst inwards as if there had been an explosion outside. And there was the sicko, forcing himself into the opening.

'Stuff . . .' he said. 'More stuff . . .'

He could hardly fit through the door. He had to stretch his arms out in front of him and roll his shoulders. Finally, with a wriggle and a shrug, he was in the room.

True to his word Felix lunged at him with his sword, but the point just sank into the side of his belly and lodged there so deeply that Felix couldn't pull it out. As he tugged at it, the man moved towards him with sudden speed, almost dancing on his toes, and one meaty hand reached out for Felix. He got him by the wrist and Felix screamed.

Courtney brought her golf club down with all her might on the sicko's wrist. There was a hefty slap and the man must

143

have relaxed his grip a little because the next moment Felix was free. He saw that Courtney, Finn and DogNut were already out of the room and he threw himself into the narrowing gap between the man and the wall, swearing with the effort. He felt the heat coming off the solid bulk of flesh, and an unholy stink of mould and sweat and shit. If the man's body hadn't been slicked with grease, Felix doubted he would have been able to get past. As it was, he was nearly trapped as the man tried to squash him against the wall with his belly, but Marco took hold of his friend and pulled him clear.

'Don't try and give the man a hug, you stupid pumplex! I know you want to kiss him all over, but you gonna catch something.'

'Shut up, Marco!'

The next moment the two of them tumbled out on to the landing, crashing into the banisters. They could hear the others clattering down the stairs below.

Felix sometimes had dreams where he was running down an endless twisting staircase as someone chased him. In his dreams he'd learnt to swing on the banisters at the corners like a monkey so that he would sort of fly from one hand-hold to another as he whizzed down. If he remembered to do it, the nightmare was turned into something fun and exhilarating. He tried to do the same now, but it was hard in the darkness and he kept falling and rolling down the steps. He was too pumped up to feel anything, though, and was laughing all the way, so relieved was he to have got away from the sicko. He fell past Courtney, caught up with Finn, overtook him, overtook DogNut, and now he was in the lead.

He was first to the front door, half running, half stumbling along the hallway. He kicked the bust of Shakespeare out of the way and wrenched the door open, not caring what might be waiting for them outside.

Mercifully, the street was clear. Felix staggered into the middle of the road and fell to the ground, laughing and sobbing with relief. One by one the others emerged. Courtney was last out and she stopped just long enough to pull down some of the stacks of newspapers and magazines so that they blocked the doorway.

'That'll hold the fat bastard up!' she yelled triumphantly as she ran out and they all hugged each other and exchanged high-fives. It quickly hit them, though, that they weren't out of danger yet. All their noise had attracted a band of sickos who were approaching along the road.

'Looks like we gotta keep on running,' said DogNut, and they sprinted away in the opposite direction. It was only when they turned the corner at the end of the street that DogNut stopped and swore. Thrashing his sides with his balled fists.

'What is it?' said Courtney, looking around for a fresh threat.

'Olivia,' said DogNut bitterly. 'Where's Olivia?'

20

Olivia was on the balcony. Tears running down her face. They'd left her. She couldn't believe they'd done it. They'd all run off without her. And now *he* was coming. The man. She'd slid the glass door shut and was standing watching as he trundled across the room towards the balcony.

She was shaking her head from side to side, unable to take her eyes off the huge wobbling bulk of the man.

'No, no, no, no, no . . .'

He reached the glass of the door and started to press his body against it, flattening his mass of fat so that he grew wider and wider. And now he pressed his face as well, squashing his nose and lips and smearing pus and snot and saliva over the window. And still he kept pressing, flattening, widening.

At last Olivia could stand it no more. She turned away and looked over the edge of the balcony. It was such a long way down. Immediately she felt dizzy and sick. The ground appeared to come nearer in a rush then speed away again, as if she was bouncing on a bungee cord.

There was a crack. She spun round. The glass had broken – jagged lines ran across it – and still the man pushed and pushed. He seemed to cover the entire window. His face expressionless. Squashed out of shape. One eye right against the glass. Staring at her. He was something disgusting and slimy in a tank at an aquarium.

The glass cracked again.

Olivia climbed up onto the brick wall that ran along the edge of the balcony. She stood there swaying, her head fizzing, tears hanging from her chin and then dropping away, down, down into the darkness. Falling had always been her biggest fear. She hated going on aeroplanes, she hated cliff tops and tower blocks and bridges.

She couldn't believe they had just left her. Run off like that. It was so unfair. She couldn't do anything by herself. She couldn't fight. They knew that. She drew in a series of racking sobs that jerked her small body as if someone was kicking her chest.

'No, no, no, no, no . . .'

Another crack. Then another. The whole window was bowing out. Any moment now it would give way and he would be there, outside, with her. Just the two of them. And he would do to her what he had done to those other children downstairs. The ones in the kitchen she had thought were waving at her. How long had they taken to die? Surely falling would be quicker? But it would still be long. The garden was so far away. And all the way down she would be alive, and waiting for the thud as she hit the ground.

Would it hurt? Or would she be unconscious before . . .

She mustn't think about that. She closed her eyes. Tried to put herself back home. Yes. It was bedtime. She was going to kiss her dad goodnight and go upstairs. She would be brave and go up by herself tonight. Listen to a story tape. The tapes were very old and worn. Most of them had belonged to her cousin who was much older than her. Paul had had them first. She'd listened to them through the thin wall and couldn't wait for them to be hers.

She loved those stories.

Dad was watching television with his new girlfriend.

No!

It was before then. Mum was still there. Even though Olivia couldn't really remember her. But she was still there. Yes, that was better. Mum and Dad together on the sofa watching TV. They were so close. On the other side of the door. All she had to do was open the door and there they'd be. She turned the handle. Kept her eyes tight shut. Didn't want to spoil the surprise.

The door was open. She sucked in a deep breath and then took a small step . . .

She wasn't falling – she was floating – and there were Dad and Mum. They were reaching out their hands to her and everything was all right.

They would catch her. They would make sure she was all right. That's what grown-ups did.

They looked after you.

They –

21

'I promised her. I said I wouldn't leave her. She was counting on me.'

'She was counting on all of us, DogNut,' said Courtney.
'It's not your fault. We all forgot about her. It was crazy
up there.'

'I can't just leave her.' DogNut started to walk off.

Felix looked alarmed. 'You're not going back, DogNut!'
he shouted, running after him. 'You can't go in there again.
He'd kill you.'

'That's not the point.' DogNut angrily shrugged Felix's
hand off his shoulder. 'The point is I promised I wouldn't
let her down and now –'

'And now she's dead,' said Felix bluntly. 'Face it. So what
would be the point in going back?'

'Exactly,' said Marco, coming over to the two of them.
'We can't change what happened. We're lucky any of us
got out, and it was thanks to you that we did.'

'I was supposed to look after her. I can't let it end like
this.'

'It ain't over, dude,' said Marco. 'It ain't over by a long
way yet. It's dark and we're still on the streets. What we
got to do now is make sure that the rest of us don't wind
up –'

'Dead!' shouted DogNut. 'She's dead and it's my fault.'

'It's been a hell of a day,' said Marco. 'We're lucky any of us are still alive. We've been through it and then some. The boat sank, the gym bunnies nearly got us, David tried to trap us in the palace, and then a humongous sicko nearly added us to his collection of dead bodies. But the thing is, DogNut, we're still here, us five. Out of the eight of us that set off this morning we've only lost one.'

DogNut laughed bitterly. 'Oh, so that makes it all right, does it?'

'Yes,' said Finn quietly. 'It does.'

He turned and started walking on. When Finn made up his mind to do something, there was no arguing. The others looked at him, and then followed, all except DogNut who stubbornly stayed behind.

'Come on,' said Courtney, returning to where he stood in the middle of the road. 'You got to try and forget, Doggo.' She gently took his arm. 'Move on. And I don't mean in a huggy-kissy, teen-advice-column way. I mean we really do have to literally move on, because it ain't safe to stay here.'

It was no good, though. DogNut wrenched his arm away and stomped off a few paces in the opposite direction. He was crying.

'DogNut!' Courtney yelled at him. 'You're putting the rest of us in danger now!'

'Then leave me alone. I'll go by myself.'

'No, you won't.' Finn had come back to see what was happening. He spun DogNut round and looked into his face.

'What's done is done,' he said. 'You're not going back in there.'

'I'll do what I bloody like,' said DogNut, his voice rising in pitch as he became more and more hysterical. 'That poor little girl is all alone in that house with a monster. And I can't leave her. I can't. I've got to go back and I've got to see for myself. Perhaps she ain't dead, perhaps I can help her, perhaps I could save her, rescue her, perhaps . . .'

Finn slapped DogNut hard in the face, stunning him into silence. Then, before he could do anything, Finn scooped him up with his good arm and put him over his shoulder as easily as if he'd been a bag of rubbish that Finn was taking out to the bins.

Finn walked on. DogNut's skinny body bouncing up and down. He struggled for a few paces before the fight went out of him. Despite everything that had happened, Courtney smiled, almost laughed. She had always known that Finn was strong, but to do what he'd done, with one arm, was beyond awesome.

'You're a good bloke, DogNut,' Finn said. 'You did enough. You got us out of there. We're not heroes. We're just kids.'

'But I won't be able to live with it,' said DogNut miserably.

'Yes, you will.'

'Yeah? And how would you know that?'

'After my mum and dad died,' said Finn, 'I tried to look after my three younger brothers. And I couldn't do it. I messed up. They all got killed. I try not to think about it. That was my old life. This is my new life.'

'I'm sorry,' said DogNut. 'I didn't know.'

'I don't talk about it. Now shut up and stop wriggling.'

'But, Finn –'

'I said shut up. How do you think I've felt all day, being

like this? My arm out of action? Not being able to do anything to help? I've felt useless. But there was nothing I could do about it. Just as there's nothing you can do about Olivia now. What happened to her, we'll all share it. OK? It's all our fault.'

'OK,' said DogNut. 'You can put me down now.'

'You won't do anything stupid?'

'No.'

Finn dropped DogNut back on to his feet and the five of them walked on in silence for a while.

They were slightly disorientated and weren't a hundred per cent sure where they were, but Marco had a pretty good sense of direction and managed to lead them back on to the Brompton Road without any major detours. The main road was busier than the side-roads, however. Small clumps of sickos skulked in the doorways of buildings.

The safest way to get past them was to run, so the kids sped up, first jogging then hammering full pelt as they started to attract the attention of the grown-ups who wandered after them.

The kids were sprinting now, as fast as they could go, trying to ignore the burning in their lungs and the tiredness in their legs.

Running helped clear DogNut's mind and he was able to close himself off from his thoughts. All he had to do was put one foot in front of the other and keep pushing himself. There was nothing more to his existence. He had to build a little box and put Olivia in it, and leave it back there in the sicko's house. He had to forget about her, just as he'd had to forget about so many other friends since the disease had changed everything forever.

It was working. He was running from her.

'Look out!'

Marco's shout alerted him to the fact that a big knot of sickos had spread out across the road in front of them.

'Keep going!' DogNut yelled, and they smashed into the grown-ups. Apart from Finn, they were all still armed. Felix had lost his spear, but had a big hunting knife. Courtney had her golf club, and she used it to crack the skulls of two slow-moving mothers. DogNut's sword slashed right and left. Marco was busy with his spear. And Finn used the heel of his good hand to shove anyone aside who got in his way. They hit the sickos so hard and so fast and so unexpectedly that they rammed their way through and out the other side before the grown-ups even really knew what was happening.

Their small victory gave the kids fresh hope and energy, and they sprinted on, feeling like they could run forever. They were aware, though, that they were picking up more and more sickos behind them as they went. True, the sickos were slow and lumbering and couldn't keep up – very few of them had anything like the speed and fitness of the gym bunnies they'd met earlier – but, nevertheless, once they had your scent they'd doggedly follow. You couldn't afford to slow down or stop until you were well away. The kids felt like they were dragging every sicko in London along behind them in a big net, drawing in more and more of them as they went.

They were all too aware that there was a shambling, shuffling, mindless army of the half dead following them. They couldn't keep running all night. If they didn't get to somewhere safe, they were going to be in trouble.

It was all DogNut's world consisted of now, running, running, running . . . About three months ago one of the search parties at the Tower had discovered a small warehouse crammed with Nike trainers. They'd carted boxes and boxes of them back to the Tower. So now the kids might not have clean clothes and fresh food, but they were never short of fresh trainers. DogNut was glad he was wearing a new pair now as he pounded down the centre of the road, his heavy sword clutched in his hand.

'How far is it?' Felix gasped. 'I can't keep this up much longer.'

'I don't know,' said DogNut. 'Just keep going.'

'You idiots!' Marco called out, half laughing, half wheezing. 'We're there! That's the museum!'

22

DogNut couldn't believe it. They'd been barely a ten-minute walk away when they'd been ambushed. If only they'd known they were so close, maybe they wouldn't have made the detour at Harrods, maybe they wouldn't have ended up in the sicko's house, maybe Olivia wouldn't have died, maybe, maybe, maybe . . .

In their panic, in the dark, eyes focused on the ground directly in front of them, they hadn't noticed the vast gothic building to their right, with two great lines of arched windows along the front, and a pair of tall towers spiking up into the starlit sky on either side of the entrance. With more towers on either end, the building looked more like a cathedral than a museum.

The museum ran down the whole of one side of the road, almost as far as they could see, opposite a row of grand houses. It stood behind a strip of open ground edged by the type of black iron railings you saw everywhere in London. A group of well-armed boys was watching them suspiciously from a small pointy-roofed gatehouse beside the main gates. They bristled when DogNut and his gang ran over, and stayed put on their side of the gates.

DogNut and his friends were suddenly hit by a wave of exhaustion and for a moment none of them could speak.

They stood there, hearts hammering, panting and gasping, doubled over, fighting for the breath they needed to talk.

Finally one of the boys from the museum walked over to the gates and looked at the new arrivals, chin raised, giving nothing away.

'Where you from?' he asked.

DogNut managed to blurt out the words 'Tower of London' and the boy nodded. He was short but beefy-looking, about fifteen years old, with spiky, gelled hair and wearing a battered leather jacket. His nose was flattened, broken. It must have happened after the sickness or a doctor would have fixed it.

'You the kids Ryan the hunter took to the palace?'

DogNut straightened up. Stared at the boy, a look of pained amazement on his face.

'You what?'

'Is one of you called DogNut?'

'Yeah. I am. But I don't get it.'

'Ryan was here before on business. Told us about you.'

'You gonna let us in then?' DogNut gasped.

The boy looked away, in the direction the kids had come from.

'They with you?' he asked, and DogNut turned to see what he was looking at.

The sickos were arriving.

'Open the gate, man,' DogNut pleaded.

'First you tell us who exactly you're looking for. See that it all checks out.'

Courtney had her breath back now. 'We're mainly looking for Brooke,' she said. 'She here?'

'You're friends of Brooke's, yeah?

'Course we are!' Courtney shouted. 'Now open this bloody gate, will you?'

'Brooke recognized your names when we told her,' said the boy.

'Just open the gate!' Marco shouted.

The boy unlocked the gates and casually swung them open.

'Nice to see you got a sense of urgency,' said Felix as he pushed past him.

The boy made a dismissive gesture and nodded to where the group of sickos had stopped and were holding back on the far side of the road.

'They know better than to come over here,' he said and waited for the last of the new arrivals to come through before slamming the gates closed and locking them.

'My name's Robbie,' he said. 'I'm in charge of security here. You cause any stink and you got to deal with me, OK?'

'Yeah. Good to meet you, Robbie,' said DogNut, and they slapped palms.

'Let me ask you one question,' said Robbie. 'How come you never asked the hunters about Brooke?'

'We *did* ask them,' Courtney protested. 'I'm sure we did.'

'We told them we was looking for David,' said Marco, taking off his helmet and wiping sweat from his forehead. 'I'm not sure we ever mentioned Brooke or Justin to them.'

'That was stupid,' said Felix.

'You calling me stupid?' said Marco.

'We're all stupid. We was so thinking about David we never mentioned the others.'

'How long ago was Ryan here?' DogNut asked.

'Couple of hours, maybe.'

157

'I can't believe we've been so dumb,' said DogNut. He wanted to punch something. If he'd only thought to ask the hunters about Brooke then Olivia wouldn't be dead now.

'It doesn't matter,' said Courtney. 'We didn't know. All that matters is we're here now.'

'I'll take you inside,' said Robbie, and he led them past some trees on to a long ramp that curved up towards the museum doors. DogNut got a glimpse of crops planted in what had once been lawns along the front of the building.

The main doors were set into a vast carved stone archway, and another guard was waiting here. He exchanged a couple of words with Robbie then opened the doors to let them in.

DogNut was impressed with the set-up. It reminded him of being back at the Imperial War Museum, where their leader, Jordan Hordern, had insisted on strict discipline and round-the-clock security. There had always been guards posted at the entrance. And since they'd moved from the Imperial War Museum to the Tower of London the routine had been even more military. DogNut wasn't sure exactly what he'd been expecting when he got here, but not this. It struck him, though, that if anyone was going to survive in London these days they'd have to be well organized and well prepared. He was thinking all this as he wandered into the massive, candlelit hall inside and was further distracted by the fossilized skeleton of a dinosaur standing in the centre, with a huge long neck and tail. So it was that he didn't really register that someone was asking him something. A brown-haired girl wearing an old-fashioned dress and carrying a lamp.

'I'm sorry, what?' he said finally. 'Did you say something, babes?'

The girl tilted her head to one side and gave him a dirty look, and it was then that he realized.

It was Brooke.

23

DogNut shouted with joy and threw his arms round Brooke, before she pushed him off.

'You dozy sod,' she said. 'You didn't recognize me, did you?'

'Course I didn't,' he said. 'Look at you! You ain't blonde no more. You ain't wearing no make-up, plus you got on some kind of weird dress out of a boring history film.'

'So you're saying I ain't pretty no more?'

DogNut held her at arm's length and studied her face. 'You're more beautiful than ever,' he said, and he meant it. 'Though I do prefer you blonde. You telling me it was fake all along? You bleached your hair?'

'Duh,' said Brooke. 'Of course. There ain't half as many blondes in this world as you think, Donut.'

'It's DogNut.'

'No it ain't,' said Brooke. 'To me you'll always be Donut.'

There was a shout from across the hall. 'Hey, what about me?' And Brooke spotted Courtney. She screamed and ran over to her, and the two of them held on to each other, dancing around, shrieking.

'I don't believe it! It's you! My God! This is so cool . . .'

'And what about Aleisha?' Brooke said at last, breaking

away from Courtney and looking around. 'Did you bring her with you?'

Courtney was instantly subdued; the life went out of her. Brooke knew what had happened without needing to ask and all she said was, 'Where? When?'

'That night,' said Courtney sadly. 'When we came across the river. After we got split up we found a boat, but we hit a bridge and it sank. Aleisha had already been wounded. She didn't stand a chance.'

Brooke hugged her friend and the two of them started crying, leaning against each other for support. DogNut didn't know what to do. Whether he should go over and try to comfort them, or leave them to it. In the end he decided this was between the girls. Not his business. He had hardly known Aleisha, but he knew that the three of them had been inseparable.

Courtney was sobbing into Brooke's shoulder. She was aware that she was soaking her friend's dress. But she couldn't stop. Didn't want to ever let go. Brooke felt warm and soft. Why had she ever thought that she didn't want to find her? They belonged together. All the tension of the day was flowing out of her, and Brooke was absorbing it. Everything was going to be all right now.

The spell was broken by DogNut who strolled up, rolling his head to loosen the tension in his neck.

'Come on then,' he said. 'You gonna show us round or are you gonna just stand there snotting over each other?'

The two girls separated, sniffed, and that was that. It was finished. They couldn't mourn the loss of their friend any more. It would hurt too much. Aleisha was gone, but they still had each other. The words Courtney had said to DogNut earlier came back to her.

They had to move on.

'Yeah,' Courtney said, looking around at their bizarre surroundings and wiping her face dry. 'I wanna see how you've pimped this place up and then you are gonna have to, like, tell us everything that's happened since we seen you last. *Everything* . . .'

'I will, girl, don't worry. Is a long story, though. Don't you want to wash and eat and rest up first? You look worse than crap.'

'Oh, thanks.'

Brooke laughed. 'Still the same grumpy old Courtney I know so well.'

'I ain't old, I ain't grumpy . . .'

'But you're still my Courtney.'

They burst into tears and hugged once more.

'Oh, not again,' said DogNut, and he made a big show of being appalled by this display of affection. Secretly, though, he was fighting back tears of his own and had a painful lump in his throat.

'Enough of that,' he said at last, pulling them apart. 'I want to introduce you to the rest of our crew.'

He called Marco, Felix and Finn over. Brooke vaguely remembered Marco and Felix, but had never met Finn before. He asked after his friends from Forest Hill School, and Brooke sadly shook her head.

'I don't recognize the names,' she said.

'It's all right,' said Finn. 'They could be anywhere.'

He displayed no emotion. DogNut knew he must be gutted, though.

'Come on,' he said, trying to lighten the mood. 'We want the tour.'

'Follow me.'

162

They walked with Brooke past the dinosaur skeleton. 'This is Dippy,' she said. 'He's a diplodocus.'

'And who's that up there?' DogNut asked as they climbed the wide stone steps at the back of the hall. 'He looks like God.'

Sitting halfway up the stairs in an armchair, as if waiting for them, was the larger-than-life-size white marble statue of a bald, bearded man.

'That's Charlie Darwin,' said Brooke, patting him affectionately on the head. 'I love his shoes. They look so real!'

DogNut studied the shoes. Brooke was right. It was hard to believe they were carved out of stone. They carried on to the top of the steps and walked through a gallery that ran along the side of the exhibition hall back in the direction they had come. There were monkey skulls here, alongside skulls from Stone Age man. Other cabinets contained stuffed apes and figures of people. There was something spooky about them in the half-light.

'What's all this?' asked DogNut. 'I didn't know they kept humans in museums.'

'It's something to do with evolution,' said Brooke. 'Showing us where we come from. I've given all the monkeys names. That one's Brian.' She pointed to a hairy orang-utan with its arms in the air.

'You need to get a stuffed sicko in there,' said DogNut. 'The latest stage in our evolution. *Homo zombiens*.'

Brooke laughed and then stopped, leaning on the wall overlooking the great hall below. From here they could see just how massive the place was. Even the diplodocus looked small.

'It's like Hogwarts,' said Courtney.

'I often think that,' said Brooke.

'It's bare big,' said DogNut. 'How many kids you got here?'

'Seventy-three,' said Brooke. 'But we don't use most of the place. Is way too big. Eight hundred people used to work here. There's other buildings, office blocks, labs, everything. It goes on forever. We just use this bit round the main hall, couple of galleries off the sides, like the dinosaur one and the mammal galleries over there.' She pointed to the opposite side of the hall. 'We close most of it down at night. It's too big to patrol and make safe. In the daytime we go all over. Except down to the lower level.'

'Why not?' Courtney asked.

'There's sickos down there.'

'For real?' said Courtney, eyes widening in fear.

'For real.' Brooke laughed and punched her playfully in the arm.

'Ain't nothing to get scared about, girl. Is just, when we got here, there was some sickos still in the museum. Staff, I guess. We chased them off, killed a load. Some went down into the basement. Is like a maze down there. All these rooms and corridors and secret hiding-places. This place is just too big to be able to control the whole thing. Goes on forever. We've locked all the doors we can to keep the sickos out, but you can hear them down there sometimes, in the sealed-off bits, moving around. Others get in from outside and they nest in the dark. They can't never get up here, though, not any more. We fixed all that. Come on. I'll show you where we all sleep.'

At the end of the primates gallery there was a doorway leading to a long room off to the side.

'This is the minerals gallery,' said Brooke quietly. 'It's big and has lots of light and can easily be secured. They

used to keep l[...]
crystals and m[...]
heavy gates this[...]
If we were ever a[...]
in here.'

DogNut looked[...]
all round the doorw[...]
thing out of a medie[...]
the odd tea light burn[...]
stretched away into the [...]
There were arched wind[...]
of square columns holdi[...]
and wood display cabinet[...]
and the kids had adapted th[...] into little
sleeping areas, personalizing [...] decorating them with
screens and awnings and bits of furniture.

'I'll show you properly in the morning,' Brooke whispered. 'Most of the kids have already gone to bed. We usually go to sleep as soon as it gets dark. I was waiting for you to arrive. Come on, though, we'll get you something to eat.'

She led them through the gallery. As they passed each cubicle space, they saw that not all the occupants were asleep. Some kids sat murmuring with friends, and they looked round curiously at the new arrivals as they went past.

A door at the end led to a short stairway that took them down to the gallery below, from where another staircase climbed to the old staff canteen. It was like being in a tunnel up here, the ceiling arched over in a semicircle with large curved windows set into the bottom. There were modern tables and chairs and it was well lit with oil lamps, similar to the one that Brooke carried.

There were three kids waiting for them.

case you turned up,'
down to a simple meal of
...ge.
... food down and Brooke watched
...ent.

... said Courtney when they'd finished. 'Why
...g such weird shit, girl?'

...oke looked down at her old-fashioned clothes and
...ghed. 'You remember Kwanele? That African kid who
was always really well dressed? Even when we was escaping
from the sickos?'

'Wheeled that little posh suitcase around the whole
time?' Courtney asked. 'Yeah, I remember him. Don't tell
me he made that dress!'

'No way,' Brooke shrieked. 'But there's this other
museum just over the road. Is called the Victoria and Albert.
We broke in there cos we saw from the maps there's this
big courtyard in the middle. We built all these planters in
there, is a well safe place to grow food, but you should see
what's in the museum itself.'

'What?' asked DogNut, intrigued.

'Well . . . Is mostly art and stuff, you know, like statues
and paintings, but they got, like, furniture, plates and jewel-
lery and things, even fashion. All clothes from history and,
like, movie-star dresses, you know, hundreds and hundreds
of them. It's wicked. We get all our stuff from there that
we need to make this place like home. Home for a king,
that is. Honestly it's like a palace in there. You got to see
it. And Kwanele, he's in charge of clothing and that. Making
the stuff fit. We dress up and we're princesses.' Brooke
stood and did a little twirl in her dress, then stopped in a
fit of giggles.

'You should get yourself something, Courtney,' she said. 'We should glam you up a bit.'

'You saying I ain't well dressed?'

'No.'

'You saying I need to be more glam, though?'

'Yes.' Now Brooke put on a simpering, lisping little girl's voice. 'You could be a lovely princess! Princess Courtney!'

'Courtney?' DogNut scoffed. 'Courtney ain't no princess.'

'You what?' Courtney turned on DogNut with an angry scowl.

'You're a queen,' he said hurriedly. 'A warrior queen.'

'Maybe we can find you a crown in the Victoria and Albert,' said Brooke, and Courtney laughed.

'So, you gonna tell us then,' she said. 'What the hell you all doing here? And why you pissed David off so much?'

Brooke smiled at her friends. 'I'm telling you, is a long story . . .'

24

'Going back to that night. I can close my eyes and watch it like a DVD, remember everything that happened, as clear as if it was, like, you know, happening right now. The rest of the time I can switch off, put the DVD back in its box and stick it away somewhere and not think about it no more. But I close my eyes now and I'm there, back on the bridge, the lorry slowly moving across, and Justin driving. Jesus, I ain't never seen a more worried-looking nerd. He was sweatier than a fat man eating chillies in a sauna. If I hadn't of been so scared I would've been laughing, but behind us half of London was blazing, and we was trying not to run over any of the kids who was squashed on to the bridge, all panicking, crazy with fear. It was hard; there was broken-down buses, broken-down cars blocking the way, people hollering. We didn't wanna get out and look, was way too dangerous, but we could hear screaming and then this, like, fresh wave of panic seemed to pass through the kids on the bridge. We couldn't exactly see what was going on behind, but when I've looked in the mirror there was smoke and fire and a mash of, like, scared faces. So we knew. We knew the sickos was attacking the kids who couldn't get on to the bridge. We just kept on driving, slowly, slowly, slowly. We was getting across, but *that*

David. What a freak! He and his boys in their red jackets and with their guns they'd got from your museum. Like little soldiers they was. I know we had a deal – he was supposed to protect the lorry and we was supposed to share some of our food with him once we was safe. I know we had a deal . . . But when I seen what he was really like I didn't want nothing more to do with him, man.'

Brooke stopped talking and took a deep breath. DogNut looked at her, sitting in the candlelight, and she was the most beautiful thing he had ever seen.

'What happened?' he asked. 'What did David do?'

'There were these kids in the middle of the road,' Brooke went on. 'They'd got into an argument, started fighting, an' we couldn't get past them. David was telling them to get out of the way, all bossy, like, and they was ignoring him, or just laughing at him. And you know what he did? I'll never forget it. I couldn't believe it. Couldn't believe anyone could do that. Not to another kid. But I saw it with my own eyes. He's pointed his rifle at one of the boys and shot him down, right through the chest. I don't know if he killed him, but, even if he didn't, how could a kid survive that? A bullet in him. With no doctors, no medicine or hospitals. I don't like to think about it. Don't like to think that it was our fault. I was shamed that David was with us. The worst thing of it was, though, that I was, like, secretly, sneakily, glad he'd done it. I know it's cold to say it, but to be honest I was glad that he'd cleared the way. The kids was moving aside finally. The road was empty. I've turned to Justin and I've told him to keep going, not wait, not stop, not worry about anyone else, just drive. I've told him we had to get as far away from David and his boys as we could. I've

169

screamed at him to put his foot down and just keep going. Outta there. And quicker now, bit by bit, we've managed to get off the bridge. We was way excited, and still scared and worried that we didn't know where Ed and the others were. And the thing was . . .' Brooke paused for a moment and turned to Courtney. 'I didn't know that you and Aleisha had got off, to go and help Ed. If I'd of known, I'd of waited, but we didn't know, did we? We was confused, but most of all we were just glad that we'd got over and got away from the fire and the sickos, and all I could think about was driving on and leaving David and his mates for dust.'

Brooke stopped again. This time she stared at the table, as if reading some message in the pattern of stains and scratches on its surface.

'There was something else, as well . . .'

'What?' Courtney asked when it looked like Brooke wasn't going to carry on. And when she raised her head they could see that she was crying.

'Something else I ain't proud of.'

'What?' Courtney asked again. 'We ain't gonna judge you.'

'It was Ed.'

'What about him?'

'I didn't want to see him again. I couldn't stomach it. I wanted to get away from him. What they'd done to his face. Justin wanted to wait for him and the others, but I wouldn't let him. Told him we could come back and find them later. Maybe I really thought we might come back. When it was calmer, when I could think straight. But right then the thought of Ed, of Ed's face, upset me too much, made me feel sick. I didn't want to ever have to look at him again. I was wrong in the head. It was all muddled up in there. All I wanted was to get away, leave all that behind, all that had happened, as if the fire would scrub it all out. I wanted to excape. And so we did. We drove on. Didn't stop. It wasn't easy. There was still hundreds of kids on this side of the river. They was pouring over the river across all the bridges, wandering in the road, wondering where to go, not knowing this part of town. Some stopping, looking for places to hole up, some moving on like us. It was wild – I was shouting at Justin, he was shouting at me . . . "Where shall we stop? Where do we go?" We needed to find somewhere safe where there wasn't too many other kids. We knew there was safety in numbers, but we also knew that our food wouldn't last long and we didn't want to share it. You get too many people in one place, pretty soon there's no food, no water. As I say, we was arguing like a married couple on *Eastenders*, and then Justin had a brainwave. I guess it was all down to you . . .'

Brooke put her hand on DogNut's.

'Living in the War Museum, the way you did, gave Justin the idea. He got it into his head that he wanted to live in a museum too!' She spread her arms and laughed.

'We didn't hole up in the war museum because we was interested in history,' DogNut scoffed. 'We went there cos it had guns, weapons. What use are a load of stuffed animals and dinosaur fossils?'

'It wasn't the stuffed animals he was interested in,' said Brooke. 'Nor the dinosaurs. It's the labs, the equipment, and all the other gear, next door, in the Science Museum. He knew there was technology in there, things we could use, inventions going back hundreds of years, things that didn't all need electricity. Things we could use to start putting the world back together. The museum is big, man, but he figured it would be easy to secure. Places like this were made to keep people out, as they got so much valuable stuff in them. No other kids had thought to come here; we knew we'd have to break in. We was only a bunch of nerds and girls and little kids, though. All the fighters had stayed with Ed. Luckily we met up with some other kids on the street, a guy called Robbie and his gang. Justin persuaded them to help us. They're all still with us.'

'We met Robbie outside,' said DogNut.

'Yeah. He's took over the fighting side of things, protecting the place, guarding us, dealing with the hunters. In those early days there was a lot more sickos around and we had some close moments. Some sickos tried to get in a few times. We killed lots of them. As I say, there's still some down below.'

'And other kids have joined you here?' said DogNut.

'Yeah, slowly. We've got a good thing going, with the gardens out front where we can grow things, and there's all these other, like, courtyards in the buildings around us. We cook things in the kitchens, we collect water from the roofs and from storage tanks, and from the Serpentine.'

'What's the Serpentine?' Courtney asked.

'Is this, like, big lake in Hyde Park. Just north of here.'

'Oh, yeah, I know. The Princess Diana fountain's there.'

'That's right.'

'It's crap. My uncle took me to see it this one time, and then we went out in a boat on the lake. It was a big deal for him. Not me. It was well boring, man.'

Brooke laughed. 'You don't change, do you?' she said. 'Always moaning.'

Courtney felt a flush of anger. Why did Brooke have to keep saying that? She *had* changed. She *had*. She tried so hard not to complain all the time, specially when she was with DogNut, but now, being here with Brooke, she was changing back. Turning into her old grumpy self. Being who Brooke wanted her to be. After the joy of meeting her old friend the confusion had started to creep back. She hated the way DogNut looked at Brooke. It made her feel jealous and angry. There she was, pretty Brooke. Thin Brooke. And here *she* was, fat, grumpy Courtney.

'Don't have a go at her,' said DogNut, smiling at Courtney. 'She's all right. She's my right-hand man. She don't moan like she used to. You better show her some respect, Miss Brooke.'

Brooke leant over and gave Courtney a big hug. 'She ain't yours, DogNut!' she cried. 'She's *my* Courtney. I wouldn't have her any other way, and now she's back I ain't never gonna let her go.' Brooke buried her face in Courtney's thick curly hair. 'I missed you so much, girl. *So much.*'

DogNut wasn't sure he could take any more of this girlie behaviour. It was getting in the way of his plans for Brooke. If he couldn't get her alone, he couldn't work his magic on her.

He was about to say something when he heard his name being called out. He turned round and couldn't believe how pleased he was to see Justin, king of the nerds.

25

Justin looked a lot older and bigger than when they'd last seen him, but he hadn't lost his air of geekiness. He was wearing pyjamas and a dressing-gown and was blinking in the feeble light.

'They told me you were here,' he said, his voice sounding cracked, like it was in the middle of breaking. 'I thought they were having me on.'

'No, boss!' said DogNut. 'Is really us! We've come to show you how it's done.' He jumped up and offered Justin a high five, knowing it would embarrass him. Justin slapped his hand awkwardly.

'How you doing, anyway, Mr Lorry-Driving Man?' said DogNut. 'You got your HGV licence yet?'

'We don't drive the lorry any more. We use it for different things now. My career as a lorry driver is sadly over.' Justin stopped talking for a moment and smiled. 'It's good to see you again, DogNut,' he finally went on. 'Really good!'

DogNut introduced the rest of his crew and Justin shook hands all round in a very formal manner. There was no way he was going to hug anyone.

'You'll have to tell us all about what you've been up to,' he said. 'Where you've been, how everyone is.'

'Everyone's cool, dude,' said DogNut.

Justin yawned. 'I'm sorry,' he said. 'I was asleep. Tomorrow you'll come to the Hall of Gods and tell the council all about what you've been up to.'

'Hold up, blood,' said DogNut, raising his hands. 'Not so fast. What the hell's the Hall of Gods?'

'It's where we hold all our meetings.'

'I see I got a lot to learn. So I'll meet the guys in charge tomorrow, yeah? In this Hall of Gods. Should be pretty damn awesome. Meeting gods and everything.'

'Well . . .'

'What's up? You saying I ain't gonna meet them? They ain't gods? Who *is* in charge here anyway?'

'I sort of am,' said Justin, shrugging his shoulders dismissively.

'You?' DogNut looked amazed. He was trying hard not to laugh. 'But you're like the übernerd, Justin. You ain't no god.'

'I never claimed to be a god. But I *am* in charge.'

'That is whack,' said DogNut.

'Sometimes brains are more important than muscles,' said Justin. 'I've sorted everything out for the kids here and they appreciate that. We don't need fighters in charge – we have a council for that.'

'A council of nerds?' said DogNut, no longer holding back his laughter.

'Yes. That's right. That's what we call it. The Council of Nerds.'

'You're joking me.'

'Knowledge is power, DogNut. Mastering science and technology is what's going to make sure we survive in the future. Here at the museum we're going to lead the way.'

'Listen, nerdo, I don't mean to be disrespectful, but mastering weapons and warfare is what's going to make sure we survive.'

'That's your opinion. But we're doing OK here, DogNut. Our way is working.'

Justin opened his mouth wide in another big yawn.

'Listen,' he said, 'I'm going to go back to bed. We'll catch up properly in the morning. You should sleep too.'

'Yeah,' said Brooke. 'I'll put them in the tree room. I'll see everyone's all right.'

'Thanks, Brooke,' said Justin, already walking away. 'Get some of Robbie's guys to give you a hand if you need. I'll see you all tomorrow.'

'Hold up,' said DogNut, and Justin paused. 'I want to ask you one thing. Make sure I got it straight.'

'Yeah? OK.'

'You know about David over at the palace? Yeah?'

'Of course we know about David,' said Justin, losing his cool, his face flushing with anger. 'Sitting over there in his palace with his little red army. Sometimes I think he causes more trouble than the bloody sickos. And he hates us. He blames us for what happened on the bridge.'

'He's right to blame you, though, really,' DogNut protested. 'You abandoned him.'

'Well . . .'

'You drove off and left him behind.'

'It wasn't my idea,' said Justin, and he looked at Brooke.

'You blaming me?' said Brooke.

'It doesn't matter. We don't want anything to do with him. He wants to destroy what we've got, get back at me and Brooke and the others. But it's not going to happen, because he can't get in here. He's like us – he can defend his palace for as long as he likes, but as soon as he crawls out of his shell he's weak. He's a threat, but only a small one. We don't lose any sleep over it. And talking of sleep I really am going to have to go to bed now. Goodnight.'

Brooke took all the new arrivals to a long empty gallery at the back of the main hall where a tree had been painted all the way along the ceiling. Some metal beds were lined up in a neat row and DogNut and his friends gratefully took out their sleeping bags and settled down.

DogNut realized just how exhausted he was. It had been a long and unbelievably stressful day. As soon as they'd got to safety his energy levels had dropped and he felt like he'd been drugged. His head hit the pillow, his eyes closed and he fell into a doze.

Brooke sat on the side of Courtney's bed and stroked her hair flat like a mother with her child.

'It's so good to have you back, girl,' she said softly. 'I didn't realize how much I missed you.'

'Me too,' said Courtney, though in truth she was still picking her way through a complicated tangle of emotions, made worse by her own tiredness. 'It's weird being here.'

'This is my life now,' said Brooke. 'Can't hardly remember nothing else. Seems so long ago, being with you on the bus, and Greg and Liam and Jack and Ed and all that. Another lifetime, like it happened to someone else. A lot's changed in this last year.'

'For all of us,' said Courtney, and she suddenly gripped Brooke's arm. 'Did they make it?' she asked urgently. 'Did they all make it? The other kids on the lorry? Are they all here?'

'They all made it,' said Brooke with a smile. 'Wiki and

177

Jibber-jabber, Zohra and little Froggie, Kwanele of course, and Chris Marker, remember him? The boy who always had his face stuck in a book. Tomorrow you'll see them all.'

'Good,' said Courtney. 'Some good things do still happen in the world.'

She started to tell Brooke about everything that had happened to her in the last year. Brooke listened, wide-eyed, not interrupting, finding out about another life.

In the end Courtney fell asleep halfway through a sentence. Brooke sat there for a long time, trying to take it all in, still not quite able to believe that Courtney was really here.

At last she stood up. She was just about to leave when there were shouts from the other end of the room; a very tall, very thin boy dressed in black was walking quickly towards the beds.

'Are you all right, Paul?' she asked when the boy got closer. 'Try not to wake anyone. They need to sleep.'

Paul looked very excited. But it was an excitement mixed with anxiety. Happiness and fear were struggling to take control of him.

'Where is she?' he said.

'Where's who?'

'Where's my sister, Olivia . . .?'

26

DogNut was struggling to make sense of what was going on. He had no idea how long he'd been asleep. He didn't even remember nodding off, and had no idea where he was. There were raised voices. A boy and a girl. Was he back at the Tower? This room was unfamiliar. It smelt different. Maybe he should go back to sleep. Not possible. Someone was shaking him.

'What . . .? Go away. I'm trying to sleep.'

'Wake up.'

'Go away.'

'Wake up.'

'What is it?'

He forced one eye open. Too shattered to open them both. Some deep part of his mind obviously knew where he was, knew he was safe, or his conditioning would have jerked him into wakefulness and out of bed, ready to face any threat.

There were no monsters, though, just a girl holding a lamp.

Brooke.

Oh, yeah . . .

It was coming back to him now. The museum. Nerd central. He sat up, groaning. Saw a boy wearing a black roll-neck jumper, black denim jacket and black jeans.

'What is it?'

'This is Paul Channing.'

'Huh?'

'Olivia's brother,' Brooke explained.

'Olivia's brother? I don't know what you mean.'

DogNut's brain wasn't slipping into gear. Too mushy. Now the boy came over to the bed, leant in closer, shook him by the shoulder.

'I heard Olivia was with you,' he said. 'Apparently one of your guys said Olivia was with you. But nobody will tell me where she is now.'

'Olivia's brother?' Things were starting to make sense, but DogNut wished more than anything that he was still asleep.

Olivia.

'I'm sorry to wake you up like this,' the boy went on. 'I've been working, checking the lower-level doors.'

'Right, yeah . . .'

'Brooke said you were in charge and . . . and I have to know. I can't see her here. Is she – Is she here? Is Olivia with you?'

DogNut closed his eyes. Fantasized about burying his face in the pillow and drifting off . . . Longed for this to be over. He didn't know what to say. Hoped that if he stayed like this Paul would disappear and he wouldn't have to face him. In the end he heard Courtney's voice from the next bed.

'She *was* with us.'

DogNut sensed Paul moving away from him towards Courtney.

'Did you leave her somewhere?' he asked. 'Did she stay at the palace, maybe? I just want to know she's safe.'

'No. She's not at the palace. She wanted to come here with us. She wanted to find you. She was very brave.'

'But where is she?'

'She didn't make it.'

'You mean . . .?'

There was a long silence. DogNut was fully awake at last and could feel the tension in the room. People breathing. Bad vibes thickening.

Then Courtney's voice again. 'A sicko got her. Wasn't nothing we could do . . . Hey!'

As Courtney shouted, DogNut opened his eyes and sat up. Paul had grabbed hold of her.

'You let her die?' he was shouting. 'You let her get killed?'

'Hey, cool it,' said DogNut, struggling out of bed. 'We nearly got her here. Wasn't Courtney's fault she was killed.'

'Oh yeah?' Paul turned on him. 'Then whose fault was it?'

Mine, DogNut wanted to scream. *My fault. I left her behind.*

'I'll tell you whose fault it was,' he said, almost shouting. 'The fat sicko that got her. All right? He collected dead kids! So don't blame us. We was only trying to get her here.'

'Maybe you should have tried harder.'

DogNut put a lid on his anger. Paul had every right to be upset. But this was all too raw for any of them to deal with right now.

'Do you know what it's like out there?' he said, his voice bumpy with emotion. He was desperate not to start crying. Knew he had to go on the offensive, though, or crack up. 'Do you?' he went on. 'Do you ever go out there? The streets at night?'

'Not really, no, not that much.' Paul had calmed down.

181

He was confused by the change of direction the conversation had taken.

'We brought her all the way here from the other side of London,' said DogNut, hoping that if he could convince Paul he could maybe convince himself that he hadn't made a monumental mess of things. 'We almost made it too, but we got trapped. We was *that* close. I'm sorry, man, all right? I'm sorry she never made it through.'

The anger went out of Paul to be replaced with sorrow and he slumped on to a bed. Courtney got up and sat next to him. Putting an arm round his shoulders she slowly and quietly explained what had happened. DogNut was grateful that the only thing she didn't tell him was how they'd left Olivia behind. In Courtney's version Olivia had died as they tried to escape.

As Paul listened, the rage came back, but it was no longer directed at DogNut and Courtney – it was focused on the sicko, the Collector. It was a black rage mixed with disgust and fear.

'I'll kill him,' he said when Courtney had finished. 'I will. I'll show you. I'll show you I can go out there. I'll find where he lives and I'll kill him.'

'Whoa, hold on, soldier,' said DogNut. 'That's exactly what I wanted to do when I realized Olivia hadn't made it. I wanted to take him on all by myself. Kill the evil bastard. But I couldn't of done it, and neither could you. You ain't going out there by yourself, OK? Your sister wouldn't want you to die for her. You wanna go kill him, fair enough. He needs to be killed or he's gonna carry on catching and killing other kids. But we do it properly, yeah? We'll take a squad. The best fighters you got here. I'll go with you – I don't mind going back there.'

'Tomorrow,' said Paul.

'Yeah. Tomorrow. If we're ready. In the daylight, when he won't be so strong. OK?'

Courtney looked at DogNut, trying to read his face in the half-light. The thought of going back there appalled her. What was he thinking of? They'd only just managed to get away themselves. The plan had been to find Brooke, which they'd done. Their mission was successful. All they had to do was rest up for a couple of days and then head off back to the Tower.

With or without Brooke.

The last thing she ever wanted to do was go anywhere near that terrible house again.

Courtney couldn't see it, but DogNut was smiling. Maybe his mind was messed up by tiredness, maybe it would all seem stupid in the morning, but a plan was forming in there. He turned it over as he drifted back into sleep. For now it looked good.

27

'So what are they up to down there then?'

'Same old same old. They're not properly organized. They live in filth. A lot of them are ill. John's a nutter. But they get by. They seem happy most of the time – when they're not fighting each other.'

'I don't know how you can stick it, Shadowman. Living with those creeps when you could be living here.'

Jester and Shadowman were sitting by the fire in Jester's office at the palace. The room was part of a small apartment, tucked up in the roof out of the way. Jester liked it like that. Private. As far as he could tell it had once been part of the servants' quarters, where one of the more important members of staff had lived. There was a bedroom, an office, a sitting-room and a tiny bathroom. He could keep himself to himself up here and not be observed by the other kids. David had a much larger suite of grand rooms with a massive office in the centre of the palace. He liked to show off his power.

Jester kept his power inside. Like Shadowman.

The two of them had been friends before the disaster. There'd been a little gang of them. They were the only people who Shadowman had felt relaxed with and able to let down his guard. Originally they were going to form a band, but that never really happened. They got as far as making up the band name – The Twilight Zone – and rock-star names for each other, and that was about it.

Jester had been called Magic-Man because he reminded the others of Derren Brown, the mind-control guy. He had the knack of persuading people to do things and think things. Then there'd been Cool-Man, Big-Man, Go-Girl and The Fox. The others had all died in the early days of the disease, except for Go-Girl, who'd left London with a group of other kids months ago and headed for the countryside. They had no idea what might have happened to her. Back then Jester and Shadowman had been living together in a big house in Notting Hill, but when that had become too dangerous they'd moved to the palace. It was much safer here. Shadowman, however, didn't like the rigid routines of the place, the feeling of being cooped up, walled in, under David's thumb, so he hadn't stuck it for long. He was restless and preferred to be alone, as far as that was possible in this dangerous city. He'd run with a couple of hunter gangs, he'd lived with Nicola's kids at the Houses of Parliament, he'd stayed a little while at the Natural History Museum. The same thing happened every time, though: he started to feel trapped and would move on.

Jester had tried to persuade him many times to come back and stay at the palace, but Shadowman kept on the go, checking in with his old friend every couple of weeks. Jester made sure he was all right and had enough food and water, because Shadowman was useful to him. He was his main eyes and ears outside the palace, the most important in a network of spies and contacts and informers. He would still have preferred to keep him under the palace roof, though, where he'd be a lot safer.

'I work alone – you know that, Magic-Man.'

Apart from David when he was trying to be matey, Shadowman was the only person left who called Jester that. Jester was a nickname he'd picked up since moving in here. It was a kind of joke at first, a way of putting him down, implying he was David's little pet monkey. He liked the name, though. It was a disguise to hide behind. He could gain more and more power without anyone seeing him as much of a threat.

'You know I don't like to get too close to people,' Shadowman went on. 'I can't face seeing them die. I figure if I just keep moving around I won't get too attached to anyone.'

'That's harsh, Shadow. You are one callous dude.'

'No, Magic-Man, that's what I'm saying – it's the *opposite*. I'm too soft. If I was harder, it wouldn't bother me so much. You're the cold one.'

'Me?'

'Yeah, you. Don't act so surprised. You're sly. Always looking for the angle. People are only interesting to you if you can use them in some way. I don't trust you as far as I could throw you.'

'So why do you still stay friends with me then?' asked Jester. 'Why do you still come and see me?'

'Because I don't give a toss what happens to you, obviously,' said Shadowman. 'So there's no risk of breaking my poor heart.'

Jester laughed. 'I believe you, dude. I believe you.'

'It's the truth.'

Jester got up and poured himself a fresh cup of tea from the big pot that was warming by the fire.

'So what about these squatters then? Are they a threat, d'you think?'

'They could be if they weren't such a shambles,' said Shadowman. 'John has dreams of power. He's like Attila the Hun, or something, wants to burn down civilization. Sees this place as the Roman Empire. He'd love to sack it. Take David's scalp.'

'Really?'

'Totally. He'd like nothing better than to come in here, take everything you've got, march out with all the fit girls over his shoulder and burn the place to the ground. That's what he likes to do, destroy things. He lives for chaos and mayhem. You know, I think he actually likes what's happened to the world. He likes that it's fallen apart. It's one big playground for him now. He can do what he wants, take what he wants, smash up what he wants, and nobody's going to stop him. He's the lord of disorder.'

'And you think he could be a problem if he gets his act together?'

'No, probably not, to tell you the truth. As long as David doesn't take his eye off the ball, John would never be able to storm this place. Not the way you've got it protected. Oh, he talks about it, yeah, tries to stir his troops up, but they're just a rabble. He knows they'd be well battered if they tried to attack you here. You can forget any plans of developing St James's Park, though. You plant anything there, or try to build anything, he'll tear it down, dig it up, kick it over and piss on the remains.'

'Where do they get their food from then?'

'They forage, break into places, nick stuff off other kids if they can. They're always raiding the weaker settlements, like the bandits in *The Magnificent Seven*. But that's John's biggest problem, actually – he can never get enough food to support that many kids. He's always taking in fresh noobs, but every day two or three kids leave, melt away to join more organized settlements. If David wanted, I could easily persuade a few to come here.'

'Maybe. I'll talk to him. So are John's numbers getting smaller?'

'Nah. As many leave, more turn up. He's got a high turnover, that's all. Kids join him for the action, the madness and the fun and games, but then they get cold and tired and hungry and fed up with the non-stop partying, and they move on to something more civilized. Except for the crazies, of course – they stay. John's people are getting more and more psycho and he keeps a hard core of nutters around him. As I say, he'll never make a big enough army to really threaten you.'

'We need the space in the park to expand,' said Jester. 'To grow more food. And the lake's a good source of water.'

'You'll never do it as long as John's camped out on Horse Guards Parade.'

'So what we need to do is attack them before they attack us?'

'You couldn't do it,' said Shadowman, shaking his head. 'They're mean, tough bastards. They'd take you apart. You're strong in defence, but not in attack.'

'That's exactly what David thinks.' Jester stood up again. He went to the window and looked out into the starlit night. 'He wants to build up our army. Create an attack force. He wants me to recruit fighters.'

'There aren't any going spare round here,' said Shadowman, kicking a log on the fire with his boot. 'All the best fighters are already in the other settlements, or with the hunters.'

Jester turned back from the window.

'We could pay hunters to do it for us.'

'No. You'd have to pay them way too much. They won't fight other kids unless they have to, if they're attacked or something. Mothers and fathers, yes, but not other kids.'

'David wants me to go on the road,' said Jester. 'He wants me to go and look for kids further out, fighters who might be tempted to join us when they see how much food we have and how safe and well organized the palace is.'

'You'd have to go pretty far.'

'What's the furthest you've ever been?'

'I mostly stay here in the centre of town where there's less grown-ups. I've been as far as Regent's Park to the north, I suppose. I've not been further than Notting Hill to the west, though, and that was some time ago. It's the Wild West over there now.'

'What about east?'

'Never risked going much further than Holborn.'

'And south?'

'No one goes south of the river any more, not since the fire.'

'So it's north or east?'

'North. Sometimes you meet kids who've strayed in from the east. Trying to get away. Apparently the city, you know, like the oldest part of town, is really diseased, heavy-duty mothers and fathers rule the streets there.'

'Some kids came through earlier. They were from the east. They're living at the Tower of London.'

'Cool. I saw them, I think. Wondered where they were from. Where are they now? We should talk to them.'

'They left. David tried to lock them down. I guess they didn't go for it.'

'Pity.'

'Thing is, though. They've got the east sewn up by the sound of it. No use trying to recruit there.'

'So it's the north then?'

'Yes. I couldn't do it by myself, though, Shadowman. I need to ask you a really big favour.'

'You want me to come with you?'

'Yes. We need a scout. Someone who's used to the streets.'

Shadowman sucked his teeth for a long time, mulling this over and staring into the fire.

'How long do I have to think about it?' he said eventually.

'Until tomorrow. If you want to come, it's usual terms, usual payment, meet in the courtyard when it's light. I can find a bed for you here if you want.'

'Nah, it's all right. There's a girl in John's camp I'm interested in. They're having a big party down there tonight. They jacked a load of beer and cider today.'

'How can you hang out with those dorks?'

'Oh, they have fun, you know, Magic-Man. F-U-N. Not like here. It's boring here. It's drab. It's dull.'

'Are you going over to the dark side?'

'No.' Shadowman laughed. 'You know what it reminds me of down there?'

'What?'

'You remember when we went to Glastonbury? It was a laugh for the first day, then it rained and the toilets were foul, there was filth and mess everywhere, too many people, non-stop music all day and night, rotten food. By day two I was knackered and dirty and strung out and you couldn't get away from it, the noise and the dirt and the crowds.'

190

'I enjoyed it,' said Jester. 'It was well cool.'

'Maybe. But, anyway, that's what the squatter camp's like. Noisy and dirty and dangerous. Fun to visit, but you wouldn't want to live there. It's like you've got two opposites – law and order here at the palace, and total chaos in the camp. You need a balance, I reckon, somewhere in between.'

'Maybe that's what we'll find in north London?'

'What? And not come back?'

'So far, Shadow, this is the best deal I've seen in London, but if there's a better one, well . . .'

'You reckon there might be something out there?'

'Only one way to find out.'

'If I come.'

'You'll come.'

Somehow the girl had kept going for hours. Running round the pitch. Escaping their clumsy attacks. They'd brought her here soon after dusk and now it was almost dawn. The great oval of sky that showed in the open roof of the stadium was growing light to the east, turning from grey to pale yellow.

She'd had three friends with her when she'd arrived. Three other girls. They'd been snatched from the house they were sheltering in and carried back here.

Her friends hadn't lasted long at all.

And once the grown-ups had eaten them their need to kill this girl had dimmed along with the hunger pains in their bellies. She was fast and she had fight in her, and one by one they had given up trying to catch her.

Now they were only playing with her.

She would wait until she thought they'd leave her alone and then run for an exit. They were always ready for her, however, and would lumber over to cut her off, slashing at her with their long dirty fingernails, snapping with yellow rotting teeth. Every time so far she'd managed to struggle free of them and return to the centre of the pitch and there she was now.

She was covered in blood from small cuts all over her

body where her flesh had been torn. Her clothes were stained black with it and her long hair was matted around her face. Her mad, terrified eyes stared out from a red mask streaked with tears. She crouched in the middle of the football pitch, panting and gasping and trembling. Fear had taken all her humanity away and she was a pathetic animal thing, a mouse in a den of cats, liable to freeze with shock at any moment.

Most of the grown-ups, with food inside them, had wandered away to sleep, but some sat in the stands, watching her. A few remained on the pitch and one of them was watching her more intently than the others. He didn't take his eyes off her. He had a great bald head on a short neck, a filthy vest with a cross of St George stretched across his belly and wire-framed glasses with no lenses in them. He had been poking his tongue into the eye socket of a severed head, trying to get at the warm brains inside. Now he threw it away into the long grass. Bored. Two skinny, starving mothers, too feeble to catch anything for themselves, had been watching him, dribbling down their fronts, and now they crawled towards the head and fought each other for it, snarling and hissing.

They could have his scraps – that's all they were good for. He was top dog and they were snivelling filth. They looked up to him. They followed him. He could get them to do whatever he wanted. He was powerful, the most powerful of them all, and they understood it.

He kicked one of the mothers in the side of the head and she fell sideways, her neck broken.

The father belched and a thin stream of brown bile bubbled from his mouth. The girl had entertained him for a while and it had triggered memories, of coming here long ago. He thought perhaps he had lived here back then, before his brain had been cooked and tangled and twisted out of shape by the disease, before his flesh had been ruined by blisters and boils and sores.

He had come here with his boy, his Liam, he remembered that much, and he had sat and watched his team. Now the grass was up to his knees, weeds were sprouting. It had changed, this place, but it was the closest thing to a home that he had. They were creatures of habit, these sick grown-ups, slinking back to the places they knew so well.

More and more of them had been coming to the stadium. Tramping in from every direction. Drawn to it, just as they'd been drawn to it before – on Saturdays and Sundays, on weekday nights when the floodlights had blazed overhead and the grass had glowed bright green.

If he really concentrated, strained and struggled and forced his mind to be still, he could remember how it had been back then, with every seat filled and all of the fans shouting and screaming and hurling abuse as the players kicked the ball.

Kick, kick, kick . . .

Back then they had followed their team. Their Arsenal. And now they followed him. He had the badge of power on his chest. The red cross on the white. He was St George. Their leader, their saviour. He would kill the dragons.

All they had wanted before was to win, to beat every other team, be champions of the world. He would make it happen now. All he had to do was beat the enemy. Beat them down until they were bloody. Kick, kick, kick . . . Kick them down and butcher them and eat them.

That was what he was. Yes. It all came back to him now.

He was a butcher. He could see himself in his shop. *Meat is life*. He could smell it in the air. The vans would arrive and they would bring in the boys and girls, and he would hang them from spikes and slit them from their belly to their throat, watch the blood draining away, pull out the guts, the heart and liver and lungs. He closed his eyes so he could see it more clearly. Licked his dry and cracking lips.

There they were in his gleaming white shop. The children hanging neatly, staring at nothing, opened up and cleaned, drained of blood so that they were white.

Chop, chop, chop, the butchering would carry on. Choice cuts. Shin, neck, breast, ribs, rump ... He hummed to himself, rocking backwards and forwards, lost in the delight of it all, the sights and sounds and smells. The words kept on coming back to him – loin, leg, shoulder, cheek – he rolled them around his mouth.

He would lay the sweet red meat out on his counter and the mums would come in, or sometimes the dads, and he would wrap the little packets of flesh and sell them.

He smiled as he hummed.

He loved the night, after he had eaten, when his head cleared and his memories returned. His special lads were nearby, finishing off one of the other girls. Cracking the bones so they could suck out the sweet marrow inside. They were the clever ones, like him. They stuck close by. His dogs. His boys. They brought him what he needed. Fresh meat. Living children. And every day he grew stronger.

Watching the girl being chased around the pitch had been fun for a while, almost like watching a game of football, but now he wanted to finish it. The girl and her fidgety scurrying movements irritated him. The young ones made him angry. He wanted to kill them all. He wanted to snap their necks just like he'd snapped the neck of the skinny mother.

Bored.

He yawned and stretched, his joints clicking. Then he belched again and spat a mouthful of bile on to the mother who sat in the grass chewing an ear. He lumbered across the pitch.

Bored.

Still the girl had not given up. She made a fresh break for it, sprinting towards the east stand. She pounded along, hoping against hope that this time, unlike the countless times she'd tried it before, *this time* would be different, she would make it to the edge and get away from this hideous place.

At the last moment a fat mother wearing a T-shirt with the Playboy bunny logo on it waddled over to cut her off and as the girl tried to duck past her she swung one of her heavy fat arms, bowling the girl to the ground. She crawled on, her breath hissing in and out of her tight throat. A father, long hair hanging down over his face, stamped on her. She squealed and rolled to the side, then struggled to her feet and limped back to the centre of the pitch.

St George was waiting for her. In the half-light it looked as if he was smiling, but the girl couldn't be sure. Grown-ups didn't really have emotions any more; they were just killing machines. There was something different about this one, though, something cleverer, more human . . .

She dropped to her knees in front of him.

'Please,' she said. 'Please help me . . .'

For a moment the light of intelligence came into his face. He cocked his head to one side, like a dog listening, and a frown flickered about his eyes. He nodded his head, opened his mouth to speak. His jaws moved up and down, his tongue waggled in his mouth, but only a gurgling sound came out.

Was it possible he understood her? That she had stirred some memory of a time when adults looked after children?

'Please,' she said again. 'I don't want to die.'

He opened his arms wide, and now he definitely *was* smiling. The girl got up and staggered into him, pressed her head against his chest and drenched his vest with her tears. He wrapped his arms round her. One hand stroked her bloody hair. He too was crying as he breathed in her scent. That warm sweet scent they all shared, the smell of life.

'Thank you, thank you, thank –'

The words were choked off as his grip tightened. Her chest was crushed so she could no longer work her lungs. She felt her ribs snapping.

Oh well, she thought, as the blackness swallowed her. At least it was all over now . . .

St George mumbled something into her hair, remembering holding his boy. Protecting him with his strong arms. Recalling the old days, the good days, when it had been the two of them against the world.

They were gathering under the dinosaur skeleton in the main hall. Some of them were excited, chattering away, unable to stand still; others were quiet and drawn into themselves; a couple looked downright sick. DogNut paced up and down, his head bobbing on his long neck, beatboxing softly, waiting for Robbie, the boy who had opened the gate for them last night. Robbie was in charge of security at the museum and would be useful to have along on DogNut's expedition.

After breakfast DogNut and Paul had gone around talking to the more adventurous kids, collecting a posse. '*Who wants to come and kill the monster?*' Afterwards Paul had taken DogNut up on to the roof and shown him the beacon fire. Despite the fancy name it wasn't much more than a pile of junk in an old brazier that when lit sent up a tall column of smoke. If any of the hunter gangs were nearby, they'd see it and come to the museum, as they knew it meant a reward of some sort if they were able to help out. Paul had explained that Robbie was the only one authorized by the council to give the order to light it. But Robbie had left early, well before DogNut had woken up, to escort a work party of kids to a nearby courtyard to harvest crops.

Ignoring Paul's protests DogNut had taken out the cigarette lighter he always carried with him and set light to the brazier, explaining that they couldn't wait all day for Robbie to get back. Paul had tutted and fretted and moaned as the junk caught light and the smoke crawled up into the clear sky. A couple of runners had been sent out to fetch Robbie, but DogNut figured once he saw the beacon smoke he'd come back quick enough. DogNut was actually glad Robbie hadn't been there to start with. It helped his plan.

Apart from the usual nightmare, he'd slept well. Long and deep. And now felt reasonably refreshed. Ready to face the Collector again. He told himself that if he took enough fighters it would be easy. First thing in the morning, confused by the bright sun, the big sicko would be a pushover. A lot of the kids in the museum wanted to help Paul get revenge for the death of his sister, but DogNut only wanted to take the best of them. Too many and they'd just get in the way of each other and make it dangerous. Most of these kids barely left the museum, unless it was to go and work in nearby vegetable patches, and weren't street tough. It had been like picking a team for a school football match. DogNut had turned away those kids that didn't look up to it.

Marco and Felix were coming. They reckoned they had unfinished business with the Collector and wanted to stick by DogNut. Finn was reluctantly staying behind. He knew he wasn't much use until his arm healed. Courtney had been in a panic, swaying one way and then the other, not sure if she could face going back to that awful place, but not wanting to look like a wimp in front of DogNut. Even now, standing here with her spear at the ready, she still didn't know if she was going to go with the war party when they set off.

199

She watched as DogNut strode into the middle of the floor and took charge.

'OK!' he shouted. 'Is everyone ready?'

There were mumbles from the kids and they shuffled into some kind of formation. Paul went and stood by DogNut, trying to look hard and failing. He obviously liked to dress all in black, with his roll-neck jumper, black denim jacket and matching jeans. They matched his hair, and with his long thin arms and legs he looked like some kind of insect.

'If Robbie don't get back soon, we'll go without him,' said DogNut.

Paul sighed, blowing out his breath to ease his tension. 'Are you sure we shouldn't wait for him, whatever?' he asked. 'He's got some of our best fighters with him.' He was very pale, made worse by his black outfit. His resolve of the night before, his determination to go and kill the Collector, was slipping away. He looked to Courtney like he'd been up half the night. Probably crying. Trying to accept that his sister was dead. The reality of being out on the streets and confronting a sicko, maybe killing him, was beginning to sink in.

'Don't worry,' said DogNut. 'We'll hang on a bit longer. The Collector is one *dangerous* grown-up. When we go in there, we want to make sure of it. Kill the bastard. You can stick his head on a pole if you like. But remember there ain't just him to worry about. There were bare sickos around last night. They'll mostly have crawled away to their sleeping holes, but they still out there and we don't want to forget it. I ain't waiting all day, though. Sun's out nice and bright now, and they don't like that. Early morning he'll be asleep, and his defences will be down. We want to get in there fast and get back here fast.'

'OK.'

DogNut mock-punched Paul. 'You'll be OK, blood. Don't fret.'

Courtney wandered off to the side and sat down on a bench, too nervous to speak to anyone. She stared at some kind of giant fossilized tortoise and prayed that DogNut would change his mind and give up on the idea of killing the sicko. She looked round as Brooke came down the wide stairs at the back of the hall past the statue of Charles Darwin. She looked so different with her short brown hair and old-fashioned dress. She had changed more than Courtney had expected in a year. She could be five years older, ten even. She headed for DogNut, who started talking at her, rattling off the words and dancing from one foot to the other. Brooke didn't look too happy. Kept turning away and fiddling with her hair.

Courtney held back for a while then decided she'd better go and see what Brooke had to say.

'You can't just come in here and stir things up, Donut,' Brooke was saying as Courtney came over.

'I ain't stirring,' DogNut protested. 'But we got to move fast if we want to kill the sicko. He might move on. And I mean, you know, maybe Olivia's still alive.'

Courtney and DogNut both knew that wasn't a possibility. This was all part of DogNut's game plan. Brooke wasn't to know that, however. She changed her tone.

'Yeah . . . maybe. OK, I see your point. Thing is, you only just got here. I was gonna show you things this morning, introduce you to some more people.'

'Laters,' said DogNut. 'When we back. OK? Plenty of time.'

'What if you don't come back?'

'I'll be back!' said DogNut, impersonating the Terminator. 'Look. We getting an army together here.'

'What if you get some of my lot killed?'

'I'll look after them good. Don't you worry. I ain't stepping on nobody's toes. I'm doing this for Paul.'

'Are you?'

'Course I am. So you gonna come with us?'

'Well . . .' Brooke thought about it. Didn't look too keen on the idea and before she could make a decision Courtney butted in.

'It's pretty dangerous out there if you ain't used to it,' she said. 'Nobody will think bad of you if you don't come. You never knew Olivia, like I did.'

'You going?' Brooke asked.

Courtney shrugged, still not sure.

'See, I'm not one of the fighters,' said Brooke. 'I got more important things to do here.'

'*I'm* a fighter,' said Courtney, standing taller and swinging her spear. God, she hoped that DogNut was taking this in. If she was going to put her neck on the line again, she wanted to make sure that DogNut was impressed.

'You coming for sure then?' DogNut asked.

'Yeah, why not? I ain't afraid.'

'My gyal!' said DogNut, and he put his arm round her and gave her a squeeze.

Before any of them could say anything else there were voices and movement from the main doors and a group of boys stepped in out of the light. They hurried across the atrium to the knot of waiting kids. Robbie was at their head, leather jacket tightly zipped, looking none too happy.

'What's going on?' he asked, his gelled hair bristling.

202

'What's it look like?' said DogNut. 'We going on a sicko hunt.'

'Who says?'

DogNut turned to Paul. 'You tell him, blood,' he said. 'This is your party.'

Paul took Robbie aside and explained what was happening. As they talked, Robbie kept throwing looks over to DogNut. Like Brooke, he wasn't happy that an outsider had come in and was shaking things up. Finally he came back and stood slightly too close to DogNut. His attempt to appear menacing didn't quite come off as his broken nose only came up to DogNut's chin.

'You ain't in charge here, Doggo,' he said.

'That's right.' DogNut shrugged and held Robbie's gaze. 'The nerds are.'

Robbie paused for a moment, weighing DogNut's pointed words.

'They look after all the boring crap,' he said at last. 'But anything to do with security goes through me.'

'Yeah, I know that.' DogNut offered Robbie a friendly smile. 'But you wasn't here so I had to start putting something together. Time is tick-tick-ticking away, soldier. You gonna come then?'

'Course I'm gonna come.'

'Then what are we waiting for? Let's go.'

As the kids marched out of the museum gates into the street, they bumped into Ryan and his hunters coming from the west along the Cromwell Road with their dogs. Compared to the kids in the museum Ryan's gang looked even more wild and fierce than they'd done before. Dressed in their furs and leathery masks, heavily armed and battle scarred, they were a complete contrast to the elegantly dressed museum kids, who carried clubs and knives mostly. Although one or two, like Robbie, had lightweight swords hanging at their belts in fancy ornamental scabbards.

Ryan greeted him, and then spotted DogNut. He loped over to him, his heavy boots scraping on the tarmac, and gave him a high five.

'You found your mates then?'

'Yeah. Is all cool. Thanks for that – we feel well dumb not talking to you properly yesterday.'

'Yeah. You *are* well dumb, Dog. So what was the smoke for? What's going down?'

Robbie put himself between DogNut and Ryan. 'I'm in charge here, Ryan – you know that. You talk to me. DogNut's just a guest.'

Ryan shrugged. 'Don't make no odds to me who I talk to. So what's up then?'

'We're going to get rid of a sicko that killed the sister of one of our boys at the museum.'

'Just one sicko?' Ryan looked amused. 'You sure there's enough of you?'

'Apparently he's big and hard to kill.'

'*Apparently?*' Ryan looked even more amused. 'You mean you ain't never even seen him.'

'*We've* seen him,' said DogNut. 'Olivia was one of our party.'

'The little girl who was with you?'

'Yeah.'

'She never made it, no?'

'That's right.'

'Harsh.' Ryan spat on the ground. 'So, you really need all these soldiers to take on one sicko? There must be twenty of you.'

DogNut shrugged. 'I don't know how well this lot fight.'

'We can fight all right when we have to,' said Robbie indignantly.

'So you need our help, or not?' asked Ryan.

'I can't offer to pay you,' said DogNut, and he nodded at Robbie. 'That's his territory.'

'I guess we could give you some food, or clothing, or something,' said Robbie. 'But not much. Quite frankly I reckon we could kill this sicko by ourselves. As you say, how bad can one grown-up be? Just cos DogNut and his gang had a hard time.'

Before DogNut could react to Robbie's taunt, Ryan interrupted. 'Tell you what,' he said. 'We'll do you this one as a freebie. I'm curious to see what this giant sicko can do.'

'Cheers,' said Robbie.

'No problem. Just remember you owe us two, now.'

'Sure.'

'Show me the way then.'

Ryan looked at Robbie, and Robbie looked at DogNut.

'Follow me,' said DogNut, and he led them eastwards towards Harrods.

Courtney really didn't want to be doing this. She could have slept all day. But she forced herself forward, plodding along with heavy feet. She wished she hadn't been such an idiot and had stayed behind with Brooke. Why did boys always have to complicate things? She loved Brooke, she really did, she just didn't want her to end up with DogNut. DogNut was hers. Courtney had to convince him that he'd be better off with a tough street fighter like herself and not a . . .

Well, whatever Brooke had become.

A house nerd.

Not that Courtney felt like much of a tough street fighter at the moment. Her guts had turned to water and all she really wanted to do was bend double and throw up. The thought of the Collector in his disgusting den terrified her more than she ever could have imagined.

Why was DogNut so keen to go back there?

Only one way to find out.

She sped up and pushed her way to the head of the column. DogNut was out in front, walking by himself, and she fell into step beside him.

'What about Brooke, eh?' she said, trying to sound like it didn't really mean much to her. 'She ain't half changed.'

'Yeah, I guess we all changed.'

'She even looks different, don't you think?' Courtney went on. 'I reckon she looked prettier as a blonde.'

'Maybe. Most girls do.'

'You think I should go blonde?'

'You?' DogNut looked appalled. 'No way, gyal. You couldn't go blonde anyways. With your hair you'd end up, like, orange, or something.'

'Don't you like my hair then?'

'Never thought about it much. Is just hair.'

'DogNut?' Courtney decided to come right out and say it. 'Why are you doing this?'

'To help Paul.'

'Really? It's not because you feel guilty about Olivia?'

'Yeah. That as well, I guess.'

'But I know that ain't all. You're being devious. You got something else on your mind. I just know it.'

'Gyaldem, eh?' said DogNut, and he sucked his teeth. 'Can't get *nothing* past them, man.'

'I can never tell when you're being serious.'

'Me either.'

'But you *are* up to something, Doggs.'

DogNut leant closer to Courtney and spoke quietly, making sure that nobody else could hear them.

'I want to *be* someone, Courtney.'

'You are someone.'

'No I ain't. I want to be important. I want to be remembered. Back at the Tower I won't never be nothing except one of Jordan Hordern's captains. But I reckon the museum is ripe for the picking. I mean, how come Justin and the nerds are in charge? Who let that happen? Why ain't Robbie running things? Ain't he got no dignity, no self-respect?'

'I dunno.'

DogNut glanced over at Robbie, checking he wasn't near enough to hear what they were saying.

'I'll tell you why, Courtney, because he is a weak-ass dope. He don't *want* to be in charge. He's scared.'

'What you saying then, Doggs? You gonna try to take over?'

'Wouldn't take much. I just need to show them all how tough I am, how I make decisions and get shit done. I wanna be top dog for a change, Courtney.'

'What for?'

'Power, girl. Power and respect.'

'What for, though?'

'Come on. I'd get all the best stuff for myself. All the best food. The best clothes. The biggest bed. All the buffest girls. And then Brooke will fall in love with me and we'll live happily ever after.'

Courtney didn't know what to say to this and she retreated into her own thoughts. She wasn't always sure that she even liked DogNut, but there was nothing she could do about the way she felt about him. Maybe what he was saying made some kind of sense. Maybe she was attracted to him because he was tough, a soldier. Big man in road.

The column of kids halted, snapping Courtney out of her thoughts. She barged to the front to see what the hold-up was and instantly wished she hadn't.

Ryan and his hunters were battering a young father to death in the middle of the road, their dogs snarling and barking. The sicko was blind, his eyelids swollen and crusted with sores. Too feeble to make it back to wherever he lived, he'd been caught out in the daylight.

The hunters were laughing, and when they'd finished one of them knelt down to slice off the dead father's ears. The boy inspected his work. He lifted up an ear that was little more than a gristly flap of skin and waved it in the face of one of his friends before lobbing it away. The other one he gave to Ryan, who hooked it onto the garland of severed ears that hung from his belt.

Ryan grinned at DogNut and gave a little waggle of his hips to make the ears dance.

'How much further, Dog?' he asked.

'Nearly there,' DogNut replied. 'Is quite close to Harrods.'

'You really reckon this giant sicko of yours is dangerous?' Ryan asked, spitting on the dead specimen at his feet. 'They don't scare us none.'

'Trust me,' said DogNut, nodding his head and walking on. 'He's dangerous.'

Ryan fell in step with him.

'Maybe we should just set his crib on fire?' he said with a wicked leer. 'Fry him up.'

Paul heard what they were saying and came over.

'You're not burning anything,' he said. 'Olivia might be in there. She might still be alive. I have to find her. That's what this is all about.'

'Yeah,' said DogNut. 'Agreed. I don't like fire. Our last safe place was burned down when south London went up in flames. Don't want to risk starting something we can't control. The sicko's den is stuffed to the roof with all crap that'll burn. Any fire in there, the place is gonna go off like a bomb.'

'So, what's your plan then?' Ryan asked, and DogNut started to tell him.

'What do you mean I stay outside?' Robbie was furious. He'd had enough of DogNut trying to run the show. The two of them were toe to toe in the middle of the street outside the Collector's house, virtually spitting into each other's faces.

'Cool it, blood,' said DogNut. 'We need someone who knows what they doing out here, yeah? Otherwise we flush him out and he gets away. And not just that. He ain't the only sicko in London. You get me? Once we in there someone got to watch our backs. Once we start kicking up a fuss, making all noise and that, the locals is gonna know we here, and any hungry ones might just be a likkle bit curious. Whoever stays out here is gonna have the most important job, yeah? When the fat man comes out, they gonna have to take him down.'

Robbie's shoulders dropped. He could see the truth in what DogNut was saying. But he hadn't given up the fight.

'So why don't you stay out here, big man, and I go in?'

DogNut made an elaborate gesture towards the house, sweeping his arm wide and half bowing.

'Be my guest, soldier. You know where to go when you get in there? Cos it's gonna be dark. Is like a maze, he got it so full of stuff. You reckon you'll know where to find him? Yeah? Cos, take it from me, you wouldn't want to be ambushed by him, and, like, *overwhelmed*.'

'Maybe . . .'

DogNut smiled and put an arm round Robbie, giving him a squeeze.

'This is the best way, brother, believe me.'

'OK. Forget it. But next time you talk to me before you start making any plans.'

'Yeah, sorry. Was just me and Ryan got to talking.'

'So who's going in with you?'

'There ain't a lot of room to move in there, so I want to keep it small, yeah? We gonna send one crew up to the top in case he's there, another lot can take the ground floor and I'm gonna take the main war party down into the cellar, where he sleeps.'

'I'm sending a small crew round the back, to the garden,' said Ryan. 'Just in case he tries to get out that way.'

'The kids going into the house need to be ones who've been in there before, though,' said DogNut. 'Marco and Felix are gonna take the kitchen. Courtney's taking the crew up to the top. I'll lead the party down to the cellar.'

'I'm coming with you,' said Paul, stepping forward.

'For real?' said DogNut.

Paul swallowed and took a deep breath. 'Of course,' he said, staring at the pavement. 'She was my sister.'

'OK, but we don't need no hero act,' said DogNut. 'You stick with me and you do what I say.'

Paul nodded.

'I'd better come along too,' said Ryan. 'And I'm bringing my best fighter. You'll need us.'

'If you say so.'

'I say so.' Ryan put an arm round DogNut. He smelt like an animal, what with all the leather and fur and bits of dead flesh hanging off him. That and the fact that he obviously hadn't washed in about six months.

'This is gonna be fun . . .' Ryan's face split into a wide smile, his long yellow teeth showing wolfishly.

'OK?' said DogNut, and Robbie reluctantly nodded. 'So that's me, Paul, Ryan, Ryan's hunter and, if you want to make sure that your guys are in on it, I'll take one more from the museum. Who d'you suggest? Someone who ain't scared of nothing and can fight up close if they got to.'

'Jackson.' Robbie nodded towards a stocky kid wearing hoodie and jeans who had close-cropped hair and a face like a potato.

'He good?'

'She.'

'She?'

'Yeah.' Robbie grinned and raised his eyebrows. 'Jackson's the hardest kid at the museum.'

He called Jackson over. She looked serious and slightly shy.

'You happy to go inside with the main team and flush the sicko out?' Robbie asked her and she shrugged.

'Why not?' She smiled now and her face softened and she instantly looked like a little girl.

'How old are you, Jackson?' DogNut asked.

'Thirteen. Why? You think I can't do this?' Jackson stopped smiling.

'Didn't say nothing. Just asking.'

Jackson sniffed. Held DogNut's gaze. Her eyes were grey and clear. She carried a short spear with a long, extremely sharp-looking head. She twirled it in her hand, like a bandleader with a baton. The tip zipping past a millimetre from DogNut's nose.

He laughed and stepped back.

'Save it for the man, soldier,' he said, and then called the rest of his team together.

'We're going in,' he shouted. 'And, remember, the show ain't over till the fat sicko croaks.'

Courtney groaned. She was back in the Collector's house. The last place on earth she wanted to be. Her feet stuck to the squishy mashed layer of paper and food and excrement that lay on the floorboards, giving the effect of walking through wet mud. The stink of it, rising from the floor in wafts of damp heat, and seeping from the walls, nauseated her. She felt like she was inside the twisting wormholes of some giant sponge that had soaked up gallons of grease and sweat and slime that was all now slowly oozing out. The air seemed to be thicker in here. It clogged her nostrils and the back of her throat, making it hard to breathe. She was panting like a dog, hard and fast, unable to fill her lungs. Her pounding heart was pushing so hard she felt as if her skin might split, and sweat lay on her in a tight cloying sheet, like clingfilm, making her itch. She wanted to scratch herself all over. But she knew she must show no fear in front of the other kids – three of Ryan's hunters and a fat boy from the museum. They were absolutely bricking themselves so she had to give them courage.

Just like dogs, the kids preferred to hunt in a large pack, and separated from Ryan, his hunters didn't look so tough. These three stuck close behind Courtney and she reckoned if they did come across any sickos they'd be out of there in a flash. They were very different boys to the cocky, swaggering bunch who'd volunteered to come inside with her. Oh, they'd been warned about what to expect – they'd even laughed about it, boasted about what they were going to do, but as they'd forced the door open and walked into the hallway they'd fallen silent. The Collector had painstakingly rebuilt the towering piles of rotting newspaper and had spent some time jamming human bones into it.

The boys had grown pale and quiet. This was like nothing they'd ever experienced before. There was an alien atmosphere in the house. Alien and evil. Very little sunlight penetrated the building. It hadn't been so obvious last night when it was dark outside, but the Collector had stacked stuff on all the window ledges, and the panes of glass were so thick with grime and dust that only a few spots of yellowish light showed here and there.

Courtney switched on her torch. It was a relief to be heading upstairs, away from what she knew waited in the basement, even though it brought back painful memories of when six of them had gone up last night and only five had come down. And there would be nothing worse than to be trapped up here again with these strangers, kids she didn't know and couldn't fully trust. A big part of her wished she could have stayed with DogNut.

Come on, girl, concentrate.

She may have got the soft option, but she still couldn't be sure of what she might find up here. What if they stumbled across the mutilated body of Olivia? She'd seen the dead bodies of friends before, but none had been mucked about with the way the Collector had torn up those poor kids in the kitchen.

Up. Keep going up.

She hustled her gang, making her way to the very top of the house without stopping. They quickly arrived at the bedroom with the balcony where they'd had their fight with the Collector. There was much more light in here. The wide sliding glass doors along the back wall were largely clear and there was a big gap in the middle where they'd been smashed. Had that happened in the fight? She couldn't remember. It had all happened so fast and she'd been in a blind panic.

Because of the broken windows the air in here was cooler and cleaner. With a strong sense of relief she went out on to the balcony and leant on the wall. A movement below caught her eye and she spotted another group of Ryan's hunters climbing the wall into the garden. They stopped and looked up and then waved to her. Courtney felt reassured that she wasn't alone.

It was nice on the balcony. Calm and peaceful. Normal. The gardens, though overgrown, looked like any other gardens, a complete contrast to the weird interior of the house.

She knew she couldn't stay out here, though.

It wasn't over.

She gulped in fresh air and spat to clear her throat. Turned back to the anxious faces of her little gang. They stood in a line, waiting for their orders.

'Take a quick look round,' she said, stepping back in through the broken windows. 'See if there's any signs of Olivia. I don't reckon she's likely to be up here, but we need to check. Then we'll work our way down.'

'And then what?' asked the museum boy.

'Then we get the hell out of here, kiddo.'

33

Paul was shaking so much it was almost funny. His whole body was vibrating, his teeth rattling in his skull. He was gripping his knife so tightly in his hand that his fingers were bone white and bloodless. Sweat ran down his arms, under his sleeves, and dripped on to the floor. He was staying next to DogNut, trying to show he was tough, and not fooling anyone. Jackson was a couple of paces behind them, then came Ryan's hunter and finally Ryan himself, walking backwards, watching their rear. They were in the basement, slowly working their way through the maze. Jackson and DogNut both carried torches. The beams crawled over the paper walls and the soggy floor, occasionally touching on a bone, or a turd, or a scrap of hairy skin, only to skitter away like startled insects.

As they came to each corner, they stopped and DogNut would carefully peer round, trying not to touch the walls if he could help it.

'This is some weird shit, man,' muttered Ryan as they came into one of the little hollowed-out antechambers. This one was filled with old radios and tiny broken human skulls. Baby skulls by the look of them.

'Ryan don't like this one bit at all,' he went on. 'Should have listened to his mum and stayed at home.'

'You believe me now, yeah?' said DogNut. 'I told you this wouldn't be no primary-school outing, and you ain't even seen the guy what built this house of horrors yet.'

'Maybe we should all stop talking and go a little quieter?' said Jackson, nudging past Paul to join DogNut at the front. 'Let's move on,' she whispered. 'The quicker we go, the quicker we get this over with.'

Jackson didn't speak anything like the girls that DogNut had grown up with. She had an unexpectedly posh accent that didn't go with the face and the attitude. What's more, she was confident enough not to put on a voice, didn't have to pretend that she was someone else. DogNut had spent his whole life trying to sound like the black kids on his estate. That was how you talked if you wanted to be cool. He admired Jackson, but she was alien to him and he didn't really know what to make of her.

Before they moved forward, she shoved Paul back and put him between Ryan and his hunter.

'You shouldn't have come down here, Paul,' she said softly. 'You're not up to this. Try to keep out of the way and not get into any trouble.'

'But I want to kill him.' Paul's face was twisted with a mix of fear, pain and anger. Jackson stared at him.

'Do you really think you could do that, Paul?'

'Yes. Of course.'

'When did you last kill someone?'

'Never. But I can start now.'

'I doubt it,' said Jackson, and before Paul could say anything else she put a hand over his mouth.

'Nobody's going to judge you, Paul. Nobody's going to think badly of you. Let *us* do it. You just try not to get hurt. That's what Olivia would have wanted.'

'I'm going to kill him,' Paul repeated once Jackson had taken her hand away. 'And you're not going to stop me.'

'OK. But for now stay back here – you're slowing us down.'

Jackson returned to DogNut and the two of them led the way down the next stretch of passageway.

34

'We mustn't let Paul come in here.'

Marco was by the kitchen door, holding it shut. He and Felix had made sure that there was nothing living in the kitchen and had then quickly secured the room in case the Collector was nearby. They had three kids from the museum with them. Two of them looked like they were about to be sick. The third one was actually being sick. He was bent double, throwing up noisily into a bucket of slops. Marco thought it was funny that he had carefully used the bucket so as not to make any mess, when the room was already covered in filth of all kinds.

You had to see the funny side of things or you'd crack. The kitchen looked even worse this morning. The Collector had added to his vile collection of broken bodies around the table and used poor Olivia's head as a centrepiece. It was almost unrecognizable, one side of it completely caved in. Marco hoped she'd died quickly.

'Please,' said one of the other boys. 'Please let's get out of here. I can't stand it. It's disgusting.'

'In a minute,' said Marco.

'At least we don't have to look no further,' said Felix. 'We know what's happened to Olivia. Perhaps we should put it in a bag, or something?'

'Put what in a bag?' asked Marco.

'The head,' said Felix. 'Olivia's head.'

'What for?'

'I don't know, to show the others. To show Paul.'

'He don't want to see that,' said Marco incredulously. 'Why would he want to see that?'

'It's proof, isn't it?'

'He don't need proof. We just tell him we found her body.'

'But we ain't found her body!' Felix protested. 'Only her head.'

'If you was her brother,' said Marco, pointing at the table, 'would you want to see that?'

'No.'

'Right.'

'So what are we going to do with it?' Felix asked. 'Maybe we should bury it?'

'Yeah, right,' said Marco, with a cutting edge to his voice. 'A tiny coffin with a head in it. That'll be lovely.'

'Marco . . .'

'Felix!' Marco interrupted him. 'That thing on the table ain't Olivia. Olivia's gone and there ain't nothing we can do about it.'

'Please, please, please, let's get out of here . . .'

Felix turned to the whimpering boy with the expression an adult might make to a baby and grabbed the face of one of the dead boys at the table. He worked the mouth so that it opened and closed like a ventriloquist's dummy, making it speak.

'Oh, diddums,' he said in a grating, comedy voice. 'Is this all too much for you?'

Then the dead boy's lower jaw came away in his hand

and a shower of rotting flesh and maggots dropped on to the table. Felix threw the jaw away and jumped back, laughing hysterically and wiping his hands on his trousers.

'You're sick,' said the museum kid.

'No, *he's* sick,' said Felix, pointing towards one of the boy's friends, who was puking on the floor. He then shifted his attention to the jawless body at the table. 'But I think this guy is the sickest,' he said. 'He really needs to see a doctor.'

'You moron,' said Marco. He was torn between laughing and screaming. He knew what Felix was doing. He was trying to avoid the pain and hurt and fear by making a joke of it. None of them could really face what was going on in their world, and they'd all developed their own ways of coping.

But Felix had gone too far. He was really freaking the museum kids out.

'Leave it,' he said. 'Hide Olivia's head so there's no danger Paul might see it. Then we'll search the other rooms on this floor, and please, Felix, don't think it might be funny to tell Paul about the head. We keep shtum about that. All he needs to know is that we found her body.'

'Yeah?' said Felix with mock innocence. 'Where is it?'

'Shut it, Felix.'

'You shut it.'

'I can't do it,' said the museum boy. 'I can't stay in here any longer. I want to go outside.' His face was wet with tears and he was shivering badly.

Marco grabbed the front of his sweatshirt.

'You stay with us,' he said. 'You've been given an order. We stick together. We're a group and we have to follow orders. OK?'

The boy gulped and nodded his head, taking strength from Marco's military attitude.

'I'm OK,' he said. 'I'm OK. We'll stick together. I won't let you down.'

'Good boy,' said Marco. 'Now let's look in the other rooms. And be careful. We don't know where the fat father is, where he might come from, and we don't know if he's alone or not. He might have some other friends about the place.'

'Yeah,' said Felix, sniggering. 'He might have invited some kids over for tea.'

35

DogNut's group had come to the end of the line. The sitting-room with the old TVs and computers and the sagging sofa where the Collector slept. At first DogNut thought he wasn't there. He could see no sign of him and there was a great mound of grubby newspapers on the sofa where his body should have been.

He absentmindedly read one of the headlines.

'Floods devastate York.'

Those were different days.

But as he looked at the writing he realized that the papers were gently rising and falling.

'He's under there,' he said. 'Under the newspapers.'

'We should just put a match to him,' said Ryan, pushing into the cramped space behind DogNut and Jackson. 'End of.'

'End of all of us,' DogNut snapped. 'I told you – no fire. We'd never get out in time.'

'OK, so what do we do then?' said Paul, his voice high-pitched and hysterical. He raised his knife, shaking sweat everywhere as his hand juddered in the fetid air.

'What do you reckon?' asked Jackson. 'Could we stab him through that lot? All do it together. Might have some chance of hitting his heart, or his liver, or something.'

'His fat gut more like,' said DogNut.

'I'm gonna stab him,' said Paul, and DogNut held him back.

'Chances are you won't kill him, just vex him. His fat's like a suit of armour.'

'I don't care if I make him angry,' said Paul. 'He killed my sister.'

'Fair enough. We do got to make him angry, I guess,' said DogNut. 'Only enough so's he chases us outside, though. Once he's out on the street we can deal with him properly.'

'I'm gonna do it,' said Paul, who didn't seem to be listening. 'I'm gonna stab him.'

'Then you'd better hurry,' said Jackson. 'I think he's waking up. I told you we should have kept the noise down.'

Indeed, the mountain of newspaper was beginning to rise, and as it did so sheets slid off it like drifts of snow from a melting roof. The next thing they knew Paul had run forward with a terrible scream and stabbed down double-fisted with his knife at the rising bulk. His hands smacked into the paper and the knife stuck fast. Then a great meaty paw reached out from under the papers and took hold of Paul's arm. It jerked him to the floor and he yelped as his face slammed into the black and sticky carpet. The Collector still had hold of him, and, as Paul tried to twist free, Jackson stepped forward and slashed at the sicko's arm with the point of her spear, then kicked it with a heavy brown work boot. There was a grunt from under the newspapers and the Collector loosened his grip. Jackson kicked his arm again and the Collector finally let go of Paul who scrabbled away, slipping on the greasy carpet. He careered into the table holding up the biggest television and it crashed down on top of him.

Now the Collector erupted upwards, throwing off the rest of the paper. All except for a few sheets that were pinned to his gut by Paul's knife like notes on a corkboard. There was a filthy rag stuffed into the hole in his side where Felix had stabbed him last night. The skin round the wound was purple and smeared with pus. He glared at the fallen television, appalled at what he was seeing, and then hissed and lunged at Paul, but Jackson deftly nipped in and jabbed her spear at his neck, just below the ear, in a quick in-and-out movement. DogNut was satisfied to see a spurt of blood pump out.

The Collector could be hurt after all.

DogNut yelled at him, to attract his attention, and slowly the huge father turned and lumbered towards the other kids. Paul seized the moment and picked up a broken table leg. He staggered to his feet and started to pummel the Collector on the back. The Collector barely seemed to notice; without looking round he swung one arm and smashed Paul across the room where he hit the wall with a wet slap. He slid to the ground, stunned.

'We've got to get out of here,' DogNut shouted. Ryan's hunter was already gone. Ryan and Jackson didn't budge.

'You get Paul,' said Jackson. 'We'll distract him.'

Now Jackson and Ryan both slashed their weapons at the father, but there wasn't the space to do any real damage. DogNut moved in and pulled Paul to his feet. He was groggy and confused so DogNut had to physically drag him into the maze.

'Run!' he bellowed.

They were all scared, panting, gasping, blundering through the maze as the Collector came after them. They could hear his feet thudding on the floorboards, hear him snorting and wheezing.

Paul was dazed, barely able to walk, let alone run. He was holding DogNut back.

'For God's sake,' DogNut snapped. 'Get your act together, man.'

Paul managed to pick up speed as his head cleared and at last they reached the stairs and went clattering up them.

'Everybody out!' DogNut howled as he neared the top. 'He's on the move!'

They burst from the cellar entrance just as Courtney came down the stairs from above and they all collided. It was a miracle that nobody was hurt because they all had their weapons at the ready. They quickly sorted themselves out and made for the front door. As the hallway had been made so narrow by the stacks of newspaper, it created a bottleneck. In the confusion and panic they were getting in each other's way.

Paul was fully alert now, but had a crazy, feverish look about him. He stopped in the middle of the hallway and shook DogNut.

'Where's Olivia?' he cried. 'Has anyone found her?'

'Get outside,' said DogNut. 'We'll sort it.'

'Where is she? Where's my little sister?'

'She's dead, Paul. Now get your arse out of here.'

'Where's her body? How d'you know she's dead?'

'You think she could live in here? We'll all be dead if we don't move it.'

Jammed in the hallway, the two of them were preventing anyone else from leaving the building. The trapped kids were yelling and shoving. They could feel the walls vibrating as the Collector clumped up the stairs.

'We'll come back for her body!' DogNut shouted. 'But please shift, Paul.'

Courtney screamed as the Collector emerged from the top of the stairs, his yellow eyes staring, drool spilling from his open mouth, blood bubbling from the wound in his neck. He smelt of shit and decay and death. The light from the open front door fell on him and as Paul got a proper look at him he became paralysed with fear.

DogNut made a quick decision. He punched Paul hard in the belly, and, as he doubled over in agony, he hoisted him on to his shoulders in one swift movement. He then staggered towards the door and out of the house, the rest of the kids following in a frenzied bundle. He made it into the centre of the road where Robbie's gang was waiting, not quite sure how he was able to carry Paul's weight, coasting on adrenalin and fear and a crazy kind of strength. Then he collapsed to his knees and dropped Paul on the tarmac.

'What happened to him?' Robbie asked, frowning. 'Did the sicko get him?'

'No,' said DogNut, fighting for breath. 'I did. Had to hit him.'

'You hit him? What do you mean?'

'Never mind all that,' DogNut gasped. 'I hope you lot are ready because there is one very angry fat man about to come out of there.'

The kids formed a long straggly line, tensed, weapons raised. The hunters' dogs were at either end, tugging at their leads.

But for a minute nothing happened. The Collector didn't appear.

Nobody moved. Nobody said anything until Courtney broke the silence.

'He's not coming out. No way am I going back in there again.'

She fell silent as a shudder passed through the waiting kids and one or two swore as the Collector's great shape appeared in the doorway. He stood there, angry and confused, studying the kids, trying to work out who they were and what he was going to do.

He blinked five times, and then slowly, slowly, slowly he shrank back into the darkness of the house as if he was sinking into a bog. He became a vague dark shape in the hallway and then there was just blackness.

DogNut spat. Swore viciously. Was about to say something when a hideous racket started up – banging and shouting and clanking.

What now?

Smoke wafted from the house and the next moment the Collector came staggering out as if he'd been shoved from behind. He squealed as bright sunlight hit him and he raised an arm to shield his eyes. The sheets of newspaper were still incongruously pinned to his belly, like a napkin in a gimmicky restaurant. They flapped in the breeze.

Marco and Felix and the three museum boys now burst out of the front door, banging pots and pans together. Felix had a rolled-up newspaper that he'd set light to. He waved it at the sicko and the boys threw their pans at him. He tottered across the pavement. The fire, at least, seemed to frighten him and Marco was goading and prodding him with his spear, all the while yelling and screaming like a mad person.

The waiting kids now formed a circle round the sicko and began jabbing at him with their own weapons, and they, too, shouted, hurling obscenities at the huge father who tried to ward them off with his massive arms. Every now and then he would let out a long high-pitched wail and try to charge out of the circle, but every time he was driven back into the centre, the dogs snapping at him.

Sharp blades flashed and flickered at him, ripping his clothes. The newspaper was getting shredded. Patches of blood were appearing on his filthy, darkened skin.

'Do him!' someone shouted, and the kids laid into him with greater ferocity.

Paul went over to Felix and Marco.

'Did you find her?' he begged. 'My sister. Where is she?'

'Yeah, we found her,' said Marco softly. 'She's dead, mate. I'm sorry. Weren't nothing you could have done for her.'

'I want her body.'

'No you don't,' said Felix. 'Leave her be.'

'No . . .'

Paul made a move towards the house, and Felix and Marco held him back.

'Leave her be!' Felix repeated.

Paul fought his way free of them and turned on the Collector.

'I'm going to kill him . . .'

Courtney stepped back from the circle of flailing kids. She couldn't bear it any longer. The Collector was disgusting. He'd killed and mutilated God knows how many children, but to see him like this, a trapped animal, she couldn't help but feel pity for him. She couldn't watch as he was worn down by a thousand tiny cuts. The kids' faces looked insane, drugged, worked up into a frenzy of bloodlust, every vile word they could think of spitting from their twisted lips.

This must have been what it was like to watch bear-baiting or a bullfight.

Hideous.

Still the cruel darting blades plunged into the father. Still the dogs' teeth nipped at him. He was making a circle of blood in the road, stamping it into the ground with his bare feet as he kept up a horrible shrieking, crying sound. His strength was seeping away from him. He couldn't last much longer. He fell first to his knees and then on to his side, and the kids just hacked and slashed at him and clubbed him and swore at him even more.

Finally he slumped forward, face down in the road.

The kids jeered, kicked him, battered him . . .

'Stop it!' Courtney screamed. 'Stop it now.'

They stopped. Startled. Stood there panting and heaving, staring at the bloody mess on the ground, unable to quite believe what they had done.

Courtney went to the body. He was still just alive, still breathing. One yellow eye stared up at her, uncomprehending.

'Can't somebody just finish this?' she said, and Paul rushed forward. He had got another knife from somewhere. He leant over the Collector and stabbed him repeatedly in the back, but it was no good; he wasn't penetrating deeply enough to finish him off.

He was crying, his tears falling on to the bloody back of the Collector as his knife chopped and chopped and chopped. At last, DogNut and Robbie managed to pull him away and Jackson took his place.

'I'll do it,' she said, and stepped on the Collector's head, holding it still. She carefully placed the point of her spear in the same spot she had stabbed him before, just below the ear, but this time she was able to angle it towards his brain.

She pressed down with all her strength. His eye went wide, and then the life went out of it.

'It's done.'

36

Just as DogNut and his crew were heading off back to the museum, another group of kids were setting off on their own expedition, a mile away to the east at Buckingham Palace.

The mood in the two parties could not have been more different. DogNut's gang was in high spirits, coasting on a wave of bloodlust and sweet victory. They laughed and shouted as they re-enacted the death of the Collector. It was true that one or two of them, Courtney included, weren't joining in, but most of them were behaving like conquering heroes returning home after a war.

In contrast, Jester's group was quiet and miserable and fearful. They had no idea what might be waiting for them out there. They hadn't met their monsters yet.

Jester himself was furious. As he walked out through the palace gates, he was ranting to Shadowman and waving his hands in the air.

'Three!' he protested, showing three fingers. 'Three kids! What does David think I can do with three kids?'

'We'll be all right,' Shadowman tried to reassure him.

'No, seriously, Shadowman, what the hell does he think I'm gonna do with three bloody kids?'

'What did he say exactly?'

'Just a load of bullshit basically. As usual. Said he couldn't spare anyone else, that he didn't want to leave the palace undefended. The bastard couldn't even spare me any of his bloody guards. I'd feel a lot happier with a couple of red blazers armed with rifles in my squad.'

Shadowman checked them out. Jester's little group was armed with spears and knives. All except for Jester, who didn't seem to have a weapon of any kind. Unless he had a knife in the leather satchel he'd slung over his shoulder.

'It's always the same with David,' Jester went on. 'He makes all these big promises, then when it comes to it he doesn't give you half what you expected.'

'He doesn't like to risk putting his precious red guards in any danger, Jester,' said Shadowman. 'You should know that.'

'What's the point in having a trained army if you never let them fight in case you lose any of them? I don't get it. Instead of sending his soldiers into battle he sends bloody civilians.'

'Are they that bad?'

Jester lowered his voice and looked round to make sure that the three kids who were moping along behind them couldn't hear any of their conversation.

'He asked for volunteers. That's all we got. Well, there were five of them originally, but two dropped out overnight. This lot weren't exactly keen this morning, either. I begged David to give me some more, but he claimed he didn't want to force anyone. They're not completely useless, but they're nothing like the best fighters at the palace. We should have had Pod and his toughest rugby players, not those three dopes.'

The three dopes in question – an older boy and girl, and

another boy who looked about thirteen – were lagging further and further behind, dragging their feet and complaining to each other.

'What are their names?' asked Shadowman.

'The couple are Tom and Kate, the little guy's Alfie,' said Jester. 'He's good company, but I've never seen him in a fight.'

'Why did they volunteer if they didn't want to come in the first place?'

'David offered them extra food, special privileges. I doubt he'll keep his promise, but . . . I don't know. They probably mainly came because they were getting bored to death in the palace with nothing to do all day except work in the vegetable gardens. I don't suppose any of them seriously thought through how dangerous this might be. Stuck in the palace behind those high walls you can easily forget what it's like in the real world. The first sign of a fight they'll probably run all the way home.'

'Yeah, well, hopefully we won't get into any fights,' said Shadowman. 'That isn't the plan, is it?'

'I guess not. The plan is simply to look for kids to recruit.'

'Yes. Don't worry, Jest. I'll keep you out of trouble and maybe we'll pick up enough kids along the way to return as a proper fighting unit. In the meantime, any sign of any strangers and we scarper.'

'I don't need to tell them that.'

'You listen to me, OK?' said Shadowman. 'Do as I say. I'm used to this. I can spot the danger signs.'

'Thanks. If you hadn't agreed to come along, I think I'd have ditched the whole thing and told David he could go off recruiting himself. I can just see him in a royal bloody carriage swanning about, waving one hand out the window at his grateful subjects.'

The two of them laughed.

'But seriously, Shadowman,' Jester went on, 'what are our chances of getting into trouble?'

'I won't lie, Magic-Man, it's dangerous. The streets round here are generally pretty quiet during the day – there's very few strangers about – but I don't know what it's going to be like the further we get from the palace . . . You scared?'

'A little. You? D'you still get scared?'

'All the time,' said Shadowman. 'And you know what? I sometimes think it'd be better if you didn't parade about in that nasty coat of yours. It just reminds me of all the mates we've lost.'

Shadowman was referring to the patchwork coat that Jester always wore. He had cut a patch of material from the clothing of all the friends of his who had died since the disaster and sewed them on to it. There were forty patches, and while lately he was sewing on fewer and fewer patches, kids still died. If strangers didn't get them, there was always illness and accidents.

'It's not supposed to remind you of their deaths,' said Jester. 'It's supposed to remind you of their lives.'

There were patches representing Big-Man, Cool-Man and The Fox, as well as other kids who had holed up in the big house in Notting Hill with Jester and Shadowman after the disaster. When they'd been forced to leave, most had made it safely to Buckingham Palace, but some were only remembered by the patches on Jester's coat.

'Whatever,' said Shadowman. 'Living or dead, it still gives me the creeps, and I don't want to end up as just another decoration for you.'

'You?' said Jester. 'No chance. You're a survivor. I reckon you'll well outlive me.' He turned round and looked at Kate and Tom and Alfie, who were plodding along about ten metres behind them, their weapons drooping in their hands. 'Can't say the same for those three, mind you.'

37

She waited for the children to go past. Squatting down by the window in the empty shop. Feeling the tension among the others. They were hungry and hurting. They wanted to rush out now. Fall on the children and tear them to pieces. But there had been hunters around earlier, and she couldn't be sure where they were now. And if the hunters were close they would come with their spears and their knives and their clubs.

How she hated the hunters.

It hadn't always been like this. At first it had been easy – children wandered the streets lost and confused. Lots of them. Weak and weaponless. Back then the ones like her had the upper hand. They feasted day and night. They got strong. But the children got strong too. The ones they couldn't kill. They banded together. Moved into safe places. Learnt how to fight back. She had been forced to join up with others and work together as a pack or die. Every day there were fewer of them, though. Some were taken by the sickness, some starved to death, some were killed by the hunters.

She knew that soon she would have to move away from this area and find somewhere easier. Somewhere where plump little children didn't have sharp blades and heavy clubs.

She adjusted her sunglasses. The sun was bright today, making it hard to think. And as she waited, trying to pull her thoughts into some sort of shape, the children moved further and further away. Before, they would have attacked without a thought, torn into them with teeth and claws. Not now. They were learning to wait. They had found a new lair, in a tube station, hidden from the hunters. But if they showed themselves, if they timed it wrong, they would be found out and attacked. More of them would die. She had to wait, find the right way to do it. There would be others. Other children. Other things to eat. Earlier this morning they had found a nice fat cat and that had helped. Their bellies were sore, though. They needed to eat again soon. Eat properly. Before too long their hunger would force them into the open; they would have no choice but to attack whoever came close.

Children, though. It had to be children.

The only thing that made the pain go away was the flesh of children.

One of the others stood, lurched towards the children, dribbling and shaking. She grunted and raised her knife. Showing her authority.

He backed away.

Not now. Not yet.

It was too dangerous to charge out into the open like the old days.

Wait until the time was right.

38

DogNut and Courtney were sitting with Brooke in what the kids at the museum called the Hall of Gods. It was the entranceway to the Earth Galleries, a section of the museum devoted to the planet, with exhibits about volcanoes and rocks and earthquakes.

Brooke had explained that the rest of the Earth Galleries were sealed off, but that the kids used this area as a meeting place. It was suitably grand. At the back a long escalator led up through a giant scrap-metal globe to the upper galleries. It hadn't run since the power had all gone off soon after the disaster, but it still looked like a stairway to heaven. Lining the approach to the escalator were two rows of statues standing on plinths shaped like half globes. They depicted the advance of human knowledge, from superstition to science, starting with a figure of God the Creator. Opposite him was a statue of Atlas holding the world on his shoulders, then there was a Cyclops, a Medusa, and finally an astronaut standing across from a scientist at work with a microscope.

The walls that towered up several storeys on either side were black with silvery-white celestial maps painted on to them. Lit by flickering candlelight the whole place looked spooky and dramatic.

Chairs had been laid out facing the statues and that was where the three children sat.

'So why does the King of the Geeks use this place for council meetings then?' Courtney asked Brooke.

'Dunno,' said Brooke. 'Maybe he just thinks it's cool. Or maybe it's to remind us of where we stand in the world. He wants to build two more statues, apparently, showing the future, one of a kid and one of a sicko.'

'So what's stopping him?'

'We got a ton of nerds here, but we ain't got any artists.'

'True that,' said DogNut, and he gave a dismissive laugh.

They had returned to the museum in triumph, telling their stories, bigging themselves up. And now they were waiting in the Hall of Gods for Justin, who wanted to show them the work he was doing at the museum. DogNut was sitting behind Brooke, leaning over on to the back of her chair so that his right elbow was pressing against her shoulder.

He probably thought he was being clever, not being so obvious as to sit right next to her. Courtney wondered why she'd bothered going on the hunt. DogNut hadn't even noticed whether she was there or not. She should have stayed behind and caught up with Brooke, tried to re-establish their friendship. They'd been apart for a year and it was difficult to go back to how things had been, particularly because of how she felt about DogNut. She was pleased to see, though, that Brooke still acted totally offhand towards him, calling him Donut and taking the piss the whole time. She'd scoffed that it had taken so many of them to kill one grown-up. Not letting DogNut enjoy his triumph. That didn't mean she didn't fancy him, though. It was just her way.

Brooke was weird with guys. Like it was all a big cruel game. If they obviously liked her, she treated them like dirt, which only seemed to make them like her more. And if they didn't like her, if they weren't attracted by her killer looks, she'd do everything in her power to change their minds. It didn't matter what she thought of them. She'd encourage guys she didn't like just so they'd hang around her and make her feel like she was the most desirable thing in the world.

Courtney wished she had that power over boys. She watched DogNut with Brooke. He was so *obvious*. She almost felt a little bit sorry for him, so desperate to get Brooke to take an interest in him.

Right now he was fishing, asking Brooke a load of questions. It was clear he wanted to know whether Brooke was attached. He wouldn't come right out and ask it, though, and Brooke was pretending not to know what he was really talking about, and not giving him the sort of answers he wanted.

In the end Courtney forced it.

'So, you got a boyfriend here then, or not?' she asked.

'Might have.' Brooke leant back in her seat. Nonchalant.

'Yeah, but have you got one?'

'No. Of course not.'

'Result!' DogNut grinned.

'I don't got *one*, I got loads,' she said. 'I am, like, *the* most popular girl here. Most of the rest of them are either nerds or mingers like Jackson.'

'Jackson's cool,' said DogNut.

'You think so?' Brooke looked horrified.

'Yeah, she's well hard.'

'Right, but would you go out with her?'

'Does she even *like* boys?'

'Far as I know, but none of them will go near her. They're scared of her.'

'She scares me,' said Courtney.

'So what about you then?' Brooke asked Courtney. 'You got a boyfriend?'

Courtney blushed. Tried to avoid looking at DogNut. Didn't know what to say. In the end she just shrugged.

'Courtney's like Jackson,' said DogNut. 'All the guys are scared of her.'

'You look better since you ain't so fat,' said Brooke.

'Thanks.' Courtney loaded the word with as much sarcasm as she could.

'No, I mean it. You're kind of hard-looking now, muscular, like an athlete. Looks good on you.'

Courtney blushed deeper. In truth she had no idea how she looked to other people. Then she got cross. Brooke had skilfully switched the focus of attention off herself and on to Courtney. She was being deliberately vague because she didn't want to tell them the truth.

'So you ain't got, like, one special guy?' said Courtney.

'No. No one here's really my type.'

Brooke's type. Courtney knew all too well what type that was. She always went for the best-looking, most popular boy around. Didn't care if she liked him or not, but it was important to her to be seen with the guy that all the other girls wanted. *The top dog.* But here that was difficult, because the guys in charge were all nerds and geeks. It was hard for Brooke to operate properly. Robbie was the closest thing to a football star, but there wasn't much going for him. He was butters, and ever since DogNut had said he was weak and not really cut out to be a leader that was how

Courtney thought about him. That left the field open for DogNut to make a move. Maybe his plan would work. And once he was king of the castle Brooke would want to be seen with him.

Unless Courtney could put a stop to it somehow . . .

'You should visit the Tower with us,' she said. 'There's lots of fit guys there.'

'Maybe I will.'

'The fittest guy from the Tower ain't home right now,' said DogNut. 'He's sitting right behind you, gyal.'

Brooke turned round theatrically and pretended to be looking for someone.

'Move out the way, Donut,' she said, 'I can't see him. Where is he?'

'Ho, ho, ho,' said DogNut. 'Lol and all that. I'm all you need, babes. Show me someone here in Nerdville can compete with me!'

'That's why you've come here,' said Courtney, smiling. 'Admit it. You're the halfway ugly guy in the country of full-on uggs. You know that back at the Tower you don't stand a chance. The guys there make you look like nothing.'

'Like who?'

'Jordan Hordern.'

'Freak.'

'Tomoki.'

'Boring.'

'Ed . . .'

Courtney was pleased to see a spark light up in Brooke's eyes when she said Ed's name. There was still something there.

'How is he?' Brooke asked, trying to sound casual.

'Cool,' said Courtney. 'He's, like, second in command to Jordan Hordern. Everyone really likes him.'

'Are you in love with him then?' said DogNut, and he made some smoochy noises with his lips.

'Me? No.' Courtney's voice shot up an octave.

'Sounds like you are.'

'No way.'

'You should hear yourself, Courtney. You're, like, "Oh, Ed's so cool, Ed's so buff, Ed's such a leader of men, Ed's got lovely shoes".'

'I like Ed,' said Courtney.

'Me too,' said Brooke, and DogNut leapt in again.

'Yeah, well, don't get too excited,' he said. 'I asked him to come along on the expedition with us and he said no thanks, not interested in finding you, said you were like ancient history.'

Courtney had to turn away to hide the massive grin that she couldn't keep off her face. He'd said just about the worst thing he could. DogNut was fun, she loved him, but sometimes he could be pretty dense. He didn't understand Brooke at all. Telling her that a boy wasn't interested in her meant that she'd do everything in her power to change his mind.

Ed was a challenge now.

There was nothing Brooke hated more than a boy not being interested in her. If DogNut had said that Ed spent his whole time writing poems about her and drawing her face on walls, she would have laughed at him and crossed him off her list.

DogNut's own naked enthusiasm was all too clear to Brooke. She would play him and tease him and offer him the odd crumb until she'd ruined his life and then go off with someone else.

'Yeah, well,' she said. 'Maybe I do need to come to the Tower with you and remind Ed just what he's missing out on.'

'Brooke,' said DogNut, laying everything on the table in a pathetic last-ditch stand. 'You don't want to go there. I came all this way to find you. *Me*, I did that. Not Ed. Don't that mean nothing to you?'

Brooke put on the sort of face you would make to a crying toddler and turned to give DogNut a playful kiss.

'Oh, Donut, you're so sweet. You'll make somebody a lovely husband.'

'There's only one person I want to marry.'

Brooke stood up, bursting with mock excitement.

'Oh, really, really . . . and I know just who it is!'

'Yeah, right,' said DogNut, leaning back in his chair and putting his hands behind his head.

'It's my girl, Courtney, isn't it?' Brooke cried.

'Courtney?' DogNut looked horrified. 'You're joking.'

'Oh, thanks, great,' said Courtney, who was still reeling from what Brooke had said. Red-faced, her cheeks burning, she jumped to her feet, not sure which of the two of them she was most angry with.

'No, Courtney, Courtney,' said DogNut, throwing up his hands. 'I didn't mean it like that. I love you to bits and all, but you're like a mate, like my sister, you ain't exactly . . .'

'Ain't exactly what?'

Courtney was going to start crying if she wasn't careful and that would blow everything big time. All she could do was turn round, kick her chair out of the way and storm off between the statues.

'I'll leave you two alone together,' she shouted as she got to the astronaut. 'You can have a good laugh about me.'

'No, no, Courtney, come on . . .'

'You *idiot*,' said Brooke once she was sure Courtney had gone.

'What?' said DogNut, looking hurt. 'What have I done now?'

'Can't you see it?'

'See what?'

'You really are a dumb-ass. Dumbo Donut, as dumb as they come.'

'What are you talking about?'

'That girl is nuts about you. You are all she thinks about.'

'Courtney? No way . . . Not Courtney . . .'

'I'm gonna go and see she's all right,' said Brooke. 'I shouldn't have said nothing. I couldn't help it. Me and my big stupid mouth. You wait here for Justin. One guy who understands women even less than you do.'

Brooke followed Courtney back into the other part of the museum. DogNut got up and was about to go after her when Justin appeared, carrying a torch.

'Sorry to keep you waiting,' he said, 'but I've been in meetings all morning.'

It was such a ridiculous thing for a fifteen-year-old kid to say that DogNut burst out laughing.

39

Justin led DogNut through the museum away from the public areas, into the warren of corridors, offices and backrooms that were hidden behind the scenes. He had grown a lot more confident in the last year, the way a nerd often can. He had blossomed from being an outsider and loner into being respected for his cleverness. He was among his own people here, and DogNut could tell that they liked him and looked up to him. He had the self-assuredness of an adult.

'Brooke told me you've had an exciting morning,' he said as they walked. 'Out there ridding the streets of filth and vermin.'

'Something like that.'

'So, Paul got his revenge?'

'Yeah.' DogNut thought about this for a moment. 'I'm not sure how much good it's done him, though. The guy's a mess.'

'He was a bit unstable before all this, if you really want to know,' said Justin. 'He's been acting weird for the last few weeks. I think he's been pretty depressed.'

'Well, he's seriously depressed now,' said DogNut. 'All the way back he was either blubbing or raving "*You shouldn't'a let her die, you abandoned her, you're all to blame, boo hoo hoo.*"'

'He has a point.'

'Come again?'

'You *didn't* protect her, did you?'

DogNut stopped and confronted Justin.

'You weren't there, Justin. You don't know how it went down. I don't suppose you get out much, don't get to see any sickos up close and personal. But maybe you remember what it was like when we found the lorry back in the day?'

'It's not something you can forget. That lorry saved all our lives.'

'Yeah, well, remember you and me sat in the cab and tried to drive the bastard?'

'Of course I do.'

'Now, think back, Justin,' said DogNut. 'You're sitting there popping cold hard sweat, crapping yourself, swearing at the engine. You remember?'

'Yes. I remember I couldn't get it started.'

'Now, tell me, at the time, did you have any idea what anyone else was up to?'

'Not really, no,' said Justin. 'I was too busy concentrating on trying to get the lorry to move forward.'

'Exactly. When you're in a fight like that, you got to look after yourself; you can't be thinking about what everyone else is up to. You don't know what's going down. Back then, in the lorry, it was just you and me.'

'Yes, but I wasn't in charge, DogNut.'

'Say what?'

'I wasn't in charge. I had a job to do. To drive the lorry. And I was doing my job. Ed was in charge, not me. He was making sure everyone else was all right. That was *his* job.'

'Ed, Ed, Ed . . .!' DogNut slapped his forehead. 'Why's everyone keep going on about Ed?'

'Ed was a good leader. And that's the sort of
leader has to do.'

'He wasn't perfect!' DogNut protested. 'He ne
that bird behind when we drove the lorry off, the
was sick, the French girl – what was her name?'

'Frédérique.'

'Yeah, her. We nearly went without her.'

'Yes, but we didn't.'

'You're confusing me,' said DogNut.

'You said yesterday that I was to blame for aba
David on the bridge,' said Justin.

'Did I? Yeah, maybe I did.'

'Well, you were right. I don't mind accepting
ibility. At that moment I was in charge. And look
knowing everything I know about David now,
did the right thing.'

'Probably.'

'OK, and you probably did the right thing
left Olivia behind. You had to think about ever
Paul's pissed off – he always will be; he'll never fo
– but you're just going to have to deal with it.'

'I didn't do the right thing,' said DogNut
'That poor little girl. I shouldn't never have left h

'You did what you had to do,' said Justin, and
open a door.

It led into a library, flooded with light from
down one side, lined with shelves and shelves of
A spiral staircase led to an upper gallery where two
leaning on the railing discussing something. Th
when Justin and DogNut came in.

'That's Chris and one of his librarians,' said J
remember Chris?'

'Yeah, the book guy. Hiya, Chris!'

Chris nodded back. Like a lot of the kids at the museum he was wearing old-fashioned clothes, in his case what looked like robes. He had grown a rather sad fuzzy beard and moustache in an attempt to look older.

'Don't mind us,' said Justin. 'I'm just showing DogNut around.' He lowered his voice and moved closer to DogNut. 'You should have seen Chris's face when he discovered the library here. You'd have thought it was a hoard of sweets and chocolate or something, not dusty old books. And it's not just these ones. There are libraries all over the place. This is mostly geological books, I think, but he's moving a lot of them out and replacing them with other ones from the different libraries, making his own collection. He even found a first edition of *The Origin of Species*.'

'Yeah?' said DogNut, trying to sound like he knew what Justin was talking about.

'He virtually lives in here now,' said Justin. 'Calls himself the Librarian. He has a study group working through all the books. Reckons the knowledge in them and the way we use it is what's going to keep us alive. I can't argue with that.'

'Why'd you bring me here?' asked DogNut, hardly listening. He was looking around the library, distracted, feeling shut in by all these books.

'He's writing his own book,' said Justin. 'Of all our stories, so that they'll never be forgotten. He writes everything down in these big ledgers he found. The lives of every kid here. It's so that we have a proper record of what's happened, so that we won't forget it, and hopefully there'll be useful information in there as well, about the sickos. *The Chronicles of Survival*, he calls them. He tells the best stories to the younger kids at night – finding the lorry, the Battle of Lambeth Bridge, the great fire – it's all written up.'

'Yeah . . . and?'

'It'd be good to get your story down, DogNut.'

'Yeah, maybe. Not sure I'd want everyone to know about what happened to Olivia, though.'

'It's part of it,' said Justin. 'And if you want to be in charge you have to think about that sort of thing. You have to be responsible for everyone. You have to make hard decisions.'

'Who said I wanted to be in charge?'

Justin sighed. He'd remained calm throughout their conversation, unlike DogNut, who was sweaty and hyped up, shifting his weight from one foot to the other, his head bobbing on his long, scrawny neck.

Justin waited for him to stop jigging and once he'd got his full attention he carried on. 'I may be a lot of things, DogNut,' he said. 'I've been called just about every name you could think of, and some you couldn't, but I've never been called stupid.'

'Did I call you stupid?'

'I've talked to everyone who went out today,' Justin continued. 'Robbie included. That's what my meetings were about. It's obvious what you're up to.'

'Oh yeah? And what *am* I up to?'

'You think you can stroll in here and take over.'

'No way, man. That's not my game,' DogNut protested. 'I don't want to step on no toes. This is your party. Whatever you been told you been told wrong.'

'OK. Good. As long as that's clear.'

'Crystal.'

'Is it?'

'Yeah.'

'Because I don't want anything to happen here that could screw things up. We've worked hard to make this a good place to live. Apart from the sickos in the lower level, it's just about perfect.'

'Yeah. Brooke told me about that. How many you got down there?'

'Don't know for sure. Not that many. You know how they love the dark, how they love to be underground. It was too dangerous to try and clear them out, so we just secured all the doors so that they can't get through to our bit. One day we ought to hire some hunters to go in and flush them out, but they don't really bother us. You remember they used to say you were never more than ten feet away from a rat in London? Or something like that?'

'Yeah.'

'But you never saw them, did you? They kept out of our way, just like the sickos do now.'

'So we safe, yeah?'

'The museum's built like a fortress, so it's easy to defend. Plus there's plenty of land to grow food on. It works well, but it's complicated. It's not just running around smashing sickos' heads in. We've moved on from that.'

'If you say so.' DogNut shrugged.

'Let me tell you what I do, DogNut,' said Justin. 'As the boy they voted to be in charge of all this. And you think about it. Think about what sort of life you want for yourself. I get up at dawn. I check with all the kids who've been on late duty that nothing's happened overnight. I personally go to every entrance and exit and make sure that they're secure. Then I check with the kitchen

253

staff what food we've got for the day. Do we need to find more? Is there enough water? Do we have enough fuel for cooking? What are the menus for breakfast, lunch and supper? Will everyone get enough ascorbic acid in their diet? Then we have morning council, where any kids with any problems, complaints, questions, whatever come and talk to me. After that I . . .'

'Yeah, yeah, yeah, all right,' said DogNut. 'I get the picture. Is boring, right?'

'Not for me it isn't, no,' said Justin. 'I find it all fascinating. But for you . . .'

'It don't have to be that way, blood,' said DogNut. 'At the Tower Jordan Hordern is a general, a fighting man . . .'

'You've seen a few other settlements recently, haven't you?' asked Justin.

'Yeah.'

'And the kids in charge – were they more like Jordan or were they more like me?'

'Well . . . I guess they was more like *you*. Nuts.'

Justin laughed. 'You're probably right,' he said. 'Now come and look at this. I want to show you something . . .'
He went over to the windows and pointed down to a big courtyard inside the museum buildings that had obviously been used as a car park.

'What am I supposed to be looking at?' DogNut asked.

'The rather large white object with wheels.'

'OMG!' DogNut cried. 'Look at that. It's the beast!'

Parked on one side of the car park was the Tesco lorry.

'Yep,' said Justin. 'We parked it there when we arrived. Hasn't left the car park since.'

'I guess the food ran out ages ago.'

'Lasted about two weeks. The lorry's still useful, though.'

'What for?'
'Safe storage.'
'How d'you mean?'
'Come with me and I'll show you.'

40

They didn't like it around here. Shadowman had led them across the wide Euston Road, and the effect had been like crossing a river from one country to another. The six-lane highway seemed to act like a boundary between the safe area to the south and the wild lands to the north. Maybe it only felt that way to Shadowman, who hadn't been north of Euston Road in over a year, but he was sure the others sensed it too. It wasn't helped by the sun going behind heavy black clouds just as they reached the far pavement. The day grew dark and chilly. In the cold gloom everywhere looked very different. The buildings here were grey and dirty and dead.

Tom and his girlfriend, Kate, picked up their pace and kept close to Jester and Shadowman. Alfie had been entertaining them by singing old disco songs. He'd gone through 'YMCA', 'Thriller' and 'Staying Alive'. That was their favourite. They'd all joined in, their high voices rising to the heavens.

'Ha, ha, ha, ha, staying alive . . .'

None of them had Alfie's energy, however, and he'd carried on singing long after the others had stopped.

But as they came past Euston station Alfie shut up as well. All they could hear now was the sound of their footsteps bouncing back off the walls of the buildings. It was so quiet. A quiet like London hadn't known for hundreds of years. The whole buzz and hum and bustle, the engine throb of a city, had been silenced. There didn't even seem to be any birds around. It unsettled the kids and made them nervous. They'd seen a couple of strangers earlier, solitary ones, badly diseased, slow and feeble. No threat at all. Laughable. One of them had even been shuffling along the pavement on his bottom, pulling with his heels and pushing with his knuckles.

Tom and Kate had perked up and wanted to attack them for the hell of it. To boost their confidence. But Shadowman had insisted they press on. Noise and the smell of blood would only attract other strangers. It was best to keep moving while the going was good. They had no idea what lay ahead, after all.

They hadn't seen any other children yet. Not one. They hadn't passed any obvious hiding-places, strongholds that they themselves might have picked to live in. The last time Shadowman had come up this way there had been lots of kids around, squatting in the houses. They must all have either been killed or had clubbed together into larger groups and moved into safer buildings, like David's group at the palace. Shadowman was wondering how far they'd have to go before they found anyone else of their own age.

'Have we got a limit?' he asked Jester, trying to break the tension of these gloomy streets.

'A limit to what?'

'How far we go. How long we stay away. You haven't really said. Do we go back tonight? Tomorrow? Next week?'

'I vote we go back now,' said Tom.

'Wait, surely we're going back before tonight,' said Kate anxiously, holding on to Tom's arm. 'I'm not staying out in the dark somewhere strange. You never said we were going to be away overnight.'

'That's because there *is* no definite plan,' said Jester. 'There can't be.'

'That's just great,' said Kate.

'No,' said Jester. 'What I mean is . . . we don't know how far we'll have to go to find any other kids. OK, to be fair, if we haven't found anyone by this evening, then we head back before it gets dark. Does that sound all right? If we *do* find other kids, though, then it might make sense to stay with them until tomorrow.'

'I vote we go back tonight, whatever,' said Kate.

'Say we do find some other kids?' asked Alfie. 'Then what happens?'

'Then we see what's what.' Jester shook his head. 'Jesus, I can't see into the future. We might think it's worth pressing on and looking for some more kids. Or we might just go back to the palace with whoever we can persuade to join us.'

'Great plan, Jester,' said Alfie sarcastically.

'I vote Shadowman's in charge,' said Kate.

'Will you shut up, Kate?' Jester snapped. 'We're not taking votes.'

Kate mumbled something inaudible.

'You're not helping,' said Jester. 'Look, this is really only a scouting party, all right? To try and find what's out there. There might be no one else, or there might be loads of kids. We might even find some who've got a better set-up than David, and decide we're not going back at all.'

'Sod that,' said Tom. 'All my stuff's at the palace. All my mates.'

'Yeah. Joke, Tom. OK? You really think there's going to be a better set-up than we've got? I don't think so.'

'So where exactly do you want to look next?' asked Shadowman.

Jester stopped walking and pulled a map out of his pocket.

'We'll head up as far as Camden, I reckon,' he said, studying the map. 'Check it out. It's the sort of place kids might end up. Then I'll decide where we go after that.'

'If you ask me,' said Tom, 'this is one big waste of time. We're not going to find anything. Nothing's going to happen.'

The words were barely out of his mouth when a stranger lurched out of a side-road no more than three metres away. He was a middle-aged father with a broken arm, the bone sticking out through the skin, his face a mess of yellow boils. It was hard to tell who was the more surprised, the father or the kids.

They all froze.

Jester and the rest of them gripped their weapons tight.

The father tilted his head to one side, staring at them with wide, lidless eyes.

'I vote we kill him,' said Tom.

'I vote we run,' said Shadowman.

'There's only one of him,' said Kate.

'Yeah?' said Shadowman. 'Try looking the other way.'

Tom turned round. Coming up the street from the direction of Euston Road were about twenty strangers. Moving fast.

'Holy shit,' said Tom.

Kate grabbed him and pulled him along the road. The others were already running. Shadowman took the lead. Streaking ahead on his long legs. He was more used to life on the streets. More used to running. So that he'd started to move the instant he saw the mass of strangers. No thinking about it, no panic, just off and sprinting.

Glancing back, though, he realized that he'd have to let the rest of them catch up. They were no different to the strangers – in a group they were strong; if they got split up, they were easy meat.

'Come on,' he yelled. 'Leg it!'

He slowed just enough for the others to draw level. All except Alfie, who was smaller and not so fast.

'Wait for me,' he shouted.

'You have to go faster!' Jester screamed back at him, as the gap widened between them.

'I can't. I'm going as fast as I can.'

'Wait for him,' said Shadowman. 'We don't leave anyone behind.'

'Hurry up, Alfie!' Jester sounded cross. Not angry at the strangers, but at Alfie. Would he have just run off and left him if Shadowman hadn't said something? Shadowman wondered about Jester sometimes. Wondered if he ever really cared about anyone other than himself.

There wasn't time to think about any of this, because the road ahead was blocked as well now. Another smaller but no less dangerous group of strangers was approaching from the north. The kids veered off to the east, smashing their way past two lone strangers, a mother and a father. Shadowman had borrowed a club from the palace for extra firepower, and he used it without hesitation to crush the skull of the mother, who crumpled on to the bonnet of a car, spraying it with a foul cocktail of bodily fluids. It was Alfie who took out the father, jabbing his spear into his guts. Unfortunately he didn't have time to yank it out again, and had to carry on without it, leaving the father staggering about in the centre of the road trying to pull it free. At last he succeeded, but it was like pulling out a plug. The father hissed as a steaming grey mass of intestines flopped out of the wound. He collapsed to his knees and three of the pursuing strangers stopped to make the most of this free meal.

Nothing else barred their way and the kids were able to run on, bobbing and weaving through the side-streets until they were absolutely sure they'd left all the strangers behind. At last they risked stopping, and leant against a wall, panting and wheezing and clutching their sides.

'Bloody hell,' Tom gasped. 'What was that? Why weren't they all indoors? Why weren't they sleeping? Don't they know they're only supposed to come out at night?'

'Maybe nobody told them,' said Shadowman.

'Seriously, guys,' said Kate, who was shaking and white-faced. 'I really do vote we go back now. This is serious. I never expected there was gonna be armies of them.'

'They weren't an army,' said Shadowman. 'They don't make armies. They don't have the brains. And none of us got hurt.'

'Yes, but bloody hell, Shadowman. *Bloody hell*. That was scary. I haven't seen that many strangers in one place since this all began.'

'Come on,' Tom pleaded. 'Can't we just go home? There needs to be more of us. This is stupid.'

'We're not going home,' said Jester.

'Why? Why not?' Kate shouted. 'Why the hell not?'

'Look.'

There were more strangers coming from the south, and once again the kids were running.

41

Justin unlocked a heavy door and took DogNut outside into the car park they'd seen from the library. DogNut had been aware of a chugging noise, like a motor running, and was intrigued to see what it was. The air was filled with petrol fumes and DogNut saw a petrol-fuelled generator standing next to the lorry.

He was surprised to see Paul fiddling with the generator. Justin seemed surprised as well.

'Are you all right, Paul?' he asked. 'You really don't need to come back to work just yet.'

'I'm all right,' said Paul, straightening up. 'It helps to be doing something.'

His eyes were red from crying, though his pale cheeks were dry. He looked very jittery, as if he might burst into tears again at any moment.

'We can find something easier for you –'

'This is my job,' said Paul angrily, cutting Justin off.

'I know,' said Justin.

'Don't you think I can do it?'

'I didn't say that. In fact, forget I said anything. Can you open the lorry for us?'

Paul said nothing, but sullenly fished a keyring from his trouser pocket. It was heavy with keys of all shapes and sizes. He selected one and slotted it into a padlock on the back of the lorry. He snapped the padlock open and slid the door up.

DogNut covered his mouth and gagged. The smell that came out of the lorry was disgusting. Sour and rotten.

'Jesus, who's died?' he said.

'About four-fifths of the population of the world,' said Justin.

'Very funny.'

There was a metre or so of clear space inside the lorry before it was blocked by hanging black drapes.

'Climb aboard,' said Justin, and the three of them clambered up. It was hot inside and the smell was worse, but Justin and Paul seemed not to notice it. DogNut was fighting not to puke up everywhere.

'How are they today?' Justin asked Paul.

'Quiet,' was all Paul said, and he yawned and rubbed his neck through his roll-neck jumper. He looked very tired.

Justin grabbed a torch that was hanging from a hook and switched it on as Paul rolled the door back down.

'We need to keep the light out,' he said.

Once the door was closed, Paul stepped over to the drapes and pulled them aside like a magician revealing a trick.

A row of bars had been fixed across the lorry and behind them sat three half-naked sickos, two fathers and a mother, chained to the side of the lorry.

Seriously freaking nuts.

Justin's torch played across the three adults, picking out features.

They didn't look too badly diseased. DogNut had seen a lot worse. These three showed some signs of the blistering to the skin that was the most obvious symptom, as if something evil was bubbling up from deep inside their bodies, but there were no signs of rot or decay or the livid fungal blooms that adults showed in the more advanced stages of the illness. There were other signs. The whites of their eyes were yellow and their skin tone in general was greyish. They looked half starved as well: desperately thin, their bones showing, their bellies swollen. They were dressed in the tattered remains of clothing that had become blackened filthy rags. They were losing their hair, the mother almost completely bald.

The three of them stared at DogNut, mouths hanging open, showing their purple gums and brown, rotten teeth. One father, the older of the two, started to drool, a long rope of saliva hanging down off his dry and cracked lower lip.

Justin sniggered. 'He wants to eat you.'

The father's tongue started to slowly squeeze out of his mouth. Muddy-coloured, swollen and blistered, it looked horribly like a turd.

'Oh, gross!' said DogNut.

'He's getting worse,' said Paul.

DogNut noticed that the other father was muzzled like a vicious dog, with leather straps tight round his face.

'He's a biter,' Justin explained when he caught DogNut looking. 'We have to be very careful, obviously.'

'Obviously. You wouldn't want your pet sicko to do you an injury.'

'They're not pets,' said Justin. 'We don't keep them for fun.'

Fun? thought DogNut. How could anyone possibly think this was fun?

He kept his hand clamped over his nose and mouth. The stench in here was appalling. There were piles of excrement on the floor and more of it was smeared up the walls. There were a couple of overflowing buckets at the back. The smell of their waste fought with the smell of the grown-ups themselves. They gave off the distinctive sour odour of decay and what the kids thought of as the sickness smell, a sort of mix of cheap sweets, school toilets and old ladies' perfume that stuck in your throat.

'We keep them out here in the car park,' said Justin, 'so that if they did escape, which I seriously doubt they ever could, they wouldn't be able to get at any of our kids. It makes everyone feel safer, knowing we don't keep them in the building.'

'Why do you keep them in the dark like this?'

'It keeps them fresh.'

'Fresh? Why? What are you planning? To eat them then? Yeah, I'll have the mother. Deep fried. She might crisp up a bit.'

'Of course we're not planning to eat them.'

'Then what the hell *are* you planning to do with them?' said DogNut. 'Teach them to dance? I mean why have you got three bloody sickos chained up out here? I don't get it.'

'Well –'

'Oh, Justin,' DogNut butted in. 'I gotta get out of here. I can't stand this smell any longer.'

'Sure, OK. Sorry. I guess we're used to it.'

He and Paul replaced the drapes, opened the door and climbed down off the lorry before Paul pulled the door back down and locked it.

DogNut stood bent over, drawing in great gulps of clean air, trying to clear the cloying stink from his nostrils. He was fighting not to be sick. Rocking back and forth, swearing, as slowly his head stopped spinning. Finally he sat down on a little camping stool that Paul obviously used.

'Right,' he said, his voice husky. 'What are they for then?'

'We need them for our experiments,' said Justin.

'Experiments?'

'We're trying to find out about the disease. Those three in there are guinea pigs. They've lived much longer than any of the others we've caught.'

'You're telling me you carry out experiments on them?'

'We take their blood, tissue samples . . .'

'Tissue samples? You mean you cut bits off them?'

'That makes it sound worse than it is. We take skin samples, saliva, anything that oozes out of them, really, excrement . . .'

'You collect their shit?'

'Sometimes.'

'You guys sure know how to party, don't you?'

Justin grabbed hold of DogNut's forearm, squeezing it tight.

'If we're going to find out how the disease works, we have to know everything about it.'

'Can't we just wait for them all to die off, and forget all about the bloody disease?'

'How old arc you, DogNut?' asked Justin.

'Fifteen, why?'

'That's good.'

'Why?'

'What happened when the disease hit?'

'Everybody over the age of fourteen got sick, the rest of us . . .'

267

'We were fine, right?' Justin was getting excited, his voice rising in pitch. 'But what happened when you got older?' he went on. 'When you turned fifteen?'

'Nothing.'

'Exactly. You didn't get ill straight away.'

'Far as I can tell, you don't get ill full stop.'

'As far as you can tell?'

'Yeah.'

'But what about in the future?' Justin asked. 'Can you guarantee that won't change? Do you know for sure you'll never get ill?'

'I got no idea, man. I try not to think about that sort of thing.'

'Exactly. You've got no idea. And do you know whether you can catch it off a grown-up?'

'No. If you get too close to them, they usually kill you, so who knows?'

'Who knows? That's right. That's exactly one hundred per cent right. Who knows? And what if you get bitten? Could it be passed on to you that way?'

'Dunno.'

'Right again. You don't know. Loads of kids have been bitten and most of them have died of some infection. Not from whatever new disease it is that killed most of the grown-ups off. There are plenty of old diseases banging about inside sickos, like cholera and typhus and, I don't know, dry rot, and if you get bitten you're just as likely to die of blood poisoning as anything else. But can they pass on the prime infection with a bite?'

'Stop asking me questions, Justin.'

'It's what scientists do. Ask questions.'

'Well, they don't ask me.'

'Listen, DogNut,' said Justin, 'so far nobody's lived long enough after being bitten for us to tell what might happen. What we need to do is test the blood of someone, a child, obviously, who's been attacked.'

'I expect you've got volunteers queuing round the block,' DogNut scoffed. 'Me! Me! Me! Bite *me!*'

'DogNut. You have to take this seriously,' said Justin. 'If we can find the causes of the illness, how it works, then maybe we can find a cure.'

'A cure?'

'Yes!' said Justin, grinning like a madman now. 'Imagine if we could turn all those sickos out there back into real mothers and fathers. All you can think about is fighting them, killing them, wiping them out. We're thinking about curing them.'

'What do you want to cure them for?' said DogNut incredulously. 'Let them die, I say. Then the world will belong to us.'

'What kind of world, though?' said Justin. 'And how will we survive in it?'

'We ain't doing too bad.'

'DogNut's right!' said Paul. He'd been lurking by the generator and DogNut had forgotten all about him. 'We should kill them all.'

'How can you say that, Paul?' asked Justin. 'After all the work you've done with us on those three in there?'

'How can I say it?' Paul was wide-eyed and getting hysterical. 'Because they killed my sister. And if you're on their side then you killed my sister too.'

'Don't be ridiculous, Paul.'

'Oh, I'm ridiculous, am I? You think it's funny my sister died?'

'No, I don't. Why would I think that? It's awful. I am really sorry for you. But this is why we need to find a cure so things like that won't happen again.'

'It won't happen again if we kill them all.'

'Listen, Paul, you really should go and rest. Lie down somewhere.'

'You don't want me here, do you?'

'Quite frankly, no. Not if you're a danger to the patients.'

'A danger to *them*!' Paul screamed. 'You've got it all round the wrong way, Justin. You're on *their* side. You all are.'

'Please, Paul, go and chill. I'll find someone else to look after the lorry.'

'Don't worry, I'm going!' Paul snapped, and he stormed off, swearing at a couple of little kids who were feeding some chickens inside a big pen.

DogNut watched him go. Not sure what to think. Paul's aggressive attitude was making it hard to feel any sympathy for him.

'He'll be all right,' said Justin.

'He did have a point, mate,' said DogNut. 'It's seriously screwy keeping those sickos in there.'

'He's been looking after them for ages,' said Justin. 'He was always good with them. Like a zookeeper. I always thought, in a funny way, he was quite attached to them.'

'It ain't right, Justin.'

'What if you got sick, DogNut?' Justin snapped, finally losing his temper. 'What if you found you had the disease? You'd want a cure then, wouldn't you? You wouldn't laugh at what we're doing here.'

'True that. But just how d'you think you're going to go about finding a cure? You? Huh? A fifteen-year-old kid?'

270

'Come with me and I'll show you,' said Justin.

'No way,' said DogNut. 'You ain't showing me any more pet sickos.'

'We don't have any more. At the moment it's just these three,' said Justin. 'No. I want to show you the labs.'

'The labs. Of course. Every mad scientist needs a laboratory . . .'

42

Jester's party were standing by the long-empty departures board in King's Cross station, tensed and alert, their darting eyes stretched wide as they adjusted to the dim light – not fixing on anything, looking in every direction for any signs of movement. The last hour had been incredibly stressful and their bodies were so pumped with adrenalin they felt wired to the mains. They gave off a pungent reek of stress and fear. Shadowman hadn't had time to tell the others to try to mask their scent, and was worried that the smell might attract any strangers who might be hiding out in here. Strangers loved dark places and the tube tunnels beneath the mainline station were a perfect nesting place.

It appeared to be deserted up here, however. Nothing moved. The shops had long since been looted. Trains that would never again go anywhere stood dead at the platforms.

They'd been driven steadily eastwards as they tried to avoid the roving gangs of strangers who seemed to be everywhere in this part of town. Any moves to go north, the direction in which they had originally been intending to head, or south, back towards the palace, had been blocked. A particularly determined group of strangers had followed them for the last half-hour as they'd meandered backwards and forwards, trying to find a hiding-place or a safe path away from the danger. In the end they'd taken a route that ran roughly parallel to the Euston Road and had eventually come to King's Cross station.

It had been Jester who'd suggested they should actually go into the station. He'd pointed out that the train tracks were wide and clear and open and some distance from any buildings. It was unlikely that any strangers would be hiding out on the rails, and if any did approach they'd be able to see them from a long way off.

As none of the others had a better suggestion, they hadn't argued, and they'd trooped in off the street.

Jester was trying to sound confident. 'The tracks run straight north from here,' he said. 'We can make good time and cover a lot of distance pretty quickly.'

'What do we want to go north for?' said Tom.

'You're not seriously thinking of carrying on with this stupid trip, are you?' Kate added.

'The best thing we can do is find some other kids to help us,' said Jester.

'What bloody kids?' Tom was getting angrier and angrier.

'Listen, Tom,' Jester pleaded, 'we're not going to find any train tracks running south, are we? Not from round here. We're on the wrong side of London. So let's just get well away from this place, OK?'

'Crap.'

'Shut up,' said Shadowman.

'You shut up,' said Tom. 'You ain't exactly been a lot of help so far.'

'Don't have a go at Shadowman,' said Jester.

'Both of you shut up,' Shadowman snapped, and Jester looked shocked.

'What –'

'Listen!'

Shadowman said this so urgently they all fell silent and listened. There was the familiar shuffling sound of approaching strangers.

'Crap,' Tom repeated. 'Crap, crap, crap.'

They emerged from the shadows into a pool of light on the station concourse, a long line of strangers much more diseased than the ones they'd seen out on the streets. Some of them looked barely human. Huge chunks of their faces were missing, and what flesh remained was swollen and bloated and popping with boils.

'Crap.'

'Too many to fight,' Shadowman shouted. 'On to the tracks!'

They raced past the departures board and vaulted over a set of ticket turnstiles, then careered along the platform. There was a long Intercity train parked on each side, the type of trains that seem to go on forever. The kids' feet pounded on the hard concrete of the platform. They might have looked like any group of passengers running to catch a train if it wasn't for the collection of diseased and rotting adults that followed them.

They ran past an endless blur of doors and windows, but at last came to the end of one train and were able to jump down on to the tracks. Then they were out past the great overhanging canopy of the station roof and into the daylight. They slowed down. Every time they were forced to run it took more out of them – their legs ached, their lungs burned, their throats were dry, their feet sore and blistered in their grubby old trainers.

They kept moving, looking down so as not to lose their footing as they stepped from one sleeper to the next, avoiding the loose clinker that lay between them.

Tom, crippled by a stitch in his side, stopped and bent over. Acid had risen in his gullet and he wanted to be sick. Surely they didn't need to run so hard now. The strangers had appeared to be a particularly badly infected bunch, and unlikely to keep up. And hopefully their fear of the sun would hold them back.

Tom straightened up.

'Oh, crap.'

Now they all stopped. Appalled at what they saw ahead of them. A tunnel, and every single train track ran straight into its huge black mouth.

'That's just great,' said Tom. 'Well done, Jester. We'll find some tracks to lead us north, will we? Have a nice walk in the fresh air?'

'How was I to know?'

'Why did we listen to you?'

'I ain't going in there,' said Alfie, staring at the dark tunnel, trying not to cry.

'We'll just have to get off the tracks,' said Shadowman, hoping to avoid another pointless and tiring argument. He'd been holding back, biting his tongue, not wanting to step on Jester's toes, but he was beginning to wonder whether he should take charge. It would at least take the pressure off Jester.

'Yeah?' said Tom. 'Good plan, Batman. I'd never have thought of that.'

'Piss off, Tom,' said Shadowman.

'Leave Tom alone,' said Kate, moving next to her boyfriend.

'All you two do is moan,' said Shadowman. 'How does that help, exactly?'

'Sod you,' said Tom bitterly. 'Once we're away from here, I don't care what any of the rest of you say, me and Kate are going back to the palace.'

'They're coming,' said Alfie.

They looked back to see that the strangers from the station were trying to slither down off the platform on to the train tracks.

Shadowman looked around – there was a bank on one side, too steep to climb. A mess of fences and building works on the other. They could run or they could fight. He saw a way to unite the group and lift their spirits. The strangers would only be able to get down in ones and twos. They were groggy and uncoordinated, they struggled with their balance and climbing was something they found difficult.

'Come on. We can at least get rid of that lot,' he said, striding over to where the first of the grown-ups was crawling across the tracks. He went straight up to it and as it rose to its feet he swung his club like a batter, splattering its brains over the back end of the train.

Tom and Kate cheered.

'Yeah!' Tom shouted. 'Now you're talking. Let's take them out!'

The next few minutes were merciless. The confused and feeble strangers carried on trying to get down off the platform and Shadowman's calculations were correct. They were arriving singly, making them easy targets. His club rose and fell, smacking into bone. Tom and Kate's swords

276

were soon covered in blood from the tips of their blades to the pommels on the end of the grips. Alfie was throwing stones and yelling madly.

Only Jester held back, shouting instructions, but keeping clear of the bloodshed.

Soon thirteen strangers lay dead or dying, and the rest of them realized they were beaten. They retreated back along the platform towards the station.

The kids cheered again and hurled insults after the limping, defeated grown-ups. They looked at each other, covered in gore, exhausted, sweaty, but exhilarated.

'Slice and dice,' said Tom.

'Mincemeat,' said Alfie.

'You still look very clean, Jester?' said Kate, staring at his patchwork coat that had only a couple of spots of blood on it. 'Didn't see you doing much damage.'

Shadowman kept quiet. He wasn't looking at Jester, wasn't interested in whether or not he'd pulled his weight. He'd noticed something. While they'd been fighting, a smaller group of strangers had emerged from the tunnel down the tracks, no doubt lured by the noise and the smell of blood. There were six of them, and they looked considerably tougher and less sick than the ones from the station.

'The party's not over yet,' he said wearily, and pointed to the new arrivals.

Jester erupted angrily. 'You think I can't do any damage? Think I don't know how to fight? Yeah? Well, watch this!' He grabbed Shadowman's club from him and strode towards the oncoming strangers who slowed down, not sure if it was safe to move in for an attack.

Jester broke into a sprint, charging full pelt at the strangers, and smacked the first one, a tall father with long fair hair, hard in the neck. He didn't go down, though, and the other strangers managed to close in on Jester so that he had no room to properly swing the club again.

'Oh, Jesus,' said Shadowman. 'We need to help him.'

The four of them dashed over and started to lay into the strangers. Tom, Kate and Alfie concentrated on the ones who were hanging back. Shadowman headed for Jester, intending to pull him free of the two big fathers who had him by his left arm. But, just as Shadowman got close, Jester swung the club back with his free hand and it struck Shadowman square between the eyes.

It was like being hit by a firework. A shower of sparks exploded in front of Shadowman's eyes and he suddenly didn't know which way was up or down. He collapsed to his knees with a grunt, and his bladder emptied, soaking his jeans. Everything had gone a sickly yellow colour and was flipping over and over. He opened his mouth to speak but nothing came out. His head felt as big as the moon and he was shivering, suddenly freezing cold.

The voices of the other boys boomed around him, but he could make no sense of them. The sound hurt him, though. He held his temples, wanting to scream, trying to hold his expanding head together.

He was dimly aware of the strangers being beaten down, of Tom and Kate yelling at Jester, then running off, Jester shouting after them.

Where were they going?

Come back . . .

I'm still here.

I need your help.

Now Jester was looking at him. His lips moving. Words buzzed in the air, but Shadowman couldn't catch them.

Jester and Alfie tried to pull him to his feet. Every time he stood, though, his legs gave way. In the end they dragged him to the side of the tracks.

'Can you walk, Shadowman . . . can you walk . . . can you walk . . .?'

Shadowman couldn't even speak, let alone walk.

'There's more of them coming . . . more of them coming . . . more of them . . .'

Where?

Shadowman tried to focus, but the image just flipped and skipped. He forced his face round towards the tunnel mouth. Another gaggle of strangers was emerging.

'We'll have to leave him . . . we'll have to leave him . . . have to leave him . . .'

No . . .

'I'm sorry . . . sorry . . . sorry . . .'

No . . .

The sky was pulsing. Shadowman threw up. Made a last effort to stand. For a moment he was up, then he was overcome with dizziness and he hit the ground with a hard, painful thump.

Everything went black.

He could taste dirt in his mouth. He opened his eyes. He was lying on his side. Staring at the tunnel.

Jester wasn't there any more. Alfie gone too.

More strangers were coming out. No chance of counting them as they jumped about in his vision. They looked to him like a horde, an army, thousands of them.

Coming along the tracks towards him.

Where were his friends?

Oh yes. They'd run.

He had to hide.

Or something.

No. He was all right. The strangers weren't coming towards him, after all. They were veering off, going after Jester and the others. They hadn't seen him where he lay in a tangle of weeds. He was safe. It was going to be all right.

And then he felt a tug at his foot.

With a supreme effort he rolled his throbbing head round to look. It was one of the strangers from the battle. The father with the long fair hair. He wasn't dead. He was slithering towards Shadowman on his belly, and he had his fingers clamped tight to his shoe.

Shadowman moaned.

It was the dead fighting the dead.

43

'We going inside that, are we?' said DogNut, bending his neck back to look up at the curved windowless walls of the building in front of him. It rose up eight storeys, looking like nothing so much as a giant concrete nut. The structure stood inside a modern extension to the Natural History Museum that was all glass and steel and hard surfaces.

'Yes,' said Justin proudly. 'It's where the museum laboratories are.'

'You sure it ain't stuffed with sickos?'

'No. Just kids. Kids and millions of specimens.'

'Why did the museum need labs?' DogNut asked as they set off up the stairs. 'Were they studying diseases, like?'

'I don't think so,' said Justin. 'I think they studied plants and animals, fossils, that kind of thing. We've found some amazing scientific apparatus. A lot of it we're still trying to work out how to use, but there's loads of things we're already using, like microscopes, computers, fridges . . .'

'I think even I could figure out how to work a fridge,' said DogNut.

'We have to keep our specimens cold,' said Justin.

'Yeah, I know. You wouldn't want your sickos to go off.'

There was an entrance to the pod on the third floor and

Justin led DogNut into the dark interior, his torch shining over the walls and floor.

'This building is called the Cocoon,' Justin explained. 'Before the disaster it had all sorts of displays and inter-active stuff in here, projections on the walls, audio playing . . .' He ran his torch beam over the walls like an archaeologist in a prehistoric cave. 'All dead now, of course, but the museum's collection of stuffed animals, seeds, insects, bones, weird things preserved in jars – that's all still here, the physical things, the real things, not digital . . . bleeps and pixels and ones and zeros.'

There was a series of sloping ramps in the Cocoon that gave occasional glimpses of deserted labs as they climbed inside it, but as they rounded a corner near the top DogNut saw light up ahead. Electric light, burning inside a busy lab full of kids.

DogNut looked at the bright lamps and the glow of monitors attached to functioning computers as if they were some kind of magic. They had a generator at the Tower and one night a week they fired it up so that they could listen to music and watch DVDs in a communal room, but it was the warmth and cosiness of the lights that the kids enjoyed most.

Looking through the windows into this bright labora-tory was like looking into another world. The world that had existed before the disease wiped it all out. Except there was an unreal quality to it, since all the scientists wearing the lab coats were children – fourteen, fifteen years old. As if they were involved in a school film project or something, playing at being grown-ups.

They were making a pretty good job of it, however. DogNut had to admit that life at the Tower was little better than medieval. This was something different.

'So you got another generator in there to power it all?' he asked.

'Not in there,' said Justin. 'The fumes would kill us. There's a couple up on the roof.'

He took DogNut inside, and they wandered among the desktops. Kids were peering in microscopes, looking at things in dishes, writing notes, reading books . . . DogNut's brain was beginning to ache.

'How d'you have time to run the museum and all this?' DogNut asked.

'Oh, I don't run the labs,' said Justin. 'To tell you the truth, I'm not great at biology – physics is more my thing.'

'I thought it was all the same. Just science.'

'No. Ah, here he is . . .'

DogNut saw a boy approaching across the laboratory floor. He was tall and wearing a grubby white lab coat over black jeans, a tweed jacket and a tatty old sweater. He had a shock of untidy dark hair and would have been quite good-looking if his teeth hadn't been yellow and blackened, jutting out like horse's teeth from rotten, receding gums.

'This is Einstein,' said Justin.

'For real?' said DogNut, grinning.

'Yeah, obviously for real,' said the boy sarcastically. 'I really *am* Einstein. Justin regenerated me from cells found in a preserved lock of his hair.'

'So it's a joke name?'

'Yes. My real name's Isaac Newton.'

'OK. Cool. Hello, Isaac.'

The boy snorted and looked to Justin then back to DogNut.

'You've never heard of Isaac Newton, have you?'

'Nope. Should I of?'

'He was only the most famous British scientist of all time, the man who discovered gravity, worked out the laws of the universe.'

'I didn't really do a lot of science at school,' said DogNut.

'You surprise me. What *did* you specialize in? Finger painting?'

'I liked history.'

'Give the man a banana. History. Not a lot of use in the modern world, but it's better than nothing, I suppose.'

DogNut stuffed his hands in his pockets. Otherwise he was in danger of hitting the boy, whose superior, sarcastic manner might have been even more devastating if his breath hadn't stunk.

DogNut made a last effort to be polite.

'So, if you're not really Einstein, and you're not really Isaac Newton, then who are you?'

'Stephen Hawking.'

'Listen, dickwad,' said DogNut, grabbing the boy's throat. 'Stop taking the piss or I'll knock your green teeth out.'

'Oh, how brave.'

DogNut slapped him and let him go. The boy looked shocked for a second and then laughed in DogNut's face.

'I can see that the world of meticulous, patient, scientific enquiry is not for you. I rather think what we do here is going to be lost on you.'

'Whatever.'

'But at least you seem to have heard of Stephen Hawking.'

'He was the dude in the wheelchair with the robot voice.'

'Bravo. Full marks.'

'Back off, both of you,' said Justin. 'This is getting stupid.'

The boy smirked and offered to shake DogNut's hand.

'My name's Orlando Epstein,' he said theatrically and not entirely sincerely, 'but you may call me Einstein. Everyone else does.'

'Yeah, right.' DogNut slapped the hand by way of a greeting. 'My real name's Danny Trejo, but you may call me DogNut. Everyone else does.'

'OK, Danny.'

DogNut didn't let his face give anything away. He may not know much about scientists, but Einstein clearly didn't know much about hard-faced, ex-con Mexican action-movie stars.

'This is all very cool and impressive, like,' he said blandly, keeping his little triumph to himself, 'but what have you actually found out?'

'Loads of stuff,' said Justin, sounding like an excited eight-year-old.

'Amaze me!'

'We've proved there's a definite link between ultraviolet light and the progress of the disease,' said Einstein.

'Yeah, and what does that mean?'

'Basically, sunlight makes the disease act faster,' said Einstein. 'It blisters their skin, accelerates the process, and we've observed the effects of UV light on their blood under a microscope.'

'Light kills them?'

'Only ultraviolet light,' said Justin. 'Like you get from the sun. Electric light makes no difference.'

'I always knew the sickos didn't like the sun. But you saying it actually hurts them?'

'Yes.' Justin nodded enthusiastically.

'And you can prove that, can you?'

'Yes.'

'How?'

'We tied up one of our specimens in the courtyard for a week and watched it die,' said Einstein.

'You mean a sicko?'

'Yes.'

'You left one out in the sun?'

'We wanted to observe it. That's what scientists *do*. They observe things and create theories based on their observations.'

'So what happened to him?'

'Her,' said Einstein. 'She burst. Splat! She couldn't have made more of a mess if she'd swallowed a hand grenade.'

'It seems the longer they stay out of the sun the worse it is when they're eventually exposed to it,' said Justin. 'Those that go outdoors in the day develop more of a resistance, like getting a suntan. We tried it with another subject, exposed him to low light levels every day, gradually increasing the time he spent in the sun. After three weeks he hadn't got much worse than the subjects we kept in the dark. Of course the sunlight irritated him.'

'It sent him crackers,' said Einstein, and he giggled. 'We had to put him down in the end.'

'When they stay in the dark, though,' said Justin, 'they stay quite calm, like the ones in the lorry. Take them outside and they lose it.'

'The brighter the sunlight, the worse it affects them,' said Einstein.

'So we got to pay more attention to the weather forecast,' said DogNut. '*Cloudy with a chance of zombies*.'

Justin laughed. 'Something like that.'

'They sound more like vampires than zombies.'

'They're neither,' said Justin, irritated. 'They're not any kind of walking dead. But we think the secret to what they *really* are is in their blood. It's *that* we need to look at most carefully.'

'We need to know if the disease is a virus,' said Einstein. 'Or if it's bacteriological, or if it's a type of cancer, or autoimmune disease, maybe it's caused by poisoning of some sort.'

'Or space dust,' said DogNut.

'It's a possibility,' said Justin. 'A disease could have come into the atmosphere off an asteroid, or a meteor, or was maybe brought back by a space mission.'

DogNut had mentioned space dust as a joke, and he decided to push it further, enjoying Justin taking his idea seriously.

'Could be an alien attack,' he said.

'Possible, but unlikely,' said Justin. 'The nearest inhabitable planet is many millions of light years away from Earth.'

'Yeah, well, if they'd set off before breakfast, they could be here before tea time.'

'That really wasn't very funny,' said Einstein.

'Whatever,' said DogNut, ignoring Einstein's insult. 'I think I get what you're doing here.'

'Do you?' said Justin.

'Yeah. You're saving the world.'

'We're trying,' said Justin, accepting DogNut's joke with a smile. 'When we've got more time I'll take you round to the Science Museum next door. That might be more interesting to you. Everything we need to rebuild the world is in there. Scientific instruments, medical instruments, tools, machines, vehicles . . . The only stuff we're lacking is chemicals, drugs, that kind of thing. If we had more troops, we could do it, but we can't spare the manpower at the moment.'

'We'd ask the hunters to get it for us,' said Einstein, 'but they're not the cleverest kids on the block. It'd take too long to explain what we're after. We need to mount an expedition, really. If we only had a good team to protect our scientists and doctors.'

'You're not *real* scientists and doctors, though, are you?' said DogNut. 'You're just kids.'

'This is all just a big joke to you, isn't it?' said Justin.

'No.'

'Have you taken on board anything we've said?'

'Yes.'

'So have you got any questions?'

'Yeah . . . What's ascorbic acid?'

'What?'

'You said before about how you had to make sure all the kids got enough ascorbic acid, and it's been bugging me ever since.'

'Is that all you've taken in?' Justin asked.

'I'm a slow thinker. Slow but steady.'

'It's basically vitamin C,' said Einstein. 'Animals make it in their bodies or else they die from scurvy. Humans, and some other animals, like guinea pigs, have lost the ability to make their own, though, and have to get it from their food.'

'Thanks. So now I know.'

'So now you know,' said Einstein.

DogNut stared at the hard-working kids at their equipment. This wasn't a world he understood. And so it wasn't a world he liked. He longed to be back out on the streets with a weapon in his hand, not having to think about things, only worrying about staying alive, fighting, killing and returning home a hero.

He was beginning to think that it had been a mistake coming here. He'd found Brooke, but she obviously didn't give a toss about him. Girls weren't really impressed by fighting when it came down to it. Only boys. And the boys here . . .

He sighed. No. Brooke didn't give a toss about him, or his plans to take over this place.

Who was he kidding? He couldn't run this place. He gave a snort of laughter.

'What's so funny now?' asked Justin wearily, expecting the worst.

'Nothing,' said DogNut. 'I think I might just take a look around if that's cool.'

'Of course.'

DogNut strolled through the lab, staring dumbly at the busy kids, not having a clue what they were doing. He wasn't cut out for this. He didn't want to be in charge of these dorks.

He didn't want to be in charge of anything. He couldn't handle being responsible. Having kids on his watch die, like Leo and Olivia. He had more in common with Robbie than he'd cared to admit. Sometimes it was better to be number two. There was no shame in it.

Number two.

Well, number three.

Maybe he should just go home. Back to the Tower. He'd at least be a bit of a celebrity there. Respected. The guy who broke out. The guy who crossed London and brought back news of the outside world.

He wandered through to another lab and was surprised

to see Finn sitting at a workbench, two girls fussing around his infected arm.

'What you doing up here with the geeks?' DogNut asked, happy to see a familiar face.

'I'm getting my arm properly fixed up.' Finn smiled at his old friend. 'These people are good.'

'These people are weird,' said DogNut.

Finn chuckled. 'I like it here.'

Before they could say anything else a breathless little kid came running in, red-faced and worried.

'Where's Justin?' he called out.

'He's through there,' said DogNut, pointing back the way he'd come.

'What's the matter?' asked one of the girls who was tending to Finn.

'It's Paul. He's gone mental.'

44

Paul was in the middle of the main hall at the museum, in front of the fossilized diplodocus. He had his knife in his hand, still bloody from when he'd attacked the Collector. The blood had dried into a blackened crust. To DogNut he looked absolutely crazy. Circling round, threatening anyone who came close, his face twisted out of shape by rage and despair, soaked with tears. Snot ran into his mouth where sticky saliva made little wires and tendrils between his teeth.

He was alternately shouting and sobbing, the words garbled, disjointed, staccato, punctuated by sobs and shuddering intakes of breath as they spilt out of him.

'You let her die that that thing that awful that fat thing uh you let him take her you you you all of you you let her uh die you're all to blame all of you look at you you're uh happy aren't you? Living here cosy and happy and stupid and happy because she wasn't your sister she was uh my sister that thing that fat thing didn't take your sister uh I know what you think I know I can hear your thoughts yes you didn't know that I can hear all of you what you're thinking I know you're laughing at me behind my back uh yes you laugh that I should be sad but she was my sister my little sister uh just so small she was coming back to me

291

coming here my sister but you wouldn't let her come would you you all wanted to kill her because it's funny to laugh at me you you uh you you don't want me to be happy you're none of you my friends Olivia was my only friend and you're all so happy that she's dead I can see you uh laughing . . . I can hear you . . . I know you . . .'

DogNut watched as Justin tried to talk him down, but he was obviously completely out of his depth. Justin knew about things, about science and maths and inventions, but he didn't know too much about people. What made them tick. He had no idea how to help Paul. DogNut wanted to wade in and slap Paul, tell him to pull his crap together and not be so dumb. He needed to be jolted out of his madness before he hurt someone, or more probably himself. The events of the day and the argument earlier with Justin by the lorry had obviously tipped him over the edge. DogNut had seen it happen to kids before. Something inside them snapped and they flipped out, retreated into madness. He often wondered why more kids didn't end up like this, the things they'd been through, the things they'd seen, the friends they'd lost. He wondered why they weren't all gibbering wrecks. He supposed that some kids just had a different gene inside. A survival gene.

How could Paul blame anyone else here, though? It had nothing to do with the other kids in the museum. If anyone was to blame, it was DogNut. He'd abandoned Olivia, not these confused nerds.

He held back, however. Figured it wouldn't be good form to start beating up on one of theirs. Instead, a concerned ring of friends had formed round Paul and they were all coming out with the sort of useless, meaningless babble they'd seen on TV programmes like *Big Brother*.

'We do care for you, Paul . . .'

'You've got a right to be angry, but not at us . . .'

'Let it out if it makes you feel better . . .'

'We all feel your pain, Paul . . .'

That was a good one. DogNut for one didn't feel Paul's pain. He had enough pain of his own to deal with, thank you very much.

He recognized a few familiar faces. There was a bunch of smaller kids, including Wiki and Jibber-jabber, Zohra and her little brother, Froggie, in a huddle at the back, whispering to each other, a couple of them actually sniggering, no doubt as a way of coping with the unsettling weirdness of Paul's behaviour.

And there was Kwanele, the dressing-up dude, looking extraordinary in some kind of embroidered Japanese or Chinese robes. Brightly coloured and with an ornate gold and silver sword in an elaborately decorated scabbard hanging from a belt at his waist. DogNut had noticed several kids with these swords and assumed they'd looted them from the Victoria and Albert museum over the road. They looked like they were more for show than battle.

And there was the book guy, Chris Marker. It struck DogNut that his robes were similar to Kwanele's, although his weren't quite as colourful. He had a group of younger kids with him and was making no attempt to join the others in trying to calm Paul down.

Robbie sidled up to DogNut and gave him a quick nudge in the ribs.

'Enjoying the show?'

DogNut shook his head. 'I can't deal with this kind of thing.'

'You're like me, Dog.' Robbie scratched his bent nose.

'We're happier out on the streets with a weapon in our hands. We don't do *domestic*.'

In the end it was Brooke who sorted it out. She pushed through the ring of kids and walked over to Paul.

'I'll cut you,' Paul cried. 'Don't come near me I know what you want I know what all of you want you want to shut me up you'd hurt me if you could you want to get rid of me like you did Olivia I know what you want you come near me and I'll stab you.'

'No, you won't,' said Brooke.

'Won't I?'

'No.' As Brooke said this, she slapped Paul hard round the face. He was so shocked and surprised he froze and Brooke quickly took the knife off him. She threw it away and before Paul could do anything else she put her arms round him.

'It's all right,' she said. 'Everything's going to be all right.'

'It's not all right . . . She's gone . . .'

'We've all lost people, Paul. We're all alone in the end. If you wanna be angry, be angry at the sickness, not us.'

Paul buried his face in Brooke's neck and gave in to his tears.

DogNut was close enough to hear him whisper five words.

'I just want my mum.'

'I know,' said Brooke, and she stroked his hair. 'We all do.'

DogNut was impressed. The old Brooke would never have done anything like this. She'd have been at the back with the sniggerers, tossing jibes at him. He looked around for Courtney. She'd want to talk about what had happened. Out of everyone here she was the one who knew Brooke the best.

Only Courtney wasn't there. DogNut realized he hadn't seen her since she'd stormed off.

He scratched his fuzzy hair and noisily blew out a long breath.

Better go look for her.

45

'We shouldn't of left him, Jester. That wasn't right.'

'We had no choice, Alfie. We couldn't carry him, could we? He was concussed.'

'But we should've stayed with him. Protected him.'

Jester said nothing. He and Alfie were hiding out in a first-floor flat on the Caledonian Road, peering out of a bedroom window from behind closed curtains. After leaving the railway tracks they'd charged around the local streets looking for Tom and Kate, only giving up when another gang of strangers had spotted them. Tired and scared, they'd looked for shelter and broken in here. They'd been lucky. There were a couple of ancient cans of beans in the kitchen and a bottle of Ribena that they'd diluted with water from their packs. As they sat at the window looking down into the road, they were eating the cold beans and sipping the sweet red drink.

The gang of strangers was still out there, hanging about on the opposite side of the road, trying to get at a scrawny cat that was cowering in a dead tree.

Until the strangers gave up and left, the two boys were stuck here.

'We should've stayed with him, Jester,' Alfie repeated, keeping his voice low.

'Really?' Jester hissed. 'Did you see how many of them there were? Huh?'

'Yeah, of course I did.'

'Well, how long do you think us two would have lasted against them? Seriously? I mean, if Tom and Kate hadn't legged it, maybe we'd have stood a chance. Maybe. They were a couple of whingers, but at least they knew how to fight. But two of us? Unarmed? Plus you're not exactly the biggest kid on the block, are you? And I'm not exactly used to fighting.'

'He was your friend, Jester. You just left him to die.'

'He'll be all right. The Shadowman can look after himself.'

'How?' Alfie looked amazed, tore his eyes away from the scene opposite and glared at Jester. 'You said yourself he was concussed. He couldn't even stand up.'

'Just leave it, Alfie. It's done. All right?'

'Jester —'

'Leave it!' Jester spat beans into Alfie's face. Alfie turned away. Tried not to think about what might have happened to Shadowman.

46

Shadowman wasn't dead. Not yet. Though there had been times in the last two hours when he'd wished he was. Finding the stranger's hand gripping his boot had shocked him into life and he'd wriggled away from him. He'd rolled down a bank and then tried to stand. As soon as he was upright again, though, he'd felt dizzy and only managed to stagger a few paces before collapsing and slipping back into unconsciousness. It was the touch of the stranger's hand that had awakened him. Alarm bells had rung inside his brain and his eyes had snapped open to find the stranger's face centimetres away from his own. He had been badly beaten in the fight, must have taken at least two hits to the face. Framed by long fair hair, it was an ugly mess, bloated and purple, the skin pulled so tight by swelling that his cheeks looked like two ripe plums with blossoms of green fungus across them. His eyes were tiny, lost in the swelling, and his nose had been reduced to black, piggy nostrils.

The stranger was no more able to walk than Shadowman. A blow or a stab in the back seemed to have broken his spine so that he trailed his useless legs behind him. He could still use his hands, though, his arms, his teeth . . .

Shadowman had kicked him away and carried on crawling.

In all this time he'd covered no more than three or four hundred metres, dragging himself through a long-abandoned building site that had been part of the new development around the station. He had no weapons. He'd lost his club and his knife, so had nothing to fight the father off with except his fists and feet. He knew he had to build up his strength and coordination before he could risk fighting him, though. For now all he was able to do was try to get away. He would start out on his belly, then get up on to his hands and knees. From his knees he'd risk a low crouch, his head pulsing in time with his heartbeat, and when the dizziness didn't immediately return he'd force himself fully upright . . .

And every time his brain would short-circuit and he'd tumble down.

And the father would catch up.

It was a pattern that had repeated itself all afternoon, like a nightmare version of the hare and the tortoise. Shadowman was faster, he got away, he passed out and the slow and steady stranger caught up with him and tried to sink his teeth into him. His mouth was a mess, the gums bleeding and swollen, the lips cracked, but he had a full set of teeth, looking incongruously white and clean in contrast to his purple skin. Shadowman had to keep those teeth away from his skin. He knew that even a small cut could get infected.

He'd lost track of how many times it had happened now. How many times he'd woken to find the father clawing at his trousers. No matter how far ahead of him he got he always caught up. The father wasn't about to give up. His legs didn't work, he was bleeding from a wound in his side, but the only thing that would stop him would be death. He might starve to death, he might bleed to death, or

Shadowman might kill him. The question was – which one of them was going to die first?

The only thing that gave Shadowman any hope was the fact that each time he woke he felt a tiny bit stronger, a tiny bit more clear-headed. He was fighting off the concussion, though his head still ached terribly. And now he'd finally woken to find no sign of the dogged stranger.

He sat up and took his water bottle off his belt, managed to force down some water and hold it down. He smiled. Closed his eyes. Felt a delicious drowsiness flood through him . . .

And the next thing he knew he was fighting over the bottle with the stranger. How could it be? No time at all seemed to have passed. One moment he was alone in the middle of the building site and the next there was the stranger's ugly face, and his bloody fingers grappling for the water. Shadowman saw that the flesh had been worn away from the father's fingertips, which ended in yellow stubs of bone. It must have happened as he'd clawed his way relentlessly across the hard ground. The horrid bony claws rattled against the metal of the canteen as they scrabbled to get a hold.

Shadowman dragged it out of his grasp and smashed it into the side of the stranger's head, knocking him away. He forced himself upright and staggered on, the building site slipping and sliding around in his vision . . . Cranes and diggers, piles of rubble, scrap, neat stacks of brightly coloured plastic pipework, deserted Portakabins.

He was able to stay on his feet longer this time and was just beginning to believe that he might at last make it clean away when he felt his brain slip out of gear, everything began to spin and he was teetering out of control. He made it as far as a big dirty cement mixer and collapsed against it. Before he lost consciousness, he wriggled around so that he was sitting with his back against it, and then he gave in to the darkness.

He wasn't fully under, though; some spark of awareness remained. He swam up out of the depths and opened his eyes. The father was creeping towards him, pulling his way along the ground, no expression on his remaining features.

Relentless.

Single-minded.

Shadowman's eyes drooped shut.

Fight it. Wake up . . .

He flitted in and out of consciousness. The periods of black-out mercifully growing shorter and less intense. Each time he opened his eyes he saw that the father was a little nearer.

He had to put an end to this nightmare. He had to stop the father once and for all. He glanced around, scouring the building site for anything he could use as a weapon. At last, about five metres away, he saw what he was looking for. A tangled heap of rusted metal, made up of the twisted steel rods that were used in reinforced concrete. He took a deep breath, flopped on to his hands and knees and set off towards it, ignoring the stones and spikes that dug into him, shredding his skin further.

He got there safely, hauled himself up and began to search through the rods. Most were useless for his purpose – they were either too long or were welded to other rods to make a framework. Just as he was about to give up and search elsewhere, he tugged at a particularly sharp-ended rod and found that it was unattached. He drew it out of the stack. It was the right length. Gasping for breath, he used the pole as a walking staff and made his way back to the cement mixer, where he sat back down in his spot to wait for the father.

Soundlessly, the stranger crept closer and closer, scraping his horrid, fleshless fingers through the dirt.

'Cme nn then,' Shadowman mumbled, struggling to form the words properly. 'Cme nng yugly bstrd . . .'

Fetching the weapon had taken a lot out of Shadowman, and, as the father got close enough to smell, he wondered if he would have the strength to do anything more than prod him with it.

He shuddered as the father reached his feet and ran his hands possessively over them, then started to edge his way up his legs, holding on to the torn material of his trousers. His mouth hung open, dribble pooling and spilling out from either side. He was shaking his head slowly from left to right, a low moan escaping from his diseased throat.

Shadowman raised the spike, drew it back, aiming for the father's face. Then he drove it forward with all his remaining strength and the sharp tip disappeared inside the father's mouth.

The angle that the father was coming at him – crawling face first – meant that the rod was forced straight down his throat and into his belly. Shadowman grunted and thrust again, twisting the spike to the side, so that the father was tipped over into the dirt on his back.

He wasn't dead. He lay there twitching and gurgling, his bony fingers groping at the spike, trying to pull it out. It was no use – a good half-metre of rod was buried inside him, like some grotesque sword-swallowing act. Shadowman didn't have the strength to finish him off. He sat there, drifting in and out of sleep as the father slowly expired.

Gradually the light faded from the day, as if mimicking the stranger's dimming life force. Still he hung on, though, his fingers moving gently, like spiders, on the pole.

There was a growing smell of blood and faeces, which seemed to become more acute as it grew dark and there was less to see. And as night fell Shadowman started to hear noises. Things moving about. Animals? Strangers? Children? He couldn't know. He couldn't stay here, though. That was for sure. Sooner or later something would come and try to eat him.

He wrestled his pack round to his front and felt inside it for his torch. He found it quickly, slid it out and snapped it on. He swore. There was a group of six strangers making their way towards him. They shielded their eyes and froze as the torch beam fell on them, behaving more like wild animals than human beings.

They were possibly part of the same bunch that had attacked Shadowman's party at the station. Friends, if that was the right word – did strangers have friendships? – of the father he had speared. He thought he recognized one of them, a mother with no hair and several missing fingers. Her companions were weak and badly gone, but in Shadowman's concussed state he doubted he could fight them all off. It had taken everything he had to beat the father and he once again had no weapon.

He wasn't going to just sit here and let them do what they wanted. He climbed up the cement mixer until he was on his feet and started to walk.

Good. Not too dizzy. No spiralling yet.

The torch lit his way. He didn't get far, though. The bald mother caught up with him, and in grabbing for his arm knocked the torch to the ground where it cut out.

He closed his eyes agin and began to cry.

He thought he'd never needed any friends. Any family. But he felt so alone now.

And then an odd thing happened. The mother gasped as a weapon struck her from behind. Shadowman heard the confused sounds of a fight. He strained to see what was going on in the darkness. As far as he could tell, another group of people was laying into the six strangers.

He was being rescued.

'Hello?' he called out. 'Hello . . .'

The fight was short and brutal. The six strangers were easily killed and then the new group came towards Shadowman, vague shapes, moving fast, organized, fit, carrying weapons and apparently well drilled. But as they got close enough for him to make out their faces in the moonlight all his hopes faded.

Not kids.

Grown-ups.

Four of them.

All fathers.

The one in front wore a Manchester United shirt. Behind him was a bare-chested father with only one arm. Next to him was a younger father wearing a business suit, a Bluetooth earpiece sticking out of one ear. Shadowman didn't have time to get a good look at the fourth one before they were upon him.

He closed his eyes again, ready to die now, too hurt and weary to care any more, hoping it would be quick.

47

Courtney was sitting holding a candle, looking up at a life-size model of a blue whale that was suspended from the ceiling in one of the museum galleries. It was an immense dark shape and she found it hard to believe that such giant creatures existed for real. She couldn't get her head round the idea that somewhere out there, in the scary depths of the oceans, whales like this were actually swimming around. She'd seen them on the TV, on nature programmes, but to see one like this, even though it was just a model, brought home to her just how humongous they were. The biggest creatures ever to live on planet Earth, according to the information signs. Before the disaster the blue whale was in danger of being wiped out. Now they were free to live and grow bigger and bigger in the oceans with no humans hunting them down.

Hanging above the model were a few actual whale skeletons, looking like aliens out of some mad science-fiction film. Squashed at the end, by the blue monster's nose, was a group of African mammals – an elephant, a giraffe, a rhinoceros. They looked like midgets next to the whales.

A voice came out of the darkness.

'There you are. I been looking all over for you.'

Courtney kept her eyes on the dangling skeletons. She

didn't really want to talk to DogNut right now. But he came and sat next to her anyway.

'Cool,' he said, taking in the exhibits.

'Did it not occur to you,' said Courtney, 'that maybe I didn't want to be found?'

'Too deep for me, girl,' said DogNut. 'My brain don't work that way. I always think if there's something to talk about you should just talk about it.'

'There's nothing to talk about.'

'Ain't there?'

'No.'

'Listen, I didn't know how you felt about me, Courtney.'

'And how *do* I feel about you then?'

'You tell me.'

'Go away, DogNut. It's a waste of time.'

'No. I really like you, Courtney, and I don't want you to be upset. I just never thought about you like, a, you know, a girlfriend or nothing. I need to make some adjustments.'

'Don't bother. I changed my mind.'

'So you *did* used to go for me, then?'

'You just made me feel stupid and small and ugly.'

'You ain't none of them things.'

'I ain't small?'

'No.'

'You saying I'm fat?'

'No!' DogNut looked at Courtney. Was she joking now? He never understood girls. It was all too tricky. She'd been crying, but now she smiled.

'I shouldn't be angry at you, Doggo. There's no reason why you should go for me. I know you came here to find Brooke.'

DogNut put his arm round Courtney.

'It's complicated, innit?' he said. 'On top of everything else – trying to find food and water and keep warm, trying not to get eaten by sickos – on top of all that we got to go through all the same old same old, girlfriends-and-boyfriends and who-likes-who and how-do-I-look and does-anyone-like-me?'

'Yeah. It's complicated.'

'But we still friends, yeah?'

'Yeah,' said Courtney, and DogNut squeezed her.

'Cool.'

Typical boy. He probably thought that was all it took. Thought it was over. That he could carry on like nothing had happened.

'Why you alone with the whales, anyway?' he asked her. 'You like whales or something?'

'Makes you think,' said Courtney. 'Where we stand in the world. We ain't top dog no more. We're just krill.'

'What the hell's krill?'

'Is what blue whales eat. I was reading the signs. They huge and that, but they just eat these, like, tiny sea insects, millions of them in one swallow, like a sort of soup.'

'You only been here one day, girl, and already you talking like a nerd.'

Courtney shrugged.

'So that's all we are now?' said DogNut. 'Krill?'

'Yeah,' said Courtney. 'We're just insects and the sickos is like blue whales, cruising around sucking us up, swallowing us down.'

'Nice.' DogNut released Courtney and stood up. 'So you gonna come back and join us humans again now?'

'DogNut?'

'What?'

'I want to go home.'

'Yeah.' DogNut sat back down again. 'Me too. This ain't our world, babes. We should leave it to Brooke.'

'You mean you'd leave her behind? After everything?'

'Yeah. Why not? She ain't interested in me. Let's go back, the two of us, where we belong.'

'Yeah. Let's do that.'

Maybe there was still hope.

48

The strangers had got into the building. Something had alerted them, and, made braver by the darkness, they'd given up on the cat and wandered across the road. They'd climbed in through the downstairs windows, and Jester and Alfie could hear them on the stairs, approaching the door to the flat.

Alfie was panicking, turning to Jester for reassurance. Jester didn't have much more of an idea than Alfie about what to do, though. The two of them had waited at the window all afternoon, hoping the strangers would give up and go away. Now it was too late.

The door to the flat was at the bottom of a short flight of stairs. The boys heard the first crash as the strangers reached it. It felt like the whole flat shook, and after the hours of silence it sounded horribly loud. Jester lit a candle and cautiously crept down to inspect the door, Alfie following, tucked in behind him for protection. They'd locked and bolted the door when they came in. Like most London flats there was heavy security. The door itself, however, didn't look very strong. The big house had been divided up into several poky flats, and not a great deal of money had been spent on the building work.

As the strangers pounded on the door, it bulged and cracked in its frame.

'Jesus, Jester, what do we do?' Alfie said, still whispering, even though it made no difference now.

'We can hold them off for a while,' said Jester, putting the candle down on the stairs.

'Yeah? And then what?'

'Then we . . .' Jester shrugged. 'We fight them off?'

'All of them?'

'Have you got a better plan?'

'You're the one supposed to be in charge,' Alfie whined, staring fixedly at the woodwork. 'Do something. Think of something. You're supposed to be clever.'

There was an almighty thump followed by an animal growl and a split appeared down the edge of the frame where it was starting to come away from the wall.

'We should have looked for another way out,' said Alfie, staring at the frame. 'While there was still time.'

'I'm not used to this,' Jester protested.

'Shadowman would have known what to do,' Alfie said bitterly. 'We should never of left him.'

'Stay here,' said Jester, snapping into action at last and bounding up the stairs. 'Push as hard as you can against the door – don't let them force it in.'

'All right,' said Alfie, thankful to be told what to do at last. He leant his weight against the door, felt the vibrations through the wood as the strangers on the other side hammered it. He swallowed hard, feeling like he was going to be sick. It made it all too horribly real, feeling the strangers throw their bodies against the door – it was like he was actually touching them. Only a few millimetres of pine separated them.

He prayed that Jester would hurry up.

How many of them were out there? They'd counted nine to begin with, but as night had fallen they'd been joined by more and more of their kind as they emerged from their dens to go hunting under the cover of darkness.

He slowly leant forward and put his ear to the door. Now he could hear their grunts and sniffs and hissing breath. Their frenzied scrabbling movements as they fought each other to get to the door.

'Hurry up, Jester!'

He jerked back as there came an even heavier thump. His arms were shaking, his hands slippery with sweat.

'Jester . . .'

'I'm here!'

There was a clatter as Jester came down the stairs carrying two kitchen chairs. Together they quickly wedged them between the door and the stairs, jamming the legs against the steps.

'That'll help,' said Jester.

'We need more,' said Alfie. 'We need to block the stairs completely.'

'OK. OK . . .'

'But, Jester, even that won't hold forever. You saw what they were like with that cat. They won't give up. They'll get in eventually, or we'll starve to death, or, I don't know what, but we have to have a better plan . . .'

Jester thought for a moment, running his fingers through his shock of stiff, wiry hair. 'I'll look for some more stuff to block the stairs,' he said, trying to sound calm.

Alfie nodded. 'OK.'

'And I'll look for another way out. A window, or something. We're not that high up.'

'Yeah. Good. But you should have looked before. You let us get trapped here.'

'I didn't think – neither did you.'

'Shadowman wouldn't have got us trapped like this,' Alfie repeated.

'Maybe not. But I'll get us out, Alfie. All right?' Jester smiled at the younger boy, a light of defiance in his eyes. Alfie smiled back. All he needed was for someone to tell him that everything was going to be all right. Jester was standing up at last, acting tough, and it gave Alfie strength and hope.

'They're all distracted here,' said Jester. 'They'll be too stupid to think of whether there might be any other ways in or out. You stay put, bang on the door, make a lot of noise. Draw them all here. Let them think we're not going anywhere.'

'OK, yeah. I get it.'

'Good man, Alfie. I'll be right back.'

Alfie watched Jester run to the top of the stairs again, and then he returned to his station. The chairs were holding. With no room to give, the door wasn't jumping so much in its frame now. Alfie's smile grew wider. It felt good to have a plan. They could get one over on the strangers. Kids could always beat them, because they were smarter. The grown-ups' weakness was their stupidity.

He banged his fists against the woodwork and was answered from the other side by a frenzied scurrying, scraping, moaning assault on the door.

'Yeah?' Alfie yelled, his voice high-pitched and hysterical. 'You hear that? That's me! Alfie Walker. Yeah? And I'm cleverer than you dumb bitches! You stupid ugly farts. Yeah, knock on the door all you like – you ain't coming in. And, if you do, I'll split you with my knife. I'll rip your rotten guts out. I'll kick your brains up the walls!'

He started to laugh as he hurled more and more insults at the strangers and came up with gorier and gorier ways to splatter them. His voice eventually started to grow hoarse and he realized that Jester had been gone an awfully long time. He turned and looked up the stairs. The candle was nearly burnt down.

Where was he?

'Jester!' he called. 'Jester, how are you getting on?'

There was no reply. Before Alfie could shout again he was distracted by a change in the noise at the door. There was a harder, sharper bang, and a crunching noise. He picked up the flickering candle and moved it closer. Then it came again – THWACK – and a big crack appeared down the middle of the door. They were hitting it with something. Something sharp. Strangers didn't normally use tools of any kind, or weapons, but some of them, the cleverer ones, the ones who weren't as far gone, would sometimes pick things up. Then it was like some deep memory would kick in and they'd find themselves back in their old lives, doing DIY on a weekend, working in the garden, chopping wood . . .

'Jester?' Alfie called. 'Hurry up. They're using a tool of some sort. They're hacking through the door, mate!'

Another crash and the point of a metal object punched through. Alfie swore and ran up the steps calling Jester's name.

'Where the hell are you?' He moved from room to room, but there was no sign of the other boy.

And then he went into the kitchen.

The window was open.

Alfie went very cold.

Surely Jester wouldn't have just abandoned him?

But that was quickly followed by another thought.

Why not?

He'd abandoned Shadowman, who was supposedly his best friend. A cold achy feeling filled Alfie's guts. He went over to the window and looked out. The sky was clouded over, but there was just enough light from the moon to see a low flat roof below. Beyond that was a small backyard and an alleyway.

Empty.

'Jester . . .?'

Alfie was crying. He wiped his nose.

'Bastard . . .'

Another crash from downstairs, followed by the sound of splintering wood, and then the noise of the strangers themselves.

They were through.

Alfie dropped his knife down on to the lower roof and squeezed out of the window. He found it hard to calculate the drop in the darkness. He hung there nervously for a moment, summoning the courage to let go, and then something struck his hand and he released his grip. He landed badly, jarring his ankles and knees. But there was no time to feel sorry for himself. He staggered to the edge and realized he was going to have to jump again. Shaking his numb hand, he looked up at the window. It was blocked by strangers fighting to get out.

He took a deep breath and launched himself off the flat roof. He landed better this time, but it still sent sharp jolts of pain up his legs and into his spine. He tried to walk and shrieked in agony. His legs were on fire.

There was a thump from above and he looked up to see that a father had dropped from the window. Alfie realized to his horror that he had forgotten to pick up his knife. There was no question of climbing back up to get it.

The father shuffled to the edge of the flat roof and jumped down. There was a horrible snapping noise and he collapsed, his broken leg bones sticking through his trousers.

That made Alfie feel a little better. He mustn't act like a wimp. He wasn't so badly hurt. He limped to the back gate, barged it open and looked both ways along the alley that ran behind the houses. No sign of bloody Jester.

He spat.

Another stranger dropped out of the window.

Alfie started hobbling down the alley, his knees killing him, swearing under his breath with every step. He wished he had his knife. He wasn't intending to be doing any fighting if he could help it – all he wanted to do right now was get away and find another hiding-place – but holding on to the knife had given him courage.

He left the alley where it joined the main road. There was nobody around. He was alone, out here on the streets with no idea where he was. There were sounds behind him. The hunters were on his tail. They could probably smell him. He tried to speed up, but it hurt too much. Tears were streaming down his face. Tears of anger and fear and betrayal and self-pity. First Kate and Tom had left him, and now Jester. He didn't deserve this.

Well, he'd show them. He'd show them he could survive. He'd got this far, hadn't he? After the sickness struck he was alone on the streets for nearly two weeks before linking up with some other kids, who he'd ended up going to the palace with.

He'd done it before – he could do it again.

Don't wimp out . . .

315

He put his hand up to dry his eyes and felt a splash of something warm across his face. A wave of nausea hit him and a terrible pain ripped through his hand.

Now what?

He whimpered. His fingers had been severed at the joints. It must have been when he was hanging from the window frame. Something had hit him. Chopped his fingers clean off.

He leant against a wall, clutching his ruined hand, and threw up.

This was bad. Really bad. He'd lost his fingers. He was bleeding. This was so bad . . .

He had to keep moving, though.

He stumbled along in the road, sobbing wildly. He had to find a hiding-place. He had to choose a house. Get inside. Off the street. Tend to his wound. He swerved into a smaller side-road. Ran past darkened houses. Trying not to think about his hand. His fingers.

Oh God.

He ran up to a front door, booted it and it swung open easily.

See. He could do it.

He walked forward in the dark. He wished he had a torch, but Jester had taken the only one. They hadn't expected to be out after dark. They should have been back at the palace hours ago. He wondered what they'd all be doing right now. Back home. Settling down to eat? Or clearing up? He had no idea what time it was. Would they be thinking about him?

Just wait till he got back and told them what Jester had done . . .

He stopped, and stood there, panting, blood dripping

on the floor, his lungs and heart working too fast. Pain taking over.

He hated being alone.

Then he felt a hand on his shoulder. He spun round.

'Jester?'

He saw a figure silhouetted against the door. Too large to be a kid. Then another hand touched him. And another. Something brushed his thighs. He smelt sour breath and the sickly sweet overripe smell of strangers. He lashed out wildly with his good hand, but it was no use. He had no weapon. He was surrounded. He'd broken into a strangers' den.

He felt breath on his face, hot and rancid. He retched and swayed, his brain melting. There was a rush of movement, teeth on his neck, fingernails raking his face. He felt a terrible pressure in his head. The teeth at his throat were suffocating him.

Oh God . . .

Mercifully he passed out before the teeth tore through his skin, and his pure, clean, undiseased blood exploded from the constricted arteries.

49

Jester hadn't planned to climb out of the window. He really hadn't. He hadn't planned to leave Alfie behind. But, when he'd pulled the window up and looked down, a plan had leapt into his mind as if it had been waiting there for him all along. It presented itself, clear and cold and perfect. Alfie was holding the strangers at the door, distracting them, and it would give him time to get well away.

He'd dropped the bits and pieces he'd been collecting to barricade the door and simply climbed out. Before he really knew what he was doing he was sprinting along the alleyway as fast as he could.

Surely it was right that one of them should survive rather than both getting killed. He was a kid and hadn't the old song always said that children were the future? They *had* to live. They had to beat the grown-ups. They had to win, whatever it took. Make it through these dark times into the light of a better future.

Better one living than two dead.

It was down to each individual to look after himself.

And anyway. Maybe Alfie would be all right. He was a tough kid. Not stupid. Maybe he'd get away just like Jester had. It was up to him. Jester wasn't responsible for anyone other than himself. If it was anyone's fault, it was David's. He hadn't given Jester enough muscle. Tom and Kate? Well, they'd scarpered, hadn't they? Blame them.

Blame anyone other than me.

And don't go whining to God about it. It was pretty clear that there was no God up there, no kindly old gent looking down, keeping score in a notebook. You did good, you did bad, it didn't make any difference, did it? This one's going to heaven, this one's going to hell, this one's going to Disneyland.

No. God wouldn't have let any of this shit happen. If you were going to believe in anything, then believe in the devil. He was much more real than God. Up there causing mischief. Laughing at the chaos he'd created.

Jester stopped running. His lungs were stinging and his legs felt rubbery. There were the beginnings of a stitch in his side.

Where was he?

No bloody idea.

Not true, Jester. You do know where you are.

In hell.

As usual.

He'd got away from the strangers, though, and that was all that mattered. With luck, any others in the area would have been attracted by all the noise and disturbance back there and he'd have the streets to himself for a while.

But were there any other *kids* around?

There had to be. It didn't make any sense otherwise. Why would strangers stay in the area if there was no food? Kids and strangers were locked in a deadly relationship. Children were the only source of fresh food, but they were also the grown-ups' greatest predators. That's why, in the end, the strangers would lose. Human beings wouldn't have survived for long if sheep had fought back, would they? Or cows . . .

Jester smiled at this thought while he stood getting his breath back.

There had to be some kids around somewhere.

But where?

He heard movement from the buildings on one side of the road. People moving about. Kids or grown-ups? You had to be careful. He sighed and moved off, plodding along the road until he was at a safe distance. After a couple of hundred metres he looked back. It was strangers. A small group of them had come out of the building and were coming after him.

He started up again, his trainers slapping down on the hard surface of the road, his patchwork coat flying out behind him, his satchel banging against his back.

He kept glancing behind him. The strangers were struggling to keep up, but he needed to put a lot of distance between him and them before he could risk holing up somewhere for the night. He careered round a bend and yelped as he almost ran straight into a stranger waddling along the other way. They knocked each other over, and Jester swore as his backside hit the deck.

He'd blundered right into the middle of a gang of about ten diseased grown-ups. He scurried backwards away from them. He'd dropped Shadowman's club in the collision and would need to get to it quickly. He scrambled messily to his feet, shoved a mother out of the way and managed to get hold of the club just as a big father made a grab for him. He lashed out and whacked the father, who went down. At the same moment another mother knocked into him and the club was pulled out of his grasp. He punched the mother, then a father, and thrashed his way out of the knot of bodies.

And then he was running again.

He was on a wide, open road with big shops on either side and a fenced-off island down the middle. And as he ran he noticed something else. At first he thought it must be a mirage, created by his panicking brain, offering up a false hope of safety. But he looked again.

Candlelight. Flickering in a sort of courtyard. He turned and aimed his steps towards it, vaulting over the railings in the centre of the road.

He careered into the courtyard. Candlelight could mean only one thing. Kids. There wasn't any other explanation, was there? Unless it was a fire. But even that would help. He could use fire against the strangers.

The light was coming from inside a Morrisons supermarket. The windows were secured and barricaded, and behind the barricades was the candlelight. Civilization. He banged on the windows and shouted to be let in.

At first there was no response then a voice called down to him from the roof.

'Get away from here. We don't let no one in.'

'You have to!' Jester pleaded. 'I'm being chased by strangers. There's hundreds of them out here, grown-ups.'

'That's why we ain't opening the doors, mate. Piss off. We don't want you here.'

'You can't lock me out!'

'Can't we?'

'Let me in, please . . .'

'We'll kill you if we have to.'

'You can't . . .'

Then Jester felt a sting in the side of his head and rubbed his scalp. Something had hit him — already a lump was coming up. Then another sting as something hit his shoulder. They were throwing stuff at him from the roof. Stones and bits of wood. He backed away.

'Bastards!' he screamed, and they swore at him.

Before they could throw anything else he retreated back out into the street, rubbing his head. More strangers had appeared. He glanced quickly in both directions, looking for any signs of light. If there was one gang of kids living around here, there might be more. He might find someone with a warmer welcome.

There! Could it be? Yes? More lights, shining out from another supermarket further along the road. He recognized the sign — Waitrose. It was where his parents had shopped before the disaster.

He ran towards it, bowling three strangers over along the way, desperate now. If he got the same response here, he was dead. The road was filling with strangers who were pouring in from all directions. And they were thickest around Waitrose.

He forced himself to move faster, his feet hammering on the tarmac, and he slammed against the front windows of the shop, roaring for help at the top of his voice, feeling like his lungs were going to burst. His shout for help turned into a scream as a mother lunged at him, teeth bared in a snarl. He battered her away and banged again on the windows.

Then he was aware of a fresh light and he looked up. Someone was shining a torch down at him.

'Let me in!'

He heard voices, but couldn't tell what they were saying. Filled with a mad fury he slammed an approaching father against the glass, and then kicked another in the guts. Jabbing left and right with his elbows he backed away from the windows, all the while yelling for help. He broke free of the huddle around him and was on the move again, darting madly to avoid a larger group of grown-ups who were trying to close in on him. The torch beam zigzagged across the road, like a spotlight in a prison-escape movie.

What were they doing up there? Were they going to help him or not?

'Please! Help me!' he wailed, his voice thin and weedy like a baby's. He tore himself out of the grip of a very determined father and ran back towards the shop. He couldn't get there, though. The strangers were going berserk. Half were attacking him, half seemed to be trying to break into the shop. The father was on him again and Jester managed to hurl him at a group of grown-ups who slammed into the glass. Shouting, screaming, punching and kicking, Jester fought his way back into the open and started running. He was forced to keep switching direction or risk being penned in by the milling grown-ups, and was soon going round in circles. Exhaustion was taking hold. His body was running on its last reserves. He had used all his energy getting to the shop and shouting for help. He couldn't believe that the kids inside were just going to watch him die out here.

And then the faces of the strangers around him were suddenly lit red and orange, like spectators at a firework display. A flaming torch was sailing through the night sky, bright against the clouds. It landed with an explosion of sparks, scattering the strangers. Jester heard kids shouting a war cry.

He clamped his hand to his mouth to stop himself from crying.

It looked like he was going to be rescued.

Maybe there was a God after all.

50

Shadowman was in some kind of tunnel. At one end was darkness, the other opened out into what he thought might be a large enclosed space. The four strangers from the building site hadn't killed him. They'd brought him here and dumped him in the tunnel. He wasn't sure exactly where here was, though, because it was too dark to see anything properly and he'd blacked out before they'd arrived. Now he was sitting propped up with his back against the wall trying to get his bearings. He wasn't alone. There were several other kids with him. All dead except for one girl, and she was barely alive. Occasionally she groaned and moved slightly, but when Shadowman had tried to speak to her she hadn't replied.

There were noises from the depths of the tunnel and Shadowman was aware of more than one adult wandering around, coming and going in the darkness. The ones who had brought him here were keeping close. Standing watch over him. He wasn't sure if it was to stop him from escaping or to stop the others from grabbing him. Just what they were keeping him alive for he had no idea. He was trying not to think ahead, trying not to imagine all the things that might be done to him. For now he was alive and feeling gradually more normal. His head was clearing and he didn't feel so sick and woozy. He was able to stay awake for much longer periods, though he still felt very tired. Even without the blow to his head he supposed he'd feel tired, though. It was the middle of the night, after all. What time was it? No idea. His watch was in his pack and his pack was gone.

His four strangers lurked silently in the gloom. Waiting for something. He had made up nicknames for them. It made them somehow less threatening. The one with the earpiece he had named Bluetooth. The one in the football shirt was Man U. The half-naked father with the missing limb was the One-Armed Bandit. The fourth member of their group was a rather ordinary-looking father. If you could describe someone as ordinary when their skin was blistered and peeling off, and their hair was falling out. It was just that compared to the other three he had no obvious distinguishing features.

The thing about strangers, grown-ups, mothers and fathers – call them whatever you liked – was they all looked the same after a while. Diseased.

These four seemed quite patient. They squatted down, leaning against the far wall, now and then standing up and going over to peer out of the end of the tunnel. And whenever another stranger came close they all jumped up and went into aggressive mode. Guarding their territory, their trophies.

Otherwise they seemed happy to wait.

Shadowman was happy to wait too, because with every passing second he grew stronger. When the time came to fight and hopefully run, he was determined to be ready.

There was a hiss and snarl from the tunnel mouth and he turned to see what had made the sound – his eyes straining to make out the shapes in the dim light. There seemed to be a father standing there, a black shape against the paler grey of the outside world. He was squat with a massive head and appeared to be wearing baggy shorts. He made a noise that sounded like he was clearing his throat and the four strangers seemed to understand what he wanted. Two of them, Bluetooth and the Bandit, took hold of one of the dead kids by the ankles and dragged him outside. Man U and Mr Ordinary then took hold of the girl who was still alive and pulled her out by her feet in the same way. She moaned and whimpered but didn't struggle. Then Bluetooth and the Bandit were back and taking hold of Shadowman. He decided not to fight, either. He needed to know where he was and what was going on before he could make any kind of escape plan.

When they dragged him out of the end of the tunnel, it was a moment before he realized where he was. It was so unexpected. In fact he had to close his eyes and open them a couple of times to make sure he wasn't hallucinating.

It was a football stadium. Overhead was a wide expanse of open sky and all around were ranks of seats. He tried to think which stadium it might be. If he was in north London, it had to be either the Spurs ground or the Arsenal. It was big enough and modern enough to be the new Arsenal stadium and that would make sense as it was the nearest one to King's Cross.

The father he had seen silhouetted in the tunnel mouth was standing in the centre of the overgrown pitch. The four strangers seemed to be looking after him. Now that Shadowman could make him out clearly he saw that he had an immense, swollen bald head, a pair of wire-framed glasses with no lenses and was wearing a football vest with the cross of St George on it. There were two dead bodies at his feet, half hidden in the long grass, and the girl who was still alive was trying to stand up. Bluetooth went over and knocked her down, then stood patiently by the fat-headed one as if awaiting orders.

Shadowman had never seen this level of organization among grown-ups before. The idea that they might have a leader, that they might work together, was something new to him. Most of the grown-ups had been driven out of the area around Buckingham Palace, so Shadowman hadn't been able to observe how they behaved, but obviously those that had survived the year since the disease first struck were changing, developing, growing. Unless it was only the cleverer ones that had survived this long. If they started to properly work together they would become truly dangerous. He was appalled, scared, and yet fascinated by what he was seeing.

He noticed that there were more strangers in the stadium seating, as if watching the spectacle that was unfolding on the pitch. Like some sort of gladiatorial games.

Or a human sacrifice.

How many were there?

Shadowman realized he had withdrawn from what was going on. He was watching all this as if it was happening to someone else. He'd always been the type to stand back and observe – now he was spying on his own death.

This would make quite a scene in a film. The grotesque swollen-headed father with the glasses, his diseased minions, the zombie spectators. All it lacked was flaming torches to give it the full Hollywood pagan-ceremony treatment.

As if on cue, a gout of flame shot up from the back of one section of seating. It seemed to be coming from one of the hospitality suites where privileged guests could watch the matches while tucking into a nice lunch. The fire spread and lit up half the stadium and then Shadowman was amazed to see a father, engulfed in flames from head to foot, come crashing out into the open, and tumble down three rows of seats. The strangers on the pitch were mesmerized. They turned as one to gaze dumbly at the rising column of smoke, and the flames that leapt and sparked as they spread along the back of the stands.

The strangers who were nearest to it were thrown into a panic. They spilt out of their seats and ran in all directions. Shadowman's gang, the more organized ones, were calmer, but he could sense fear taking hold of them.

Something was attacking their den. For the moment they forgot about Shadowman and stood there, confused and angry. It was all the opportunity he needed, but if he tried to run would his legs betray him again? Would his brain short-circuit and send him flip-flapping to the ground like a puppet whose strings had been cut?

He had to risk it. He wasn't going to be offered a better chance of escape than this, and if he delayed a moment longer the strangers might remember him and get back to work.

Now or never, Shadowman.

What did Nike say? Just do it . . .

He took a couple of deep breaths, filled his lungs with oxygen and lurched forward. He took a few wobbly steps and his legs held up.

Now run!

He broke away from the gang and aimed for the nearest stand. He wasn't about to go back into the players' tunnel – it was too dark in there and he had no idea where it led

— but there would be openings in the stands leading to the exits. It would mean getting in among the strangers. He just hoped that they'd be confused and groggy and panicked.

Miracle of miracles, his legs stayed firm, his brain stayed focused. He vaulted over an advertising hoarding into the seats and felt a rush of life and energy surging through his body.

So long, suckers . . . The Shadowman is out of here!

51

'You can't leave.'

'We can and we are.'

DogNut was standing by the diplodocus in the main hall at the museum with Courtney. Morning light was streaming in through the windows. They'd packed their gear and had been about to round up Felix and Marco when Justin had appeared, bustling in from one of the side galleries. Now he was hyped up and anxious.

'You give us one good reason why we can't go,' said DogNut.

'You promised me you'd tell your stories to Chris Marker, for *The Chronicles of Survival*.'

'Did I? I don't remember promising nothing.'

Justin grunted and rubbed his scalp, shifting his weight from one foot to the other.

'Well, yeah, OK,' he said. 'Maybe you didn't promise, but I asked and I thought you'd agreed.'

'Didn't agree to nothing.'

'It's important to us,' Justin pleaded.

'We need to get back, Justin,' said DogNut apologetically. 'We've done what we set out to do. We found you lot – now we need to go and tell them back at the Tower. They're the ones who need to hear our stories.'

'Yes,' said Justin, 'I appreciate that, but, well, we've shown you everything we're doing here, and . . . and the least you can do is tell us how you've survived. It would be a huge help to us.'

'What d'you mean?' said DogNut. 'I don't see how it helps anything.'

'It's a very valuable resource.'

'*A very valuable resource*,' said DogNut, mocking Justin's nasal tones.

Justin's face flushed red, and he raised his voice angrily. 'You can take the piss, DogNut,' he snapped, 'but we happen to think it's important.'

'Well, how long's it going to take?' said DogNut.

'All you have to do is tell your stories, starting with what you can remember of when the disease first struck, and finishing with your arrival here.'

'Yeah,' said DogNut. 'So I'll ask you again, brother, how long do you think it'll take?'

'I don't know, a few hours? They've got to write it all down.'

'A few hours?' DogNut's face was a picture of amazement. 'But we need to make an early start. That ain't gonna work.'

'Leave tomorrow,' Justin pleaded. 'What difference will one more day make? It would mean a lot to us . . . It would mean a lot to me. I'll give you stuff for the journey, food and water. If you'll just do this one thing for me.'

'I don't know . . .'

'He's right, Dog,' said Courtney. 'What difference would one more day make?'

'I thought it was you that wanted to go!' DogNut protested.

'I don't mind.'

'I'll tell you what,' said Justin. 'If you agree to stay and tell us your stories, I'll give you an escort. I'll get Robbie to pick some fighters and go with you, at least some of the way.'

'On one condition,' said DogNut.

'What?'

'Jackson comes along. That girl is well hard.'

'Deal.'

DogNut sighed and put down his pack. 'All right,' he said. 'Agreed. One more day. We'll talk to Chris.'

'Thanks, DogNut,' said Justin, and he shook DogNut's hand.

52

The squirrel ran across the grass, its body and tail moving in a series of flowing S shapes. It stopped. Sat up on its hind legs, its whole body shaking. There was no way it could go any further in this direction. It turned and darted back the way it had come. Again its path was blocked. It raced off in another direction. It was panicking, running shorter and shorter distances as the net tightened round it. Scurrying, stopping, turning, twitching, jumping . . .

The gym bunnies weren't going to let it reach a tree. They'd been chasing it for the last half-hour, and they were determined to catch it.

They were getting used to the sunlight, staying out longer each time, growing braver. They'd risked coming into the park this morning. There was nobody else around and their hunger was driving them crazy. They'd stripped bark off the trees and pulled up plants to get at the roots. And then they'd seen the squirrel. Scared it out of a tree down on to the ground.

Now it was surely trapped.

The mother moved forward. It would be her kill. She held her knife tight in one hand. All she had to do was grab the animal and slit its throat. It skittered away across the grass, chittering and squeaking. She dived, missed. Another sicko lunged. Another kicked it and it flew back towards the mother who at last managed to get a hand to it. She held it up to show the others, grinning. She was proud of them. They were learning to work together properly. They were a team.

The animal wriggled in her grasp, shrieking, scratching and biting her fingers. She put the knife to its scrawny neck and cut deep, severing its head. The bright red blood foamed out and she quickly put it to her mouth, drinking it down, feeling it hot against her tongue and lips.

A father picked up the head and popped it into his mouth, crunching it like a sweet.

The mother sat on the grass and stretched the animal's small body out, stuck the knife into its belly to get at the guts.

It felt so good she smiled with joy. The knife was helping her think straight. The familiar feel of it in her hands was awakening old memories. She was becoming stronger, clearer-headed, more able to hunt and kill.

She stuffed the warm guts into her mouth, tossed the squirrel's body to her pack and stood up.

Raised the knife to the sky. Felt the energy from it pulse through her body. Stared at it, clutched in her ragged fingers. Her eyes twitching in her head as they tried to focus on the blade. Transfixed by the light that lanced off it. Letting it flicker across her eyes. Showing the others in her pack that she wasn't afraid. That she had the willpower to resist.

It was a tool, and tools were what had given mankind dominance over every other living thing on the planet. Just holding the knife had cleared her head and boosted the intelligence that made her the natural leader of the pack. And the powerful electric force that flowed through her from the cold, hard handle of the weapon brought back memories. Memories of all the things that she had lost. A glimpse into the perfect golden world she had lived in before the sickness had wormed its way inside her, wriggling and burrowing through her flesh. It had taken root in her just as the knife was doing now. She could see writhing tendrils snake out of the handle and dig into her flesh, joining with her veins and arteries. The power of the knife would banish the disease. She could see black lines on her skin. Was it a picture, perhaps? A picture of the disease?

She smiled.

See.

She was growing clever again. The knife was the key. The rest of the pack, they were too stupid to understand these things; all they could do was follow. Like animals. Hunting together.

Soon they'd go back underground to their new den by the tube tracks. They could only take the brightness for a little while. They'd rest, strengthened by this tiny meal, drink the water that rose up through the ground. And tomorrow they'd be strong enough to risk attacking any children who came past. As long as it was a small enough group. She would fall on them and she would gut them like she had gutted the rat thing.

She chuckled, blood dribbling from between her teeth.

Tomorrow.

Tomorrow they would eat properly.

They'd found some children in the night, hiding in a building. The children had tried to use fire to drive them away. But the fire had turned on them, and they'd burned up. She dribbled as she remembered the smell of roasting meat, a pool of spit forming at her feet.

The children were in the kitchen, cooking.

When they'd finally got to them there was nothing left, just charred bones. So she'd brought the pack out to hunt in the daylight. She had to help them.

She was their mother . . . Was that right? Where had that thought come from? Was she the mother of the children who'd been cooking in the house? Or was she the mother of the pack? Was she the mother of them all?

Mother. Definitely a mother.

Before the worms had got into her body she had had real children. Not roasted ones. Babies of her own. Delicious babies. No, not delicious. That came later . . .

She snarled. Shook her head, trying to pin down her thoughts. They were tangled up, the threads of disease inside her, the roots of the knife inside her, the black lines on her skin, twisting and knotting, one thing leading to another . . .

Concentrate.

Where were her babies now? Where had she left them? She had no idea what had happened to them. The hard bright light bounced off the blade and drove deep into her brain. She moaned and her mind emptied. For a while no thoughts troubled her. No memories bubbled to the surface. She saw no pictures except the confusing black scrawl on her wrist. Then the blade turned, the light switched off and her mind flowered back into life. Thoughts came crowding in. She wasn't looking at a picture of the disease, or roots from the knife, the black lines on her wrist were a tattoo. A Celtic tribal knot. Her boyfriend had one the same round his wrist . . .

337

What had happened to him? She had an image of a body covered in boils. The smell of decay. A man screaming as his face split down the middle. She pushed the memory aside and searched for happier ones. A hospital bed. A baby in a cot. A home. Polished wooden floors the colour of honey. A television. A running machine in a gym.

That was the most powerful image – the gym and all its machines. All working away together, parts of one giant machine. And there *she* was, watching the TV as she ran. And ran and ran and ran. Pictures on the TV now, of hospitals and doctors in white coats, talking. Not the same hospital. Not the one where she had had her baby. That was a different memory. She snarled again. No matter how hard she tried to hold on to the good memories, the bad ones were stronger. Sickness. Death. Pictures on the TV of the disease spreading. Ambulances. Hospitals overflowing with patients. Men in white coats talking . . .

That was all they'd ever done. Just talked. They hadn't found a cure. There hadn't been time . . .

The light stabbed at her eyes again and her memories twisted away from her, as if someone had pressed the delete button. Her screen was blank. All her memories were gone and she was back, tangled in the lines on her wrist.

Dirty. She tried to rub them off, and realized she was holding something in her other hand.

A knife.

Yes.

She had to hold on to it. Never let it go. It was power. Power over the children and power over her pack. She sniffed the air. Watched the dancing sunlight on her blade. She'd been thinking about something. What was it? Why couldn't she fix her mind on one thing? She took in a long shuddering breath. Her lungs burned, scarred by illness. Her skin itched. Her eyes were raw; they felt like they'd been peeled. Her brain was too big for her head; the pressure gave her a permanent headache. Only one thing made the pain go away, made her thoughts slow down, only one thing gave her calm.

The blood that ran in the little ones' veins. The flesh that wrapped their small thin bones. The life they held inside. A shame the ones in the house had got burned up, a terrible shame. It had forced her out in the daylight.

Well, from now on she was going to walk in the light. She had feared it for too long. If they hadn't been disturbed by the hunters, forced from their den, maybe they'd never have learned.

It hurt. It confused them. But if they were careful they could survive it.

It wouldn't be easy.

Small steps.

An hour a day. No matter how much it hurt.

Like going to the gym.

Enough. Time to go back into the darkness. She hissed to the pack and led them out of the park. As they walked down the street, shrinking from the sun's rays, she saw something glinting. Something she needed. She walked closer.

It was a shop, and lined up in the broken window were glasses, and there, at one end, was a model head wearing sunglasses. She laughed.

Clever.

Use tools.

That was how it worked. That was what would make her strong. The mother of the pack. The rest of them were useless. They had no idea that they had once used tools, driven cars, worked in offices; their hands hadn't just been for stuffing their stupid faces.

'You're fired,' she grunted – the first words she had spoken for as long as she could remember – as she reached in for the sunglasses. Ignoring the broken glass that gashed her arm.

She lifted the glasses off the dummy. Raised them to her face. As she put them on, she started to laugh.

She had been queen of the night, now she would be queen of the day too. Tomorrow she would catch some children.

She turned her face up to the sky and screamed at the sun.

'You're fired. You're fired. You're fired. You're fired. You're fired. You're fired. You're fired. You're fired. You're fired . . .'

53

Shadowman was lying on his belly, looking out through the bottom of a floor-to-ceiling picture window. The rest of the glass was filthy with dust and grime, but he'd cleared a patch just big enough to give him a good view of the outside world without being spotted.

He was four floors up in a flat opposite the smouldering Arsenal stadium. It had been a mad scramble getting away, battling through the slow and confused strangers who lived in there. His gang of four had given chase, but he'd been too fast for them. They may have been cleverer and less diseased than most of their kind, but they were still clumsy and unco-ordinated. The worst part had been when he'd gone through to the back of the stands and down the access stairs to try to find a street exit. He'd ended up running round and round the lower level until he'd stumbled across an open gate. The inside of the stadium was full of filth, human waste, dying strangers, rotting bodies, piles of unrecognizable rubbish. It was probably all this that was burning now.

Once he was out he'd decided he couldn't get very far away. He was still light-headed from the concussion and didn't want to risk moving around too much in the dark in an area he didn't know. He would put himself in danger of stumbling across more grown-ups.

Once he was sure nobody was on his tail he'd chosen this place to hide out. It was an old industrial building that had been turned into modern flats. He was hoping that any strangers in the area would congregate with the others inside the stadium, but he was still very careful when he broke in. Normally this would have been just the sort of place where they build their nests. He still had a box of matches in his pocket and he'd gone straight down to the basement to thoroughly search it by their juddering light. Then he'd worked his way up to the top. Any doors that were firmly bolted he'd ignored. Strangers didn't use locks. The whole of the top floor was a large studio apartment that must have been quite swanky in its day, with polished wooden floors and exposed brickwork on the walls that were hung with abstract art. The door had been hanging open, however, and the place had been ransacked. When the disease had first struck, when half the police force was off sick, and law and order had broken down, hordes of looters hit the streets. Their frenzy didn't last long, though, as they themselves had quickly fallen ill. In a few short weeks it was over.

This apartment hadn't escaped the vultures. Anything useful and usable and valuable had been carried off. There was broken glass everywhere, smashed furniture. He was pleased to see that there was no evidence of recent use by grown-ups, however. Like the rest of the building it was deserted, so it suited his purposes perfectly.

First he'd secured the door and wedged it shut. After that he'd tidied up a little and found some old bedding in a cupboard. Together with the cushions from a sofa he'd made a bed by the window and settled down. He figured that if he could stay close to the strangers it would give him an advantage. He would know where they were and what they were doing, and with any luck he could stay hidden from them. The air was full of smoke and the bitter stink of burning rubbish, which would mask any scent he might be giving off. He would learn their movements, study their behaviour, and when he was strong and rested he would set off back to civilization. He hoped that would be sooner rather than later. He mustn't rush it, though. He felt pretty terrible. There was a big lump on his forehead where Jester had hit him that was round and hard and shiny, and his head thudded in time with his heartbeat.

He had dozed off and on through the night. Waking to squint out through his little spyhole and follow the progress of the fire. It had lit up the whole sky, illuminating the streets as well as any floodlamps. The stadium was set back far enough from the surrounding buildings for the fire not to spread, and it seemed to be reasonably well contained, so Shadowman found it comforting rather than frightening. Now and then strangers would spill out and mill around in the road, not sure what to do. Some of them fought each other in their frustration.

It was quiet now. The sun was riding high in the sky. He warmed himself in the little patch of light that was spreading across the floorboards. He didn't think he would sleep any more. He was stiff and aching all over. His neck felt like it had seized up. He hoped Jester hadn't done any permanent damage.

Jester. Just to think of him made his headache ten times worse. How could he have deserted him like that? Left him there to be eaten by strangers?

He'd always known that Jester was self-centred and hard-hearted – that was how he'd survived for so long, after all.

But he'd never expected his friend to just dump him. If he ever met him again – and how likely was that? There was no saying that Jester had got away himself – Shadowman thought that he could easily kill him. He really thought he could do it. He pictured himself shoving his knife into his belly.

Only he'd lost his knife, hadn't he. His knife and his precious pack. He was completely defenceless. He'd need to find a new weapon before he strayed very far from his den.

He coughed. Felt a harsh rasp in his throat. He was very thirsty. He had his precious canteen still fixed to his belt, but it wouldn't last long. He had to think about finding more water. He could go a few days without food if necessary, but more than twenty-four hours without water and he'd be in serious trouble.

All in all, the message was clear.

He couldn't stay lying here any longer.

He slid back from the window. There didn't seem to be any strangers about, but it was best to be careful and never let his guard down.

He did a few exercises to loosen up his muscles. Tried rolling his head on his stiff neck. Groaned. Massaged his temples. Then he took the A to Z out of his pocket, glad that he'd stuffed it there the last time he'd looked at it, rather than into his pack, and looked up the Arsenal stadium.

There it was, just off Holloway Road. When he felt up to it, the walk back to the palace, if he was left alone, could be done in two or three hours, probably.

If he was left alone.

Who knew what waited for him outside the doors to the building?

A haze of smoke hung in the air, even here inside the

apartment, and it made him cough again. He had to find water before he could think of doing anything else.

Shadowman had explored enough of the city to know that a building like this would be likely to have water storage tanks in the roof. These could be a useful source of drinking water, so long as it hadn't gone stagnant. He searched for a hatch of some kind and eventually found one in the ceiling at the top of the stairwell. He stood up on a chair and pushed it open. An access ladder slid out. He pulled it down then climbed up into the roof space. He sat for a while to get his breath back. He found even the smallest movements tiring. Then he lit a homemade torch that he had constructed out of a chair leg wrapped in strips of torn-up sheet. There was just room enough to stand here, and the roof space was enormous. He soon spotted a couple of large water tanks, protected by plastic covers. He eased the cover off one of them and waved his torch over it. It was three quarters full and there was no smell. The water looked clean – no animals had crept in and drowned, or used it for a toilet. He drank the last of the water in his bottle then refilled it from the tank. It would be better boiled, but his guts had got used to eating and drinking all sorts of things that they would have rejected before the disaster.

Feeling more confident he set off back towards the hatchway, and that was when he saw them.

Three wooden boxes behind an old chimney breast. He opened them to discover they contained a secret emergency stash that someone had hidden up here.

They were filled with cans and packets of dry food, another box with a pair of binoculars, a tool-kit and an emergency medical kit, including water purification tablets, and, next to them, a large holdall packed with weapons.

Three knives, a machete, two baseball bats, even a crossbow with twenty steel bolts.

He shouted in triumph and punched the air, shouting, 'Yes, yes, yes, yes, yes . . .' over and over again, tears running down his face.

This was salvation.

Forget Jester.

Forget that loser. The Shadowman was back on track.

He could hardly believe it. It was as if some God with a warped sense of humour had decided he'd had enough for a while, and it was time to give him a bit of good luck.

He was reminded of playing computer games. Just when you were out of ammo there'd be a bonus to collect. Something to keep you going through to the end of the level.

He snuffed out his torch and sat down among the boxes, overcome with emotion. He hadn't realized just how strung out he was. He'd been running on nothing more than adrenalin and fear for a day. He'd been that close to breaking.

Nearly an hour later, well armed and well fed, back to something approaching an even keel, he climbed down the ladder and returned to his spyhole to check whether the coast was clear.

He'd made the decision to move on. Finding the stash had been a sign. He'd been given the tools to get back to civilization.

It was still quiet outside. He laced his boots up tightly, stuck a knife in his belt, loaded the crossbow and left the apartment, carefully closing the door behind him and wedging it shut again. If there were any problems, he could come back here.

He started down the stairs, treading softly, staying alert and focused.

He made it down without incident and peered out into the street.

It was deserted. All he had to do was start walking . . .

He paused. For a moment gripped by doubt. His confidence had been jolted yesterday. For months he'd been on top of things, and then . . . In a few short hours it had all fallen apart. He'd realized just how vulnerable he was.

He took some deep breaths. Told himself that he could do it. Told himself he was going to get back to safety. They'd been fools, him and Jester. Wandering off for a picnic in a minefield. He knew it wasn't going to be easy getting back to central London. These outlying areas were wilder than he'd ever imagined. David and the other kids like him in the large settlements might have been pompous pricks, self-important little Hitlers, but at least they'd cleaned up the streets and made them relatively safe. This was war around here.

Come on . . . Just do it . . .

He was about to step out of the doorway when some sixth sense told him to wait. Maybe his ears had picked up a tiny sound, maybe his keen eyes had spotted a movement, maybe there was a new smell of rot in the air, but whatever it was he was suddenly tingling all over and his muscles locked in place.

Don't move. Wait. Be careful.

He shrank back behind the security desk in the reception area, and looked out into the street.

They were starting to appear. Strangers. Pouring out of the stadium, like the crowd after a match. At their head was St George in his grubby vest, then came his associates, the gang of four – Bluetooth, the One-Armed Bandit, Man U and Mr Ordinary, the man with no name.

Behind them . . .

An army.

That's what it looked like. An army of strangers, not exactly marching in step, more a shambling mob, but moving with a purpose nevertheless. The fire must have got so bad they'd been forced from their hiding-place into the open, the bright sun.

So many of them. It took ages for them all to pass. Shadowman held back. Waiting for his moment.

Finally the last few stragglers shuffled past and he got ready to head off in the opposite direction.

Except . . .

What were they doing? Where were they going? He remembered his revelation of last night, about how dangerous the strangers would be if they properly united. If they could join others like themselves, band together into larger and larger gangs, be a real army.

Until last night such a thought would never have entered his mind. Now, though, he was seeing something horribly new and dangerous. He had to follow them. He told himself that he was only making sure that he knew where they were, so that he could avoid them, but he knew it was something more than that.

Know your enemy.

And they *were* the enemy. A real threat. This organized rabble. This terrifying . . .

What?

What could he call them?

He'd always liked to name things. If you put a label on something, it was yours – you owned it. That was why he was so frustrated at not to be able to think of a proper name for the fourth stranger in St George's little gang of lieutenants.

He'd spent his life following, observing, naming . . . Now he could put his skills to good use. He sneaked out into the road and set off after them. The secret survival hoard had been a sign. But it was a sign that he had misread. He'd been given what he needed, not to go back to the palace, but to survive on the streets here and keep an eye on the strangers.

There was only one thing. If he was going to spy on this army of the sick, he'd need to give them a name.

It would come to him.

54

DogNut, Courtney, Marco, Felix and Finn were in the library where Chris Marker and his assistants had set up camp. Chris was sitting at one end of a long table with a huge leather-bound volume open in front of him, writing carefully by hand on the blank creamy-white pages. Assistants sat on either side of him, all writing away in similar ledgers. There was a peaceful air of quiet study. The assistants were listening intently to DogNut, looking up now and then, before tilting their noses back to their work.

They'd been here all day, Dog Nut's team, taking it in turns to tell their stories, and now it was his turn. He was the last to go and not enjoying it. He'd been telling them everything he could remember about what had happened since his mum and dad died and he'd had to face up to the new reality of a disease-ruined world. He had told how he'd left his council block and joined Jordan Hordern's crew. How they'd fought their way into the Imperial War Museum, and how they'd lived there until they'd been forced to leave by the fire.

As he talked, the sun slowly went down and one of Chris's assistants lit a row of candles that had been placed down the middle of the table. They gave a comforting, mellow glow. Courtney felt like she was in some medieval film, or the sort of programme you used to get on the BBC about monks and things.

DogNut paused, scratched his stubbly head. Not sure how to carry on. His voice was hoarse. He was tired of talking. The day had seemed to go on forever. He couldn't believe that he had delayed going back to the Tower for this. He'd been so keen to get here and now the thought of spending just one more night was torture. He looked out of the window. Getting darker all the time.

Whatever happened he was leaving first thing in the morning.

'Go on,' said Chris, pen hovering over the page.

'Look, I ain't any good at this,' said DogNut. 'I don't know what's important. I don't really know how to tell stories, only jokes.'

'You're doing fine,' said Chris Marker. 'Don't stop now. Let *me* worry about how to make it into a story.'

'How you gonna do that, though? It's just, like, stuff that happened.'

'There are stories everywhere; you just have to untangle them.'

'You reckon?'

'Yeah. So go on then.'

DogNut went on. He told the story of how he and his friends had found Ed fighting for his life at Lambeth Bridge. How they'd got split up from everyone else and ended up drifting down the river on the tour boat. He told about their arrival at the Tower, and then it had been left to him to tell all that happened in the last year. How Jordan Hordern had organized them into military units. How they'd made the Tower secure and protected it. How they grew food. The fights they'd had. The things they'd found. The friends they'd lost.

Courtney and the others chipped in now and then, adding their own memories, filling in the gaps for him and correcting some of his mistakes. He wasn't very good at telling it clearly. He kept stopping and starting and going off on side stories and forgetting what he was talking about, but Chris Marker remained patient, occasionally asking him to clarify something or repeat it so that he was sure he understood correctly.

And then finally DogNut came to the story of their journey here. Of the boat trip back up the river, of meeting Nicola and her kids at the Houses of Parliament, of Bozo and the hunters. He laughed about their short stay at the palace and outwitting David. He didn't laugh when he came to the part about the Collector. He mumbled and muttered and became very vague when he told about leaving Olivia behind. Courtney saw he was having difficulties and took over, quickly filling in the last part – arriving at the museum and going back with Paul and Robbie and the others to kill the Collector.

Once DogNut was done Chris put down his pen and looked up, rubbing his eyes, which looked feeble and watery in the candlelight.

'Thank you,' he said, closing the book.

'Not sure what use any of that's gonna be,' said DogNut. 'The only thing I know for sure, talking about it, is I want to be back there at the Tower right now.'

'You never know what's going to be important in the future,' said Chris. 'There are loads of stories in London. There are kids out there now going through the same things as you, and they're all parts of one big story. The story of our survival, of fights and victories, and defeats and death, friends being killed, enemies being slain.'

'Slain?' said DogNut. 'Nobody says "slain". You even sounding like a book.'

'Why not?' said Chris, and he tapped the leather cover of his ledger with his fingertips. 'We're all in a book – *this book*. We're all in the story. Tonight we're writing down your part in it, DogNut.'

'Yeah, great,' said DogNut. 'To be honest I didn't understand any of what you just said.'

'Everything you've done since you left the Tower,' said Chris patiently, 'all the people you've met, it will all have an effect, and who knows where it will all end? It's like dropping a stone in a pond, ripples go out in all directions.'

DogNut snorted through his nose. He was beginning to think Chris Marker was half mad. He'd never really known him before. This was the most he'd ever heard him say. Somehow this weird kid had come alive here, in this world of books.

'There you go again, Chrissy-Boy,' he said. 'Hitting me with your deep stuff. You ain't making it no clearer, bruv. Let me tell you.'

'I suppose what I'm saying, DogNut, is that you're part of history. We don't know yet how important a part, but you're in there all the same.'

'Is anyone really gonna be interested in reading about me, though?'

'I'm interested,' said Chris, 'and others will be too. We're the new generation. We're the survivors. We're making a whole new world here. In the future, kids are going to want to know what happened. How it was. I think your journey, crossing London, could be really important, because you've taken the first steps to uniting all the kids around London, drawing us all together. It's like someone coming from the other side of the world, like Marco Polo travelling to China, or Columbus arriving in America. You'll all be important figures to future generations. You'll all be heroes.'

'Future generations?' DogNut scoffed. 'If we're lucky.'

'We're going to make it, DogNut,' said Chris.

'Who says these *future generations* are gonna want to remember, though?' said DogNut. 'I'd of thought they'd want to forget all about this.'

'No. History is important . . . You know what Winston Churchill said?' asked Chris.

'We'll fight them on the beaches, or something.'

'Yeah, he said that, but he also said that history is written by the victors.'

'What's that mean then?'

'It means that if you win a war you can write the books and say you were the good guys and the losers were the bad guys.'

'Yeah, OK, I'm on it. So what?'

'I think it works the other way round as well,' said Chris. 'If you write the history, you'll *become* the victor.'

'You lost me again.'

'If we make our own history, if we tell stories that bring us together, we'll be stronger. It'll give us something to believe in. The sickos can't do that – they're no better than animals – but *we* can. Every battle we win we have to tell the story over and over, so that we can win more battles. People love stories. They've told stories since even before they could write. Myths and legends, stories of heroes and villains, gods and monsters. Real things happened, the story got told and then the stories became legends. That's what we've got to do – tell our own heroic stories.'

'I don't feel like much of a hero,' said DogNut, and

354

Courtney laughed. 'Plodding across London, letting poor little Olivia die.'

'It depends how you tell the story,' said Chris, and he smiled at DogNut. 'You're Jack the giant-killer, and the Collector was an ogre in his castle, the Cyclops in his cave, the Minotaur in his labyrinth. Olivia was the virgin who was sent off to be sacrificed, and you're the guys who tried to save her, who slew the monster once and for all so that nobody else would be eaten by him.'

'Yeah, maybe when you put it like that it don't sound so bad . . .'

'That's the power of storytelling. That's why we have to control the stories – to control history. What was the Collector's version? It was the story of a poor lonely man, the last of his kind, just trying to survive, and being ambushed in his den by vicious killers. That would make it very different. If we told it that way, we'd feel sorry for him, and then it'd make it harder to kill other sickos in the future. That's why *we* have to tell the stories, so that we're the heroes and the sickos are the monsters. We tell it our way.'

'What are you saying, book-boy?' DogNut was shaking his head slowly. 'I keep thinking I got it and then you hit me with more words and it goes out my head.'

'I'm saying you're going to be a hero, DogNut, whether you like it or not.'

55

Jester was sewing a patch on to his coat by the glow of a fire. It was a small piece of material he'd cut from an old T-shirt of Shadowman's. He'd found the shirt in a pile of clothes that Shadowman had left at the palace. Jester had brought it along with him in his satchel . . .

Just in case.

He had no doubt that Shadow was dead. This way he'd always remember him. When he got back to the palace, he'd find out whether Kate or Tom had made it. He doubted he'd ever see Alfie again, and would have some explaining to do if he did. Probably, though, he would distribute Alfie's belongings among the other kids, and hold one item of clothing back.

To cut a patch from.

He put down the needle and thread, and stared into the fire, watching the embers. It was the closest thing to television any of them had now. You could stare into a fire and imagine it was anything you liked. You could be staring into another world. Witnessing the eruption of a volcano. The birth of a planet. The lights of a giant city from the air . . .

Or just a fire.

He rubbed his face. It was very late. Apart from the

guards they'd posted around their camp, the others were all asleep. He was lucky. He knew that much. He'd stumbled across a group of kids who knew how to look after themselves. Two groups of kids, if he was going to be accurate. Each group had been holed up inside a different supermarket, and he gathered that they didn't exactly get on. That was useful information. He'd tuck it away in case he needed to use it later. After he'd been rescued he'd managed to persuade both groups that they'd all be a lot better off at the palace. He was good at that kind of thing. Talking people round. And he knew that once he got these kids to the palace, if he wanted to keep them there, doing what David told them, he was going to need to use all his powers of persuasion, his skill at bending the truth. He was going to have to convince them that they were looking at something white when it was actually black.

These were tough kids who weren't used to being told what to do by anyone else, but if he could make them believe that the palace was the best place to live in the whole of London, then David would have the best army around. It was going to be difficult. Not everyone took to David. Not everyone wanted to live under his rule. He drove Jester himself up the wall sometimes.

Yeah. He was going to be busy, and was already planning his strategy now. The Holloway kids weren't all fighters. They had younger kids with them who would appreciate the greater safety and security on offer at the palace, so that was a start. It was their leaders who were going to be the most trouble. Although on that front Jester had had a little luck. Arran, the leader of the Waitrose kids, had been killed in a pitched battle with some particularly nasty grown-ups.

A girl called Maxie seemed to have taken temporary charge, but he wasn't sure how much authority she had. She'd be easy to deal with. The leader of the second group of kids, however, the ones from Morrisons, the bastards who had initially chased him away, was going to be harder. His name was Blue, and he was one tough case. David was going to have to offer him something he really wanted. Failing that, Jester would have to arrange for poor old Blue to be taken out of the picture. Jester wasn't ever going to forgive him or his crew for driving him away with stones.

He'd get his revenge. He just had to wait for the right time. There was no hurry.

For now he just had to get them safely to the palace. When they saw the good life to be had there, it should soften them up.

The downside to Arran dying was that they'd all been held up for hours waiting for him to give up the ghost. And then Maxie had insisted on burning his body. By the time they'd reached Regent's Park it had been dark, and they'd been attacked again, this time by wild animals. In the end they'd decided not to push on any further until it was light. Now they were camped out in a railed-off public garden at the end of the park. Guards patrolled the perimeters, a couple more kept watch from the roof of a groundsman's hut. Jester felt perfectly safe. Having seen these kids in action, he was more than a little impressed.

He was tired. He'd sleep soon. For now, though, he was trying to make plans while it was quiet. How easy it had been in the old days, with mobile phones and email and Facebook. He could have had a long chat with David and warned him in advance of their arrival. Told him to lay it on thick, prepare a feast, put on a show. They could have banged their heads together until they'd come up with a solid plan. Instead he was having to fly solo for now.

Never mind. He was sure it would all work out fine. It wasn't far to the palace from here, certainly not more than an hour. They'd be there before lunchtime tomorrow. In the end his trip had been successful, more successful than he'd ever dared to imagine. He'd hoped to maybe find a few strays and outcasts who might want to join up with a larger group for protection and instead he'd found these tough and well-organized *warriors*. It was a shame he'd lost Alfie along the way. And probably Kate and Tom – God knows where they'd ended up. Good luck to them.

And then there was Shadowman. That was a *real* shame. He'd liked Shadow. The closest thing to a best friend he'd had in the world. In the end, though, Shadow had made a sacrifice for the greater good. Look what Jester was bringing back in exchange for his life. At least thirty new recruits. If there was anybody up there in the sky keeping score, couldn't they see that Jester had done the right thing? What use was it living in small scattered groups around London? They needed to be in one big group. That was the future.

Surely Jester had done more good than bad.

No, not *bad*, wrong.

He had done more right than wrong.

Hell. Had he even done wrong at all? It wasn't his fault Shadowman had walked inside his swing. If you wanted to blame anyone, blame the strangers, blame the bloody grown-ups who'd left the world in this mess.

Don't blame *him*. Not Jester. All Jester was doing was surviving. That's what mattered now. To get through all this and rebuild the world.

Yes. Everything he had done was for the future of mankind.

When he'd finished sewing on the patch, he would sleep well tonight.

And if Shadowman himself was up in heaven looking down at him, he was sure he'd understand.

56

The strangers weren't going to give up. They'd been besieging the house since before it had got dark. How long ago was that? A few hours, definitely. From his new hiding-place, in a burnt-out family home a safe distance away from the action, Shadowman had trouble seeing exactly what was going on in the darkness. He could hear well enough, though. Hear the strangers' grunts and yowls, the creak of breaking wood, the occasional snap. There were kids inside that house and the strangers intended to get at them no matter how long it took.

He'd followed them all day. At first they'd meandered aimlessly about the streets with no real purpose and he'd moved from house to house behind them, keeping far enough away that there was no danger of them smelling him, but close enough that he wouldn't lose them. It wasn't difficult. They moved in a slow, shuffling mass, stopping every few minutes and, for no obvious reason, milling in the road, before switching direction and wandering off again. Even if the leaders got too far ahead Shadowman always kept one eye on the stragglers – he couldn't let his guard down – and kept his other eye in the back of his head as smaller groups were constantly appearing out of nowhere, curious to see what was going on. In the past

Shadowman had seen rival gangs of strangers attack each other, like packs of wild dogs, but that hadn't happened today. These strangers, under the leadership of St George, were working together as an army, just as Shadowman had feared.

Finally, after a long stretch of this random behaviour, he'd noticed a change come over them. They'd become more alert, excited, and had started to move faster. He, in turn, had had to move faster to keep up, taking more risks as he darted from one safe cover to another.

Intrigued as to what might have caused this change in them, he'd braved flanking the crowd to see what the leaders were up to. He'd managed to work his way far enough round the side to get a reasonably good view. St George was acting as if he was on the scent of something. Kids most likely. There was a purpose to him, and the rest of the strangers responded to it. They'd moved steadily south, sticking together, shambling along a little faster. Shadowman had let them pass him by and then fallen back to his position at the rear.

Perhaps twenty minutes later the strangers had become severely agitated and Shadowman assumed they must be moving in for the kill. They'd grown very excited, and now lots of small fights had broken out among them. Then they'd halted. Shadowman had been following their progress in his A to Z and had worked out that they were about halfway down Camden Road. Once again he'd wanted to sneak forward to see what was happening, but couldn't risk it. In this fired-up state the strangers were unpredictable and a lot more dangerous. Instead he had to wait frustratingly at the rear, trying to read what was going on in their increasingly disturbed actions.

They'd waited in the road for ages before suddenly lurching forward in a drunken sort of charge. What followed was evidently a battle of some kind. Shadowman was too far away to see what was happening, but it was clear that a big fight was in progress. He hoped that whoever they were attacking were well armed and well prepared. He could do absolutely nothing to help. He was one boy against an army. He toyed with the idea of firing his crossbow into the back of them and told himself not to be so stupid. It would only put him in danger of being discovered. His skill was watching and waiting and following. Information was power. In a war a well-placed spy was more valuable than a foot soldier.

He could hear distant shouts and screams, the sort of sounds you used to hear coming from school playgrounds from several streets away. At one point he could have sworn he heard a car's engine, but thought he must have been mistaken.

The fight didn't last long, maybe half an hour at the most, but he knew how tiring fighting for even that short length of time was. With your body flooded with adrenalin, your every muscle working hard, your stressed heart thumping, you can't keep it up for long. On top of that, swinging your weapon, hitting someone and being hit in return takes huge amounts of strength and energy. His dad had been a big boxing fan, and had made Shadowman watch old DVDs of Muhammad Ali in action. A round only lasted three minutes, but the boxers would finish each session dripping with sweat, utterly worn down. Shadowman knew from experience that when you were fighting for your life it was much, much harder. He'd seen kids in fights with strangers just give up, unable to cope any longer, and let themselves be killed.

He had time to think about all this as the battle raged down the road, and then, as quickly as it had started, the fighting stopped and the strangers started to drift back the way they'd come. There was no way of telling who'd won the fight. Many of the strangers were bloodied, some with quite serious-looking wounds. He'd waited until he'd spotted St George and then set off after him. It was hard to read emotions in grown-ups' blistered, subhuman faces, but there was a definite, defeated, angry mood among St George's little gang, who all appeared unharmed. Once again they'd wandered with no real purpose, and once again they collected strays as they went. Their black mood had only lifted when they'd stumbled across a house where two older strangers were trying to break in. Shadowman realized straight away that there must be kids hiding inside.

A territorial dispute had quickly broken out between the two old fathers and the angry new arrivals. There followed a brief, bloody fight that ended with the deaths of the fathers. Then St George and his gang had set about trying to break in themselves.

Shadowman had taken out his new binoculars and studied the area. The house stood in a large square with a fenced-off garden in the centre. It had probably once been a rich man's home, but now looked like something out of a war zone. Whoever was inside had managed to barricade it pretty well; all the downstairs windows were blocked. He wondered how long the kids had been in there holding out against their original attackers. As he swept his binoculars over the site, he spotted the dead body of another stranger. An elderly mother who had been half eaten. Maybe she had been part of the siege party and the kids in the house had killed her? The fathers had probably eaten some of her to keep going, but what they really wanted was the fresh young meat inside. The body looked like it had been dead for a while, the blood around it dark and dry, which meant that the siege had probably been going on for some time.

Since he'd arrived, Shadowman hadn't seen any signs of life from inside the building. He knew there must still be kids in there, though, or else St George would have given up and wandered off long ago.

He'd worked his way closer, moving from building to building, and had ended up in this burnt-out house. The fire must have happened fairly recently because there was still a strong smell of smoke and charring hanging over it. That would help to mask his scent, which was why he'd chosen it. He didn't think there was any chance of them discovering him here, but he kept his loaded crossbow by his side just in case. He had a pretty good vantage point, up on the third floor, peering out from a gap in the broken masonry. The roof was open above him, showing the cloudy, starless sky. He wished it had been a brighter night so that he could have seen more of what was happening, but couldn't risk getting in any closer in case they sensed him.

Now his binoculars could only just pick out the shapes of the grown-ups in the darkness. It was weird to see the control St George had over them. They seemed to respect his authority. What's more, they all appeared to understand what he wanted them to do, even though he could only communicate with grunts and clumsy gestures, or by occasionally shoving one of them into the attack. They were working together as one unit, like a swarm of ants, sharing a single mind. Shadowman shook his head and told himself not to be crazy. There was no way the strangers could have developed a form of telepathy along with their boils and blisters, when the disease hit them. Or at least – he hoped not. For all their sakes . . .

The strangers were slow and awkward and St George's gang were the only ones who could use tools of any kind. Sooner or later, though, they were going to get into the house and kill the occupants. If there were enough kids in there to beat the besiegers, they would have attacked them by now, got rid of them. The fact that they hadn't told Shadowman that there weren't enough kids to mount any kind of useful assault.

They were doomed.

The strangers had been steadily working away at the house all night. Right now a knot of them was hammering at the front door while a second gang was tearing at a downstairs window. Others were busy round the back. It was only a matter of time before they got in.

Once again Shadowman felt utterly helpless. Stuck out here, only able to watch. There must have been thirty, maybe forty strangers by the house. If he waded in, he'd just be one more casualty. An attack would achieve nothing.

It made him sick, though, imagining how terrified the kids inside there must be right now.

Then a ripple of excitement passed through the strangers, and they surged towards the front door.

They were in.

Shadowman closed his eyes. He could hear them, crashing about. There were shouts. Kids' voices, high and frightened. Screams . . .

It felt like it was never going to end. At least the kids

weren't giving up without a fight. Maybe they would take down some of the strangers before they died.

And then at last Shadowman opened his eyes and dragged the binoculars to his face. They felt like they were made of lead. He didn't want to look.

It took a moment to get his focus. The strangers were dragging two bodies out, a boy and a girl, the boy dead, the girl still alive and struggling feebly. Shadowman could just make out the shapes of St George, with his bloated head, and the One-Armed Bandit. He could picture the rest of them, Bluetooth, Man U and the one without a name. Picture how excited they would look, how triumphant. How miserable that girl would be, knowing this was the end now.

The strangers dumped the bodies on the ground. The girl sat up. Then tried to stand. With a jolt Shadowman realized that he recognized her. There was something distinctive about the way she moved. He strained at the binoculars, wishing he could see more clearly.

Then the girl shouted defiantly at the grown-ups.

There was no mistaking that voice.

It was Kate.

The dead boy must be Tom.

Then Shadowman's view was completely obscured as the strangers crowded together, snarling and hissing, jostling to get closer to their catch. Kate stopped shouting. He knew what the strangers would be doing now. He'd seen it often enough before. The way they tore bodies apart to get at the meat and the blood. Gouging with their fingernails, ripping with their teeth, pulling limbs away from bodies with their adult strength. It was a long, slow and messy business.

Without any knives it's hard work butchering a human body.

Shadowman noticed that he was weeping. He beat the sides of his head with his fists. He felt so utterly useless. Maybe he should have sacrificed himself, just to show Kate he cared.

In despair he aimed his crossbow at the shapeless mass of bodies and pulled the trigger. The bolt shot through the night air, invisible and silent. He had no idea if he'd hit anything, but in a moment a pack broke away from the feeding frenzy. He watched them lolloping this way and that, confused, directionless. They couldn't possibly have seen where the bolt had come from, though, and soon gave up to go back to their meal.

Shadowman fitted another bolt and kept the bow trained on them.

Idiot. What had he achieved other than losing one of his precious bolts? He doubted they'd find him up here – they wouldn't know where to look – *but even so* . . .

Stupid.

If he was going to survive, he was going to have to close his emotions off. If he panicked, if he lost control, if he attacked in a stupid rage, they would kill him, just as easily as they'd killed Tom and Kate.

Kill him and eat him.

And he couldn't let that happen. He *wouldn't*. He was witnessing something new here, something terrifying, and when he'd seen enough he had to warn other kids about it.

The grown-ups were getting their act together.

57

'You sure you're not coming?'

'I'm sure. I was lucky to get here like this.' Finn raised his arm, which now hung in a clean new sling. 'I'm not risking it out there on the streets again until it's fully healed. And you've got to admit there's a better chance of that happening here than back at the Tower.'

'You just like having them nerd girls play nursey-nursey with you.'

Finn laughed and put his good hand on DogNut's shoulder. 'I'm knackered, Doggo,' he said. 'It's only when you stop it hits you. Feel like I could sleep for a thousand years. I probably shouldn't have come in the first place. I mean, I haven't exactly been a lot of use, have I?'

'Couldn't have done it without you, Finn. You carried me . . . Quite literally.'

'Things would have been different if I'd had two arms.'

'You gonna keep on looking for your mates when you're feeling better?'

'I need to talk to some of them hunters, see what they think. Where I should look. If there's any point.'

The two of them were sitting in the sun on the steps outside the museum. DogNut had his armour ready, his pack by his side and he was cleaning his sword.

'I'm sorry you never found them,' he said, holding the blade up to the light.

'Yeah, well, I'm glad you found what you were looking for, Doggo.'

'I ain't so sure about that,' said DogNut, and he scratched his bony head. 'I found something, but it wasn't what I expected. I think maybe I was supposed to have stayed at the Tower. I don't know. Is all too deep for me. It just don't feel right here.'

'Are Felix and Marco going back with you?'

'Yeah. We'll stick together. We're a team. Go back where we belong.'

'And Courtney?'

'Yeah. And Courtney.'

'You gonna be all right? Just the four of you?'

'We'll be OK. We made a deal with Justin. Robbie's gonna come with us, escort us part of the way. He's OK, you know, Robbie is. Didn't get him at first. But turns out we got a lot in common. Neither of us wants to be king of the world.'

'So which way are you going back?'

'We gonna cut across to Hyde Park Corner, the same way we came up from the palace, then head along to Trafalgar Square and shoot down to the river from there. That's where we'll say goodbye to Robbie.'

'You sure about that?'

'No probs. It's a straight run to the Tower from there, and we'll have the river protecting our right-hand side. It sucks that we ain't got our lovely rowboat no more, but we setting off nice and early and, well – we made it here, didn't we? We'll make it back.'

'Good luck,' said Finn, and he gave DogNut a hug. 'Say hello to everyone for me, won't you?'

'Will do, soldier. And, remember, we all heroes now, whatever happens!'

Courtney was waiting for DogNut with Marco and Felix down near the main gates. She looked up at him, the daft boy, all skinny like a big awkward lizard. He should have been on display in one of the glass cases here. He was almost a fossil already, just hard bones with no flesh on them. Since he'd told her he was going to go back to the Tower and leave Brooke behind a great happiness and calm had settled on her. She hated that it took someone else to make her feel this way, but that was how it was. She had a tough fight ahead of her still convincing bony-boy that she was someone he might actually want to hook up with, and be more than just a mate, his battle buddy. She had time now, though. Time and space. There was a big hole in his thoughts and feelings where Brooke had used to be. She just had to fill that hole.

She smiled. She was much bigger than Brooke. She was really going to have to squeeze herself to fit in a Brooke-sized hole.

She watched as DogNut said his goodbyes to Finn and trotted down the steps, slipping his sword into its scabbard. And then he did something she never expected. He kissed her. Just once. Quickly. On the lips.

'What was that for?'

'You had the kind of face that was asking for it,' he said.

'What's that mean?'

'It means I'm in a good mood today, gyal. You wanna argue about it?'

No. Courtney didn't want to argue. Instead she kissed him back, then giggled like a five-year-old. Marco and Felix made some crude remarks and DogNut swore at them good-naturedly.

Then it was all hustle and bustle as they checked their weapons, strapped on their odd pieces of armour, slung their packs across their backs and marched over to where Robbie was chatting to his mates by the gatehouse.

'All set?' he asked when they walked up.

'All set,' said DogNut, and he grinned at Robbie. 'Look at you. You can't wait to get rid of us, can you?'

Robbie laughed. 'It ain't like that.'

'Ain't it? I reckon you only agreed to excort us to the river just to make sure we was really going.'

'Well . . . Now you put it like that.'

'Yeah. You *know* it, soldier. Just remember we might come back one day, though, screw up your life one more time.'

Robbie laughed again. 'I like you, DogNut,' he said. 'You're a mad bastard but I like you.'

'Cool. So shall we go?'

'We're just waiting for one more,' said Robbie, looking over towards the museum.

DogNut counted heads. There were three other boys and Jackson.

'One, two, three, four, five. That's what you said, wasn't it? Five guys named Mo.'

'There's one more added on.'

'Who is he?'

'She.'

'You got more like Jackson? Yeah! Now you talking. She is one mean girl.'

'Not exactly.'

'Who then?'

Robbie didn't need to answer. Instead he nodded towards the museum steps where Brooke was hurrying down, a narrow, decorative sword in one hand. She had changed out of her weird, old-fashioned dress into heavy boots, jeans and sweatshirt and her hair was tied back. She had a pack ready over her shoulder.

Courtney couldn't believe it. What was she playing at? But DogNut smiled widely.

'You look the business,' he said when she arrived. 'But what you doing, girl?'

'What's it look like I'm doing? I'm coming with you.'

'You joining the excort?'

'No. Like I said, Donut, I'm coming with you.'

'With me? How d'you mean exactly? *With me?*'

'You are really special-needs sometimes, Donut. Try and keep up. I am coming to the Tower.'

Courtney felt like screaming at Brooke, telling her to stay where she belonged, but instead she just smiled. 'That's great,' she said.

'Thought you'd like to have me along,' Brooke beamed. 'And watch your arses for you.'

'I'll watch *your* arse.' DogNut leered and Brooke gave him a dirty look.

'I still don't get it, though,' DogNut went on. 'I thought you liked it here. I thought this was it for you.'

'Unfinished business,' was all Brooke said, and she marched to the front of the group where Robbie was opening the gates. DogNut raised his eyebrows at Courtney and she gave him what she hoped was a look that said, *How amusing, typical Brooke!*

Yeah. Right. *Typical Brooke.*

She could have killed her.

58

The hunger was terrible, an intense, churning pain, as if some sharp-clawed beast had crawled down her throat in the night and was scraping at her belly from the inside. Maybe it was the squirrel she had eaten, come alive?

Could that happen?

She didn't know. It was so hard, trying to think. There was another animal inside her head, a rat, gnawing at her brain. She moaned and rubbed her stomach. The squirrel had hardly made a difference at all. There had been so little to go round. One of the others had found a nest of mice, down in the tunnels, the young ones still pink and bald. But these scraps of meat had only made things worse, reminded her stomach that there was such a thing as food.

And then more had turned up.

Friends.

That was the word, wasn't it? They were her friends. They'd been scattered by the hunters and had been wandering the streets. Now they were starting to arrive in the tunnels. They'd somehow known to come here.

To their queen.

But there were more mouths to feed now. If they didn't eat again soon, and eat properly, they'd start turning on each other. She remembered eating one of her older friends.

He wasn't strong enough to fight and hunt, and he wasn't strong enough to defend himself. He had kept them going for days.

She was all right. She had the knife. She was in charge. None of them would dare attack her.

She was their queen.

All she could do now was wait. It was like fishing: you picked your spot and you sat there and you hoped that sooner or later something would swim past.

She clutched her knife to her chest. Licked her dry lips. They were smeared with blood from the day before, like lipstick.

They had water, down below, under the ground. It rose up through the dirt. But if they didn't eat today it would all be over for them. She couldn't hold the pack together any longer. It was all down to her. She had to look after her children.

Wait, watch and wait, and be patient.

They would get a bite sooner or later.

She was sure of it.

59

Not having to worry about any younger kids, they were moving fast, almost jogging. Felix and Marco were at the front with Robbie and Jackson. Then DogNut and Brooke, side by side. Behind them came Courtney, walking by herself, and bringing up the rear were the three other boys from the museum.

DogNut had an intense feeling of excitement. He was back where he belonged, on the streets. There had been something creepy about the museum. He didn't know what to think about Justin and Einstein and their experiments, about the three sickos locked up in the lorry. He guessed it had to be done, if they were going to find the cause, and maybe even a cure for the disease. That would change everything. But it felt wrong, somehow.

Whatever.

If he was going to be honest with himself, he also felt uncomfortable being around Paul. No matter what anyone said, he hadn't looked after Olivia properly and Paul ranting all over the place and going fruitcake was a constant reminder.

Was he running away then?

Yeah. Probably.

He'd tried to run away from the ghost of Leo and what

had happened in the bank, but had only landed himself in a worse nightmare.

You can't really run away. He'd learnt that.

It felt good while you were running, though.

They saw no living thing all the way to Hyde Park Corner. There was a dead sicko by Wellington Arch, but no other grown-ups were feeding off it. They were all tense skirting the back wall of Buckingham Palace. They kept expecting David to appear at the head of a column of red blazers. Would he try to arrest them and lock them up in the palace for treason? It was stupid to be scared of other kids, but David's presence rested over this part of London like a great dirty stain.

As it was, they got past without incident. Seeing no one. Everywhere was quiet as the grave. They came to Green Park and slowed down. Walking along in the sun like this, it might have been a time before the disaster. A stroll through London on a quiet Sunday morning. Brooke was walking by his side. Chatting away. DogNut was hardly listening. It was weird. Once he'd accepted that she didn't want him, he'd got used to it pretty quick, and now she was just another person. She didn't bother him. If he didn't mean anything to her, then she didn't mean anything to him.

Lost in his thoughts he didn't register that she'd asked him a question, and it was only a nudge in the ribs that brought him back to their conversation.

'Sorry, what?' he said. 'What did you say, babe? I was, like, distracted.'

'I know you were. You ain't been listening to a word I've said, have you?'

'Some of it,' said DogNut. 'I've listened to some of it.'

'I was asking about Ed.'

'That's probably why I wasn't listening.'

'Well, listen now.'

'Why? What's the matter?'

'Nothing's the matter. I just want to know how he is.'

'How he is? I've told you. He's cool.'

'Yeah, but how does he, like, you know, how does he *look*?'

'He looks like Ed.'

'Stop pretending to be a moron, Donut. You know what I mean. How's his face?'

'Oh that, yeah. It looks the same.'

'What's the same?'

'Twisted. Bad, I guess. I don't think about it much, though, to be honest. I've got used to it. But, you know, like, sometimes you forget and you look at him and you think . . .'

'It's well bad, yeah?'

'You know what?' said DogNut. 'I always thought having a scar would be bare cool. But it ain't like it is in the movies. That side of his face looks all mashed up. Sort of, like, screwed tight.' He made a face, scrunched up and leering. 'It's a half and half face, you know, like Two-Face in *Batman*.'

'Who?'

'Harvey Dent.'

'Who's he?'

'Don't you know *Batman*?'

'Not really.' Brooke shook her head and shrugged.

'Well, what I'm saying is that Ed won't be winning any teen polls for most gorgeous boy in the world no more,' said DogNut, 'but you don't need to worry about him. As

I say, you get used to how he looks. Don't make no difference to anyone at the Tower. And I'm still as gorgeous as evah,' said DogNut, pouting and displaying himself like a model.

'Donut, you never been gorgeous. Not even to your mum. You're too thin and your neck's too long, and your eyes are too close together and your mouth's too big. You're always fidgeting. You get on people's nerves . . .'

'Stop it, I'll blush.'

'I was horrible to Ed,' said Brooke quietly. 'When it happened, I was so shocked. I reacted badly. I was a cow, as usual. Looking like that don't make him no different. When I told Justin to drive on after we've crossed the bridge, I didn't want to see Ed no more. I wanted to get away from him. That was part of it, you know, part of why we left you all behind.'

'We was floating down the river, babes, didn't make no difference to us.'

'Yeah, but I didn't know that, did I? I should have waited for you all.'

'What happened to you, Brooke?' DogNut asked. 'You ain't the same mouthy cow you used to be.'

'A lot's happened in the last year, Donut. A whole lot. I guess I've grown up. Losing Aleisha and Courtney . . . At least I *thought* I'd lost them. It's great to have Courtney back, you know. Sucks about Aleisha. But, like, in my mind, I know it's harsh, but in my mind she was already dead. You gotta think that way, not hope and dream, you gotta think straight and carry on, not get dragged down by your bad thoughts. And I thought I'd never see none of you again. And so, you know, like, I thought I'd lost everything. And it made me realize what was important – friends. Helping each other, working together. Not how you look, or what anyone thinks of you, or trying to always be one up on everyone else. Living at the museum there, we've got our own, like, little world. It's great. I can be myself there. I don't have to pretend to be some kind of hard-assed street bitch shooting her mouth off the whole time and putting everyone down.'

'Pretend?'

'Yeah. We all of us pretend, Donut. You too. We show people what we think they want to see.'

'You even talk different.'

'So do you.'

'Do I?' DogNut looked amazed.

'You used to talk like you was fresh off the boat from Jamaica,' said Brooke. 'You still do a bit, when you want, but nowhere near as much as before. Me too. Used to be the only way to be cool. But we neither of us black, Donut, admit it. And, no matter how hard we try to talk like we was, it's never going to change the colour of our skin.'

'True dat!'

Brooke laughed. 'I guess after a while you start to talk like the people you hang out with,' she said. 'You mixing with all different sorts now at the Tower, you talk different. And me . . .'

'You becoming a nerd then?'

'Maybe I am, Donut. The queen of the nerds. But it ain't so bad. I never was that girl, really, the old blonde Brooke. All that chat. All that front. I learnt it and used it and I thought I was top girl. But most of the time I was just horrible to people and used my mouth as a weapon. What's important now is surviving. As a team. That's all. End of.'

'So this is the new you then – Sister Brooke, the lovely nun. You'll be singing "The Sound of Music" next.'

'Are you trying to set me off, Donut?' Brooke narrowed her eyes at him. 'You want me to have a go at you, I will. I ain't lost it none. Just you see.'

'I believe it, gyal.'

'So, do you want it? Do you want to feel the full force of Hurricane Brooke?'

'Yeah, why not?' DogNut grinned. 'I miss the old you.'

Brooke took hold of DogNut's hand. 'It was sweet of you to come find me, Donut.'

'Sweet? It nearly killed me.'

'Why'd you do it?'

'You know why. I thought maybe I was still in with a chance.'

'Still?' Brooke raised her eyebrows. 'Where did "still" come from? You wasn't *ever* in with a chance, boy.'

'Was I never?'

'No not ever. I mean, I always liked you . . .'

'Is all right,' said DogNut. 'I knew it was Ed you was hot for. Dumb of me to think I could make that go away.'

'I blew it with Ed,' said Brooke. 'I couldn't handle the fact that he wasn't a hunk any more. You believe I could have been so shallow . . .? I don't have any fantasy that Ed might want to see me,' said Brooke. 'Like you told me, he never came with you on this journey. I'm not going to the Tower to fall at his feet and beg him to be my boyfriend.'

'So, why *are* you coming?'

'I don't know, to say sorry, I guess. When you told me he was still alive, I felt something inside, like a kind of jolt. Not good, not bad, just a pain. Unfinished business. Life is short, Donut, and we don't want to go through it carrying no regrets. Things unsaid. Apologies left cold. There's a lot of bad things in the world, Donut. I've seen terrible things happen to people. The least I can do is say to poor Ed that it don't matter what he looks like.'

'Hold up!' said DogNut, letting go of Brooke's hand. 'Why've they stopped?'

The two of them had been so wrapped up in their conversation they hadn't been paying attention to what was going on around them.

Robbie's group was standing in a line, looking at something.

'What's happening?' Brooke asked no one in particular, and then froze, her mouth hanging open, unable to make sense of what she was seeing.

A cloud of pure white was moving across the road, silent and gleaming in the sun. It was such an unexpected sight that it was a moment before she realized that it was a flock of birds. Swans. About thirty of them, calmly wandering from one side to the other, their heads held high on long necks. As she stood there, goldfishing, warmth spread through her. It was such a beautiful thing, so peaceful and quiet and innocent.

She started to smile. She couldn't stop herself. She looked around and saw that the other kids were smiling too, like a bunch of toddlers at a petting zoo. Nobody made any stupid comments, or suggested throwing something at the swans; nobody wanted to break the spell in any way.

Life was returning to the capital. Animals that would have been kept away before by noise and pollution, by cars and people and the clamour of city life, were starting to colonize the place and make it their own. Now the kids started to cheer. The swans turned to look at them, a bit snooty, but didn't walk any faster or try to fly away. They just waddled casually on, until the last of them had gone into Green Park and the street was empty.

Brooke blinked. Had it been a mirage? A dream?

'Come on.' Courtney shouldered past her. 'Let's keep moving.'

Brooke held DogNut back for a moment then linked arms with him and they followed Courtney. She was silent for a while then leant closer to him.

'Enough about Ed. What about Courtney?' she asked, her voice lowered.

'Courtney? She's all right, I talked to her. She's cool.'

'Don't hurt that girl.'

'I never would. I told you, I talked to her.'

Brooke shoved DogNut roughly away, and he stumbled in the road, surprised.

'Brooke. Don't be like that –'

'Shut up, DogNut. I saw something.'

'Shit . . .'

DogNut glanced wildly about, and then he saw it too, four sickos skulking in the shadows to their right behind a row of arches.

'Hang about!' he shouted, and the advance party stopped. Robbie, Jackson, Felix and Marco looked round, then trotted back to join DogNut and Brooke. Courtney stayed where she was, standing alone. Robbie's three other boys hurried to catch up with them from the rear.

'Bloody sickos!' DogNut hissed, drawing his sword.

'We can handle them,' said Felix.

'Unless there's more.' DogNut quickly took in where they were, checking for any cover. He'd been stupid, distracted by the swans and his conversation with Brooke. This wasn't a stroll in the park. The world was still dangerous.

They'd come down a long straight stretch of road, wide

enough for four lanes of traffic, and had entered the top of Piccadilly. Now, instead of open greenery on one side, there was a tall building whose front was built out over the pavement, forming an arcade that ran the length of the block. DogNut saw a sign announcing that it was the Ritz Hotel. It was here that the sickos waited.

On the other side of the road there was a run of airline offices and a Boots chemist.

'Should we leg it?' said Brooke, who was less used to being out in the open.

'We can handle them,' Felix repeated. 'Take them down and we don't have to worry about them no more.'

DogNut hesitated, unsure of what to do. In his confusion he wasn't acting quickly enough. He was in danger of panicking. He looked to Robbie who was similarly unsure.

'Cut them down,' said Courtney. She needed to take her anger out on something. Watching DogNut and Brooke saunter along hand in hand had made her feel sick to her stomach. Before anyone could stop her, she gripped her spear with both hands and advanced towards the four sickos.

'Come on then!' she shouted. 'I'm all yours!'

The others had no choice but to follow her. DogNut felt a flutter of panic. They shouldn't be fighting unless they absolutely had to. He looked up at the sky and cursed.

When were they ever going to be given a break?

60

The four sickos sidled away. Hanging back in the shadows. Almost as if they were waiting for the kids to get to them.

Don't be stupid.

DogNut swore under his breath. The sickos didn't have a plan. They weren't clever enough for that.

As he got closer to them, he swore again.

He recognized them.

'Gym bunnies!' he said.

'You what?' Brooke looked frightened.

'The ones we saw the other day, on the way to the palace. I told you about them. There was a whole load of them.'

'A whole load of them?' Brooke looked even more worried.

'That was two days ago. Ryan and his hunters have been on their ass. Maybe there's only these four left?'

'Let's finish them off,' said Felix.

'No, wait,' said DogNut, and there was such anxiety in his voice that all the kids froze. Including Courtney.

Nothing happened.

'You've lost it, DogNut,' said Felix. 'The old days we'd have merked these creeps without even thinking.'

Only one thought went through DogNut's mind. *I don't want to be in charge. I don't want to muck it all up again.*

Felix and Marco hurried to catch up with Courtney who was now stalking the cowering sickos as they edged towards the end of the arcade. Robbie's group ran to cut them off, but as they drew near they realized that the sickos weren't alone. A larger group of gym bunnies had been hiding round the corner in a side-street and they suddenly emerged, moving fast towards Robbie's group.

Staying in a tight pack.

Organized.

And these weren't sickness-ravaged weaklings – they looked worryingly fit and muscular and ready for a fight. Some were nearly naked, showing skin that was disfigured with boils and wounds that wouldn't heal, but, rather than make them look weaker, these blemishes simply made them appear more frightening.

'All right,' said Felix, staggering to a halt in the road. 'Now I suppose we'd better run.'

But it was too late. A third, smaller, group of sickos now appeared from the opposite side of the road. The kids had fallen into a trap. Distracted by the four lone sickos, they'd let themselves get surrounded. There must have been at least twenty-five sickos ringing the group of ten kids. More than two against one. Not the worst odds, particularly as the sickos weren't armed, but the chances of getting out of this fight unhurt were slim.

DogNut hawked up a big green gob of phlegm and spat it on the ground.

If only he hadn't hesitated. If only he'd ordered them all to run while there was still time. No chance of that now. Not until they'd broken out of this ring of grown-ups.

'Stick together,' he shouted. 'We need to punch our way through.'

But Robbie's gang either hadn't heard or were ignoring him, because they charged forward without waiting for DogNut and the others. They hacked down a couple of fathers but were immediately swamped by half the remaining sickos.

Now was DogNut's chance. There was a big gap in the ring. He could easily get through.

Only that would mean abandoning Robbie.

No. Not again. Nobody was going to call him a coward. He was a hero, wasn't he?

'Help them!'

He ran at the sickos, sword swinging through the air. He took one out, but had to be careful in case he cut any of his friends. Courtney joined him, stabbing at the grown-ups with her spear. Brooke dithered, holding back, her narrow sword limp in her hand.

'You're going to have to fight!' Felix yelled.

'I don't know how.'

'Just kill them.'

Felix didn't have time to say anything else, because they were on him. Five of them, trying to get in close so that he couldn't swing his own sword. He was forced to use short, less powerful jabs and slashes, using his elbows and kicking out as well if more than one came at him at once. Marco fought his way to his side and together they managed to turn the fight back against the grown-ups.

Two of Robbie's gang were down on the ground and bleeding, but Jackson managed to break clear of her attackers, battering them out of her way with her spear, a cold, steely look in her eyes. She had one arm round Robbie whose neck was a bloody mess. She joined up with DogNut and Courtney.

'He's hurt,' she said bluntly.

'I can't move my arm,' Robbie groaned.

'We have to get back to the museum,' said Jackson.

DogNut saw Jackson's two friends lying in the road, unmoving.

'What about them?'

'Leave them,' said Jackson. 'They're too badly wounded.'

'But . . .'

'Leave them!'

Jackson powered ahead, not letting any sickos stop her as she ploughed her way through them back towards Green Park, the one remaining uninjured boy from the museum helping her.

'Stick together!' Marco yelled. 'We have to stick together.'

'We're trying to stick together, stupid,' said Felix.

Nobody could follow Jackson, though, as the sickos turned their attentions to DogNut's gang. Felix and Marco were completely swamped. The boys fought back and in a moment there were three dead gym bunnies at their feet, but that only made it harder for them to move without tripping up. As they fought to get clear of the pack, they kept slipping and stumbling. DogNut and the others couldn't help them as they were all engaged in a fight of their own. DogNut and Courtney were protecting Brooke who had dropped her sword and was now completely unarmed. She was trying to scream, but the breath caught in her lungs and no sound came out.

Jackson hadn't deserted them, however. She'd taken Robbie to safety and left her boy watching over him, and she now came belting back down the road to smash into the sickos, freeing Marco and Felix.

'Run!' she bellowed.

The kids didn't need to be told twice. In a moment they were all staggering back down the road the way they'd come, exhausted. The battle had been short but intense, and it had drained their strength. They limped and hobbled, trying to ignore all the cuts and bruises they'd sustained.

The surviving sickos weren't through yet, though. Nothing would make them give up now. They set off after the kids, bloodied and dribbling, their breath hissing through rotten teeth.

Jackson went to Robbie and got under one arm, her friend propping him up from the other side. The eight of them pushed on. They'd cleared the Ritz and were back by Green Park. A little further along was the entrance to Green Park tube station. A thought flashed through DogNut's mind that they should steer wide of it. A tube station was the sort of dark subterranean place that sickos liked to hide out.

But the sickos were behind them, weren't they, and, besides, he was too tired to say anything. Jackson was first past the entrance, carrying Robbie, then Courtney, but as Felix and Marco came level with the steps leading down to the station there was a shriek and a mother wearing sunglasses came flying out, knife in hand, which she brought slicing down across Felix's face.

He yelped and the next thing they knew, several more sickos, bigger, harder and less diseased than the rest, followed the mother out.

Jackson froze in her tracks. 'Hang on!' she shouted.

'No! Keep going!' DogNut shouted back at her. 'Get Robbie to safety! We'll catch you up . . .'

There was a scream from behind and DogNut spun

round to see Brooke being wrestled to the ground by two of the faster sickos from the pursuing pack. He and Courtney ran to her and laid into them, dragging them off Brooke and hacking at them. But the delay had given the other grown-ups from the first attack time to catch up and DogNut and Courtney were soon in the thick of it again. DogNut's sword arm ached, his knees were trembling, his lungs on fire, as he cut down as many sickos as he could. Courtney was gasping for breath, she wouldn't let up. She stood over Brooke, protecting her from any attack.

They'd had to leave Felix, though, and, blinded by the knife wound, he was defenceless. A mother fell on him and knocked him sideways, so that he collapsed over a dead body. This was all the other sickos had been waiting for: five of them dropped on to his back, clawing at him with their fingers and ripping at him with their teeth.

'Get off! Get off me,' Felix sobbed, sounding like a little kid. Marco kicked at the sickos, slashing with his knife. It was no good, though – there were just too many of them – and he himself toppled over, landing on his friend and smothering him.

'It's all right, Felix,' he said. 'I'm with you. It's all right. You're not alone.' He felt for Felix's hand and held it tight, as more gym bunnies blocked out the light, swamping them.

Brooke got to her feet, trembling uncontrollably, and stood behind DogNut and Courtney.

'We're going to be overwhelmed,' Courtney said as more and more sickos arrived from every direction. Everything she had ever feared was coming true. A young mother slashed at her with long nails, raking down the side of her cheek, and Courtney retaliated by clubbing her full in the face with the shaft of her spear. The mother's face split open and she collapsed.

But it was only one. How many more of them were there?

Overwhelmed. She'd always thought it was a stupid word, and the more she used it the more stupid it seemed, like it shouldn't have been a real word.

'It ain't going to happen, babes,' said DogNut. 'I know what you're thinking, but we ain't gonna be overwhelmed. We can do this.'

'No, we can't.'

'Yes, we can.' DogNut kissed her fiercely, the briefest of kisses, and then he raised his sword above his head. 'Let's do this. You and me, girl, let's take it to them! DogNut and Courtney against the world!'

'Yeah . . .'

Side by side, they charged at the sickos, weapons a blur, hacking to left and right. For a few seconds it looked like they might do it. Sickos fell wounded around them. It couldn't last, though. Courtney was right. There were too many.

Brooke stood there, too terrified to move, watching in frozen panic as sickos converged on her friends.

Two fathers got close to Courtney and clung on to her spear, dragging it down. She snatched her knife from her belt and lashed out at them with her free hand, but the bigger of the two deflected her blow and the blade cut deep into her own arm. She hissed with pain and let go of the spear. She was filled with a terrible rage and gouged great chunks out of the fathers before they dropped dying at her feet. Before she could recover, however, she was jumped from behind by two more of them.

DogNut meanwhile was too hemmed in to do much more than barge sickos out of his way. A searing pain in his ankle stopped him dead, and he looked down to see that a fallen mother had got hold of his leg and sunk her teeth into him. He stamped on her with his other foot and stabbed down, taking her in the neck.

'Courtney!' he shouted, but didn't know if she could hear him.

Where was she?

'Courtney!'

There. He forced his way over to her and pulled the sickos from her back. She was bleeding from small cuts all over her, and her right arm was red from shoulder to fingertips, but she was still battling with her knife. DogNut took hold of her and started to drag her away, ignoring the sickos that grabbed at him from all sides. All his energy was ebbing away. He wasn't sure how much longer he could keep this up.

'Come on, Courtney,' he said. 'Don't give up. You and me, girl. You and me.'

'You and me, Dog,' said Courtney.

'Love you, girl . . .'

'Love you, too . . .'

As Brooke stood watching helplessly, she spotted the lead mother moving in fast towards the two of them, holding the knife. She was a horrible sight, with her sunglasses and her mad grin.

Brooke sobbed. It wasn't right. Sickos didn't carry weapons. They were too stupid. And this mother was smiling.

'Look out!'

It was no good. The mother came up behind DogNut and plunged the knife deep into his side between his breastplate and his backpack. He howled and the mother laughed.

DogNut fell to his knees.

Overwhelmed, he thought. Courtney was right after all. Overwhelmed. He couldn't get a fix on what was happening. One moment he was in the pit at the bank, with sucking mouths fixing on to him, the next he was back at school, playing football, now he was in class, struggling to make sense of algebra, then he was with his mum, arguing about something . . .

Don't argue, Mum, he thought. *Can't we just be friends? We don't have long.*

Why don't we have long, darling?

Because I'm dying, Mum. Can't you see? I'm in the pit at the bank and sinking under all these mouths. Sickos, Mum, too many of them, so don't argue.

But you have to do your homework.

It's algebra, Mum. You know I can't do algebra.

You have to try.

What's the point, Mum? I'll never need to use it in my life.

Well, you might one day . . .

Might I? I ain't needed it so far and it looks like I ain't going to be around for much longer. I don't think algebra would've saved me today.

Saved you from what, darling?

Don't you ever listen, Mum? I told you: I'm dying. There's sickos, Mum. I've been overwhelmed. This time I'm not going to get out. They're going to drag me down, down in their rotten flesh.

Are you by yourself, darling? I can't bear the thought of you dying alone.

No, Mum, I'm with my friend. I'm with Courtney . . .

Courtney . . .

He called out her name.

'Courtney,' he said. 'I'm sorry . . .'

But Courtney was already dead. She'd gone down hard and cracked her skull on the edge of the pedestrian island in the middle of the road. Already sickos were tearing at her body.

Brooke could stand it no longer. She wasn't going to watch her friends die and do nothing. Screaming, she ran towards DogNut, shoving sickos aside. They dropped back, startled by her fury. She made it to DogNut and put her arms around him. He was still alive.

'Can you stand up?'

'What?'

Brooke grabbed DogNut's sword. It was sticky with blood. With her other hand she pulled DogNut to his feet and then circled her arm round him, holding him up. Three mothers came at her, sticking their spotty faces right in hers, like mocking kids in a playground, salivating, their eyes somehow dull and mad at the same time.

'Get away from me, you ugly bitches!' Brooke screamed, and sliced the sword across their throats in one hard determined thrust. Blood spattered her front and the mothers staggered back, clutching at their wounds with twitching hands.

I did it, she thought. *I got them. I can do it.*

She wasn't sure she could do it again, however. She'd been lucky. Now the sword felt unbelievably heavy. She waved it uselessly at the ring of sickos that had formed around her.

It was only her left now.

Let them come. Let the gym bunnies kill her. She couldn't take any more of this. She looked at the bodies of Felix and Marco and Courtney.

And then she felt DogNut stir and moan.

No. She thought. *I will not let it end like this.* She wasn't ready to die yet. As long as she had a breath left in her she would protect DogNut. She had to survive. Otherwise who would ever know what had happened here? Who would tell the story of the death of heroes?

She became aware of the lead mother smiling. She looked like she might have been quite beautiful once, with a good body, fit. Now she was just this ugly thing, with boils and spots across her face, eating away at her. Her teeth black. She knew she was the winner today. Brooke cursed her.

She darted in and Brooke swiped at her. Missed. Felt a blow to her face. A cold, dazzling band of pain across her forehead. Blood gushed down and she couldn't see anything.

Oh no . . .

DogNut's hand felt for hers, took the sword from her. She felt him moving, swinging the blade. Felt his body red hot against hers. In this moment she loved him more than anything in the world, more than anyone.

'You're still in with a chance,' she whispered.

'I knew it . . .' he croaked.

Brooke wiped the blood out of her eyes.

The mother was standing there. Eyes hidden behind the sunglasses. Showing her black teeth in a sick grin. The girl was hers now. She looked at her knife, hardly able to believe that she could control it. She licked her lips. The other sickos, the ones who weren't already ripping into the dead bodies, were holding off, waiting for her to move in for the final kill.

She raised the knife and stepped forward, and at the same moment something distracted the rest of them. They turned as one and charged off across the road.

The mother grinned wider, lifted her knife higher, drunk

with its bloody power. Brooke held her gaze. Clutching DogNut tight. With one last desperate effort DogNut swung the sword. It flapped feebly at the mother's face, doing nothing more than knock the sunglasses off.

The mother paused. Brooke looked into her eyes. Saw some last glimmer of humanity there.

And then an extraordinary thing happened.

The mother grunted as an arrow struck her in the right eye. She tilted her face upwards, wailed and toppled over backwards. The next moment another group of the bunnies went down beneath a swarm of arrows and other missiles. There was movement off to Brooke's left. A group of kids was approaching from the north. They looked street tough and hardened, working together like a smooth killing machine – a well-drilled unit. There were archers out on the flanks and several kids with slingshots. A boy at the front with a spear was moving expertly, a deadly killing machine. Brooke picked up silly details like the shaved patterns in his hair.

Another boy, with flame-red hair and a slingshot, ran over.

She was being rescued. Maybe there was some hope left in the world after all. A muscular-looking black kid with a club smashed two sickos aside. There was a girl alongside him, with short scrappy hair, wearing a leather jacket. In her bewildered delirium, Brooke thought that the girl could make more of herself.

Maybe she could show her how.

In a few seconds all the gym bunnies were dead. Battered to the ground or pierced by arrows. If Brooke hadn't seen it for herself, she wouldn't have believed it. Wouldn't have believed that a bunch of kids could destroy sickos so easily.

It was the most efficient and deadly attack she had ever witnessed.

She realized that she had slipped to the ground and was holding DogNut in her lap, her bloody hand gripping his jacket tightly.

The muscly kid came over to her, said something. She couldn't understand the words. Her head was filled with a ringing sound. She tried to speak, but she didn't think that anything came out.

The boy said something else and she thought that maybe he was saying that she was all right now, safe . . .

Safe . . .

A shadow fell across her and she heard another voice. Struggled to see who was speaking. She was feeling faint and distant, as if she was watching all this in a film about someone else. Shock was setting in. Turning her to stone. There was blood pouring down her face. She didn't have the energy to wipe it away. The day was growing dark.

Another girl appeared, took some stuff out of a first-aid kit, said something to her, might as well have been speaking Chinese.

Chinese . . .

Brooke laughed.

Someone was easing DogNut out of her arms. She wanted to tell them not to hurt him. Then the flame-haired boy was back with some other people, so many of them . . . Who were they all?

They put her on to a kind of stretcher. Where had they got that from? She tried to thank them, but the words only seemed to form in her head.

As she was carried across the road towards the park, she looked for her friends. There was no sign of them or the dead bodies of the sickos. The road was clear. She must have dreamt it all. There hadn't been a fight here . . .

That couldn't be.

Her head hurt.

So much blood.

She closed her eyes and gave in to the darkness.

61

David was waiting in his office at the palace. It was a grand room with a marble fireplace, oil paintings on the walls and a large dark wooden table in the centre that David kept polished to a glass-like shine. Tall windows looked out over the gardens where children were busy working in the vegetable plots and he often stood gazing out at the activity, secretly smiling at how well he had done for himself. Here he was, in the queen of England's old home. And everything he could see out there belonged to him. The lake full of fresh water, the food growing in the rich soil, the children themselves. When the disease had struck, it had felt like it was the end of the world, most children had fallen into a paralysing despair, many had been killed, or had died of disease and neglect and starvation. But not David. He had seen the whole thing as a massive opportunity. Here was a new world that he could take control over.

And why not? Children needed someone strong in charge. They didn't have to like him, just as long as they did what they were told. He was keeping them alive, wasn't he? Looking after them. Offering them a future. Once the hard part was over, once the last rotten, diseased adult had been hunted down and exterminated, they could do whatever they wanted. London was theirs. England. The whole planet. Theirs for the taking.

David saw himself as an entrepreneur. He'd always enjoyed watching *The Apprentice*, and had dreamt of going on it when he was older. Well, now he didn't have to be an apprentice. He was the boss, wasn't he? He was Lord Sugar.

There was still a lot of work to be done, though. He knew that. Until every kid in the area recognized his authority he couldn't relax. Hopefully his meeting this morning would lift him another step up the ladder.

He walked over to the mirror that hung above the fireplace and checked his appearance. His mother had always told him that appearances were important. First impressions. He needed to look like the boss, with an air of authority. He smiled at what he saw.

His mother would have been proud.

He was wearing a suit and tie. His dark hair was neatly cut and combed to the side. His pale, freckled skin was clear and spot-free. Not like some kids out there who looked almost as bad as the pustule-covered grown-ups. He was only fourteen, but had the manner of an adult.

He liked what he saw.

Even so, he patted his hair flatter and fussed over his tie knot. He had to admit he was slightly nervous. This meeting meant a lot to him; it wasn't just about power and business. There was more to it than that. He had other plans, and he'd started to put them together the first time he'd met her.

Nicola. The girl from the Houses of Parliament, the one who called herself prime minister. She could call herself whatever she wanted as far as he was concerned. It was just a name. She wasn't in charge of anything except her own

scrawny little bunch of kids. Even after she agreed to everything, which he was fairly confident she would – hadn't
she asked for this meeting? Yes, even afterwards, he would
let her keep the title. Let her think whatever she wanted
to think. Let her pretend to be in charge.

Nicola. He wished he didn't feel so fluttery. But there
was something about her . . .

He turned away from the mirror. Embarrassed. Unable
to hold his own gaze any longer.

He knew what that something was. She was pretty.
Beautiful, really. With her long red hair and her green eyes.

A princess.

That was how he thought of her. Royalty. He pictured
the two of them, side by side, king and queen. Their two
worlds united. The two of them united. Like Kate and Will.

He blushed. He was getting ahead of himself.

That wouldn't do. He had to maintain his self-control.
Not get carried away. The business deal was the important
thing to get sorted today. The rest of it? Well, with any
luck that would follow, but he mustn't let it get in the way
of their negotiations.

He had no idea what she thought about him. He wasn't
bad-looking, not film-star material, but not ugly. His
freckles were annoying, and people had always teased him
about them . . . The main thing, though, was that he was
important. Important and powerful. Girls were attracted
to that sort of thing, weren't they? Especially now that
they needed looking after. He might not be Action Man,
but he was tall and healthy. He had that air of confidence.
He was a king rather than a warrior.

And girls went for those types.

Didn't they?

He was pretty sure they did. Although his own experience of girls was fairly narrow. He had no brothers or sisters and had gone to an all-boys school. That was why he was nervous. He didn't want to behave like a fool around her and give himself away. He wanted to come across as grown up. In control.

He was aware, though, that there was a special power that girls had. It was nothing to do with strength, or cleverness, or authority. It was to do with . . .

He was blushing again. He poured himself a glass of water from the cut-glass carafe he had carefully placed on a silver tray that sat on the gleaming table top.

There was a knock on the door and he moved to the fireplace, stood in the pose he had rehearsed, copied from one of the paintings at the palace, showing some general or other posing with all his medals and honours. Legs apart, chest out, hands behind his back, a superior half smile on his lips.

'Yes?' Dammit. He'd wanted his voice to sound deep and manly, and it came out strained and pinched, sounding to his ears almost like a squeak.

'She's here, David.'

'Bring her in.'

The door opened and Pod, his chief of security, came in with Nicola.

She was as beautiful as he remembered. And she was wearing a long green dress that matched her eyes. That pleased him. He didn't like girls to wear jeans, unless they were working. In his opinion girls should look smart and feminine . . .

No. Don't think like that. You'll start blushing again, you idiot. Be businesslike.

'Hello, Nicola,' he said, pleased that his voice had settled down. It came out sounding much more relaxed. 'Come in. How are you?'

'I'm fine, thanks. How are you, David?'

'Very well.' He turned to Pod. 'Did everything go as planned?'

'Yes.' Pod grinned. Pleased with himself. 'I brought her up the back way, by the servants' stairs. Nobody saw her come in. Nobody will see her go out. This meeting will be completely secret.'

Now David turned to Nicola. 'You didn't come all the way up here from Westminster by yourself, though, surely?'

'No. I brought some friends and we paid some hunters to escort us. The others are waiting over the road in your safe house.'

'Good. I think it's best this way. No need for anyone else to know our business for now.'

'I suppose so.'

David looked at Pod, who was standing there in a rugby shirt, the collar turned up. He wasn't the brightest kid in the palace, but he was loyal and knew how to follow orders.

'You can leave us now, Pod, thanks.'

'Will do, boss.' Pod said goodbye to Nicola and went out, pulling the door closed behind him.

'That's better. We're alone now,' said David, and instantly regretted it. It had come out creepy. He had to keep this businesslike. To cover his embarrassment he indicated that Nicola should sit at the table and he poured her a second glass of water.

'So,' he said, handing her the glass. 'There's a lot we need to talk about.'

'Yes. I suppose there is.'

Nicola looked a little awkward and nervous too. That was good. David sat down. Drank some water. Wiped his lips. Looked up at her. Important to maintain eye contact.

'Do you want to start or should I?'

'Well, you invited me here,' said Nicola, keeping her eyes fixed on his. He looked down before he could stop himself. *Damn.*

'But it was you who originally suggested we should meet up,' he said, and forced himself to look her in the eyes again.

'Did I?' Nicola shrugged. 'Maybe. I can't remember exactly how it came about.'

'You sent Ryan Aherne over with that letter.'

'Yes, but only after I got *your* letter . . .'

David forced a laugh. 'Well, let's not argue about that. It doesn't really matter how it came about, does it? The thing is we *both* wanted a meeting.'

'Sure,' said Nicola.

'I've tried to get you to meet me properly before,' said David. 'What changed your mind?'

'I suppose it started the other day when those kids arrived from the Tower of London.'

'Yes. You know they came here afterwards.'

'Yeah. They seemed all right at first, I suppose. It was only after they'd gone that I started to think it was all a bit weird.'

'Weird?' David took another sip of water. His throat was dry.

'Was it a coincidence that they came to ours?' Nicola asked. 'They had a story about looking for some friends, but . . . You don't know, do you? You can never be too careful. Anyway, we had a sitting and it came up that perhaps they'd been spies of some sort.'

404

David tried not to smile. Of course it had come up. His plants at the Houses of Parliament had been *told* to bring it up. To spread unease. *They* were the real spies.

'I agree,' he said. 'I don't think they were all they seemed. When they came here, they immediately started poking around and asking a lot of questions. They were very curious, wanted to see everything. I knew them from before, you know?'

'Yes, I think they told me that.'

'I know their leader,' said David. 'A boy called Jordan Hordern. He's – how can I put it? Well, if you met him, you'd know what I meant. Let's just say he's the kind of guy who wants to be in charge. From what I gather it's a hard life over at the Tower of London. I wouldn't put it past him to be thinking of looking for somewhere else to move to. He could well be probing our weaknesses, checking us out, planning to take over.'

'That's exactly what we were talking about in parliament,' said Nicola, leaning towards David excitedly. 'I think it's getting more and more important that we establish some proper stability around here. It's ridiculous that we're all living so close to each other and yet it's almost as if we're enemies.'

'You're so right,' said David seriously. 'We must never forget that the real enemies are the grown-ups. We shouldn't be competing with each other; we should be working together.'

Nicola drank some more water. David watched the movement of her throat as she swallowed. She carefully set her glass back down on the table.

'The other thing is that gang in St James's Park,' she said.

'The squatters?' said David. 'What about them?'

'They're raiding us nearly all the time now,' said Nicola. 'They come steaming in and take food, supplies, water. There's nothing much we can do to stop them, except lock the doors. But we can't stay cooped up inside forever. They wait for someone to come out and just . . .'

'Steam in,' said David.

'Exactly. We don't want to get into a fight with them, but they're making things really difficult.'

'It's the same for us,' said David. 'We wanted to develop the park, you know, grow food there, and they just dug everything up and attacked our guys. I agree – we definitely need to do something about them.'

'What can we do, though?' asked Nicola. 'We can't attack them.'

'Why not?'

'Well, they're kids. I made some promises during the election.'

'You had an election?' said David, amused. 'I didn't notice.'

'It was just an internal thing,' said Nicola. 'Every year the kids at Westminster vote on who's going to be, you know, prime minister. This year they voted for me because I promised them a few things.'

'Like what?'

'Like never to attack other kids . . . And . . .' Nicola laughed, embarrassed, unsure whether to go on.

'You can tell me.' David was still very amused by Nicola's situation.

'I promised never to have anything to do with you.'

Now David laughed. 'Well, we all make promises we can't keep, Nicola. Now that you're in charge I suppose you've realized that it's not as easy as it looks, is it? And sometimes you have to change your mind about things. They'll get over it. If you sort things out for them, make their lives safe and secure, they'll forget all the promises you made to get elected, and they'll keep voting for you year after year after year.'

'I hope so.' Nicola frowned. 'I mean, I think if I can stop the raids by the squatters, as you call them, then I'll be popular. But how *can* we stop them? What can we do? We can't go wading in there. They're not adults. They're not diseased. They're just kids.'

'They may be kids,' said David, 'but they're not obeying the rule of law. As you say, we need to establish order round here, and they're just pushing things towards chaos and anarchy. We can't let that happen. You and I, we've worked hard to make things better, to rebuild. If they're going to behave the way they do, then I think we're justified in turning the water cannons on them.'

'You've got water cannons?'

David laughed again. 'No. It was a metaphor. I just mean there's no reason why we shouldn't come down heavily on them.'

'You'd attack them?'

David crossed his arms and leant back in his chair. 'Yes,' he said. 'I'd only be doing to them what they'd like to do to me. What they *have* done to you. We need to bring them into line and we can only do that if we're united.'

'Even if we unite, though,' said Nicola, 'we don't have enough fighters. Certainly not ones who'd be happy to attack other kids.'

'Leave that to me,' said David. 'I'm working on something. But we have to think further ahead than just cleaning up the park. It's about more than just attacking the squatters. Yes, they're a common problem we share, but we share loads of other problems as well.'

'Are you suggesting an alliance of some sort?' asked Nicola.

'I am. A union between your camp and ours. You wouldn't have to change anything. You could keep all you've got and run things how you liked at Westminster, but we'd be working together. We could hold regular meetings, share resources, information, fighters.'

David went over to a little side table and picked up a pile of papers.

'I've drawn up a contract,' he said, sitting back down. 'It's more than just a treaty – it's a sort of constitution.'

'I don't know,' said Nicola as David pushed the papers towards her across the shiny table top. 'It's all a bit sudden.'

'Why did you come here?' said David, pressing on now that he felt he had the upper hand.

'To talk.'

'About what?'

'Well . . .'

'About something like what I've proposed.'

Nicola thought about this for a few seconds before replying.

'Yes,' she said at last. 'Something like this. But, as I said, you're not exactly popular at Westminster. Quite a few of the kids there came from here. You're seen as being a bit, well, *bossy*. The idea of teaming up with you would scare some of them. They'd think you were just trying to take over.'

'That's where the royal family comes in,' said David, smiling broadly, but trying not to look smug.

'What do you mean?' Nicola was more than a little confused.

'Haven't you heard?' said David. 'We have members of the old royal family here.'

'I'd heard rumours,' said Nicola, 'but I never believed any of them. I thought it was a joke.'

'It's not. It's all true. We found them here when we arrived. None of the big names, unfortunately. I think they're all dead, or in a bunker somewhere. My lot are mostly minor royals, but royals nevertheless. It's always been my dream to reinstate them on the throne. That way, it will appear that they're in charge, and people won't worry so much about what I'm up to.'

'Let me get this straight, David.' Nicola looked bemused and appalled. 'These are adults? Diseased mothers and fathers?'

'Think of them more as dukes and duchesses.'

'But diseased?'

'Yes. Don't worry, we keep them safely locked up in the dark, so that they don't degenerate too badly.'

'I don't want to be ruled by a bunch of zombies.' Nicola was shaking her head, her eyes wide.

'You wouldn't be, Nicola. They'd just be figureheads, something to put on the stamps. They'd just represent an old order. Stability. Tradition. Something to unite everyone. Kids need that sort of thing. You and me, we'd hold the real power.'

Nicola stared at the papers in front of her, trying to take this all in.

'I don't expect you to sign anything now,' said David. 'Take the agreement away with you and study it. Make any changes you think it needs. It's nothing complicated, but . . . You're like me, Nicola. We both like rules, structure. We both like things to be organized. Perhaps our beliefs might be slightly different, but in the end we both want what's best. Best for our kids, best for the future, best for the country, if you like. Together we can be strong and we can deal with any future threats. At the moment, fighting off the grown-ups is what's holding us all together. Once the last grown-up's been killed and we don't have a common enemy there's a danger that everything will just fall apart. There'll be more problems like the squatters, and who knows what Jordan Hordern might be plotting? This is the first step to properly uniting everyone in London. We can make alliances with more and more kids, all join together under one banner. We can clean out all the grown-ups in this area. Work out how best to use the hunters. Be ready to deal with people like Jordan Hordern. Make London safe. Then we really could call ourselves king and queen.'

'I beg your pardon?'

'Well, you know what I mean,' said David, desperately trying not to give himself away. It had come out without his meaning to say it. 'I'm talking metaphorically again. You know, we'll be, like, joint rulers. Not husband and wife.'

Nicola leant forward, put her elbows on the table and rested her chin in her hands. She smiled at David in a slightly superior, mocking way that he found unnerving.

'It sounded just a little bit like you were coming on to me there, David.'

'No, no, not at all . . . Don't be silly.'

'Why? Don't you like me?'

'No. Well, yes, obviously, but that wasn't what I meant. I just meant that, well, you must admit, Nicola, that if we were together like that, not that *that* was what I was suggesting, but just consider it for a moment, if we were, it would really seal our union.'

Nicola raised her eyebrows.

'You're a dark horse, aren't you, David King?'

David sniffed and became very businesslike, leafing through some pages of notes.

'Why don't you take the agreement away, study it and we'll meet again in a few days . . .'

'I don't know if I really want to make some sort of official deal,' Nicola interrupted.

'What do you want then?'

'I want to be safe. I don't want the squatters to attack us again. I want to know we're not going to, I don't know, be invaded by you or anyone else.'

'OK,' said David. 'Here's the deal. To prove to you why we'd be better off working together, what if I promised to deal with the squatters, bring them into line, slap them down?'

'Could you?'

David stood up and struck his manly pose. 'Yes,' he said. 'And, if I do, will you promise to sign the agreement?'

'OK, sure. If you think you can do that. If you can really properly deal with them and stop them raiding us, I'll sign, we'll form an alliance. We'll be king and queen of London.'

'Of England, surely,' said David.

Now Nicola stood up and came round to David. She stood slightly too close to him and he could smell soap and clean hair and something else. Something mysterious and feminine.

'You'd like that, wouldn't you?' she said.

'Yes.' David's throat felt dry.

Nicola leant even closer. 'Me being your queen.'

'Well . . .'

There was a knock at the door. Nicola laughed and backed off.

It was Pod again. David told him to come in. Nicola watched as he strode over to David and whispered something in his ear. David smiled, nodding his head happily.

Evidently it was good news.

'OK, Nicola,' he said, rubbing his hands together. 'I don't think there's anything more we need to talk about. Pod will escort you back to your friends. Do what you need to do, discuss it with whoever you think needs to be in on it, and then we'll meet again in, what? A week from now?'

'OK, yeah.'

Pod led Nicola away and David hurried through the palace to the main function room at the front of the building where he found six of his boys waiting for him in their matching red blazers. David inspected them quickly. They had their rifles with them and looked smart and alert.

'We'll go out on to the balcony,' he said, giving them a final once-over. 'You know the drill. Look like soldiers. Look impressive.'

They all nodded. Straightened their backs. David took a deep breath and went out through the central French windows on to the balcony. His guards followed, falling into position on either side of him. David leant on the stone balustrade and looked down.

The other palace kids were gathered on the parade ground. They'd just let in a group of new arrivals who were marching towards the palace. David quickly assessed them. There were maybe twenty-five, thirty, armed boys and girls of all ages. Two of them were carrying a makeshift stretcher with a girl lying on it, her face heavily bandaged. At the head of the party was Jester, looking full of himself. There was no sign of the other kids who had set off with him two days ago.

'Magic-Man!' David called down to his friend, spreading his arms in a welcoming gesture. Everyone looked up at him. *David*. The boy who owned all this.

'Well done, Jester,' he shouted. 'We didn't think we were ever going to see you again.'

'You didn't doubt me, did you, David?' Jester shouted back.

'Never! But where are the others?'

'They didn't make it,' said Jester, and the effect on the palace kids was immediate. A wave of moans passed through them, followed by mumbling. David tutted, chewed his lower lip, and then made sure he put a smile back on his face. It was bad news to lose anyone, but at least Jester had brought plenty of new recruits back with him. He wondered if they were any good or whether they'd be just more hungry mouths to feed.

As if Jester could read his mind, which David sometimes thought he could, he answered the question for him.

'But this lot,' he cried, 'you should see them in action. They're skilled fighters, David. They're going to really make a difference.'

David's smile grew wider. This was turning out to be a very good day all round.

'Well, come on in!'

62

They never discovered Shadowman's hiding-place in the burnt-out building, and he'd spent the long night there listening to them feed. St George and his gang first, and then the others, who fought over every last scrap of flesh and skin and bone. Finally, the most diseased, the weakest, had come to the table and Shadowman had had to watch them in the grey light of dawn as they licked the road clean of blood. Now he could see more clearly the mess they'd made. There was almost nothing left of Tom and Kate.

As the day dawned, some of them had started to drift away, first in ones and twos, and then in larger groups. Wandering off to find somewhere to sleep until it got dark again. The last to leave were the toughest, the ones who didn't fear the daylight, St George and his boys. They trooped up the road past Shadowman's hiding-place, looking pleased with themselves. St George at the front, his great fat head too heavy for his neck to hold upright. Then Bluetooth and the One-Armed Bandit, followed by Man U and . . .

Shadowman had to hold back a laugh. His bolt *had* hit something when he'd fired it into the night. It had hit the last member of the gang. The one he'd been struggling to name. It stuck out of his shoulder – either it was too deeply embedded to pull out, or he simply hadn't bothered to try. He didn't look too troubled by it. He almost seemed to wear it with pride. Like a medal. Shadowman wept with joy at this tiny victory. Not only had he wounded the bastard, but he'd given him a distinguishing feature. He was no longer just a faceless stranger.

When you named things you owned them.

A big smile spread over Shadowman's face as he finally worked out what to call him.

Spike.

63

That bit there was a road. It ran beside the train tracks and led to the forest. Past the forest was the city, with all those houses and parks and fine buildings – the cathedral, the stadium, the row of theatres, the shopping centre. Next to the city was the farm. Where she lived. It was just like the one she'd made playing Farmville on Facebook. The hours she'd wasted on that! She tended her new farm just as carefully now as it hung above her. She planted seeds and pulled up vegetables. She milked the cows and fed the chickens and exercised the horses. Her sheepdog, Baxter, rounded up the sheep. She could look after this place, keep the animals well fed and safe and happy. Nothing bad was ever going to happen here. Not like in the real world. Not like the cold, heartless, unfair, unfair, unfair place London had become. Where she could do nothing to save her friends.

Her imaginary world was warm and sunny and bright. Everyone smiled all the time and there were no wolves to frighten the sheep, no foxes to get into the hen-house, no grown-ups to shoot the rabbits. No grown-ups at all. Anywhere. Not even healthy ones. And her farm was a private place. No one else knew the secret road to get there. There were just the three of them, Brooke, Donut and Courtney, sitting at the kitchen table, eating freshly baked bread and soft-boiled eggs and drinking cold milk. Sitting side by side, laughing and chatting.

Never mind that this farm didn't exist, nor the city, nor the forest, nor the network of roads, that they were all just made up out of the stains and cracks and blotches that covered the ceiling above her bed.

Never mind . . .

She could lie there for hours, suspended somewhere between wakefulness and sleeping, staring up and wandering about in that imaginary world. She'd sunk so far into her depression that she'd reached a numb place, where nothing mattered any more. Nothing was real. She was detached from her body, oblivious to the pain that blazed around her wounded head. They gave her painkillers now and then, but they did little to help. She sensed they were rationing them. Pills like these were rare and precious these days. They probably wanted to keep them for their own. They'd stitched her face, though. She had felt them tugging and gouging and gathering her skin together where it had been sliced through clean to the bone across her forehead.

At first she hadn't known where she was. Hadn't cared. Had simply drifted in her dream world. Slowly, slowly, however, despite her trying not to, she had started to tune in to what was going on around her. They'd brought her to Buckingham Palace, where David and his followers lived. They'd carried her upstairs to some kind of sick-bay. It was quiet and peaceful in here, lit only by the soft glow of tea candles. Girls came and went, dressed as nurses. It was one of them who had stitched her, a girl called Rose. She seemed to be in charge. She gave Brooke her pills, took her temperature, fed her, took her to the toilet . . .

How long had she been here? A day? Two days? A week? Years . . .

She had no idea. Time had ceased to have any meaning for her. She just lay on her back and stared up at the ceiling as the seasons came and went on her farm.

She had to stay up there, among her animals, because there were places she couldn't go, memories she couldn't face. Every now and then she settled into a deep calm; she would be floating on pink fluffy clouds counting sheep, sliding on a rainbow, or sitting at that kitchen table with her friends. There were times when she'd feel warm and safe and well fed, cared for, looked after . . .

And those were the most dangerous times, because her defences would drop and suddenly the memories would come screaming back at her. How Donut and Courtney had come all the way across London to find her. How she had been reunited with them only to have them snatched away from her. The friends she hadn't seen for a year and had thought must surely be dead. Slaughtered by sickos.

Unfair. Unfair. Unfair.

Tears would well in her eyes and soak her pillow. Sometimes she woke up crying, and one of the nurses would come over and ask her how she was and wipe away the tears and stroke her hair and Brooke could pretend that everything was OK.

She would never reply when they asked her things. She hadn't spoken a word since she'd come here. Didn't think she would *ever* speak again. What was the point? What was the point of anything? Living or dying or talking or laughing . . .

All she could ever look forward to in the future was a life of pain and loss. They were all just children – what

418

chance did they have? They could play at soldiers, or scientists, or nurses and doctors, but they were just as helpless as the cattle on her farm, the chickens and sheep, they were just farm animals, waiting to be eaten by the grown-ups.

She hadn't dared look in a mirror at what a mess the mother had made of her face. To make it worse the wound had become infected. The nurses had covered it with disinfectant and antiseptic, but it had burned. At times she thought the infection must be burning right through to her brain. Sending her mad. She thought about Ed, once so handsome, remembered what the cut had done to his face, and she knew that she would look just as bad if she survived. She would be a freak, a monster, like the disease-ruined mothers and fathers who wandered the streets. Was this God's punishment for how she'd treated Ed?

Or was it just shitty luck?

She knew she must look bad because when Rose and the girls inspected her wound they winced and grimaced and said things like 'poor girl'.

Poor girl.

She also gathered that her whole face had swollen up from the bruising and infection. Her eyes were puffy and blackened. She must look more like a corpse than the old Brooke. *The most beautiful girl on the bus.*

They'd wrapped bandages round her head. She suspected it was as much to hide what she looked like as to keep the wound safe. They had to change the bandages all the time as they began to smell.

There was one good thing about being unrecognizable and not talking. Nobody knew a thing about her. Who she was. Where she had come from. David had come in once, glanced briefly at her, before turning away. He hadn't recognized her and had talked about her as if she wasn't there. Had told Rose to keep her here as long as possible and not let any of the newcomers see her again, or try to talk to her. That was fine with Brooke, but Rose had questioned him about it.

'I want this new lot to stay,' he'd explained in that snooty, slightly impatient tone of his. 'At the moment they think that the palace is the only option. The less they know about the other settlements the better. Once they realize the benefits of living here, they'll not want to go anywhere else, but until then we have to be careful. Who knows where that girl's from, but probably from one of the larger settlements, Westminster or the museum. As I say, the less this new lot know about all that the better. And, besides, doesn't that girl need rest and calm or something? Isn't that how it works?'

'I suppose so, yes.'

'Good . . .'

Good.

That girl.

As far as he was concerned she was a nobody. If he ever realized who she was, he would come back to gloat. And probably worse. She knew he'd never forgiven her for abandoning him on Lambeth Bridge during the fire. And it wasn't just him; there were other boys here who might remember her. The boys from his school who still wore the geeky red blazers.

For now she had to stay hidden, drift off into her cloud world where nobody could find her. And when she was strong enough, if she lived, she would think about maybe trying to get away from here. That was the one spark of life she had left. Getting away from David. When she was tired, when the memories came back to taunt her, she couldn't care less, would have been happy to die, but now and then that one tiny thought popped into her head, and she felt her heart beat faster. Somewhere deep inside her something was struggling to live.

Gradually, as time passed and the burning in her head faded, she started to listen to Rose and the other girls, the nurses, who talked quietly as they went about their business. She gathered that the kids who'd saved her were from Holloway, in North London, and that David's second-in-command, Jester, a boy she'd heard about but never met before, had gone off looking for new recruits and brought them back here to the palace. Four other kids had set off with Jester but none of them had returned. Things didn't look entirely black, though, because the new arrivals were apparently great fighters. Well, she'd seen enough of them in action to know that, hadn't she? Now David was hoping that they'd help him get rid of some hooligans who'd made camp in a nearby park and were causing a lot of trouble.

All this stuff was going on around her. People with their own lives, their own problems. And it meant nothing to her. She drifted in and out of sleep, lost herself in the marks on the ceiling, and the next thing she was aware of was a boy in the bed next her. He also had a bandage round his head. He, too, had had a blow to the skull. She thought he might be the muscly black kid who'd rescued her at Green Park, but she couldn't be sure.

He was out cold, completely unconscious. Brooke listened to the girls and picked up that he'd been hurt in a fight with the hooligans.

David came back, this time with Jester. Brooke recognized him from his famous patchwork coat. The two of them talked to Rose, completely ignoring Brooke who might just as well not have been there. David explained that he wanted to keep the boy – his name was Blue – under guard. He left two of his red blazers to do the job. They sat outside the door and made sure nobody came in or out without David's permission.

The boys didn't take their job very seriously; they spent a long time in the sick-room chatting with the nurses, flirting, drinking tea, playing cards. One of them was spotty and grumpy, the other one, who had a big nose and was called Andy, seemed quite nice and was obviously pretty bored with being a guard. Listening in on their chat, tuning in to another world, helped Brooke to tune out of her own problems. She could almost imagine that when she closed her eyes she was listening to a play on the radio or something. One of her mum's boyfriends had listened to Radio Four all the time, and there always seemed to be a play of some sort on. He never worked, just sat at the kitchen table all afternoon rolling fags and listening to the radio. Said it was 'far superior to television' and that only morons wasted their time watching TV. The thing was he was a moron himself, happy to sponge off Brooke's mum who was out at work all day, and the radio drove Brooke nuts.

Now, though, it was a useful, comforting memory of cosier times, and she could pretend that the disease, the sickos, the death and despair, were all just part of a radio series. Maybe, after all, nothing more would go wrong . . .

64

They'd been following the boy for ten minutes, holding back, not letting him see them. He'd been creeping round the wall of the Buckingham Palace gardens, going backwards and forwards, distracted, as if he kept changing his mind about what he wanted to do. Once he'd tried to climb over the wall, but had quickly given up. The wire and the spikes at the top had defeated him. He'd been round to the front twice, keeping low, and had peered through the railings of the parade ground, making sure he wasn't seen by the boys on sentry duty in the boxes.

It was a dark night, so it was hard to see him clearly. All they could say for certain was that he was about fifteen, he was wearing dark clothing, he was very thin and his behaviour was odd, confused.

Now he was making a complete circuit of the wall, muttering to himself.

'What's he want? Does he want to get in, or not?'

'I don't think he knows.'

The boys following him were two more of David's boys from the palace, their red blazers looking grey in the half-light. They'd been sent out here by Pod as part of the increased security that had been put in place since DogNut and his crew had got out over the wall. The security had

423

been bumped up even further following the attack on the squatter camp and all that had happened since then. These two had missed most of the excitement, but had heard about it. How one of the kids from Holloway had taken on the squatters' leader, John, in single combat to settle the argument between them and David.

The Holloway kid had won the fight, but Pod worried that the squatters might not stick to their agreement.

Pod had told them that the palace was now on red alert. Whatever that meant.

Actually, they knew what it meant. It meant their job was as much to stop anyone from getting out as getting in.

'Do you think he's from the camp?' one of the boys whispered.

'I dunno. Don't think so. He arrived from the west. He's alone. He doesn't look dangerous to me.'

'Shall we grab him then?'

'I dunno.'

'I think we need to talk to him.'

'After you . . .'

65

David was sitting at the table in his office, writing up his diary for the day, when Pod knocked and poked his face round the door. David slid the diary under some papers. No need for Pod to know he kept it. Wouldn't want anyone to get any ideas about reading it. There were too many secrets in there. One day, though, it would be very valuable. His own personal record of events. The sort of thing that would be kept in a museum.

'What is it?'

'We have a visitor,' said Pod, trying to keep from smiling too broadly. He was evidently very pleased with himself.

'Is it Nicola?' David asked rather too quickly, sounding more excited than he had intended.

'No.'

'Oh . . . Who then?'

'A couple of the guards spotted him wandering around in the road outside. Looked like he was trying to get in.'

'Who is he, Pod?' said David with growing irritation.

'He's from the Natural History Museum.'

'Oh, right. Anyone we know?'

'No. But he's got an interesting story to tell.'

David leant forward over the table and smiled at Pod. 'Where is he now?'

'We're keeping him down in the guardroom out of the way. Apart from me and the two boys who brought him in, nobody knows he's here.'

'And they know to keep quiet?'

'Of course they do. They're well trained.'

'It's just with everything going on here at the moment we have to be very careful,' said David. 'I don't want the new arrivals talking to anyone from the museum.'

'I know,' said Pod. 'But this guy might be just what we need to solve your museum problem big time.'

'You're either going to have to bring him in, or tell me more about him, Pod. You can't keep teasing me like this.'

'I'll go and get him.'

'And get Jester too. He needs to be in on this.'

'All right.'

Pod hurried out and David stood up. He went over to the windows and looked out towards the gardens. It was black night outside so all he could see was his own reflection looking back at him. Could he dare to hope that all his plans were going to fall neatly into place so quickly? Not that anything was guaranteed. The Holloway kids were a deadly fighting force, but they were difficult to deal with and didn't like being told what to do. He had their leaders safely tucked away in the sick-bay under armed guard, which was a start. And John was beaten. He finally had the squatters under his control. Nicola would have to stick to her agreement. She might not realize it, but she was his, and all her kids were his too. He rubbed his hands together. If this boy that Pod had found was all he had implied, then maybe the museum kids would be his soon as well.

It was all happening scarily fast, everything at once,

but he'd been planning for a long time, setting it all up. That's what it took. Not violence, not shouting and screaming and running around with a big stick, but careful planning and intelligence. Thinking things through. Organization. So that now he could let all the pieces slip into place.

He'd have a lot more to write in his diary tonight.

No matter. He liked to stay up late. Didn't need much sleep. Up late and up early was what worked. Some kids liked to sleep all day, but not him. That was no way to get things down.

He grunted. Out of the corner of his eye he'd caught the reflection of one of the paintings. A full-length portrait of some long-dead princess or other. For a moment she had looked like Nicola.

Nicola . . .

He was trying to keep a cool head and a clear mind, but thoughts of her kept jamming the gears. He remembered her sitting there opposite him at the table. Remembered her getting up and coming over to him. Standing too close. She'd been mocking him, he knew that much, but all the same . . .

All the same.

He remembered the smell of her, the flecks of gold in her green eyes . . . Oh yes, he'd thought about her a lot lately. Pictured her standing by his side on the balcony. Pictured her . . .

Pod came back in. He had a boy with him who looked pale and thin and slightly crazy. There were dark rings round his eyes, as if he hadn't slept for days. His hair was a mess, and as David watched he scratched his scalp with dirty fingernails, then rubbed his neck. There was an agitated, fidgety feel to him. His gaze flicked around the room. Seeing ghosts in the shadows.

David poured him a glass of water. Handed it to him. He drank it down in one long gulp.

'This is David,' said Pod.

'Yes, I know,' said the boy. 'I know who David is.'

'Were you looking for me?' David asked. The boy stared at him, sussing him out. He sniffed. Put the glass down carefully on the table.

'No, not really. Yes, a bit, yes and no.' He giggled nervously. 'I wasn't sure what I was looking for . . . Something. Something or other. Or both. Or neither.'

'You're lucky you didn't come across any strangers out there,' said David. 'Any grown-ups.'

'Lucky?' The boy gave David a withering look. 'For me? Or for them? I kill grown-ups. I destroy them. I see any I'll strangle them. I'll kick their balls off. I'll smash their sick faces into their heads. I'll stick my knife into their guts and twist it.'

He mimed the action, leaning towards David and breathing foul sour breath over him.

David backed off. 'Sit down,' he said, and the boy sat, looking like he could spring up out of his chair at any moment. He was dressed all in black with a slightly grubby roll-neck jumper that he kept fiddling with, picking at the material.

'What's your name?' David asked.

'Paul,' said the boy. 'Paul Channing.'

66

They'd brought his head out on a pole. Poor doomed kid, he hadn't stood a chance. His face looked peaceful, calm even, but he must have died screaming in terror. And once again Shadowman had been able to do nothing more than watch. For two days they'd been trying to get at the boy. He'd been hiding inside a Waitrose supermarket on the Holloway Road. Close enough to where Shadowman kept his secret stash of weapons and supplies to allow him to sneak back there whenever the action slowed. He could eat and drink and rest, and each time he returned he found the grown-ups still hard at work, nibbling away at the defences.

Shadowman had found a good look-out spot in a tiny flat above a carpet shop opposite the supermarket. It was high enough and the road was wide enough that he didn't need to worry about being detected. He'd dragged a bed over to the window and, using pillows to prop himself up, he could lie there and watch what was going on through his binoculars.

The supermarket had been well fortified and Shadowman had been holding out some hope that the strangers might give up and go elsewhere.

No such luck.

Eventually they'd smashed their way past the barricades and got inside the shop. The place was so well fortified he'd assumed that there must be loads of kids hiding in there. In the end, though, there was only the evidence of this one dead body. This grisly, battered head on a stick. Why the others had abandoned the boy he had no idea.

There were loads of grown-ups gathered here now, every day more and more of them turned up, and all the while that they'd been attacking the shop they'd grown more confident.

St George was triumphant. He was a diseased commander at the head of an army. He paraded up and down the road, using the severed head as a banner.

Shadowman felt a cold fear grip him. The army would move on now, sweep through London like a swarm of locusts, devouring everything in their path, collecting more strangers as they went. St George was the leader, Spike, Bluetooth, Man U and the One-Armed Bandit were his generals, and the rest of them were his horde. Hadn't Genghis Khan's Mongol army been called the Golden Horde? This lot were hardly golden. They were a rabble, but they still needed a name.

If he named them, he would feel like he had more power over them.

What to call them, though?

The Horde?

The Mob?

The Enemy?

It was there, in the back of his mind, the word he was looking for, but he couldn't tease it out.

The right word.

The right name for this terrible ragged army.

No point trying to force it.

It would come to him.

67

'I used to live at the Natural History Museum,' said Paul. 'Not any more. They don't want me there. I don't want them. They laugh at me.'

'Yes, you told us that,' said David patiently.

'I hate them. I hate them all. I just want to hurt them. I want them to know what it feels like. To feel like I do. I want them – You never met Olivia . . .'

'I did meet her, actually,' said David. 'She came here on her way to find you. I offered to look after her and keep her safe, but the others took her away. DogNut and his friends. They wouldn't let her stay here, even though she begged me. They took her to the Collector. They gave her to him.'

'The others, yes,' said Paul, nodding his head violently. 'Yes. They did that. Because they hated me, you see? They wanted to get back at me.'

David fixed Paul with an intense stare. 'It was them all along, Paul, don't you see it?'

'Who?'

'All of them,' said David. 'Brooke and Justin and all of them at the museum. They were working with DogNut and the others. They made a plan together.'

'Did they?'

'Of course they did!' David almost shouted at Paul, who was gripping the edge of the table with white-knuckled claws. 'DogNut always had a plan. Jester overheard him when he was here, didn't you, Jester?'

David looked at Jester, who was watching from by the fireplace. They'd been working on Paul for a long time as his muddled brain went round and round in circles.

'That's right,' said Jester. 'I heard them plotting. They were talking about how they'd secretly made a plan with Brooke . . .'

'No. Not Brooke,' said Paul. 'I don't think so. Brooke was nice to me. I liked her, I needed her help, but she disappeared. I looked for her. I wanted to talk to her.'

'That was all part of the plan,' said David. 'Can't you see? They were all in it together. Brooke and DogNut and the other kids at the museum.'

'Justin?' Paul's eyes were wide and staring.

'Yes, even Justin. He's the one in charge, isn't he?'

'Yes, he is.'

'Does he like you, Paul?'

'Nobody likes me. Because I can't fit in. That's why they make me work with the sickos.'

'Tell us more about the sickos,' said David, leaning back in his chair.

'They keep three of them. In a lorry.'

'A Tesco lorry?'

'Yes. They keep it in the car park. There are three sickos in there. It's my job to look after them. To feed them and clean them out. To keep them chained up and muzzled. That's all I'm fit for. They won't let me grow food, or work in the library, or the science labs . . . No, all Paul the idiot is fit for is cleaning up after sickos.'

'What would happen if they got out?' Jester asked.

'What do you think? They'd attack. That's all sickos ever want to do. If the sickos got into the museum, that'd show them. That'd show them . . .'

'Three sickos couldn't do much harm, Paul,' said David.

'There are others,' said Paul, grinning. 'In the cellars below the museum. That's where we caught the ones we keep on the lorry.'

'You know that was my lorry, Paul,' said David. 'They stole it off me.'

Paul laughed, too loudly, and for no apparent reason, then stopped, too quickly.

'Tell us about the sickos below the museum,' said Jester.

'Like rats down there. Too many to get rid of. They're locked out, you see, but if they could do it, if they ever got past the locked doors, they'd come into the museum. Nobody could stop them. Nobody.'

'You must have guards? People protecting you?'

'Robbie got hurt. He's out of action.'

'Who's Robbie?'

'He's supposed to be in charge of security. He got hurt. The sickos could easily do it, if they got through. They could destroy it all, punish them all. Then the bloody bastards would know what it's like to feel pain.'

'You could stop that happening, Paul, couldn't you?' said Jester. 'That's your job.'

'Yes. I guard the sickos on the lorry. I check the doors in the lower level, make sure everything's locked. That's how I got away from the museum without them knowing. Hee hee hee. They don't know! I got out through a lower-level window. Robbie got hurt. Robbie's in bed recovering. Security's a joke.'

433

'Did you make sure the doors were still locked when you left, though?'

'Yes, yes. There were sickos down there, but they kept away from me. They knew I'd kill them. I wanted to kill the sickos on the lorry, but after they all turned against me Justin said I wasn't allowed to be near them any more. They won't even let me do that now. I'm useless. But I'm the only one who really knows how to look after the sickos. I understand them. The only one.'

Paul frantically rubbed his neck, like a dog with fleas.

'They hate you,' said David.

'Yes.'

'But you could show them, teach them a lesson, teach them how useful you are,' said Jester.

'And teach them what it's like to feel pain,' David added.

'Could I?' Paul's eyes went very wide.

'You have to,' said David. 'They had an arrangement with DogNut, about Olivia. They gave her to the Collector to keep him quiet, so that the rest of them could get safely to the museum. He was blocking their way, wasn't he? And they had to give him something.'

'They had to give him your sister,' said Jester. 'It was all planned. That's why they brought her from the Tower. To sacrifice her. And they arranged the whole thing with Justin and Brooke.'

'Yes, yes, I really think that's what happened, I really do.'

'The whole thing was planned to hurt you, Paul,' said David.

'Yes.'

David tried not to smile. This was working almost too well. He and Jester just had to keep telling Paul the story

434

he wanted to hear and they could get him to do whatever they liked.

'You mustn't let them get away with it,' he said. 'They have to be punished, and you're the person to do it. You have the power in your hands.'

Paul raised his hands and looked at them. They were shaking, like an old man's hands, the fingernails bitten right down to the flesh.

'They must be made to understand,' said Jester.

'Yes.'

'You're going to go back there, Paul,' said David.

'Back there? No. No, I can't . . . I've got away. I want to live with you now, David. Don't you see?'

'I do see, Paul, but there is one thing you need to do before you can come here.'

'OK.'

'It's important, Paul. You won't be happy until you do it.'

'OK, OK . . .' Paul sobbed. 'I want to be happy. I do, I really do, but I don't know how to any more.'

'Don't cry, Paul, everything's going to be all right. You did the right thing coming here. We can help you. We understand. But first you have to do just one more thing.'

'OK, yes. Yes. Tell me what I have to do.'

68

Brooke had been miles away, wandering the outer roads of her sky kingdom, when they'd come in. She was so deeply lost in her fantasies that she might as well have been unconscious. As she'd stared at the ceiling, she'd been only vaguely aware that more kids were arriving. For a while there'd been a crowd. She'd registered raised voices, an argument about something, shouting . . .

Not her argument.

Nothing to do with her.

She'd let herself go, fallen asleep.

When she'd surfaced again, it was quiet. The crowd had gone. Even Rose and the nurses had gone. The boy was still in his bed, but there was a girl with him now, lying on one of the other beds. She was the one with the scrappy hair and the leather jacket that she'd seen after the battle. Her name was Maxie. They were talking to each other and slowly Brooke tuned in to their conversation. They were discussing their problems, but there was something else. Brooke sensed that they didn't know each other that well. Perhaps had even started out not liking each other very much. She also sensed that they wanted to get to know each other better. That they were growing closer.

They began to talk like lovers, and as Brooke listened she

felt a thaw within her. The cold dark block around her heart started to melt and she was gradually, step by tiny step, led back from fantasy into reality. She began to appreciate that she wasn't the only one who hurt. She remembered Paul, what she'd said to him when he'd freaked out at the museum. She'd told him that he wasn't alone. Told him not to be selfish with his pain. Not to blame the world. And that's what Brooke began to understand now.

She wasn't alone either.

She had lost Donut and Courtney, but she didn't have to cope with all this by herself. She could talk to someone, just as these two were talking now. She could share with them. She could sense that Blue and Maxie cared for each other and the kids they looked after. They'd lost friends along the way, just like her, but they were showing that you could make new friends. They couldn't ever properly replace the people they'd lost, but they could still matter. Life had to go on.

Real life.

Maxie and Blue gave her hope, and the more she listened, the more she learnt about them and got involved in their stories, the more she liked them. What was Chris Marker always banging on about, surrounded by all his books? She'd never really got it before, when he'd talked about all the stories in London, how they were going on all around them, all the time, and how some of the stories were the same, kids going through the same experiences, and sometimes they joined together. Maybe this was meant to happen. Maybe her story had taken a turn and these other kids were going to become an important part of her life. Maybe it was time for her to rest for a while and let their story take over?

As the time ticked past, showing on the face of an old-fashioned wind-up clock, she listened and learnt. She put herself in their story. And the marks on the ceiling slowly became just that – marks. The cities and forests, the roads and train tracks and little villages faded away, to be replaced by cracks and stains. The last to go was the farm. Courtney and Donut were still there, in the kitchen, sitting at the table, drinking tea, chatting happily. They'd always be there if she ever wanted to visit them, but for now she had to say goodbye.

There were problems in the real world to deal with.

It was clear that David was holding Maxie and Blue prisoner here in the sick-bay. He was trying to keep them from their friends so that he could take over their crew. The two of them were plotting how to get away, escape from the palace, just as Donut and Courtney had done the other day.

They were talking about it now and had come up against one problem.

'. . . say we did get out, yeah?' Blue was asking Maxie. 'Where would we go?'

'We've got the whole of London to choose from,' Maxie replied. She was posher than Blue, spoke differently. In the past Brooke might have laughed at someone like her, mocked her and teased her. Not any more. She knew that it made no difference where you came from, how you'd been brought up – the disease affected you all the same. They'd all lost parents, friends, brothers and sisters. They'd all had to fight to survive. They were all the same.

Just trying to get from one day to another.

What if they *could* escape? Get away from here. All of them, together.

438

For the first time since she'd lost her friends, Brooke wanted to get up out of bed, to run and shout and fight. To kick back against the world that was trying to get at her. The world of grown-ups, and disease, the world of David . . .

69

'Do you think he'll go through with it?'

'If he can. He's just mad enough.'

Jester giggled. 'I'm not sure we really should have done that,' he said.

David looked at him and shook his head. 'You loved it, Jester. You can't fool me. It's what you're good at. Persuading people. Working your magic. You *are* the magic man.'

'Yeah, but is it white magic or black magic?' said Jester.

'It's all the same. When this is over and we've won, we'll write the history books, and we'll both be waving to the crowds on the cover. Everything's coming together right now. This is how it's meant to be. We've struck a blow against Justin and his traitors. We'll fatally wound them, and they'll come crawling to us for protection. We won't offer it to them, though, not at first. We'll let them stew a bit and then march in with our new army and save their wretched socks. Then we'll be holding all the cards.' David paused, let a smile take over his face.

'Just remember,' he said. 'Justin and Brooke. They're mine.'

He went to an ornate drinks cabinet that stood in the corner and selected a decanter of whisky. He hated the taste of the stuff but he'd seen enough films in his time to know that when something like this happened you had to celebrate with a drink. A drink and a cigar.

He took the cut-glass stopper out of the decanter and sniffed the pungent, eye-watering amber liquid inside.

'Drink, sir?'

Jester laughed. 'Why not?'

70

Blue and Maxie were still talking, still plotting. Blue kept coming back to the fact that they didn't know the area. These were unfamiliar streets to him.

'We don't know where's safe.'

'There must be other kids,' said Maxie, who seemed more hopeful of escape. 'This can't be it.'

'Nowhere else is going to be as well set up as this,' Blue went on. 'Nowhere else is gonna be as safe. David's the only one round here who's organized.'

Now Brooke heard a third voice, and at first she didn't understand where it had come from.

It simply said, 'David's a liar.'

She recognized that voice. So familiar.

Of course. It was her own voice. She'd come back from the dead. Spoken without meaning to. The other two kids sat up and looked over at her.

'What did you say?' Blue asked.

'David's a liar,' Brooke repeated. 'He's been lying to you all along. Why do you think he's been keeping me out of the way up here?'

'Because of your injuries?' said Blue.

'They're not as bad as they look,' said Brooke, and it was as if a tap had been turned on. All the words that had been growing inside her came tumbling out in a rush. She was saying things she hadn't even thought. The sentences came out fully formed without seeming to pass through her brain.

'When you cut your face, there's a lot of blood,' she said. 'Rose fixed me up pretty well. I'm going to look like hell, but it's only skin. David didn't want me mixing with you lot, though. He didn't want me talking. Once it was clear they were keeping me prisoner I made sure I didn't speak, hardly even moved. Just listened . . .'

Best not tell them that she'd gone a little crazy. That could come later. Best appear to be on top of things. She needed their help and didn't want to scare them off.

'I don't get it,' said Blue. 'Where are you from?'

Good question. Where *was* she from?

'The museum.'

She hadn't meant to say that. She'd meant . . . somewhere. Some safe place with her mum. A place that didn't exist any more.

'Museum?' said Blue. 'What museum?'

'Natural History Museum,' said Brooke, and once more the words came pouring out. She told them about her life there, and how they weren't the only other kids around, that there were other places to go, and then she tried to tell them about her expedition with Donut, but that was when the words ran out. It was too soon to talk about that. She stopped before the tears came, and the words dried up.

'It's all right,' said Maxie.

Yes. It *was* all right. She did have somewhere to go. A safe place. And she needed to get back there. She needed to connect with the friends she'd left behind at the museum. With Justin and Wiki and Jibber-jabber, with Kwanele and

Zohra and Froggie . . . So many of them. So many faces. So many stories. With Maxie and Blue's help she could get back there.

Maybe some small good had come out of the seemingly senseless deaths of Donut and Courtney.

She had linked up with these new kids.

They had things to do together.

Stories to tell.

It was fate.

'I just want to go home,' she said.

71

David and Jester were both gulping, laughing and grimacing. They clutched their throats in theatrical displays of choking. The room was full of thick cigar smoke and the reek of whisky. David took another puff of his cigar and then tried another tentative sip from his glass. He coughed and Jester laughed even harder. David joined him. Soon they were both slumped in chairs laughing helplessly. David laughed so hard he blew a candle out and that only made the two of them laugh harder.

'Whisky is disgusting,' David gasped, once he'd got his breath back.

'You'll grow into it,' said Jester. 'Remember you're just a fourteen-year-old boy. It's easy to forget sometimes.'

'We've had to grow up fast,' said David, and he put his glass down on the table.

'You should get a coaster for that,' said Jester. 'Or you'll make a ring.'

David gave him a dirty look, then dipped his fingers in the whisky and flicked some at Jester who yelped and swore.

'I'm not that grown up just yet, thank you very much,' he said. 'I'm not ready for my pipe and slippers.'

'Look at us, though,' said Jester. 'Sitting here in Buckingham Palace drinking whisky and smoking cigars and plotting to take over the world. Can you believe it? How did it happen?'

'Crazy, isn't it,' said David, and they began to talk about the past, everything that had happened to them, the twisted interconnecting paths that had led them to this room in this building on this night. The whisky they'd managed to force down had warmed their guts and they congratulated each other, bigging themselves up drunkenly. They babbled on, discussing how well their partnership worked, and sniggering at how stupid everyone else was, how easy they were to manipulate.

All in all, they were very pleased with themselves.

What could possibly go wrong with their plans?

There was a knock on the door.

'Who is it?'

'Jonathan.'

David looked to Jester. Then back at the door. Jonathan was a junior guard. It wasn't normal for him to interrupt David when he was in a meeting. Only Pod and Jester had the authority to do that.

David rested his cigar in an ashtray, waving smoke away from his face.

'What do you want?'

'There's a problem.'

'Well, yes, I assume there's a problem, or you wouldn't be bothering us. What sort of a problem?'

Jester hauled himself out of his chair and went over to open the door. He glared at Jonathan who looked nervous and sweaty.

'Well?'

446

'I–it's the royal family,' he stammered.

'What about them?'

'They've got out.'

72

Stupid. How could he have been so stupid?

To doze off. Here. Exposed like this, within spitting distance of the strangers' army. To drop his guard so disastrously . . .

Dead stupid.

After St George had brought the boy's head out on the pole the strangers had somehow set fire to the shop. How they'd done it he had no idea. Had they really remembered how to use matches? Cigarette lighters? Or had it been an accident?

He didn't know, and he'd watched helplessly as flames had climbed into the night sky. Then the strangers, with nothing to unite them, had milled about in the road, grunting and hissing and brawling with each other, as the supermarket steadily burnt down behind them. It had looked like nothing much more was going to happen tonight. Some of them had even broken up into smaller groups and found places to sleep.

At some point Shadowman had fallen asleep too . . .

And now they were here.

They hadn't all gone to sleep. Some had obviously started roaming the streets, looking for more food, their senses alert. After all, there had only been that one lone boy in

448

the supermarket. He wouldn't have fed that many of them. As long as they'd been concentrating all their efforts on getting at him they hadn't bothered with anyone else. Now they were bored and hungry and fired up by St George.

And no one was safe.

Anywhere.

A noise must have disturbed Shadowman because his eyes snapped open and he was awake in a split second, his brain on a tight trigger. The supermarket was still on fire and there was a dim flickering orange glow in the room. He had just long enough to clock several large bodies bundling through the door before they were on him.

He'd been lying on his back on the bed, his weapons laid out next to him ready for action. There was no time, though, to get to them. By the time he was awake, a big father with no hair was pawing at him. Shadowman brought his hands up to protect himself and discovered that he was still holding his knife. He hadn't totally dropped his guard. He slashed at the father's forearms and rolled off the side of the bed.

He hit the floor with a thump and found himself surrounded by a forest of legs. He thought there must be five or six strangers in the room. The light from the fire over the road did little to lift the darkness. It was hard to see anything in here, which was worse for him than it was for them, as they acted as much on smell as on sight, whereas he had to rely solely on his eyes. His only advantage was how cramped it was in the room. The clumsy strangers were bumping into each other in their eagerness to get at him. He stayed low, scuttling across the carpet, avoiding grasping hands and slashing at the grown-ups' lower legs. One went down heavily as he sliced through the tendons

449

in his ankles. He lay there moaning and thrashing about, spraying blood all over the place as his useless legs kicked out.

Shadowman bumped up against the wall and two fathers cornered him, making a grab for his clothing. Shadowman forced himself on to his feet, powering up with all his strength and headbutting one of them in the chin. The father's head jerked back and Shadowman heard a clack as his jaws were forced together. He got a glimpse of a bleeding mouth. He elbowed the second father in the throat, lashed out with his knife and pulled away from the two of them.

He had to get to the bed and reach his other weapons. He needed the machete.

But one of the other strangers hit him with something in the back of his head and he reeled across the room, stunned. Another managed to get hold of his cloak and jerk him back. As he went, he had enough sense left to push off hard with his feet so that he fell back with some force against whoever it was that held him. They crashed into the wall and he heard the hiss of air pumped from liquid-filled lungs.

Shadowman's head cleared and he was filled with a wild energy. He knew he was fighting for his life. He whirled round blindly, his knife cutting anything it hit. He didn't scream or shout. He was trying desperately not to make a sound in case it attracted the whole army. If that happened, he had no chance. He had to hope that this was just a small hunting pack.

He felt fingernails scraping down one arm, tearing at the material of his jacket. At least they didn't seem to be armed.

No sooner had he had that thought when a long arm came flying out of the darkness and struck him in the chest with some sharp object. His ribs ached from the blow, as if one of them had snapped, and he felt wetness under his shirt.

He stabbed towards the attacker with his knife and it connected with something soft and stuck fast. He'd hit one of them. He pulled them into the light from the window. It was a mother. His knife embedded in her cheek. He tugged it free and as the unseen weapon battered him on the back he threw himself at the bed. His injured ribs sent a jolt of pain through his torso and he stifled a cry. There was a little more light here and he managed to get his hands on his loaded crossbow. As he twisted round, he fired off a shot point blank at the father he had head-butted. It got him in the chest and he toppled backwards, arms windmilling.

He jumped up from the bed.

That was three of them down.

Which meant there were only three left.

It was far from over, though. The remaining three came at him in a group, swamping him with their bodies. He had no time to reload and dropped the bow, wishing he had gone for the machete instead. As he struggled to bring up his knife arm, one of his attackers took hold of it; another was trying to bite his throat. The third one was at his back, pounding him with his weapon. All three were pressed against him and the smell was awful. Fighting off panic, he once again powered backwards, knocking the stranger over behind him. The biter was still at his throat. Quickly Shad-owman brought his knee up then kicked down, aiming at where he thought the biter's knee might be. He connected with a satisfying crunch and the father shrank away from him, hissing with pain.

Shadowman was still only getting odd glimpses of his attackers as they stumbled about in the half-light. He looked round at the stranger who had his knife hand and saw a puffy mother's face, swollen with boils and growths, twisted and misshapen. His knife was still out of action, so he would have to fight like a stranger now. If they could scratch, then so could he. He reached over and jabbed at the mother's eyes. As his nails made contact with her lower eyelids, he tugged down hard. It was like ripping off an especially sticky bandage. There was a tearing noise and half the mother's face came away. Shadowman was left with a handful of skin and pus. The mother loosened her grip just enough for him to be able to bring the knife up at last. He plunged it into the guts of the father with the broken knee, followed it up with a quick slash to left and right across the mother's neck and he was left with only one assailant.

The father with the weapon who he had knocked over.

He'd scrambled across the floor and got to his feet on the other side of the room. Now he was holding back in the darkness, blocking the doorway.

Shadowman was fighting for breath, dripping with sweat and blood, and worse. There were countless small wounds all over his exposed skin, but as far as he could tell none of them was life threatening. His ribs burned, his throat was horribly dry, his legs shaking, his heart thumping, but he was still upright.

And so far he was winning.

He knew he had to keep going while he was ahead. Not let up.

He raised his knife and winced. His whole arm ached and he felt like he had wrenched his shoulder.

Ignore it.

Fight through the pain.

The last stranger stepped into the light.

With a jolt Shadowman realized he recognized him.

It was the One-Armed Bandit. He was naked from the waist up, the stump of his missing arm wagging. He was holding a sharp stone in his remaining hand. The sort of thing a Neanderthal might have used as a tool.

Heavy and dangerous-looking, but nothing compared to Shadowman's knife. If he held his nerve, this would soon be over.

The Bandit came closer. His gums were massively swollen, as if he was holding two sausages under his lips. The tiny yellow stubs of his teeth looked like little lumps of sweetcorn. He appeared to be smiling, but Shadowman knew that it was just the way his lips were being forced back by his puffed-up gums.

He swung the stone through the air as he moved closer and closer to Shadowman, his breath bubbling in his throat.

Shadowman charged. And it all went wrong. He hadn't seen the one whose tendons he'd cut lying on the floor in front of him. The father flung his arms round his legs and brought him down. Shadowman swore for the first time and stabbed the father in the chest. He instantly knew that this was a mistake as the blade caught in his ribs. And, as Shadowman tried to tug it out, the One-Armed Bandit fell on him.

To make it worse, the father he had stabbed wasn't dead. He was writhing and gurgling and feebly trying to pull the knife out. Shadowman was sandwiched between him and the Bandit, who was battering him with the stone again. He was too close to do much damage, however, and

Shadowman was able to twist round and punch him in the face, splattering his nose and cutting his top lip open. The Bandit groaned, rolled fully on top of him and put his mouth to Shadowman's neck. Luckily his teeth were so deeply embedded in his inflamed gums he couldn't properly bite. The feel of his wet, blubbery lips was revolting and Shadowman thought he might be sick.

He fought it and kept his focus. The first thing was to stop the stabbed father from straining against him. Shadowman took hold of the Bandit's wrist and used his hand to hammer the knife in deeper. The stone connected with the knife handle and drove it down. One, two, three. At last the father fell still and the Bandit dropped the stone. Then Shadowman did something dumb.

He let go of the Bandit's wrist.

The hammer blows must have loosened the knife and broken some of the father's ribs as well, because now the Bandit's fingers closed round the handle. Before Shadowman knew what was happening the Bandit had slid the knife free and was trying to stab him. Shadowman managed to react just in time, grabbing the Bandit's hand and holding the knife in the air above him.

The pain that pulsed through his tensed muscles was excruciating. His arms shook with the effort. He knew he mustn't let go. The point of the blade was aimed straight at his left eye. It hovered there, only centimetres away, dripping blood on to him. He blinked some away and swallowed hard.

The Bandit's sour breath felt hot on his skin and his horrible, leering face pressed closer.

As Shadowman lay there, locked in this lethal embrace, the stranger's weight crushing him, the fire in the supermarket must have flared up, because, for a few precious seconds, the room was brightly lit. Out of the corner of his eye Shadowman spotted the machete lying half a metre away on the carpet.

The only problem was it would mean freeing one hand to reach for it and he wasn't sure he was strong enough to hold the Bandit's knife off with just the other one.

He would have to risk it, though, as the knife was creeping ever closer to his eye.

Do it now.

Do it quickly.

There was no choice.

He barked out a harsh swear-word and in one swift movement he groped for the machete, picked it up and swung it.

The next moment he was still holding the hand that held the knife, but all the weight had gone from it. He had sliced clean through the Bandit's arm, which flopped down harmlessly, spurting blood.

The full, unsupported weight of the Bandit slumped on to Shadowman, suffocating him. He couldn't use the machete again; the two of them were too tightly entwined. Instead he kept hold of the severed hand, turned it and stabbed the knife into the side of the Bandit's neck.

'That was for Tom and Kate,' he said, tearing the blade through tendons and arteries. 'And the boy over the road . . . And for me . . .'

73

It was taking him an awfully long time to die.

His name was Jamie. He was thirteen. Paul had been pretty friendly with him once. Then Jamie had found a new gang to hang out with. They'd probably been laughing at Paul behind his back. Not any more.

Jamie had been checking the lower levels at the museum by himself when he'd come across Paul. He should never have been by himself. If Robbie hadn't been recovering from his attack, he would have made sure the patrols were properly organized. As it was, it just made Paul's job easier. He'd smiled at Jamie and before he knew what was happening Paul had put his hands round his neck and started to squeeze.

He'd never realized before how strong he was. Nothing could shift his fingers from Jamie's throat. No matter how hard Jamie struggled. He squeezed as hard as he could. How long did it take for someone to die?

Jamie was still thrashing about now over a minute later. Paul reckoned he must be doing it wrong and shifted the position of his thumbs. He felt a spasm pass through the boy, and then at last he was still.

Paul eased him to the floor and then dragged him over to the door. He stopped to get his breath, fumbling for the keys in his pocket. It was hot down here. It always was. Even in winter it was a couple of degrees warmer than upstairs.

And it smelt.

It was them. The sickos that lived down here. Lurking in the abandoned rooms underneath the museum. For the most part the kids just ignored them, safe in the knowledge that the diseased, mushy-brained grown-ups could never open the locked doors.

Not the sickos, no.

But he could.

The lamp that Jamie had been carrying had blown out when he'd dropped it. Paul picked it up and relit it. He put it on the floor close to the door and pushed the key into the lock. He turned it. This was the last door. Once he'd done this he would go up to the car park and let the three sickos off the lorry. And after that he could sit back and watch the fun.

He pulled the door open. There was a knot of sickos pressed up against it on the other side. Crushed together in a tight huddle. One stared at him, but the two nearest ones looked blind. They were thin as skeletons and slow moving. Their skin was pale, hardly blemished by sickness, their eyes sunk deep in dark sockets. Paul noticed a skittering movement among them and saw that rats were crawling all over them. One fat greasy specimen hung off a mother's ear, its teeth gripping the lobe. She didn't seem to notice. Another sat up, straight-backed, on the shoulder of a young father, sniffing the warm air. And then it went back to where it had been gnawing a hole in the father's skin.

One rat jumped down and trotted off, a lump of unidentifiable grey flesh in its mouth.

The sickos started to stir. Those that were able to crawled towards him; others simply stretched out their hands; one or two appeared to be dead. One came close and sniffed him, then moved on. Paul spat on him and then dragged Jamie's body closer.

'Here,' he said. 'It's supper time. Eat your fill. Get your strength up. You've work to do. There's more like this up there. A whole building full of them.'

The rest of the sickos started to move, breaking away from the huddle, ignoring Paul and slithering towards Jamie's body. One put his hands on him, feeling with blind fingers over his face, and as he did so Jamie's eyes fluttered open.

Even after all that he still wasn't dead.

Never mind. He soon would be.

He looked at Paul with a helpless expression. Tried to say something. A mother put her fingers in his mouth.

Paul leant over him. 'I want to show you something, Jamie,' he said. 'My little secret.'

He held on to the top of his roll-neck jumper and pulled it down, then lifted the lamp to illuminate his exposed skin.

There was a horrific scar below his right ear. It hadn't healed properly. Pus oozed from a sticky hole. The skin was ragged and lumpy around it. It was a mess, but you could still tell what had caused it. The scar was in the unmistakable shape of two sets of teeth.

Paul laughed. 'That's what they do to you,' he said. 'The grown-ups. That's what my one on the lorry did, before I muzzled him. That's what they'll do to you.'

He straightened the neck of his jumper and stood up. Jamie's eyes pleaded with him.

Paul turned and started to walk away along the corridor.

It was time to let the night come down.

Shadowman had gone round the room in the flat making sure the strangers were all dead, methodically cutting the throats of any who showed signs of life. And then a noise had drawn him to the window.

St George was doing a sort of war dance on top of a car. He was stamping up and down, hammering out a rhythm with his feet, lit by the lurid reds and yellows of the dancing flames from the burning supermarket.

His army was transfixed, watching him with upturned faces. He was their god. One by one they'd joined in with him, stamping, beating their fists in the air, and now they were systematically wrecking every car on the street in an orgy of senseless violence.

Shadowman was shaking uncontrollably. His head felt light. Nausea rose in his gullet and he fought the urge to pass out. He was sopping with sweat and blood and worse. There were tears dripping off his chin. He was crying, biting his tongue to keep from howling. Finally his knees buckled and he collapsed on to the bed, unable to stand any longer. He curled up into a foetus, hugging his knees. Around him on the floor lay six dead bodies.

He realized that he had been absolutely terrified. Scared beyond all understanding. He had been in a place he never wanted to go again. They had done that to him, St George and his bloody army. And they were going to do it to others. They were going to spread their terror wherever they went.

He had killed one of St George's lieutenants. And he wasn't going to let it end there. He would overcome his terror. He would kill the rest of them, when he could, one by one – Man U, Spike, Bluetooth – he'd find a way. A way to punish them for what they'd done to his friends.

And when he got the chance he would kill St George.

And then he would go to the palace and look for Jester and kill him too. Snuff him out for his betrayal. That was what would keep him going. That was what would get him up off this gore-spattered bed. He would ignore his wounds, his hunger and his thirst. Revenge would drive him on.

He forced himself back to the window. The army was starting to march off. He had to follow them. That was his role now.

He would do it.

Even though they scared him to death.

He packed up his weapons. Took a drink of water from his canteen.

He was ready.

The army had a name now. He'd known it all along. Known what to call them.

The Fear.

THE ENEMY attacked.

THE DEAD awoke.

THE FEAR spread . . .

NOW the story continues in

THE
SACRIFICE.

Read on . . . if you dare . . .

Small Sam wasn't dead. He was walking across the inner grounds of the Tower of London with his friend The Kid and a load of other children. They were heading for the White Tower, a big square lump with smaller towers at each corner that sat bang in the middle of the castle on a small hill. Sam, who was something of an expert on castles, knew all about the White Tower. It was the keep, the first part of the castle to be built here, started by William the Conqueror in the eleventh century, with stone specially brought over from France, and finished by his son, William the Second.

Sam felt like he was living in a dream. He had always been obsessed with knights and fantasy. He'd lost count of the number of times he'd seen the Lord of the Rings films. And now here he was, actually living in a real-life castle. Some of the other kids even wore armour and carried medieval weapons, though they were having to leave them at the door as they filed inside.

The boy in charge, General Jordan Hordern, had called a council of war, and everybody in the castle was expected to attend, even newcomers like Sam and The Kid.

Once inside they climbed to an upper floor, where there was a big room with windows on all sides. They found places to sit on the wooden benches that were arranged around the edges. Sam, who had visited the Tower several times, tried to remember what this room used to look like. He couldn't picture it. The local kids had removed the exhibits and returned it to how it must have looked in the Middle Ages. There were banners and pennants hanging on the bare stone walls, candles lighting the dark interior. A long table had been set up across one end and behind it stood four guards with halberds, the double-handed weapon that looked like a cross between an axe and a spear. There was a smaller table to one side where two girls and a boy sat, writing on loose sheets of paper.

Ed came over to where Sam and The Kid were sitting. It was Ed who'd found the two of them a few days ago, wandering, tired and wet, along the road that led to the Tower, and he'd taken it on himself to look after them. He still couldn't quite get his head round the fact that they'd survived for so long out there by themselves, and had made it here alive. It was up to him now to make sure they stayed that way.

'You just sit here and listen, OK?' he said. 'Just watch.'

He glanced at The Kid. He was an odd boy, odd and unpredictable, and had his own way of talking. He was prone to speaking out and Ed didn't want him to pipe up during the council.

'What's going on?' Sam whispered.

'To tell you the truth, I'm not sure, but I have to be over at the council table with the other captains. I'll explain anything you don't understand afterwards.' He looked at The Kid again, holding his gaze.

'Don't be tempted to join in.'

'Aye aye, skippy. Message received and misunderstood.'

'Seriously, Kid, zip it.'

The Kid zipped it, miming the action.

'Right now I'm as much in the dark as you are,' Ed went on. 'General Hordern called a special meeting of the council, so I guess he'll tell us what's going on.'

'That's him there, isn't it?' said Sam, and Ed turned to see a black kid with thick glasses come into the room flanked by two more guards.

'That's him. I better go. Remember. Zip it.'

Sam watched Ed go and take his place with several other kids who were settling down at the long table.

Sam felt safe with Ed. He'd been a bit scared of him at first. He had an ugly scar down one side of his face that pulled it out of shape, but he'd soon learned that Ed was kind and friendly and not frightening at all. Sometimes, though, Ed would go quiet and stare into the distance. Sam didn't say anything, but he knew that Ed was sad about something. He didn't need to ask what. They were all sad in their own ways. They'd all lost family and friends.

Sam and The Kid had been left alone for their first couple of days at the Tower. They'd been given food and allowed to sleep for most of the time. Now they were feeling more normal and Ed had offered to show them around properly. They'd just been getting ready when they'd been told to come to the meeting.

Jordan Hordern sat down, flanked by four boys and three girls. He waited, blank-faced and unreadable behind his thick glasses that were held together by sticking plasters round the bridge of the nose and one arm.

He waited for the room to fall silent. Didn't have to say anything. It was understood.

He looked around.

General Jordan couldn't tell anyone, but the truth was that he could hardly see anything at all any more. It wasn't just that the lenses in his glasses were scratched and old – his eyesight was steadily getting worse. There were dark patches in the centre of his vision. It was still clear around the edges, so he had to look sideways at things to see them properly. He'd never liked to look people in the eye before, and now it was nearly impossible.

He wouldn't let the idea enter his thoughts, but it was there, lurking in the back of his mind. He was going blind. What use would he be then? How could he keep his position in charge here at the Tower if he couldn't see anything?

It was important that nobody knew. For now he had unquestioned power over everyone at the Tower.

The kids sat in absolute silence. He was pleased. He'd known teachers at school who could never get a class to shut up. Jordan had given them hell, and now here he was, just a boy, able to control more than a hundred kids.

Sam couldn't take his eyes off the general. Jordan scared him. There was a stillness and a coldness about him. He was like a statue, or a big old crocodile at the zoo. Sitting there without moving. Who knew what weird thoughts were going on behind that calm exterior.

Sam could feel the tension in the room. As Ed had explained to them, nobody knew what this meeting was about, but by the look of Jordan it was something serious.

At last the general spoke.

'OK,' he said. 'Let's get started.'

Sam had been expecting something medieval, full of *verily*s and *thee*s and *thou*s and *aye* instead of yes. It was a surprise to hear Jordan talking so normally. But why not?

They weren't really in the Middle Ages, were they? They were in the middle of London in the twenty-first century.

'This is a special meeting of the war council. In fact it's a military tribunal. Which means it's a trial. '

The kids on the side table started writing furiously. A hum and murmur went round the room, but it was quickly silenced when Jordan raised his hand. Everyone was looking around, though, trying to work out who wasn't here. Who might have been arrested.

'Last night a boy was caught trying to steal food from the storerooms. As you know, when I took control I drew up a list of rules, and stealing is one of the worst crimes on it, especially stealing food. You all know the rules. So there's no excuse for breaking them. However. I intend this trial to be fair. So I will give the suspect a fair hearing. Bring him in.'

All heads twisted round now towards the doors as a boy was shoved through them, his hands tied behind his back, an armed guard on either side of him. He was tall and fair-haired, and had a bruise on one side of his face. His shirt was slightly torn. He looked like he'd been crying. His eyes all red and swollen. Mixed emotions – fear, anger, defiance, hatred and embarrassment – flickered across his features.

The boy was made to stand in front of the big table and his hands were untied. All eyes in the room were on him.

'What is your name?' Jordan asked.

'You know my name, Jordan, you arsehole,' said the boy, and a couple of the kids giggled. Jordan didn't react; his expression didn't change; he didn't even blink. He remained cold, blank, patient.

'Tell us your full name.'

'No.'

Jordan raised his head now and stared at the boy. He so rarely looked directly at anyone that the effect was quite powerful. The boy dropped his own gaze.

'Bren, *Brendan*, Eldridge.'

'And what have you been charged with, Bren?'

'Oh, for God's sake, this is stupid. This isn't a proper court. We're all just kids. I know I did wrong. So give me a slap and let's get on with our lives.'

'What have you been charged with, Bren?'

'Stealing! You know it's stealing. OK? I stole some tinned fruit. Big deal, boo hoo. Naughty me.'

Jordan looked over towards the side table.

'The charge is stealing food.'

'Big deal,' said Bren.

Jordan paused for a few seconds before going on. 'Without food we die,' he said.

'Tell me something I don't know.' Bren gave Jordan a dismissive look.

Jordan ignored him. 'Stealing from other kids is one of the worst things you can do,' he continued. 'If we don't look out for each other, we're all going to die. Therefore, Brendan, I reckon stealing food is as bad a crime as murder.'

'Oh, come off it, Jordan. It was just some tinned peaches.'

'Was it?'

'Yes, it was. You know it was.'

Again Jordan turned to the side table.

'Make a note of that. The suspect has admitted to stealing the peaches.'

'Hey,' said Bren. 'No, I didn't. I was talking hypothetically.'

'I'm going to call Captain Ford for evidence,' said Jordan,

and he nodded to the boy sitting on his right, who had long straight black hair and Japanese features. The boy stood up.

'For the record, can you state your full name and occupation, rank and regiment?' said Jordan.

'Seriously?'

'Just do it, Tomoki.'

'My name is Tomoki Ford. Captain of the Tower Watch.'

'Can you tell us how you happened to catch the thief?'

'Alleged thief,' said Bren. 'If we're going to have a proper trial, then I'm innocent until proven guilty, aren't I?'

'You've already made a confession,' said Jordan.

'I wasn't under oath.'

'We don't bother with that. You already said you stole the can of fruit.'

'Prove it.'

'OK,' said Tomoki. 'About ten days ago Captain Reynolds of the Service Corps came to see me. He told me that he believed someone was stealing from the Tower stores. He'd noticed some small things had gone missing, and when he checked he found out that other stuff had gone as well.'

He took out a piece of paper from his pocket and showed it to General Jordan.

'I've written it all down. Do you want me to read it out?'

'No, just give it to the clerks afterwards.'

'OK, so, anyway, Captain Reynolds got his team to check much more carefully every morning and evening. It was soon obvious that stuff was being nicked nearly every night. Just small amounts – the thief probably thought that it wouldn't be noticeable. I told you about it a week ago.' This was addressed to the general, who nodded. 'And you told me to put a special watch in the stores. We built a hiding place and took it in turns to stake out the stores all night. We saw Bren come in just after midnight – he had his own key – and we saw him take three cans of peaches away in a backpack. We followed him back to his room in the Casemates and arrested him.'

'All right, all right. This is boring,' said Bren. 'Three cans of peaches. I admit it.'

'Once we'd locked Bren up we searched his room,' Tomoki went on. 'And we found all this.'

Tomoki paused as three kids brought in boxes packed with food. The murmuring started up again. Someone whistled. Bren's head drooped and he looked ashamed.

'Do you admit that you stole all this as well?' Jordan asked.

'Yes,' said Bren quietly.

'Were you working alone?

Bren nodded and Jordan asked Tomoki if he agreed.

'We don't think there was anyone else in on it. That's why we followed him, to make sure.'

'Do you want to say anything else, Bren? I can't really see the point, but if you want to.'

'No. I don't want to say anything. Just . . . I'm sorry, I suppose. It was stupid.'

'OK,' said Jordan. 'So if nobody has any objections then I reckon you're guilty.'

'Yeah. OK.'

Tomoki sat down. 'So, what's the sentence then?' he asked.

'As I said.' Jordan stared at Bren. 'I think stealing food from other kids is as bad as murder. So the sentence is death.'